"Joanna ... to my father."

Matt Sinclair folded his arms and stared across the parking lot. "They were married for two years. I was only seventeen at the time. Pretty much out of the picture, thank God."

"Obviously you didn't care for her," Kate said.

"Frankly, no. Sorry if that offends you."

Kate inhaled deeply. She hadn't come to Joanna's funeral for any kind of confrontation. All she'd wanted to do was pay her last respects to the woman who'd once saved her life.

"I do—did—care for Joanna," she said, "and I don't believe in speaking ill of the dead. Especially at a funeral." She brushed past him to head for her car.

"Those are fine sentiments," he replied, raising his voice as she kept walking. "And you're welcome to them. But Joanna Barnes ruined my father. I'll never forgive her for that."

Matt watched her car zip out of the parking lot and disappear down the quiet, tree-lined road. He didn't like the uneasy feeling in his gut when he recalled the hurt in her eyes. As if she couldn't comprehend why he was attacking somebody she cared about.

But that somebody was J——— ——— ———d himself. The last pers——— ——— ———y.

ABOUT THE AUTHOR

Reading and writing have been lifetime passions for Janice Carter. She wrote her first novel at age twelve in school notebooks. As a teenager, she wrote daily serializations of romance novellas for her classmates. "Publishing a novel was always a dream," she recalls. "But for a long time, the business of living got in the way of writing. I traveled around the world and saw many exotic sights. I married and had two amazing daughters. There was little opportunity or inclination on my part to write until one autumn I impulsively decided to take a romance writing workshop at a local college. I was hooked! That year I began to write my first romance novel and sold it two years later to Harlequin Intrigue."

Janice lives with her husband and two daughters in Toronto, Ontario, where—during the year—she works as a teacher-librarian in an elementary school. Her summers are spent on a small island on Lake Ontario where she has her morning coffee and watches great blue herons fish off the rocks. Then she adjourns to her "writing room" and indulges in her favorite occupation.

Books by Janice Carter

HARLEQUIN SUPERROMANCE

593—GHOST TIGER
671—A CHRISTMAS BABY
779—THE MAN SHE LEFT BEHIND
887—THE INHERITANCE

Summer of Joanna
Janice Carter

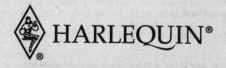

HARLEQUIN®

TORONTO • NEW YORK • LONDON
AMSTERDAM • PARIS • SYDNEY • HAMBURG
STOCKHOLM • ATHENS • TOKYO • MILAN • MADRID
PRAGUE • WARSAW • BUDAPEST • AUCKLAND

ISBN 0-373-70995-1

SUMMER OF JOANNA

Printed in U.S.A.

For my beautiful daughters, as always

ACKNOWLEDGMENT

With much appreciation to my editor of many years,
Zilla Soriano, for her intuitive good sense
and gracious guidance.

CHAPTER ONE

SHE COULDN'T TAKE her eyes off the coffin.

It sat, resplendent beneath a spray of leaves and white lilies, in the very middle of the raised dais in front of the altar. Kate closed her eyes, fighting the pain that swelled up from the pit of her stomach. Just get through this, she reminded herself. Then give in to grieving for Joanna when all the questions have been answered, especially those beginning with *why*. Until then, stay calm, in control and, most of all, stay angry.

The organist segued into another interlude as mourners continued to slide into the pews. Kate raised her head, glancing left to the center aisle. The church was filling up. Joanna would be pleased. Or so Kate imagined. For how much *could* she say about someone she hadn't seen for nineteen years? Kate lowered her head again and squeezed her eyes shut, bringing back that sultry July day at Camp Limberlost. The day she'd met Joanna Barnes.

THE RAFT WAS TOO FAR AWAY. Kate knew that from the start, but it almost seemed to beckon to her, a refuge from the gang of kids lying in wait down by the canoes. If she turned around to confront them, she'd probably get into another fight and she'd already had her last warning. One more and she'd be put on a bus and sent back to the city. Which wasn't such a bad thing, she figured, since she hated the place, anyway. But there was only her foster mother and little kids, including a new baby, at home. The rest of the summer was already booked for baby-sitting.

So the raft it would be, she decided, wading into the shallow water of Whitefish Lake. But distances were deceiving in the midday glare, and Kate wasn't an experienced swimmer. Less than a yard away from the raft, she could barely keep her head above the water. Her legs seemed like lead weights, pulling her down, as her arms flailed the surface.

"For heaven's sake, take my hand so I won't have to come in after you."

The command—really a peeved drawl—came from the raft, and Kate barely caught a glimpse of a bronzed arm reaching toward her as she went down for the second time. Her own arms kept thrashing but contact was made. A strong grip pulled her to the raft's edge where a beautiful face, framed by an ear-length swoop of jet-black hair, loomed over her.

An angel's face, Kate was thinking as she clung to the ladder at the side of the raft, and was suddenly glad she'd gone to confession before leaving for Limberlost.

"Catch your breath before you climb up," the woman said. "I've just slathered myself with sunscreen, and I don't want it to come off if I try to haul you out." Then she disappeared from the edge and shifted toward the center of the raft.

Kate waited until she knew she could pull herself up on her own. When she finally rolled onto the warm, dry surface, she lay on her back, her chest heaving.

After a moment, the woman raised her head from the paperback she'd been reading and said, "I'm Joanna Barnes and you must be one of the Bronx kids."

Kate shot up. "My name is Kate Reilly and I'm *not* one of the Bronx kids. I live in Queens."

Joanna Barnes shrugged, turning her attention back to her novel. "Whatever," she said.

THE ORGAN SWELLED to a crescendo as the minister walked toward a podium a short distance from Joanna's casket. Kate rose with the others, reaching automatically for a hymn book and the page the minister directed the congregation to. But she could still see Joanna sprawling on a beach towel, apparently oblivious to the eleven-year-old kid gawking at her.

"ARE YOU RELATED to the people who run this place?" Kate asked when she'd caught her breath.

"My parents," Joanna mumbled from behind her book.

Kate tried to connect the white-haired plumpish couple she'd met her first day with the beautiful woman in the bikini, but couldn't quite do it. She swiped at a drop of water hanging from the tip of her nose. "So do you work here, then?"

The novel came down. "Hardly." There was the faintest of smiles.

"I haven't seen you before and I've been here a week."

The crimson smile widened. "I don't exactly hang out with the campers. But I used to work here when I was a kid. My parents have owned Limberlost for twenty years."

"Did you like coming here when you were a kid?"

"We lived here year-round in those days."

"You *lived* here?"

A peal of laughter burst from Joanna. "For several years—until I finally made my escape."

"That's what I'd like to do," Kate muttered bitterly. "Make my escape."

"It's not that bad here...or is it? I've forgotten what it's like to be a kid in a godforsaken place like Limberlost."

"The place itself isn't that bad," Kate admitted. "And

neither are the counselors, except for Mary Lou Farris—or the ferret, I call her. Your parents seem pretty nice," she added, not wanting to offend the person who'd saved her life.

"Then it's the other kids," Joanna guessed.

Kate nodded. "They all knew one another before they came here. And I'm the only one from Queens."

Joanna shook her head. "Kids can be mean. Usually Mom and Dad try to get a mix from all over."

"If I'm lucky, they'll send me home soon, anyway."

"You miss home that much?"

Kate pictured her foster mother walking wearily around the cluttered house, rocking the baby and snapping orders left and right. She herself would be chasing the two-year-old away from the family cat. She'd been in that particular foster home almost four months.

"No," she finally mumbled.

"Maybe even Limberlost can look good compared to other places—and other people."

Kate gave that some thought before asking, "Are you on a holiday here, too?"

"Not really. More like on leave. At the moment I'm unemployed and between marriages," she said. "What my dad calls footloose and fancy-free."

Kate wasn't certain what the phrase meant, but she thought it a good one for the woman sitting next to her. The painted fingernails and matching toes seemed to go perfectly with the splashes of color on her bikini. Up close, Kate could see that her makeup was also perfect, which made her wonder how she'd made it to the raft without getting wet. Her eyes drifted past Joanna and spotted, for the first time, the tip of a paddleboat tied to the far side of the raft.

They sat in silence for a while. Then Joanna put her book down and, turning to Kate, said, "I'm sorry about lumping you in with those other kids. I can see now that you're an entirely different type.''

That was when Kate decided Joanna Barnes was an okay person—for an adult.

THE MINISTER'S resonant baritone drew Kate from the past. He'd begun to speak about Joanna, and in spite of herself, Kate's attention began to wander. Mainly because he wasn't talking about the woman she'd known briefly for a week when she was eleven years old. He referred to the well-known fashion writer and columnist, world traveler, friend of many and wife. Kate's ears pricked up at that. Had Joanna married again?

She peered discreetly around, trying to guess which somber-suited man in the congregation had been Joanna's latest husband. Trouble was, the small church was full of black-suited men. In fact, she just realized, there seemed to be more men than women.

She wondered briefly if any of Joanna's family were here, then remembered the reference in the obituary to Joanna's late parents. She frowned, trying to recall their faces. The minister coughed, then, lowering his voice, alluded to the cause of Joanna's death. He knew every euphemism for suicide, Kate thought. But his oblique references only revived the anger she'd been feeling since she'd read Joanna's obituary in the *New York Times* three days before. No way, she'd fumed, would Joanna Barnes commit suicide. Not in a million years. And especially not just before their promised reunion—a promise made nineteen years before at Camp Limberlost.

AFTER THAT FIRST MEETING, Kate found herself swimming out to the raft every afternoon. Those few hours had saved Kate's summer for her. The remaining week at camp flew by. Joanna talked about growing up in the country, laughing at Kate's reference to it as "wilderness." She brought a cooler pack with pop and snacks out to the raft, letting Kate indulge in the junk food forbidden at camp.

"I plan to head for Manhattan soon," Joanna said, after revealing that she'd had her first lucky break—a fashion article published in a local newspaper. "If I'm ever going to make it in this business, that's the place to be."

"Maybe I could visit you," Kate suggested impulsively.

Joanna smiled and murmured, "Maybe."

Kate's excitement fizzled. Joanna's reply had been the first typical adult comment she'd made all week. Kate figured she might as well have added, "But not likely."

Then Joanna leaned over and said, "Look, I can't make promises like that because I've no idea where my life is going to go from here. I'm going to be thirty years old this September and you're…"

Kate's heart sank as she waited for Joanna to say "just a kid."

But instead, she'd scrunched up her forehead and said, "What? Twelve?"

"I'll be twelve on August 15."

"There you go. I was close enough. Anyway, I guess I don't have to spell it out for you—the big difference in our ages. You're on the verge of becoming a teenager…sort of, and I'm on the verge of—"

"Becoming a woman?" Kate suggested.

Uproarious laughter at that. "Let's say, a more mature woman. Going into my thirties, I hope not to repeat the mistakes of my twenties."

"I can hardly wait until I'm the same age as you and I can go anywhere and do anything."

Joanna nodded. "It's pretty good, believe me. And what you gotta remember is, you can also *be* anything. Don't forget that one."

They sat without talking again for a long while. The sun

was lower in the sky now and the west side of the bay was in shade. "It must be past five," she said. "My turn to help set up for dinner."

As she edged toward the ladder on the far side of the raft, Joanna suddenly put out a hand. "I hate to tell you, Kate, but I may even be leaving tomorrow sometime. Something's come up." She frowned and glanced away for a second as if she didn't want Kate to see her face. "But I just had a great idea," she enthused, turning back to Kate with a big smile.

Kate's insides churned. "What?"

"Well, since it's unrealistic for us to expect to get together on a regular basis, how about if we promise to meet someplace—we can decide where later—exactly nineteen years from today, July 14. You'll be thirty—just about my age now. You can fill me in on how your life has turned out and I'll…well, I don't even want to think about it, but I'll be looking at the big five-oh coming up. We'll both be dealing with an age milestone. Sound like a good idea?"

"Yeah! But…what if one of us forgets?"

Joanna pursed her lips thoughtfully for what seemed a long time. Then she said, "We won't because I'll send you a reminder card every year—like a countdown."

"Do you think you can remember to do that?"

"I promise you, Kate Reilly, that if I get one thing in my life together, it will be that. Okay?"

"How will you find me?"

"Jeez, you're brimming with good questions. I knew from the start you were a smart kid."

Kate beamed.

"Let me see…you give me your address before I leave and as soon as I get to New York in September, I'll set up a postal box number for you. I'll pay for it until you reach the age of…what? Twenty? Then you can pay on your own."

"Nineteen," Kate said. "Because I'm going to make it on my own before I'm twenty."

"That's what I want to hear! Okay, then. Deal? Shake?" Kate stuck out her hand.

YOU PROMISED, JOANNA, and since you've been keeping that promise for the last nineteen years, I know you wouldn't have let anything stop you from meeting me last week.

The organist swelled into the next hymn as everyone stood. Kate now had an opportunity to scan the congregation in front and to the left of her. She thought she recognized a few people in amazing outfits. Perhaps she'd seen them in some of the many news clippings she'd saved over the years—articles and pictures featuring Joanna and various fashion-world celebrities.

She'd acquired quite a collection. It was one of the things she'd considered taking to their reunion, to show Joanna how she'd tracked her life through the years. But then she realized how pathetic that might look—as if she hadn't achieved a life of her own. And she had. A very satisfying, rewarding life, though teaching elementary school was probably a bit tame by Joanna's standards. But not bad, Kate thought, for a kid who'd been shuffled from one foster home to another.

After the hymn ended, the minister rose to introduce the eulogist—Joanna Barnes's husband, Lance Marchant. Kate straightened. So, Joanna *had* remarried. Was this man number three or four? she wondered. A tall man in a navy pin-striped suit stood from a front pew and headed up onto the dais, pausing to place the palm of his hand on the end of the casket. Someone behind Kate blew a nose.

Joanna's husband was a handsome, white-haired man who looked very familiar. *Lance Marchant.* The name rolled around in her mind, teasing her memory. Where had she seen him and why hadn't she known about the marriage? Especially given her habit of snipping any mention of Joanna in the papers. She might have missed the announcement, or perhaps, for some reason, Joanna had kept the marriage under wraps. Another piece to add to the puzzle that was growing around Joanna Barnes.

Lance Marchant cleared his throat, cast a quick glance at the casket and began to speak. As eulogies went, Kate assumed his speech was the standard fare. Not that she was any expert, since this was only the second funeral she'd ever attended. He did refer to their brief marriage of less than a year, but claimed to have known Joanna Barnes almost twenty. Kate's antenna rose at this. If she herself had first met Joanna nineteen years ago, then he must have known her earlier.

He continued extolling the talents and—with humor— the foibles of Joanna Barnes. It was an eloquent speech, Kate had to acknowledge. But that was the problem. Instead of a tribute delivered by a grieving husband, it had come across as a piece put together by some clever speechwriter.

When he finished, Lance Marchant stepped down from the dais and suddenly stumbled. Kate's heart leapt; she wondered if he was going to topple onto the casket. But he caught himself, placing his hand on the gleaming oak surface and staring down silently for a moment, as if communing with his wife one last time. Kate squirmed. She couldn't think why, but the scene embarrassed her.

Lance raised his head and walked down the aisle out of the church. As he passed Kate's pew, she caught a close-up of his face—flushed now, jaw set in a tight, steadfast line. The other mourners followed in hushed respect. Kate sat until the last person passed. Then she stood and, on rubbery legs, made her way to Joanna's casket.

There was so much she wanted to say, but finding the starting point was difficult. The whole purpose of their getting together again on the nineteenth anniversary of Kate's

stay at Camp Limberlost had been to compare the courses
of their lives. Joanna Barnes had certainly not been a substitute for the family Kate never had, but she'd represented
a kind of continuity in her life. No matter how many foster
homes or bad times Kate had gone through, she'd always
had that annual card to look forward to. And true to her
word, Joanna had never forgotten, although once she'd
been late.

Kate touched the casket, then flashed to the eulogy scene.
She quickly withdrew her hand. It was too late to talk to
Joanna now, and here wasn't the place. She started to turn
away when four undertakers from the funeral home filed
through a side door.

"Are you finished, ma'am?" one of them asked quietly.

Kate could only nod. The tears she'd tried to hold back
welled up. She dabbed at her eyes with a tissue. The men
bent to release the wheel brakes of the stand the casket
rested on and lifted up the cloth that skirted it.

"Where…where will she be buried?" Kate asked.

"Mrs. Marchant is going to be cremated. We'll be taking
her back to the funeral home from here."

"I see. Thank you," Kate murmured, and averted her
face, unable to watch Joanna Barnes wheeled out of her
life forever. She closed her eyes, listening to the muted
rumble of the casket as it rolled along the carpeted aisle.
There was the sound of a door opening and, seconds later,
thudding shut. Silence roared through the empty church.

Kate clutched the back of a pew to steady herself.

"Can I get you something?" a voice asked from behind.

She turned and looked up, making eye contact with a
man who seemed to tower over her. He wasn't smiling and
his eyes were serious.

"Something?" she echoed. "Like what?"

A single eyebrow on his pale face rose at her question.
"Uh, well, since this is a church…say, a glass of water?"

"Thanks, but I'm not sure you could even get a glass of water here. Everyone's gone."

He shook his head. "They're all outside, being social the way people have to behave at a funeral. Maybe even talking to reporters."

"Reporters? *Here?*"

"A couple, anyway. Too bad Joanna can't talk to them herself—she'd be in her element, wouldn't she?"

Kate stiffened at the edge in his remark. "I wouldn't really know," she said, and began to walk down the aisle toward the open front doors of the church. She heard him follow.

"Sorry," he said. "That didn't come out the way I intended. Just that, you know how Joanna loved the limelight."

He caught up with her. "Are you a relative of hers?"

"No." Kate kept walking.

"Then…a close friend?"

"Not really."

As she reached the entryway, he reached out his hand to stop her. She swung around, staring down first at the hand on her forearm and then up into his face. A nice face. Nice enough to be in some of the fashion articles Joanna used to write. Maybe he had been, she thought. There was curiosity in the face, too. But the eyes—gray, she decided—were intense.

"Not really?" He repeated. Then he frowned. "You're not a reporter, then?"

"No, for heaven's sake. I met Joanna a long time ago. End of story." She turned her back on him and headed for the door.

"Sorry again," he called after her. "I've been trying to find someone she was close to."

"I can't help you there, but her husband is probably right outside."

"He's the last person I'd talk to."

That stopped her. Kate pivoted around. "You're not a relative?"

"No."

"Friend? Colleague?"

"Hardly." The edge returned to his voice.

The emotional fatigue of the past few days suddenly overwhelmed Kate. She was tired of this little game and only wanted to leave the church and go home. "Then I suppose neither of us has any relevant information to exchange." Kate swung around and stepped out the church door into the glare of a July afternoon.

Lance Marchant was holding court at the foot of the steps leading up to the church. He craned his neck as Kate exited, frowning momentarily before turning his attention back to the small group of reporters interviewing him. As Kate passed, she became aware of a brief flurry of interest from the reporters, but it quickly evaporated when Joanna's husband failed to acknowledge her.

Kate had to smile. So much for her fifteen seconds of fame, she thought. Then she remembered why she was there—and why the reporters were there. Walking briskly through the knots of people milling on the church lawn, she headed with grim determination to the rental car parked in the lot beside the church.

The day was already gearing up for more record heat. Kate was grateful for the air-conditioning that had made the drive to Westchester more tolerable. When she'd read that Joanna's funeral would be held outside New York City, she'd decided to rent a car rather than travel by public transit. She hesitated at the entrance to the lot, scanning it for the small white Escort.

"Lost your car?"

She turned, thinking the man from the church had followed her to the parking lot. But the man a few feet to her right was another stranger. He was short, balding and red-faced from the heat. His baggy tan slacks dipped beneath a bulging stomach, and the rumpled sports jacket looked as though it had been acquired at a secondhand clothing store. His white shirt, straining at its row of buttons, clung to him in unsightly patches. He threw the cigarette he'd been smoking onto the pavement, ground it under his heel and huffed his way toward her.

Watching him made Kate feel cool. "When I got here, there weren't so many vehicles," she said.

He glanced behind her at the lot. "Uh-huh. And most of them limos."

Kate suddenly noticed a sleek black limo angled in front of the Escort, blocking any quick exit she might have made. "Great," she muttered. She pulled the material of her navy blue sleeveless dress away from her damp skin. Five more minutes in this lot, she figured, and she'd look like the man standing beside her.

"Problem?" he asked.

Kate sighed, tugging at the dress again. "My car—it's behind that black limo in the second row."

"Uh-oh. Hopefully the owner won't be long. Unless he—or she—is attending the postfuneral reception in the church manse."

Kate fanned herself with the rolled-up funeral service program. "How long will that be?"

"You're not going?"

"No. I'm not family and...well, it wouldn't be appropriate." In fact, she was thinking, it would be downright awful to have to mingle with a bunch of strangers, picking up snippets of talk about Joanna.

"Not family, eh? You in the fashion trade, too, then?" His eyes, small and deep-set in his fleshy face, swept over her.

''No, I'm a teacher,'' she replied, wishing he'd go away. What was it with all the questions? she wondered.

She glanced around to see if the owner of the limo might be walking their way, but all she saw was a group of uniformed drivers standing smoking under a tree in the far corner of the lot.

''Friend of Mrs. Marchant, then?''

Kate turned her head. He was almost her height, making the top of his glistening forehead about even with her nose. His face was tilted up, allowing a brief glimpse of trickles of sweat dripping off the folds of skin beneath his chin. Kate looked away.

''Guess I'll see if one of those drivers can move the car,'' she said, moving off, hoping to put some distance between herself and the man.

But he followed. ''Were you a close friend of Mrs. Marchant's?''

The way he used her married name told Kate he wasn't exactly Joanna's bosom buddy, either. She stopped and turned toward him. ''No, I wasn't. Why are you asking?''

''Just curious about why you came to the funeral.''

Kate narrowed her eyes at him. ''And what business is that of yours?''

He'd taken a handkerchief from his trouser pocket and was now mopping his forehead with it. ''Guess I should have identified myself. Sergeant Tom Andrews, Westchester County Police.'' He started to extend the arm holding the handkerchief, then apparently thought better of it.

The introduction didn't exactly warm Kate to him. Instead, she wondered why he'd taken so long to get around to it. ''And?'' she prompted in her best schoolteacher voice.

He straightened at her tone, tucking away the handkerchief and digging in his jacket pocket for his badge. Kate scarcely had a glimpse of it before it was stowed away again. "Just making a few inquiries of the funeral guests, that's all, Miss...?"

"Reilly. Kate Reilly. Is it customary for the police to attend the funeral of a suicide victim?"

He seemed to look at her with new interest. "Police like to get information on any death where there are unusual circumstances."

A calm stillness settled over her while a tiny voice inside whispered, *I knew it! I knew it!* "And...what are the unusual circumstances around Joanna Barnes's death?"

He frowned. "Sorry, I can't get into the details. What exactly was your connection to Mrs. Marchant, or Miss Barnes?"

"I met her when I was a young girl. We haven't seen each other in nineteen years, but she corresponded."

"She ever talk about being depressed? Suicidal feelings?"

Kate bit down on her lower lip and shook her head. After she'd managed to regain control of her voice, she said, "No. We...uh, we weren't close enough for her to talk about things like that."

He kept his eyes on her, nodding his head thoughtfully. "I see. Okay. Well, thank you very much, Miss Reilly. How about if I find out which one of those guys over there belongs to the limo blocking your car? I've got to talk to them, anyway."

"Thank you. I appreciate it," Kate murmured, his question still pounding in her ears. *She ever talk about being depressed?* If only Joanna had written about her personal life more, rather than elaborate on information Kate had already gleaned from newspapers and magazines.

Then what, Reilly? Think your knowing her better would have prevented Joanna from killing herself? She closed her eyes. The small voice inside her was shouting *yes! yes!* No matter how hard she'd tried over the past few days, she couldn't shake the thought that she might have had some influence over Joanna had she known her better.

"Sure you don't want that glass of water?"

Kate jumped.

"Easy. I didn't mean to frighten you. I thought you saw me coming."

Kate squinted. He was standing with the sun behind him, and at first she didn't recognize him. Then she caught his reference to water and managed a weak smile. The man from the church. "Thanks, but I'm all right. I was…lost in my thoughts."

He stepped out of the sun to join her in the patch of shade. "Need a lift anywhere?"

"I have a car, but thanks, anyway." Remembering the police officer, she turned her head to peer around his shoulder toward the limo drivers across the lot. Sure enough, she saw one of them talking to the officer. Then the driver sauntered toward the limo parked in front of her car.

"The black limo?" he asked, following her gaze.

Kate had to smile. "No. The white Escort behind it."

"Aah. I'm sorry, I should have introduced myself sooner," he said. "Matt Sinclair." He extended a hand.

Kate placed her hand in his. "Kate Reilly."

"A friend, but not a close one," he added.

She smiled again. "Yes. You were a friend of Joanna's?"

"I knew her," he said, finally letting go of her hand. "Family connection."

He was being vague and Kate couldn't understand why. Instinctively she stepped back, taking a second, longer look at Matt Sinclair. Unlike the policeman, he seemed cool and unperturbed by the sweltering heat. Everything about him spelled good grooming, from the cut of his lightweight summer suit to the plain silk tie knotted unobtrusively at the throat of a crisp white shirt. Grooming, she thought, and money, too. One of those limos in the lot probably belonged to him. His thick black hair was perfectly trimmed, and his eyes, still fixed on hers, were definitely gray. But not a cold gray, she thought, recalling how they'd looked in the church. Now they seemed to flicker with specks of color. Or was that glint amusement, instead?

"Do I pass?" he asked.

Kate looked away. She was certain her face had reddened, and not from the heat. "So you're related to Joanna, after all. You mentioned a family connection?"

He folded his arms across his chest and stared across the parking lot. Kate turned her head, too, watching the black limo roll into another place. He shifted his attention back to her and mumbled, "By marriage."

"By marriage?" she repeated. "A cousin or something?"

He shook his head. "She was married to my father." He paused, fixing his eyes on hers. "For two years."

"When?"

"Eighteen years ago. I was seventeen at the time. Pretty much out of the picture. Thank God," he muttered bitterly.

"Obviously you didn't care for Joanna," she said.

"Frankly, no. Sorry if that offends you."

Kate inhaled deeply. She hadn't come to Joanna's funeral for any kind of confrontation. All she'd wanted to do was to quietly mourn and pay her last respects to someone she'd met and liked.

"I do—did—care for Joanna," she said, "and I don't believe in speaking ill of the dead. Especially at a funeral." She brushed past him to head for her car.

"Those are fine sentiments," he replied, raising his voice as she kept walking. "And you're welcome to them. But Joanna Barnes ruined my father. I'll never forgive her for that."

Kate kept walking, fixing her eyes on the white Escort

and not noticing the policeman until she bumped against him as he passed.

"Goodbye, then, Miss Reilly. Maybe we'll meet again," Matt Sinclair called after her.

She reached the door of her car and slipped the keys from the side pocket of her purse. She wanted only to leave as quickly as possible, determined not to look back at the two men behind her. Both of whom, she suspected, were staring after her.

When the engine and the air-conditioning were running, Kate accelerated out of the lot and made a sharp turn onto the main street. She glanced at the rearview mirror and saw that the two men were now standing together as they watched her car drive away.

When the church and parking lot were out of sight, Kate pulled over at the first convenience store. She told herself she was desperate for a cold drink, but what she really needed was to wait for the trembling to stop.

CHAPTER TWO

MATT WATCHED her car zip out of the lot and disappear down the quiet, tree-lined street. A swirl of conflicting emotions threatened the grim determination he'd felt earlier when she'd rushed to defend Joanna Barnes. He wondered why he cared so much. Probably everybody else at the funeral had also been friends with Joanna.

He wiped away the sweat beginning to bead on his forehead. For the first time he questioned his motives. He didn't like the uneasy feeling in his gut when he envisioned Kate Reilly's pinched red face and the angry flicker in her jade-green eyes. It wasn't the anger that had struck a nerve, but the almost simultaneous hurt. As if she couldn't comprehend why he was attacking someone she obviously cared for.

Except it's Joanna, buddy. The last person he could think of to deserve such fierce loyalty from a friend. Matt expelled a mouthful of bitter air and spun around to go back to the church. The man standing to his right said, ''She's definitely worth pursuin', don'tcha think?''

Matt grimaced and kept right on walking.

THE FLAT THROBBED with heat. Kate headed straight for the kitchen and flicked on the small air-conditioning unit she'd just bought. She peeled off her dress and, seconds later, was standing under a cool shower in the bathroom. Was it her imagination, she wondered, or were those really wisps of steam pluming off her body? Or was she still angry at how the afternoon had played out?

She raised her face to the fine spray, and the band of pain across her brow began to ebb. But a pulse of disappointment was still there, right at her temple, when she finally stepped onto the bath mat. It came from the sense that she'd been robbed of her day of grieving for Joanna.

Kate rubbed a towel over herself before slipping into a cotton nightie that instantly stuck to her damp skin. She was suddenly reminded of the short, pudgy police officer at the funeral and grimaced as the pounding in her head amplified. Together with the Ivy League lawyer-type, the two men had succeeded in wiping out all thoughts of Joanna, leaving behind an ugly smear of doubt and innuendo.

The air-conditioning was going full blast by the time Kate returned to the kitchen to get a glass of ice water. Splurging on the unit had been an act of desperation, driven by forecasts of a hot summer in the Big Apple. So far, she hadn't regretted the purchase, even though it had removed a significant chunk from her already tight budget. Kate took a long swallow from the frosty glass, then rolled it across her forehead.

Perhaps she ought to have signed up for another summer-school course, after all. At least she'd have had a few hours of daily relief working in an air-conditioned building. But having the whole summer off had been part of the plan. Time for Carla, as promised. And time with Joanna. *As promised.*

Kate closed her eyes, fighting a stab of pain. A week ago, the whole summer was an uncharted map. The thrill of anticipation—*of promise*—had yet to draw lines on that map; to mark days and nights of events that Kate had only recently allowed herself to dream about. She'd been finally going to see Joanna again. Finally to tell her how that summer's meeting long ago had changed her life. How it had fixed a real place in her childhood, a place called hope.

Maybe Joanna could be repaid through Carla, Kate thought. *Carla.* She hadn't telephoned to confirm their weekly get-together. Signing on as a mentor and Big Sister to thirteen-year-old Carla Lopez had stemmed from another promise Kate had made to herself, years ago. Somehow, in some way, she'd help another troubled teenager the way Joanna Barnes had motivated her.

Glass in hand, Kate strolled to the living room to check her voice mail. She quickly punched in her password when the beeper indicated a message. Carla's piping tones unspooled from the tape.

"Hi—Kate? I know tomorrow's our day, but something's come up so, uh, I can't make it. Talk to you later. Bye."

Kate frowned. She called Carla's foster home and, after several rings, finally reached Rita Santos, the teen's foster mother.

"Nope, she isn't here, Kate. Took off about an hour ago. Didn't say where she was headed. As usual."

There was a moment's silence. Thoughts of Carla filled the void. Kate felt more annoyed than worried. Carla's street sense was twice what hers had been at the same age. Of course, by thirteen Kate had already met Joanna and was working on her goal to get out of Queens.

"No doubt she'll turn up with some excuse," Rita said. "If not, guess I'll have to call her worker again. Sorry she let you down, Kate."

"No no, don't say that. Carla's not letting anyone down—except maybe herself. I'll call back in the morning, but if…you know, there's a problem, please call me. Even if it's the middle of the night."

"Sure. Meantime, I wouldn't sit up worrying, I was you."

"Okay, Rita. Talk to you soon." Kate hung on to the receiver a few moments longer, thinking about the ominous turn Carla's behavior had taken over the past few months. Rita had had about as much as she could take from the girl, who'd been with her for almost a year.

The pity of it was that Kate knew Carla really liked her current foster home. Only she liked her gang of friends more. Keeping Carla away from that gang had been an ongoing project for Rita, Kate and Carla's social worker, Kim, for several months.

Kate still remembered vividly her own desperate efforts to be part of a group that wasn't controlled by adults. Fortunately for her, the vow to make good and show Joanna Barnes that she could, had supplanted her need to be a gang member. It was a goal that took her off the streets. She was determined to do the same for Carla.

For now, though, she could do little but hope that Carla would have the sense to go home. Kate prowled around her small apartment. It was barely past nine and the city was just now succumbing to the cooling embrace of dusk. She'd eaten a fast-food dinner on the way home from dropping off the rental car, so didn't have to worry about conjuring up a meal from the meager contents of her refrigerator. Still, she was restless.

She peered out the bedroom window through the geometric frieze of the fire escape on the other side of the glass, over the treetops and row houses of SoHo. Last summer she'd flung open the window and lain awake most nights in fear of intruders taking advantage of the heat wave to climb to her second-story flat. But now, thanks to her air-conditioning, she was both safe and cool. Except that she felt like a prisoner, barricaded against the heat and the night.

She stared down into the street and watched couples stroll in the balmy evening air, envying them. She could understand why Carla preferred the street to the family room, dominated by a blaring TV and the constant bickering of youngsters. On summer nights in the city, the streets were alive with excitement, anticipation.

Kate let the venetian blind drop, hiding the night away. Loneliness overwhelmed her. Thinking she'd be busy doing things with Joanna, she'd turned down a chance to travel out West with a friend and colleague at her school. Now, except for outings with Carla, the summer loomed empty and unpromising.

She wandered around the room, pausing before the mirror above her dresser. Her chin-length, damp, reddish-brown hair framed her face in limp tendrils, making her look like a waif out in a storm.

Kate moved away from her reflection—no comfort there—and slumped onto the edge of the bed. Too early for sleep. Too wound up for television. Ginny, the tenant downstairs and also a friend, was visiting her parents for a few days.

Maybe she ought to go down to the streets and look for Carla. Her quick smile vanished just as abruptly. No, she warned herself. Worrying about Carla, making sure she was all right, could be a full-time job if she was foolish enough to make it one. Both she and Rita Santos had already come to that conclusion.

Thoughts drifted back to the afternoon. Joanna's casket. The flowers. *Had Joanna liked lilies?* So much she didn't know and now, no possibility of ever learning. Impulsively, Kate went to the closet, drawn there by a need to find some clue, some hint in the few letters she'd received from Joanna Barnes over the past nineteen years. *Why, Joanna? Why?*

The album sat on the shelf above the clothes rack. Kate carried it to the bed, stacked the pillows against the headboard and made herself comfortable. Then she opened the first page.

August 15, 1982. Today is my birthday and I got my first real birthday card in the mail. It was from Joanna! She's kept her promise and I'm going to keep mine. The one I made to myself the last night of camp. Not to get in trouble anymore. Not to ruin my life.

Taped beneath the scrawled entry was the card from Joanna. Its message read simply:

Happy Birthday, twelve-year-old! Don't celebrate too much. Manhattan's amazing and I'm loving it. Watch for my byline in the papers—whenever. Have a great year and see you in eighteen!

Joanna

Kate passed her hand along the card's glossy surface. She'd read the card more than a dozen times the day it arrived. It had been the first piece of personal mail ever to be delivered to her. She remembered, too, the way her foster parents and their children had stood openmouthed in surprise as she read the card. And the questions that had followed.

Who is this person, Kate? Where did you meet her? What's this all about, anyway?

She'd been afraid then that somehow the whole thing—the cards and the promised reunion with Joanna—would be snatched away from her. But in the end, her partial explanation had satisfied her foster mother, who'd only muttered a last warning—*I just don't want you to get your hopes up.* Kate hadn't appreciated the irony of that comment until many years later.

Kate sighed and quickly flipped the page. This one—a

postcard from Paris—had caused a real stir in the household because no one else had even *known* anyone who'd gone to Europe. Weeks before its arrival Kate had rushed to check the mail every day. *She might forget. Don't get your hopes up.* But Kate had had the blind faith of a child. And she'd never been disappointed.

Suddenly she couldn't take any more. Her only memories of Joanna Barnes were now permanently sealed behind plastic in an ordinary photo album. She'd never have the chance to transform all those bits of paper into a real person. Kate closed the album, sank back onto the bed and stretched out her arm to click off the table lamp. Street light dappled the room with a pale rainbow of color. But Kate closed her eyes to the summer night, turned her head into the pillow and cried.

KATE DIDN'T HEAR from Carla until two days after Joanna's funeral, but she suspected the girl had tried several times to call her. There'd been a few hang-ups on her answering machine. She figured Carla had already been read the riot act from Rita and Kim, so she kept her voice light and neutral.

"Hi, Carly! What's up?"

There was the slightest of pauses, as if Carla had been expecting another response.

"Uh, not too much. Guess you heard I got grounded."

"Yes."

Carla cleared her throat. "Well, I don't know why everyone was so ticked off at me. I was okay. Not in any trouble or nothing—until I got home, anyway."

"Maybe they were worried, Carla."

"Yeah, right!" she scoffed. "More like Rita was thinkin' she'd lose that check every month."

Kate sighed. She'd heard the line before. "Is that fair? I don't think Rita's in this for the money."

A longer pause this time. Then Carla mumbled, "Maybe not. But I wasn't doing nothin'. Just hangin' with my buddies."

Kate counted mentally to ten. She'd had this conversation with Carla so many times she felt like screaming. *Why aren't you getting this, Carly? What does it take from all of us?* Finally she said, "It's all about communicating, Carla. Let people know where you are and when you're coming home. Call, for heaven's sake."

A hoarse laugh drifted through the line. "If I'd'a called, Rita would've told me to get home. And I was having a good time—you know, with my buds."

Kate knew better than to malign Carla's friends. She'd seen Rita do it and it always brought Carla rushing emotionally to their defense. Besides, she'd heard all the excuses. Carla could pull them out of the air like a magician popping rabbits from a hat.

"So now what?" Kate asked, softening her voice.

"My last chance. Kim said next time she'll have to send me to a group home. Out in the *suburbs!*"

Kate might have laughed at this final indignity, obviously a fate worse than death, were it not for the catch in Carla's voice. The threat of a group home was now suddenly very clear to her. Kate sighed again. It had taken six months of "last chances" for that sober reality to register with Carla.

"Carla, be cool, okay? Look, my plans for the summer have altered a bit. I'll have more time than I thought. We can do some things together."

"Like go shopping?"

Kate smiled at Carla's raised inflection on the last word. "Sure. Things like that. Maybe check out a museum or art gallery, too."

"Yeah," Carla murmured, less enthusiastic now.

''I'll call you tomorrow about two and we'll set a definite time and place. All right?''

Carla agreed and hung up quickly. *Before I changed my mind?* Kate wondered. Or because she had an incoming call? Kate shook her head as she set the receiver down. In spite of Carla's attitude, she hadn't yet crossed the line into serious trouble. Kate just hoped she could deflect the girl from that course before it was too late.

The remainder of the afternoon was spent in completing errands that Kate had postponed. She was grateful for the chance to be busy, thus removing thoughts of Joanna from her mind. Until she returned from feeding her neighbor's cat and picked up the phone to order a pizza. There was a message for her from the law firm representing Joanna Barnes.

Kate sat down on the armchair next to the phone and listened. The cheery voice on the line requested her to attend a reading of Joanna's will the next day at ten in the morning. *Please bring some identification.* After the message finished, Kate sat and stared into space, her sweaty palm clamped onto the receiver.

WHEN THE ELEVATOR DOORS parted, the man who'd spoken to her in the church after Joanna's funeral was standing on the other side. The look of incredulity in his face must have matched her own, Kate thought, for they stood gaping at each other until she murmured a faint ''hello'' and stepped out onto the carpeted hall.

He'd obviously been about to enter the elevator, but turned on his heel to follow her into the reception area.

''Miss, uh…''

''Reilly.''

''I don't know if you remember me—Matt Sinclair, from Joanna's funeral.''

''It was only four days ago.''

He looked offended at her brusque tone. "Right. So you're here for...?"

Kate flushed with annoyance. Subtlety definitely wasn't his style. "I've an appointment with Collier and Associates. Why do you ask?"

"Sorry. I suppose I'm being rude, but I'm just curious. Are you here for the reading of Joanna's will?"

Kate raised her chin to stare directly into his face. A handsome face, in spite of the knotted eyebrows and the glint in his eyes. Too bad he was so irritating.

"Yes, I am, Mr. Sinclair. Not that it's any concern of yours." She started to walk toward the reception desk where a young woman was watching them with interest.

He reached out a hand to her elbow. "I take it, then, that you're more than just an acquaintance of Joanna's, after all. Since you're a beneficiary."

Kate stared blankly at him. She'd been tormented by that very realization all night. *What exactly was I to Joanna?* But she wasn't about to confide in someone like Matt Sinclair.

"And I suppose, since you were about to leave, that you are *not*. A beneficiary," she clarified, and looked pointedly at his fingers splayed lightly on her arm.

Coloring, he dropped his hand. "No. I've been to see Marchant—his offices are farther along."

Kate swung around to head for the desk.

"You just seemed different, that's all."

She stopped and faced him again.

"From Joanna's pack of friends," he said.

Kate's eyes swept over him from head to toe before she resumed her course to the receptionist and asked for Mr. Collier. From behind, she heard the elevator door open and close. When she turned to head for the man's office, Matt Sinclair was gone.

The brief walk down the hall was long enough to calm

her, although Kate knew her face was still warm when she tapped on the lawyer's opened office door.

"Miss Reilly? Come in, please." Greg Collier rose from his desk chair.

He was in his mid-fifties and had the air of a suave used-car salesman. Or so Kate thought after a mere five minutes into their conversation. When he asked her if she'd known Joanna long, she derived some satisfaction from his surprise when she replied, "About nineteen years." She followed him into a small boardroom where a handful of people sat around an oval mahogany table. Lance Marchant was pouring coffee from a stainless-steel jug at the head of the table and glanced up as Kate walked into the room.

Her arrival appeared to puzzle him momentarily, but he recovered almost instantly, setting down the jug and beaming in her direction.

"Kate Reilly?"

When she nodded, he moved around the chairs to her side, extending his right hand as he did so. "I'm Lance Marchant, Joanna's husband."

"Yes," she murmured.

He frowned, studying her face. "Have we met?"

"I was at Joanna's funeral," she explained.

"Aah." He nodded his head thoughtfully, obviously conducting a quick mental search of the day and still coming up blank. He was about to say something more when Joanna's lawyer went to the head of the table, pushing aside the tray of coffee items as he withdrew a sheaf of papers from a briefcase. He put on his reading glasses cleared his throat and gestured toward the table.

"Shall we begin?" he asked, pausing while Lance returned to his chair and Kate sat down. "As all of you know, you've been requested to be here today for the reading of the late Joanna Barnes's will, dated April 1, 2001." He glanced over the rim of his glasses to smile. "Yes, that was

Joanna's idea of a little joke, though she assured me the will's contents were quite serious.'' He then began to read the legal preamble and Kate found her attention shifting to the others around the table.

Lance Marchant took a place to the right of Greg Collier. The lawyer's secretary sat on his left and was jotting on a steno pad. The elderly woman sitting across from Kate had been introduced as Joanna's housekeeper, and the thin, nervous-looking man with an earring in his right ear and a designer scarf knotted with a flourish around his neck had been her assistant at the fashion magazine where Joanna had worked as staff writer for the past five years.

Where were her other friends? Kate wondered. All the people she'd seen draped around Joanna in the newspaper and magazine pictures she'd clipped over the years? And *family?*

Kate peered down at her hands, clenched together on her lap. Her eyes filled with tears—as much for herself as Joanna. She'd thought herself immune to the sense of alienation that having no family produced. But here it was again, her pain on display for this roomful of strangers.

If only Joanna had called, made some kind of personal contact. But then what? Would we have had a real friendship? Would it have been a substitute for the family I've never had?

She chomped on her lower lip, forcing her mind back to Collier's recitation of the will. There was a mild gasp from the older woman when the lawyer revealed Joanna's bequest of a few thousand dollars. Likewise for the assistant, who received a smaller sum and all of Joanna's office furniture and equipment. Kate almost missed her own name, except that everyone at the table looked at her.

'' 'To my dear friend and co-conspirator, Kate Reilly, I leave Camp Limberlost and all its assets, in hope that she will rediscover the magic of a summer long ago. Kate, I can't tell you how much our contact over the years has meant to me, and wish you all the best for a wonderful life. I have complete confidence in your continued success.'''

Kate stared blankly at the others. She was stunned as much by Joanna's personal message as by the bequest. Tears welled up again and someone handed her a tissue, with which she quickly dabbed at her eyes. Joanna's lawyer was clearing his throat again, waiting a discreet moment before continuing.

The rest of Joanna's estate had been left to Lance Marchant. Through the labyrinth of legalese, Kate gathered that Joanna hadn't owned very much personally beyond whatever she'd possessed jointly with her husband. When Greg Collier was finished, he asked the beneficiaries to stay behind long enough to sign some papers. While the housekeeper and assistant were doing so, Lance Marchant sidled over to Kate.

Still reeling from the will, Kate missed the first part of his comment.

"Sorry?" She blinked.

He smiled. "I said that I'd no idea Joanna had such a good friend in someone so young. She seldom discussed her friends, unfortunately."

Unsure what he meant, Kate gave a tentative smile. What was he really thinking after learning his wife had left property to a virtual stranger?

She was saved from responding when Greg Collier approached with some documents. "Miss Reilly? Congratulations," he said, as if Kate had just won a lottery. "If I can get you to sign these papers…"

"Of course," she murmured. "Then I have some questions for you, if you don't mind." She went through the motions, still disbelieving the whole morning from the moment she'd stepped off the elevator into Matt Sinclair's insinuating face. She was half aware of Lance chatting politely to the housekeeper and assistant while seeing them to the door. When she finished signing on all the lines Greg Collier had indicated, she looked up at the two men smiling benignly down at her.

"Well, then," Collier said, rubbing his hands together, "more coffee, anyone?"

"Please," Lance replied, pulling out a chair across from Kate.

Collier spoke softly to his secretary, who took the papers Kate and the others had signed and left, closing the door behind her. "Coffee, Miss Reilly?"

She felt she was being set up for something. "Yes, thank you," she said, waiting while the lawyer poured and handed round the coffee with a tray of cream and sugar. Then she spoke, deciding not to let the two men take the lead. "I'm as puzzled by Joanna's bequest as I'm sure you both are. Although I met her nineteen years ago, I haven't seen her since. We corresponded only sporadically."

Greg nodded at Lance, then at Kate. "That's pretty much what Joanna explained when she had me draw up this will in the spring."

Kate flushed at the knowledge that people had been discussing her.

"I'm sure you must have some questions about the property," he continued, stopping as Kate began to shake her head.

"Actually, I've questions about Joanna's death that I'm hoping—" she glanced quickly at Lance, then back to the lawyer "—neither of you will mind answering."

The smile disappeared from Collier's face. He sat down beside Lance, who was staring into his coffee cup. "Of course, Miss Reilly," he said. "Ask away."

"It's just that, you see, Joanna and I had this promise to meet on July 14. It was meant to celebrate our meeting nineteen years ago. W-well," she stammered under Collier's blank look, "it's a long story and I won't bore you with it. I just can't believe that she'd...she'd commit suicide, knowing how much the reunion meant to both of us." She stopped, unable to continue.

Someone cleared a throat—Collier, Kate guessed. But it was Lance who spoke. "Kate, I understand what you're saying. I've been tormenting myself with the same doubts. I'd always considered Joanna and I to be the perfect match for each other. I loved her deeply, and I know she was very happy with me. That's what makes it so hard for me to believe she could..."

Kate's ears burned. This statement from a bereaved husband made her own disbelief sound like pathetic whimpering. She kept her head down, unable to look either of them in the eye.

Collier broke the silence. "As much as we all want to have an answer for this...tragic situation, sometimes there just isn't one that we can accept with any degree of comprehension." He paused, then continued, "Now, about this piece of property, Miss Reilly. I'm not certain of the current market value because I understand that it's been closed as a resort for several years. Most likely you'll want to sell it, and I'd be happy to have someone give you an estimate of its worth."

Kate's head shot up. "Oh! I...I've scarcely had time to think about even owning Camp Limberlost, much less selling it."

Collier chuckled. "I suppose all this does take time, but the summer will be the best season to show the property and all its potential." He looked to Lance for agreement.

Lance simply nodded, keeping his gaze fixed on Kate. He wasn't signaling his feelings about the camp either way, Kate realized. She had no idea how he felt about her inheriting it. Tongue-tied, she stared at the men.

"Owning it will most likely prove to be a greater disadvantage than asset,'' Collier added. His voice dripped like honey from a spoon.

"I know Joanna hasn't spent any time there since her father died almost eight years ago. And he closed it down a couple years before that, so…'' Lance shrugged.

"I've heard the whole area has gone downhill,'' Collier said, glancing at Lance and shaking his head. ''Too bad. I understand it was once a prime resort.''

"I think so,'' Lance murmured. He smiled across the table at Kate. ''You'll want to take a few days for this,'' he assured her. ''To let it all sink in. Believe me, as a developer, I know only too well what a headache owning a piece of property can be. Especially land and buildings that have been neglected. Let Greg—or me—know as soon as possible. We'll help you get the best possible price for it.''

Collier nodded heartily. ''Always available.'' He pushed his chair back and stood up. ''Now, if you'll pardon me, I must get back to work.''

Kate struggled to her feet. These two were good, she decided. If they shoved a dotted line at her at that moment, she was certain she'd sign without a second glance. Except for a sudden clarifying thought. *If Joanna willed Camp Limberlost to me, she must have really wanted me to have it. So no way am I going to give it up that easily.*

"Thank you for everything, Mr. Collier. I promise to get back to you as soon as is realistically possible.''

He patted her arm. ''You do that, my dear,'' he said, and left the room.

Kate reached for her purse, slung across the back of her chair. She felt Marchant's eyes on her and, when she straightened, knew from the amusement in his face that her own was beet red.

"Collier can be…well, shall I say, a bit paternal.''

"Is he a personal friend?'' Kate asked.

"Only socially—he's my lawyer, too, of course."

"Oh," she murmured.

"Which doesn't mean that I can't be objective about all this." He waved his hand into the room.

Confused, Kate followed the movement.

"The will—the inheritances and so on," he explained. "Joanna and I agreed when we got married that we'd each hold on to our own assets. Of course—" his voice dropped and he lowered his head "—we'd been discussing any future possibility of divorce, not…death." When he raised his head, his eyes were red-rimmed and tired. He managed a faint smile. "You obviously meant a lot to Joanna for her to include you in her will. And I know at some point in time that camp of her parents must have been worth a lot. It's just that—" he paused to shake his head "—Joanna was sometimes prone to what we used to call flights of fancy. A real romantic."

Kate felt herself nod, though she wasn't certain she agreed. The Joanna she remembered had seemed to have both feet firmly planted in the real world and to know exactly what she wanted.

"At any rate, I think the occasion of an inheritance, whatever that inheritance may be, is cause for celebration. I'd be honored if you'd be my guest for lunch."

The invitation capped a morning of surprises. Kate heard herself consent before she had time to even process the invitation. As she left the boardroom, Lance Marchant's hand guiding her at the small of her back, she had the feeling she'd played her cards exactly the way the two men had anticipated.

CHAPTER THREE

PARTWAY THROUGH LUNCH, Kate felt herself begin to unwind. She sipped her white wine, chosen after much deliberation by Lance. The ritual had amused Kate. She knew little about wine and was certain her own choice would have been based strictly on cost. The meal was impeccable, too. Another score for Lance, who was obviously a regular at the upscale restaurant, one Kate had read about in the papers, never imagining she might be eating in it some day.

In fact, there'd been so much deference shown to Lance as soon as they'd stepped inside that Kate began to wonder if he was a celebrity in his own right, regardless of his connection to Joanna Barnes. She pondered this throughout the salad course, racking her brain to determine where and when she'd seen or heard his name. She also scolded herself sharply for not reading the papers more carefully. Headlines were her specialty, along with a skim through the fashion and entertainment pages.

She began to think that maybe Lance Marchant was okay, after all, in spite of his smooth manner. Before ordering, they'd made small talk, discreetly skirting around the morning's events as if none of the business of death had taken place.

As the salad plates were removed, Lance referred to Camp Limberlost and Kate thought, here we go again. But rather than renew his pitch for selling it, he'd asked what she recalled of the camp.

"I didn't like it at the time—not until I met Joanna."

"She was there? When *was* this, exactly?"

"Nineteen years ago this month. What year would that be?" She screwed up her face, mentally counting backward.

"It would have been 1982."

Kate laughed. "That was fast. You should be teaching my grade eight math class."

He gave a dismissive shrug. "I use numbers all the time in my job. Were you there with your family?"

"No. I was with a bunch of kids from here in the city. Courtesy of a joint social-service program and the generosity of Joanna's parents."

Marchant frowned. "Oh. You mean like..."

"Kids with problems. Not delinquents," she added quickly, noting the expression in his face. "But, you know, kids at risk."

He nodded. "I don't mean to be nosy. Just didn't realize Joanna's parents were into that sort of thing."

Kate was tempted to ask, "Like *charity?*" but sensed he really wasn't being insensitive. Besides, she wanted to think she'd grown out of all that stuff—the feelings of defensiveness, of apologizing for being an orphan on the social welfare register.

"Did you know Joanna then?" she asked.

He nodded. "Joanna and I go—went—a long way back. But we weren't dating or anything. Just friends."

"Have you ever been to Limberlost?"

"I'm a city man. My idea of a holiday is a resort on some Caribbean island, five-star and all-inclusive."

She joined in his laughter. "You and Joanna both, I'm sure."

His face sobered. "Yes, for sure. That's why I can't figure out her being there. She always talked about how she'd made the Great Escape."

"I remember her mentioning that she was between hus-

bands then. I thought that was such a daring thing to say—
to a kid, I mean.''

Lance opened his mouth as if to add something, but the
waiter arrived with their main courses and the next few
moments were devoted to murmurings about the food. Kate
had almost forgotten what they'd been discussing when he
asked, toward the end of the meal, ''Do you remember
much about that summer? How old would you have been?
Don't answer if you consider that a rude question,'' he said,
grinning.

The way he put it, refusing to answer would seem childish. ''I was turning twelve in August. That's why we decided to meet this year.'' Kate angled her fork across her
plate and leaned forward. ''I was on the verge of adolescence and Joanna had just turned thirty. We'd been moan-
ing about our problems and getting older et cetera and she
said, wouldn't it be great to meet when we were both at
another milestone? To compare notes on how things had
turned out.''

''I guess your memory of the place wouldn't be very
vivid.''

Kate laughed. ''Oh, it's pretty vivid even now, trust
me.''

''How do you mean?''

She shrugged, unsure whether she really wanted to trip
down memory lane with someone she scarcely knew. ''I
wasn't really having a good time there until I met Joanna.
I was a typical city kid, afraid of everything with more than
two legs. Plus the other kids had been there before and
knew one another,'' she said.

''Aah,'' he murmured sympathetically.

The waiter appeared to gather the rest of the plates and
asked if they'd like dessert or coffee. Lance looked questioningly at Kate.

''No thanks, Mr. Marchant. I should be going.'' Kate

looked at her watch, realizing she hadn't called Carla yet. So much for setting an example.

He asked for the bill and, turning back to Kate, said, "Please call me Lance. And I insist on driving you home. My car is being brought up to the front door by the valet right now."

Knowing she'd get home much faster than by subway, Kate agreed. She'd hoped to glean more information about Joanna over lunch, but as they left, she realized Lance Marchant had been doing most of the asking. Perhaps the ride back home would elicit something about Joanna she hadn't yet read in a newspaper.

A blast of heat greeted their exit from the restaurant. Lance tipped the valet, who'd driven up with his red convertible sports car.

"Where are we going?" Lance's face was smilingly inquisitive.

"I live in SoHo. On a dead-end street off Bleecker, near Sullivan."

His tanned forehead crinkled in thought. "Near the university?"

"Past."

"Fine. The drive'll be longer than to the restaurant, but you don't seem to be the type to worry about a hairdo," Lance said. He ushered her into her seat, got behind the wheel and shifted into Drive. The car jerked forward and squealed out of the parking circle. He was laughing when he braked at the first stoplight. "Sorry again. I've just had it tuned prior to selling it. Joanna doesn't—didn't—like it, and my campaign manager advised that I drive something a little more sedate."

"Your campaign manager?"

He nodded. "Yeah. I'm running for Congress in the fall election. Lance Marchant? Republican ticket?" he added, obviously trying to jolt her memory.

Kate was embarrassed at her ignorance. "Oh, I'm sorry. I don't keep up much with politics."

He stared at her thoughtfully until the light changed, then shifted gears again. The breeze and traffic noise made conversation impossible, eliminating Kate's hope of talking more about Joanna.

But when the car slowed for a traffic halt, she managed to say, "The reason I find it hard to believe Joanna would...would commit suicide is not just because of our meeting, but I read in a gossip column that she was expected to be made editor of *Vogue*. That would've been the pinnacle of her career. I just can't believe that..."

Lance took his hand off the gear knob and patted her arm. "I've tortured myself with these same doubts, Kate, believe me. Perhaps she learned that she didn't get the job, after all. Certainly no one there has called to express sympathy. That must mean something." He paused then, having to move with traffic. Other than shouted directions about getting to Kate's neighborhood, all talk ceased until Lance pulled up in front of the row house where her flat was.

"Wait!" Lance said after Kate thanked him for the lunch and ride.

She turned, halfway through the opened door. His wind-tousled hair and trendy sunglasses made him seem dashing and much younger than his years, she thought. He had the kind of classic good looks that appealed to women of all ages, and Kate suddenly realized she herself wasn't immune to his charms herself. Well-established, well-dressed, trim and self-assured. But there was more. The gallant and attentive manner, the way he'd seemed to hang on to every word she'd uttered over lunch. He certainly fit the image of a winning politician.

"There is something," he said, glancing quickly away when he'd caught her attention.

She watched him clench and unclench his hands around the steering wheel. Finally he murmured, "The thing is, Joanna and I hadn't really been living as, well, as man and wife—if you get my drift—for several months. And as hard as I try, I can't pinpoint a reason for it. She was incredibly involved with her work, but that was nothing new. I had my own business to run, too. I think it all started when I decided to run for Congress. She was supportive, of course, but part of her seemed negative about the whole thing." He shrugged, helpless. "Maybe the thought of all the limelight—"

"Joanna loved the limelight!" Kate blurted. "At least, I'm sure she did. She often sent me press clippings of herself."

Kate could see her house reflected in his sunglasses. She wished she could see his eyes, to read what he was feeling.

"That she did," he agreed. "But on her terms. She knew how to manipulate the media, as many celebrities do. Inside, she was an intensely private person."

It wasn't the picture of Joanna that Kate had in her memory, but she could see how it fit with other facts. There'd only been a single card every year, even though Joanna had spent most of the nineteen years in the same city as Kate. And the few references to a personal life in those cards had been mainly a repetition of what Kate had already gathered from the media. The week with Joanna at Camp Limberlost had revealed more about the woman than the following two decades. The impact of that realization struck Kate with physical pain. *Because now it was all too late.* Tears edged her eyes and she averted her face. She wiped the corners of her eyes with her index finger.

"Kate?"

When she turned his way, it was her own drawn face she was seeing now in his sunglasses.

"Give me a call about the property as soon as possible.

Don't leave it too late. Summer's prime showing season for lake properties. And, uh, whatever you decide, I hope we can see each other again. *Soon.*''

There was no mistaking the suggestion. Kate was speechless. The man had just buried his wife. Her friend.

As if sensing his indiscretion, he quickly added, ''I didn't mean that the way it sounded. Simply that I knew very few of Joanna's colleagues, but I do know that you must have been very special to her. Otherwise she wouldn't have included you in her will.'' He paused and lowered his voice. ''It would be nice to get together again and just talk. Do you know what I mean?''

Kate nodded. ''Yes, of course Mr....uh, Lance. And I will call you or Mr. Collier as soon as possible. Thanks again for lunch and the ride home.'' She slid out the door, closed it and waited by the curb as he drove off. When the red car zipped around the corner of her street, she turned toward her house. Matt Sinclair was leaning against the brick planter box at the foot of the steps.

HE'D BEEN FEEDING a parking meter a few yards away when Lance Marchant's car screeched to a halt in front of Kate's place. So he waited at the meter, watching the two of them chatting until Kate got out. Matt knew the surge in his blood pressure was from a long antipathy for Marchant, but the cozy sight rankled even more. When the red Porsche sped off, he strolled over to greet Kate.

She was in the same dress she'd worn to Joanna's funeral, and her face looked just as red as it had that day, too. *The heat or the thrill of Marchant's company?* He'd pegged her for an unassuming schoolteacher. Now he wasn't so sure. Her chin-length hair fanned up and away from her face, whipped into a froth of knots by the car ride. As she marched toward him, he saw that, although the expression in her pinched face was most definitely schoolteacherish, her manner was no longer unassuming. For a moment he had a frightening flashback to his prep-school days, standing before his headmaster.

"You've been following me!" Her voice peaked in anger.

Matt forced back a smile. "Actually, I was here before you. Likewise for this morning at the elevator." He waited a beat. "Maybe it's the other way around."

The lame attempt at humor failed. She hadn't registered a single word, but came right up to him to repeat her accusation. So close that he sniffed the residue of wine and garlic on her breath. The sudden image of her and Marchant laughing over lunch chilled him.

He raised his palms in a surrendering motion. "Whoa! Doesn't the word *coincidence* mean anything to you?"

"*Coincidence* was the meeting this morning. *This* is no coincidence. How did you get my address?"

"Phone book?" he countered.

She narrowed her eyes but calmed down, taking a step backward. "What is it you want, Mr. Sinclair?"

"Make it Matt, please. Could we go somewhere for a cold drink and a talk?"

"I've been eating and drinking for more than an hour, and frankly, I don't see how I could possibly have anything to say to you."

She started to move past him but he placed his hand on her arm. Looking down at the hand and then up at his face, Kate said, "You have an unpleasant habit of doing that and I'd like you to remove your hand this instant."

Matt's hand flew off her arm as if she'd taken a ruler to it. He tried again. "Look, after seeing you this morning I realized there were a lot of questions you must have about Joanna and, well, the things I said about her the other day."

"Go on," she said.

The stare made him think she must be a good teacher.

Probably never had to raise her voice. Just fix those eyes—
what color were they, anyway?—on an unruly kid and order would prevail.

"There's a coffee place around the corner. Why don't
we go there? Not for long. I'll leave whenever you tell
me."

She frowned as she considered the invitation, then nodded curtly and began walking toward the corner. He had to
lope to keep up with her, in spite of the difference in their
heights and leg length. She only came up to his shoulder
but had no trouble keeping enough distance between them
to make him feel like a pup on a leash.

The blast of frigid air as they stepped into the coffee
house was nothing to the cool appraisal she gave him as
he ordered iced cappuccino for them both. Her face could
have been chiseled from Siena marble, he thought. Not a
hint of emotion.

She got right to the point. "You wanted to tell me something about Joanna."

He tipped an invisible hat to her. She was good. Making
it look like the wanting and telling were both on his side
when he could see, even under that neutral expression, that
she wanted—no, *needed*—to hear whatever he had to say.
He thought for a moment, knowing how important it was
to choose his words carefully.

"My father and Joanna got married when I was seventeen, as I think I told you the other day. My mother had
died just six months earlier." He paused to stare down at
the table for a long moment before raising his face back to
her. "I was in Europe at some fancy boarding school my
parents decided I needed at that point in my life."

The waitress arrived with their cold drinks. When she
moved away, he went on. "I got a telephone call about
their marriage just the day before," he explained. "They

were in Las Vegas. It was all a last-minute thing. That's what my father claimed, anyway.''

The bitterness in his voice just slipped out. He swallowed some of the frosty cappuccino, reminding himself to relax. It was a long time ago.

''To make a long story short, they got married and were on the verge of divorcing two years later when my father died of a heart attack. The last time I saw Joanna was at Dad's funeral. I was nineteen and hardly knew her. We exchanged a few words and that was it.''

''You were going to tell me why you disliked her so much.''

Matt forced himself to keep his voice neutral. ''To give Joanna her credit, she never tried to take anything out of the marriage that my father hadn't actually given her. So after he died, she willingly handed over all my mother's things—some jewellery and photographs—as well as most of Dad's personal papers and such. But she certainly managed to go through most of his liquid assets in those two years, and they'd been substantial. Dad had been a highly paid executive at the bank. By the time taxes and lawyers were paid, there wasn't much left, anyway.''

''And?''

He flushed with annoyance. She was cool, all right. Not a murmur or flicker of sympathy during his whole speech. Suddenly he wanted to blurt out the whole of it. See if that finely sculpted marble would crack under the heat of what he'd say.

''A while ago I learned that she hadn't returned everything of Dad's. I've been trying for several months now to get hold of some papers of his. They weren't important to her, but they are to me. That's why I was at Marchant's office this morning. To ask about them.''

''What did he say?''

He wasn't expecting the question. She was obviously

more interested in Marchant's response than in his story, and he felt a surge of irritation. Then she sat forward in her chair, folding her elbows on the tabletop. Her iced cappuccino, still untouched, was sitting in a widening puddle of condensation. Merely keeping eye contact with her blue-green and very direct gaze obliterated his rehearsed reply. Matt wet his lips and glanced down at his own empty glass.

"Mind?" he asked, indicating hers.

"Go ahead," she mumbled.

Matt took a long swallow. "Lance told me he hadn't found any of my father's papers among Joanna's things."

Kate shrugged as if to say, what did you expect?

"But after I left his office, I thought the papers might have been stored at that camp of her parents. Can't recall the name."

"Limberlost," she said. She was sitting straight as a poker now, all ears.

"Right. I wondered if you could look for them for me."

Kate tilted her head questioningly. "Say again?"

He cursed under his breath. Well, he thought, there was no going back now. The proverbial cat was definitely not only out of the bag, but scampering across the table.

"Perhaps I'm speaking out of turn, but I heard that you'd inherited the camp from Joanna and, uh, I was wondering if you'd look for the papers for me. At the camp."

"Where did you hear that?" she demanded. "Who told you I inherited the camp?"

She leaned across the table, the end of her nose almost touching the iced cappuccino sitting in front of him.

He made an effort not to pull his head back. In spite of the dizzying warmth of her breath enveloping his face, he managed a casual shrug. "I don't know. I…I guess Marchant. When I saw him this morning."

She eased back into her chair, a faint smirk on her face.

"I don't believe you. Your meeting with him was before the will had been read."

Matt knew he'd never come up with anything convincing enough to sway that haughty, self-assured expression in her eyes, but he made a stab at it. "I'm sure he mentioned it. How else would I know?"

The rhetorical question hung over the table. After a long moment, Kate pushed her chair back and stood up. "I don't know who you are—oh yes," she said, holding up a palm, "you *say* you're Matt Sinclair and your father was married to Joanna and so on, but we haven't really been introduced at all, have we? I mean, you could be just *anyone* telling me whatever you want, and you still haven't explained why Joanna was a target of your hate. I've no idea how you learned about my inheritance, but seeing as it's got *nothing* whatsoever to do with you, I'm leaving."

Color bloomed in her face again, and in spite of the frizzy hair and a bra strap drooping off her shoulder, Matt knew that she was mustering all her reserves to make a dignified exit. He remained in his seat as she marched to the door and left without a backward glance.

Strike three. So now you've blown all three encounters with Kate Reilly. Way to go, champ.

KATE KEYED IN HER password so hard she chipped the end of her index fingernail. With the telephone receiver clamped in one hand, she patted down her hair with the other. Then she noticed her bra strap hanging limply from under the shoulder of her sleeveless dress and swore. The safety pin must have unfastened. She should've taken a few extra minutes that morning to sew the damn thing. Knowing that she'd left the café disheveled as well as angry added to her conflicting emotions about Matt.

Her voice mail clicked on, repeating Carla's message.

"Hi, Kate, it's me, Carla. It's already two and you

haven't called yet. Are we still on for shopping tomorrow? Can you call and let me know later, 'cause I'm going out right now. Bye.''

Kate hung up and swore again. In spite of the casual tone of Carla's voice, she knew from experience what a broken promise meant to a troubled teen. She replayed Carla's message. Hadn't she been grounded? If so, why was she going out? Kate rapidly punched in Carla's number, but the line was busy. Reluctant to play telephone tag, she hung up and headed into her bedroom.

She'd forgotten to close the blinds before leaving that morning, and the room, filled with sunlight for hours, was like a Swedish sauna in spite of the air conditioner pumping away in the kitchen. Kate rushed to the window and reached for the rod. Glancing downward, she noticed a man standing on the pavement a few feet away from the entrance to her row house. Matt Sinclair.

Kate frowned. She'd managed to put the coffee-shop scene out of her mind for five minutes and now the whole humiliating event surged back. She leaned closer to the window. He had his back to her and seemed to be swaying from side to side, his right arm raised. Kate pressed her nose against the glass to get a better look. Then she realized what he was doing. Talking on a cell phone. She almost laughed, except he chose that moment to crane around and look up at her window.

Ducking to the side so he couldn't see her, Kate continued to watch him talk and survey her windows. Finally he tucked the phone into his suit jacket pocket and stepped off the curb to a silver-gray car. As he unlocked the car, he glanced up once more. Kate jerked her head back again and waited before chancing another peek. He was inside the car now and pulling away from the curb. She watched him drive down her street to the main intersection, then turn right.

Stepping out from her hiding nook, she yanked the blind rod and the slats swooshed noisily into place. Her fingers were still trembling as she unzipped her dress, letting it fall onto the floor. A wake of lingerie marked her path to the linen closet and bathroom.

Seconds later, a full spray from the shower nozzle cooled her body temperature to normal. A brisk scrubbing with her loofah sponge had her skin pink and glowing. If only, she thought ironically, she could eliminate all memory of Matt Sinclair and his annoying habit of dropping into her life every few days. No, not days. Make that *hours*.

Kate used the corner of her towel to clear a circle in the steamy mirror. She tapped her reflection lightly. *Why do you care so much, anyway? Matt Sinclair is nothing to you.*

By the time she'd dressed and poured herself a tall glass of ice water, she was ready to call Carla's foster home again.

"Rita? It's Kate Reilly calling. Is Carla there?"

A slight pause on the other end, followed by a muffled exclamation and a wail. "Shh! Hi, Kate. Sorry, just had to change arms there. I've been rocking the baby all afternoon and she just this second fell asleep."

"I suppose the phone woke her. Sorry about that."

"No, no. It's okay. She's gone back to sleep again. Worn out. Like me," she whispered.

"Is she sick?"

"Teething. She was up all night, too. Look, Carla's taken off again. I should call Kim. I…I don't want to, Kate, but she really left me in the lurch. Promised to be home all afternoon 'cause you were calling. I'd hoped to catch a nap…."

Her voice drifted off, as if she were too exhausted to even finish the sentence.

Kate didn't know whether to be angry at Carla or herself.

If she'd called on time, would the girl have stayed? Who could tell with Carla?

"Okay, Rita. I'll call again tomorrow."

"It doesn't look good."

Kate sighed. "Yeah. It sure doesn't." She said goodbye and hung up. She understood Rita's reluctance to call Carla's social worker. It seemed like a betrayal of loyalty, going behind Carla's back to discuss her. That was how Kate would have interpreted it, when she'd been in Carla's shoes. But now she could see the other angles. What worried her was the fear that she'd no longer be able to get through to Carla herself.

Kate wandered into the darkened living room and flopped onto the couch. She felt drained of energy and initiative. No wonder, she thought, considering all that had happened that day.

Lunch in the most exclusive restaurant she'd ever been in, not to mention a ride in a foreign car that probably cost more than her annual salary. Two strange encounters with Matt Sinclair. She shivered. *What's his problem, anyway?*

And how did he know which flat was hers, because he'd seemed to look straight up at her windows on the second floor. She took another sip of water, set the glass down on the coffee table beside the couch and lay back. A nap would be nice, she decided, plumping the pillows behind her. If she could clear her mind of all the unpleasant thoughts— Carla, in trouble again. Matt Sinclair. She sighed and closed her eyes. A brighter picture appeared.

Camp Limberlost. Now hers.

CHAPTER FOUR

"I SAID I WAS SORRY."

Kate closed her eyes and breathed a sigh of relief.

Carla hung back on the door stoop. "I wanted to phone, honest. But the others started laughing and calling me a baby," she continued, her dark eyes fixed on Kate's face, willing her to believe.

And Kate wanted to. Except that she'd heard it all before in a hundred different ways, so that even Carla's turned-down mouth and slumped shoulders failed to arouse pity. But the hint of moisture in her eyes did the trick, because Carla never cried.

"Come inside," Kate said gently, standing aside as the girl slinked past. Instead of making for her favorite canvas hammock chair as she usually did, Carla stood in the center of the room, hugging herself tightly. She was a pathetic sight, but Kate resisted going to her.

"Care for a glass of lemonade? I was just getting one for myself." And without waiting for a reply, Kate headed into the kitchen. The few extra seconds gave her time to put together some kind of strategy. Confrontation, she knew only too well from her own turbulent adolescence, was like turning up the heat. Too much sympathy would offer an escape route that Carla had already learned to use to her advantage. Of course there was also appealing to reason. *With an emotionally charged teenager?* Forget it.

After handing Carla her drink, Kate casually sat down on the couch. She sipped, wondering how long it would take Carla to follow suit. Three seconds later, Carla perched on the edge of the wicker armchair Kate had bought at a yard sale. It was a horribly uncomfortable chair and Carla never sat on it. Kate had to stifle a smile. A sign, perhaps, that the teen wanted to punish herself? She waited, taking a longer drink of lemonade. Finally Carla began to talk.

"Okay, see, there's this girl I met. She doesn't live near me, but a couple of subway stops away. She belongs to this gang. And, like, she's been trying to get me in."

Kate reached over to set her glass onto the coffee table. She was afraid if she held it a moment longer, it would shatter from the force of her grip. *I've been too complacent,* she thought. Assuming that Carla's problems could be solved with shopping trips and sleepovers. How could I have forgotten so easily? But then, by the time she was Carla's age, she'd already met Joanna Barnes and made her promise to take a different path from the neighborhood kids.

"Go on," Kate said, keeping her voice as neutral as she could.

Carla glanced up at Kate for the first time since she'd entered the flat. The expression in her face begged for understanding. "They're nice to me, Kate. That may be hard for you to believe, but they are. They don't try to get me to do, you know, bad things like shoplift or smoke dope."

"Do *they* do those things?"

Kate realized at once it was the wrong question to ask. Carla stared down at her lemonade and simply shrugged. After a moment she mumbled, "I don't know."

But of course she did, thought Kate, *and I've just made her rush to their defense.* She tried to make amends. "It's okay, Carla, I'm not asking you to snitch on them. Forget I mentioned it. Go on."

But there was a wariness in Carla's voice now and she

spoke in a stilted way, as if talking to her social worker. Or a teacher.

"Anyway," Carla said, "I told Rita I'd help her out when I got home and I would have, only…"

"Only?"

She swallowed a mouthful of lemonade, then said, "I didn't realize how late it was, and Toni—that's my friend—said if I waited a couple more hours, her boyfriend would drive me home when he got off work."

"She has a boyfriend? How old is this Toni?"

"Sixteen."

Kate took a deep breath. "What are the ages of the rest of the kids? In the gang, I mean."

"I dunno. Maybe fifteen up to eighteen or so."

"Carla, you're only thirteen."

Carla raised her head, eyes flashing with anger. "Yeah, but they don't hold that against me, you know. They think I'm, like, cute and funny. They even call me their mascot."

Kate resisted responding to that, in spite of images of inflated birds and oversize fluffy dogs.

"And you couldn't have called Rita? Or even me?"

"Like I said, they'd have teased me. Besides, what would have been the point by then?"

Kate leaned forward on the couch. "It might have meant that Rita wouldn't have worried half the night, wondering if she ought to phone Kim or maybe the police."

"The *police?*" Her face paled.

"Carla, if you'd stayed out an hour longer, Rita would probably have called them."

"So much for trust."

Kate sighed. Here we go again. "You have to *earn* trust. There've been too many other times like this. Rita feels that she's expended all of her options. She doesn't know what to do anymore."

Carla lowered her head, seemingly intent on picking at

a scab on her finger. But Kate noticed the trembling across her shoulders. After a moment, Carla wiped her nose with the back of her hand. Silently, Kate went to the bathroom for a box of tissues, which she placed in Carla's lap. Then she sat down, waiting for the girl to stop crying.

When Carla had used two or three tissues to daub her face, she set the box down on the coffee table and looked across at Kate. "I know I've been giving Rita a hard time, but...but I don't mean to. I like Rita. She and Eddie have always been good to me. Strict, but fair. I've been with them for two years now and I want to stay with them. If they still want me." She glanced away, her chin wobbling again.

"They do want you, Carla. They've never stopped wanting to care for you. It's just that they've never raised a teenager before and—"

"A problem teen, like me."

"No, Carla. A teen with some problems, yes, but that's all. The important thing is to keep talking to them. Don't be afraid to just go to them and say, 'Look, I know I screwed up and I'm going to try harder the next time.' They'll be more sympathetic if they see that you really want to change. Trust me, after all, I'm your Big Sister."

Carla's big brown eyes, damp with tears, fixed on Kate. "I hope you'll always be," she whispered.

"I will be." Kate felt the prick of tears in her own eyes, but forced them back. "You know, I just had a great idea Carla. I've inherited some property in the mountains and—"

"Wow!"

"Yes, though I don't know yet how exciting that is because I haven't seen it for years. I was thinking of renting a car and driving into the mountains for a couple of days. If I get permission from Rita and Kim, would you like to go?"

A confusion of emotions battled in Carla's face. "Would it be, like, camping or something? Would there be wild animals there? 'Cause I'm not real good with stuff like that."

"Me, neither. No camping—there's a lodge with beds—but it may be a bit dusty and cobwebby. Think you could handle that?"

"Yeah! It'd be cool, just you'n me. Will you rent a car with a CD player?"

Kate laughed. Typical teen—getting right to the important things. "If there's one available. If not, we may have to settle for tape cassettes. Anyway, this means I'll have a few phone calls to make. Shall I try to plan it for the day after tomorrow? Is that too soon for you?"

"I think that'll be okay." Carla frowned. "Do you think my behavior is going to make them say no?"

"I don't know, Carla. That's up to Kim and Rita. But I do think another apology and a real effort to help out over the next couple of days will influence their decision."

Carla stood up. "I will, Kate. Thanks for...everything." She reached out and gave Kate an awkward hug.

It was the first sign of physical affection Carla had ever shown to her, and Kate knew to play it down. She smiled and tapped the girl's chin lightly with her finger. "I'm always here for you, Carla, remember that. Now, you'd better head home and I'll start making my calls."

After she'd closed the door behind the girl, Kate sagged against it. Yesterday's impulsive idea to visit Limberlost was now a commitment. She didn't know whether to curse herself or praise her ingenuity. She took a deep breath and moved away from the door. If she was going to make her promise to Carla a reality, she had a lot to do.

"MISS REILLY? Greg Collier here, returning your call."

"Thanks for getting back to me so quickly, Mr. Collier. I wanted to talk to you about Camp Limberlost."

"Ah! You've made a decision already?"

"Well, no, not really. I thought I'd like to visit it before deciding anything."

After a slight pause, he said, "I see. Now, tell me, Miss Reilly, do you know that area at all? Other than having gone to Limberlost once as a child?"

"Uh...no, but to tell you the truth, it's a chance to get out of the city for a couple of days." Kate mentally chastised herself for feeling the need to make excuses. Wasn't the property legally hers now?

He must have picked up a cue from her voice for he quickly went on to say, "Of course, and please don't let me discourage you. Just want to remind you that things may be a bit rough up there—the camp hasn't been used for a number of years."

The urge to speed into the mountains was starting to wane. "Well, if things are too bad I can always head back to the city," Kate replied. "How do I go about getting a key for the place? Or is there even such a thing?"

"Oh, yes. Apparently the place has been looked after by a couple who live in the nearest village. Now, what was the name..." There was a sound of drawers opening and papers shuffling. Then, still talking to himself, the lawyer mumbled, "Ah, here it is. Tippett. Bill and Verna. They live in Bondi, which is about ten miles from the camp. How about if I give him a call and let him know you're coming? He'll need to see about electricity and so on."

"That would be great. Now, I guess I'll have to get directions."

"Do you have a fax machine?"

Kate smiled. "No, I'm afraid not."

"No problem. I'll have my secretary courier a map to you ASAP. When shall I tell Bill Tippett you're going?"

It appeared she had to nail down the date. "I'm thinking the day after tomorrow."

More paper noises. "Uh, that would be the twenty-fourth?"

The twenty-fourth of July. Ten days after she was supposed to meet Joanna. Kate couldn't speak for a moment. If things had turned out differently, perhaps she and Joanna would have been making the trip to Limberlost together. And Carla might have had a chance to meet her and…. She closed her eyes.

"Miss Reilly?"

She took a deep breath and said, "Yes, the twenty-fourth."

"Righto. If there's a problem with Tippett getting the place ready, I'll get back to you."

"Please tell him I don't expect miracles. I'm quite prepared to rough it."

"I'm sure there won't be any miracles, Miss Reilly." He laughed. "When you get back to New York, let me know if I can help you with the property in any way. Whatever you decide."

"Yes, I'll do that. Thanks, Mr. Collier."

His voice boomed across the line. "Only too happy to help out."

As Kate put the phone down, she couldn't help but think of a hungry shark streaking through a school of fish. She'd heard too many lawyer jokes, she told herself. Still, was it her imagination or had the man really been trying to put her off visiting Limberlost? Kate shrugged. What did it matter, as long as she and Carla had a chance to get out of the city? Now all she had to do was get permission for the girl to come with her.

Easier said than done. It seemed to Kate that she'd been dealing with bureaucracy all her life—filling out forms to go to camp, to go on school trips outside the city, to get braces on her teeth. Growing up a ward of the courts had meant a lifetime of dealing with committees and agencies rather than individuals. The years after Joanna had been relatively stable, but only because Kate had decided that cooperating with her foster parents was more likely to lead to the goals she'd set for herself.

So she knew exactly how to phrase her request to Kim, Carla's caseworker. The woman was fair and would realize the break from routine would benefit Carla. Still, Kim said she wouldn't be able to get back with an official okay until late afternoon the next day. Kate decided to book a rental car for the twenty-fourth on the assumption that Carla's permission would be given.

Everything was proceeding well until Rita called early the next morning while Kate was finishing her first cup of coffee in bed.

"Carla's taken off," she said.

Kate sagged against the headboard. "What?"

Rita gave a loud sigh. "It's not as bad as it sounds, but she left in a huff right after breakfast. When I reminded her she'd have to do laundry for your trip north, she said she probably wouldn't be allowed to go and what was the point. Then just as she walked out the door, she hollered back that maybe she didn't want to go, anyway."

"She's just setting things up so she won't be disappointed if it doesn't work out. But it's going to. Kim seemed very supportive. You haven't spoken to her about it, have you?"

"Kim? No, I thought I should talk to you first."

"Do me a favor, then, Rita? Wait until I get back to you. I'm going to have a talk with Carla. Where does she usually hang out with her friends?"

"They could be a couple of places. Either at the basketball hoops at the school playground or at the parkette at Vine and Broadview. It's about two subway stops south of our place."

"Right. Is that near where her friend Toni lives?"

"You know about Toni, eh? She's bad news, that one."

As soon as Kate hung up, she dashed into the shower and dressed in cutoffs, T-shirt and sneakers. Rather than take a fanny pack or wallet, she shoved her subway pass and a twenty-dollar bill deep into her shorts pocket. Then she searched in the bottom of her closet for her baseball cap and pulled it down over her hair, tucking the side tendrils back behind her ears and under the cap. She looked about seventeen, which was fine with her. As long as she eliminated her schoolteacher persona. She had a feeling that wouldn't carry much weight with Toni and her gang.

Soon after, Kate arrived at the Brooklyn neighborhood where Carla and her friends hung out. They weren't at the basketball court. Okay, she thought. On to the parkette. She didn't want to think about what she'd do if Carla wasn't there.

But she was. Coming up from the subway exit, Kate spotted a group of kids across the street. She paused at the top of the stairs, watching them. The parkette was merely a slightly-bigger-than-room-size piece of sunburned grass a few yards from the intersection. A scattering of benches were chained to concrete posts, and there was a rusting combo of swings and teeter-totters around which a handful of mothers, shoulders drooping from the pull of plastic shopping bags, chatted as they watched their children shuffle from one swing or slide to another. It was only after ten, but already the heat was sucking energy from everyone, injecting them with a listless apathy. Except for the knot of teenagers who'd taken over the best benches—the ones in the shade at the edge of the sidewalk.

The large-framed girl standing, arms on hips, in the middle of the sidewalk was the focal point. The others around her were laughing at her impersonation of a suited execu-

tive type who'd just strode past them, cell phone clenched
to his ear as he gesticulated with his free hand. The girl
was good, Kate had to admit, watching her mincing mim-
icry of the man's walk as he signaled his reactions to the
phone conversation to the world at large. Then another pas-
serby appeared.

Just a kid, but seriously obese. Laden with two bulky
shopping bags, he waddled out of the corner fruit-and-
vegetable store and headed their way. He was wearing
shorts that ballooned out from his thick legs and a crumpled, wide-brimmed sun hat that might have sheltered an
elderly woman's head thirty years ago. Kate licked her dry
lips, waiting for the gang to notice him.

Suddenly there was a flurry of elbow-poking as the girl
was alerted to her new target by the kids around her. Kate
looked at Carla, sitting at the farthest end of the bench with
her knees tucked up against her chest. She, too, was looking
at the boy, slowly making his way toward them. But she
wasn't laughing, Kate noticed with relief. Instead, she
dropped her chin to her chest, as if hiding from what she
knew was coming.

Oh, Carla. There's hope for you yet.

Time to make my move, Kate thought. She sprinted to
the corner, making it to the other side of the street just as
the light changed. The girl had planted herself in the center
of the walk, planning to block the boy's way. She turned
her head back to the others behind her, saying something
that produced laughter from the bench-sitters. All but Carla,
who now had her face completely buried in her upraised
knees.

Kate marched toward them, easily overtaking the boy,
who'd slowed his pace when he'd caught sight of the gang.
Initially Kate had hoped to get Carla aside and talk to her
in private. But now she realized she couldn't avoid a con-

frontation with the performance artist herself. Was this the notorious Toni?

So she stopped dead center and mere inches from the girl, enjoying the surprise and then outrage that flitted across the teenager's face.

"Where's Carla?" Kate asked, her voice strong and confident.

The girl's eyes narrowed, shifting from the approaching target to Kate. "Carla who?"

"Carla Lopez." The second word was spoken like a taunt that conveyed the tag *stupid*.

Carla raised her head, and her eyes widened in disbelief. The boy was forgotten by the gang as all eyes shifted her way. Kate stepped forward, shortening the distance between her and the girl. When the girl stepped back, Kate knew she had the upper hand.

"So who are you?" the girl asked, her tone challenging.

Kate noticed Carla lower her feet to the pavement, start to get up off the bench.

"I'm her big sister, and I suppose you must be Toni."

"Her *sister?*" Toni echoed with a glance back at Carla. The others looked back to Carla, as well. Sister? This was news to them.

"You don't look like no Lopez," jeered an acne-faced girl beside Toni.

Kate simply shrugged. She brushed past Toni to Carla. "Coming, Carly?"

Carla's eyes flicked from her to Toni, held there a moment long enough to raise Kate's blood pressure, then back to Kate. "Okay," she whispered.

Kate draped her arms across Carla's shoulders and the two stepped forward. But Toni wasn't ready to let them go so easily.

She moved directly into their path. "She really your sister, Carla?"

"Well…yeah," Carla mumbled.

"How come you never talked about her?"

"I don't tell you everything!" Carla hotly declared.

Kate silently applauded the girl.

Toni raised her eyebrows. "So, you leavin' for lunch or somethin'," she sneered, "or you leavin' the group for good?" The others stood round their leader, arms folded across their chests and nodding agreement.

Kate swallowed. Carla wasn't ready to make that kind of a choice yet, and certainly not so publicly. She said, "What's the big deal? I've come to get my little sister because I need her for something. Besides, it's my job to look out for her, isn't it?" She scanned the faces of each and every one. Then focused her attention on Toni.

"You got a big sister or brother?" she asked.

Toni flushed. Someone behind her burst out, "Yeah. In Sing Sing," then sputtered in a hard laugh that died as soon as Toni swiveled her head round to glare.

"Whatever," Kate said casually. "A brother?"

Toni gave a jerky half nod.

"So if he were here, he'd be looking out for you, too. Right?"

A more affirmative nod this time.

"'Course he would," Kate continued. "That's what big sisters and brothers are for." She searched their faces again, waiting for disagreement. When none came, she said, "Then I guess you guys won't mind if I take my little sister away for a bit—family business, you might say." Kate reached down for Carla's hand and started to walk.

Toni hesitated a second before standing aside. As they moved past her, she gave Carla a seemingly playful poke on the shoulder. "See you around, Carla."

Kate kept walking, pulling Carla along. She felt the girl look back, but didn't slow her pace. When she heard Carla say, "Maybe," she knew everything was going to be okay.

It wasn't until they got to the subway entrance that Kate relaxed enough to stop. Instead of lecturing the girl, she gave her a big, breathless smile. "We made it," she said, giggling.

Carla, clamping her hand to her mouth, dissolved into laughter. "I couldn't figure out who you were at first," she said. "You look so different in that hat, with your hair all hidden. When you said you were my big sister, I almost fell off the bench."

"Yeah. Well, I meant every word, Carla."

The girl straightened up, meeting Kate's gaze with an instant sobriety. "I know you did, Kate. That's how I got the nerve…you know, to just…"

"Walk away?"

The girl nodded. "Thanks for coming," she mumbled. "I…I…"

"You didn't look like you were having a good time," Kate said.

Carla shook her head. "Toni can be real mean sometimes."

Kate made no comment, letting that realization sink in. Then she said, "Let's go," and the two ran down the steps into the subway.

NEITHER SPOKE UNTIL they reached Carla's station. As they exited onto the sidewalk, Kate said, "By the way, I've rented a car and Kim's going to call me later today. She sounded very positive about your coming with me to Camp Limberlost."

Carla stopped and looked up at Kate, an anxious frown creasing her brow. "But, well, do you think Kim'll still feel that way after today? I mean, when she hears that I walked out on Rita again."

"Rita didn't call Kim."

"She didn't?"

"No. I asked her to wait until I had a chance to see you."

There was a thoughtful silence from Carla, followed by a husky thank-you. When they reached the triplex where Carla lived, Kate said, "I'll call you as soon as I hear from Kim. In the meantime, you might want to do some packing. You'll need a bathing suit, towel and change of clothes. I figure we'll stay two nights. That should satisfy the needs of two city girls."

"Rita said she'd buy me a sleeping bag."

"Good idea! I'll have to pick one up for myself. Okay, that's it, then." She smiled down at the girl. "We're going to have a great time. Talk to you later." As she turned to leave, Carla reached out a hand to her arm.

"Kate, I won't mess up again. I promise. And I really did want to get away from those kids. I was just too chicken."

Kate shook her head. "You came, didn't you? That said everything." She waved goodbye and headed back to the subway to get a train to Manhattan. Partway, she realized she was dying for a cold drink and recalled a terrific coffee shop on the edge of Little Italy, just a few stops from her flat. An ice-cold latte was definitely in order, after her encounter with Toni and friends.

Exiting the shop, chilled drink in hand, she strolled along to the next subway station, thinking she might find a store on the way that sold sleeping bags. Good for Carla for thinking of it. She herself had blithely assumed there'd be clean, pressed sheets on the beds. If the camp had deteriorated as much as Greg Collier had implied, she'd be lucky to have cobwebs and spiders swept away. Kate shivered. *God, I hope so.*

Luck was with her and she came upon an outfitter store just a block from the subway. By the time she'd made her purchase, she realized it was almost three. She wanted to make sure she had an answer from Kim before the woman left work for the day. Clutching the bag under her arm, she jogged the remaining distance. Later that day, she realized that if she'd been looking where she was going and hadn't bumped into the woman pushing the stroller out of a grocery store, she might have run right past Lance Marchant.

Swearing under her breath as she stooped to pick up the sleeping bag after her collision with the stroller, Kate paused to rub her scraped shin. When she straightened, she noticed a bright red convertible pull out from the curb. There couldn't be too many cars like that, she thought, even in New York. She walked briskly toward it, reaching the edge of the curb just as the car arrowed out of the space.

When the driver turned to check oncoming traffic, she saw a shock of white hair and realized that he was definitely Lance Marchant. She almost waved, except that he was looking to his left and not in his rearview mirror. Kate glanced back to the store in front of the parking space. It was one of those all-male sports bars. A dingy-looking one at that. Not some place a man like Lance Marchant would hang out.

She'd just stepped off the curb onto the empty parking space to jaywalk to the other side of the street when a sleek black limousine shot toward her. Kate jumped back onto the sidewalk. There was a flurry of Italian spoken behind her, and as she turned to look, a trio of dark-suited men in sunglasses hustled another man out of the bar and into the rear door of the limousine.

The door slammed and the car, having barely come to a halt, snaked out onto the path of traffic exactly as Marchant had. Must be some kind of celebrity, Kate guessed. Maybe the bar was one of those exclusive places that only the very wealthy knew about. She smiled at the idea, stepped off the curb again and, for the second time in two minutes, was almost run over. This time a battered white van roared into the lane of cars just as Kate was about to take advantage of a break in the traffic.

She swore aloud and would have run alongside the van as it chugged forward into the traffic. But she stopped in her tracks, recognizing one of the two men sitting in front on the passenger side, his finger pointing ahead as he talked to the driver. It was the police officer who'd spoken to her after Joanna's funeral.

Kate watched the van merge into the mass of cars until it disappeared. What was his name? Anderson? Anders? Andrews? Yes, that was it. Somebody Andrews. She was certain it was him. What was he doing here? And Marchant, too. Seeing two men from Joanna's funeral in the same neighborhood and virtually at the same time was a little too coincidental.

CHAPTER FIVE

KATE HUNG UP the receiver and exhaled a breath of relief. No problem. Carla could accompany her to Camp Limberlost. She made a quick call to Rita, speaking afterward to Carla to arrange a pickup time for ten the next morning.

Rita came on the line again after. "I don't know what happened today—I mean, she was a bit sketchy with the details—but that girl has been wonderful since you brought her home. She even volunteered to take the baby for a walk after dinner!"

"Well, let's keep our fingers crossed."

"Exactly," agreed Rita. "One day at a time."

Kate rang off and sank into the armchair next to the phone. She was wrung out by the day's events, but at the same time, coasting into second gear mentally, charged by the bustle of activity and the way things were working out.

By the time she'd arrived at her flat, it was almost five. There'd been an accident on the subway line and she'd had to walk the last few blocks. But Kim had left a brief message confirming permission for the trip.

And there'd been a large brown envelope awaiting her—map and instructions from Greg Collier, as promised. Kate pulled the envelope out from under the stack of mail she'd collected on her way upstairs and opened it. Glancing at the map, she was at once struck by the distance she'd have to drive. Bondi was about fifty miles from Plattsburg, and the camp, another ten beyond. She estimated that the trip would take four or five hours, with refreshment stops included. Collier had even enclosed information about facilities available in Bondi. Gas and a small grocery store. Well, what more did she need?

But as she tucked the papers back into the envelope, anticipation of the trip was swamped by a wave of uncertainty. Her only journey outside the city as a kid had been that one summer at Limberlost. As an adult, she'd traveled with friends into the surrounding countryside and once had flown to Florida for winter break. That was it. Her whole travel experience. What if she got lost? What if the rental car broke down? What if she and Carla were attacked by killer mosquitoes or trapped in the lodge by a prowling bear? She didn't even know how to build a fire. *I must be crazy to think I can do this.*

The shrill peal of the phone almost propelled her out of her chair. She fumbled for it, knocking the receiver onto the table before getting it safely to her ear, and then couldn't identify the voice at first.

"Everything okay there?" were his first words, and Kate scanned the room, thinking she was on some kind of closed-circuit video.

"Sounded like something fell. It's Matt Sinclair. I, uh, was wondering if you might be free tonight for dinner. I know it's last minute, but I'm in your neighborhood and thought I'd give you a call."

It was a moment right from Kate's past—complete loss of speech resulting from shock at the unexpectedness of the call. She flashed back to tenth grade when the red-haired boy from her chemistry class had invited her to the semiformal. Reluctance and pleasure at being asked battling it out inside her. And just as she'd done years ago, she mumbled a graceless assent that implied she'd nothing better to do, so why not.

"Great," he replied, although his voice suggested otherwise. "Can I pick you up at your place in, say, half an hour?"

"Sure," she said, and hung up quickly. *Before he could change his mind?*

Half an hour meant a brisk shower—not enough time for a shampoo and blow-dry, so she slicked her hair back with gel, spiking it for a trendy look that somehow didn't quite work. The dress part was easy. She'd impulsively bought a designer reproduction at a local shop in late spring. The filmy overdress of aquamarine with floral organza floated seductively over a deeper blue mix of chiffon and Lycra, designed to cling. Spaghetti straps meant a strapless bra and Kate tossed undergarments out of her drawer, searching for the one she'd purchased with the dress.

The shoes, she thought. Where were they? Scrambling on hands and knees in the floor of her closet, she came up with not only the shoes but the set of test papers from last year that she thought she'd thrown out by mistake. Pushed them aside—water long passed under the bridge. Forced herself to slow down, sensing that rushing into a dress that even a sharp fingernail could damage forever was a bad move.

She poked through her small wooden jewelry box—a Christmas gift from Carla—for the silver-and-aqua earrings purchased along with the rest of the ensemble. Finally, standing in front of the full-length mirror attached to the back of her closet door, Kate had the whole outfit together for the first time since she'd bought it months ago. *You're such a social butterfly,* she murmured to her reflection.

She gave herself as objective an appraisal as possible. Hemline okay. No bulges that weren't supposed to be bulges, at least. She blessed good genes, though heaven only knew where they'd come from. The color of the dress was fabulous, she had to admit. Especially against hair shining, helped by the gel, like autumn leaves—chestnut, shot with crimson and gold. Awarded herself a nod of approval just as the entry buzzer rang.

Which she knew right away he seconded, given the expression on his face as she opened the door. Obviously it was his turn to be speechless, and Kate found herself enjoying the moment. The look in his eyes was almost an...awakening. An awareness of her as a woman, rather than as a former friend of Joanna's. It was a heady feeling for her, one she'd not experienced for some time.

IT WAS THE KIND of restaurant Kate had seen in movies. Small, intimate, candlelit. Attentive waiters but not intrusive. The food exquisite. French, Matt informed her. Bistrostyle. Meaning, he explained further, some innovative chef had learned to reproduce the best of home-cooking from various regions of France. It all meant little to Kate, who'd only recently graduated from take-out Chinese to Thai. Eating in expensive restaurants was still a celebratory experience for her, rather than a regular occurrence as it probably was for him.

There'd been little conversation on the drive from her flat. Other than polite questions about how long she'd lived there, where she taught and how she liked her job. Kate had the feeling he was putting in time. Certainly, there seemed to be an unspoken pact not to discuss Joanna Barnes or anything to do with her.

"You mentioned that you were in my neighborhood earlier," she said in the lull between main course and dessert. "Were you there on business?"

"Oh!" He sounded surprised. "Guess I haven't given you my own bio yet."

She smiled. "Is that what I've been doing? Giving you mine?"

He shook his head, disarming her with a megawatt smile. "No. Don't think that. I've been wanting to make amends ever since you left me at the café the other day. I'm afraid the events of the last few weeks kind of wiped out any rational thought I might be capable of. You must have begun to view me as a bit of a nutcase. I'm not really as obsessive as I've appeared, believe me."

"So?" she prompted, enjoying the upper hand.

"I'm a lawyer. Hope that isn't going to ruin the evening," he quickly added.

Kate waved a dismissive hand. "No, no. Go on."

"I do corporate law, a lot of financial advising, as well."

"Like your father?"

His eyes clouded. "What do you mean?"

Little alarm bells went off. Kate searched for the right words, sensing she'd just set foot on a patch of quicksand. "I thought you said he was a banker."

He seemed to relax a bit. "Oh, right. Banking has been in my family for several generations. I broke with tradition a bit, though the influence is obviously still there."

"Do you have any brothers or sisters?"

"Nope. Just me. How about you?"

Years of explanation had produced a party line for her own past. "I really don't know. I grew up a ward of the courts. The story I got when I was ten was that my mother had to hand me over to Children's Aid when I was about a year old because she couldn't support me. Must have been a single parent. Anyway," she said, rushing on, weary of the tale now herself, "I spent most of my childhood in a variety of foster homes until I was eighteen and evicted from the social-welfare nest."

He didn't speak for a long time, just fixed his charcoal-gray eyes on her. No pity in them, she noticed gratefully, but something more like assessment. A kind of reevaluation.

"You've come a long way," he finally said, adding, "I don't mean that to sound like a commercial. Just that obviously you've created yourself, achieved all you have on your own. That's a considerable accomplishment.''

And because he hadn't gushed sympathy as most people did, Kate was once again unable to answer; this time, the words were choked back by the lump that had formed in her throat. She looked down at the table, praying she wouldn't spoil the evening herself by sniffling over dessert. Fortunately the waiter had good timing, and while he was setting chocolate soufflé and crème brûlée before them and taking orders for coffee, Kate had a chance to compose herself.

''Mmm,'' she moaned, dipping her spoon into the soufflé. ''Sure you don't want some?''

''No thanks. Chocolate isn't my thing.''

After the coffee was delivered, he said, ''I suppose you'll be driving up north soon.''

Kate's eyes shot up over the rim of her coffee cup. ''Up north?''

''Didn't you say you were going to have a look at the resort Joanna left you?''

''Uh, yes, I guess I did. As a matter of fact, I'm going tomorrow.''

''So soon? Any special reason?''

At first she was tempted to be vague about her plans. It was a habit formed in childhood to counter interfering foster parents and social workers. She knew she ought to be less suspicious of ordinary questions. Besides, the dinner had been wonderful and, she had to admit, the company, as well.

''I have this little sister,'' she said.

''I thought—''

''Not a biological sister. You've heard of Big Brothers?''

He looked blank.

''It's a charitable group of men who befriend and act as

mentors and role models to kids at risk. There's a group for girls, too. Called Big Sisters.''

"And you're the big sister.''

"Right. And Carla Lopez—that's her name—is my little sister. I've had her for almost two years now. She's just turned thirteen. We get together at least once or twice a month. Go shopping, go to movies, visit the museum, and so on. The idea is to expose girls like her to cultural and educational opportunities they don't get at home.''

"So this girl, Carla—is she at risk, as you say?''

"Unfortunately, though she's lucky to have a great foster home now. I don't know a lot about her background—we just get facts that we need to know—and I'm bound by confidentiality issues, but I can say that she comes from a very turbulent family experience. Being in a consistent and stable environment is what can save her from…from the streets.''

"She's lucky to have you as a role model,'' he said.

He didn't know her well enough to make that kind of observation, but she blushed at the compliment, anyway. "Well,'' she continued, "I thought it would be an opportunity to get Carla out of the city for a couple of days, as well as check out the property.''

"See if you want to keep it?''

Her shrug conveyed the implausibility of that. "Realistically, what would an impoverished schoolteacher who's spent her entire life in New York City do with a few acres of land in the Adirondacks?'' She gave a self-deprecating laugh. "I'm sure I couldn't even pay the guy who's been looking after it to continue the job.''

"So the trip is…''

"A trip down memory lane. That's all.'' As soon as she said it, she knew that was exactly the purpose of going up north, in spite of her excuse about Carla. *Face it, Kate. Whether Carla comes or not, you have to go just to lay*

Joanna's spirit to rest. She stared down at her empty coffee cup, unable to meet his gaze.

The waiter appeared to remove their dessert plates and inquire about coffee refills. Kate shook her head and murmured, "I should go. Have to pick up my rental car early in the morning."

As Matt ushered her out of the restaurant, his hand rested lightly on her bare back, just above the edge of the dress. Kate felt the instant prickle of goose bumps and shivered.

"Chilly?" he asked, lowering his head to murmur in her ear.

The line of bumps streaked up the side of her neck. The shock of the sensation caused her to stumble against him. The hand on her back moved to her shoulder while his other arm reached out to keep her upright. Kate laughed nervously, embarrassed by her clumsiness.

"That'll teach me to have an extra glass of wine."

"I don't think two glasses count for much," he said, his lips still poised above her left ear.

She tossed her head and stepped away. "One more than usual," she said. "I'm not much of a drinker, I'm afraid."

He followed a couple of paces behind as they walked to his parked car. On the drive home, the silence between them became unbearable for Kate. She gushed about the dinner, thanking him for the invitation twice before realizing she was making a complete fool of herself. Not that his manner suggested it. He was quiet, politely listening to her rave on. By the time they reached her brownstone, she was certain the dinner date would be their last outing.

The car engine purred gently after he shifted into Park. She felt his eyes on her and knew something more was expected. An invitation upstairs didn't seem appropriate; nor was it a gesture she wanted to make. Still, he was so damn silent.

Then she remembered the bizarre coincidence of that afternoon. She almost mentioned seeing Lance Marchant, but bit the sentence off as it began to form. Mere mention of that name would totally ruin the night. But there was the policeman—Andrews.

"This afternoon I was walking back from dropping off Carla and happened to see that man from Joanna's funeral. The cop."

Nothing in his face moved.

"What cop?" he asked.

Kate frowned. She'd had a distinct impression of the two men standing side by side as she drove away that day. "You came out to the parking lot to talk to me. When I was leaving?"

No response.

"Before talking to you, I'd met a man who introduced himself as a Westchester County police officer. He...he asked me some things about Joanna." She began to stammer, nervous under that penetrating stare.

"Go on" was all he said.

"Well, I thought you might know him, that's all. When I drove away, it looked as though you two were talking to each other."

"I vaguely recall someone nearby as I watched you leave."

She squinted at him in the dark. It hadn't seemed like that at all to her, but why couldn't he remember Andrews otherwise? "I saw him driving this white van today. He looked strange. Wearing clothes like a street worker or someone. Not police type clothes."

"Are you sure he's a policeman?"

"He said he was, but how do I know? And what would he be doing in the city if he worked for Westchester County?"

Matt sighed and shook his head. He appeared tired—or bored—by the whole tale. "I've no idea. Who can say?"

"Anyway, I know his last name is Andrews, but I can't recall his first one." She screwed up her face, gazing out at the street for some memory prompt. "Kind of unusual, but not really. Not Bob. Not Ted."

"Not Dick or Harry?" He laughed.

She turned her face back to his. "That's it. *Tom.*"

He looked puzzled.

"You know—Tom, Dick and Harry."

"Oh, right," he said. He rubbed his eyes. "I'm starting to feel a bit fatigued myself."

Something had changed, Kate realized. Though she didn't have the faintest idea what it was. Perhaps she'd bored him with her rambling. Well, whatever. She remembered enough about the dating game to know when the date was over. She reached out her right hand to the door handle and pressed down, releasing the catch.

"Thanks again, Matt. It was a…a nice evening. The dinner was great."

He stretched out his right hand to her shoulder, starting to toy with the narrow strap of her dress. Then, perhaps thinking better of the gesture, abruptly removed his hand to the steering wheel.

"The pleasure was all mine, Kate. Enjoy your trip."

She opened the door and slipped out, managing to step onto the curb, cross the pavement and negotiate the steps up to the front door without stumbling once. For that, she was grateful. Then she turned once to wave goodbye and the car surged ahead, right on cue.

WHEN THE TELEPHONE rang as Kate was pouring her second cup of coffee next morning, her heart leapt into her throat. *Oh, please, don't let it be about Carla.* She took her time answering, postponing the inevitable. Disappointment and cancellation of all plans. But the male voice at the other end brought a sigh of relief.

"Kate? Lance Marchant here."

Of course, she thought. Why shouldn't it be his turn, now that she'd managed to run into all three men from Joanna's funeral in a scant twenty-four hours?

"Oh, hello."

"Hope I didn't wake you, but I wanted to catch you early before you left."

Did everyone know her plans? "Left?" she parroted, deliberately playing dumb.

"I played a round of golf yesterday afternoon with Greg Collier. He happened to mention you were heading up to Limberlost today."

"Oh, *did* he?"

"Yes, and I wondered if you could do me a favor..."

Kate reined in the sarcasm this time as it obviously had gone right over his head. Besides, he had been nice to her. So what if he and Joanna's lawyer discussed her affairs? "What is it?" she asked, attempting a more pleasant tone.

"A few years ago Joanna stored some documents up there for me. Nothing important—old tax returns and so on. I was moving residences at the time and she offered to look after some of my stuff. If you're planning on selling the place, or even keeping it—" he chuckled, as if the idea was completely far-fetched "—I thought I'd better get hold of the stuff."

"I see. But how would I know what to look for?"

"I know that's a problem. Maybe what you could do is simply check around—see if there are any boxes of papers and so on. Then sometime I could drive up there myself and go through them. It just means saving me a trip, that's all. To tell you the truth, I'm not even sure they're still at the lodge. It's possible she'd already removed them and brought them back here." He chuckled more exuberantly now. "Guess I'm revealing the state of my personal house-keeping."

"Sure, I'd be happy to look for you," she said.

"Wonderful. Let me know when you get back how everything went." Before ringing off he gave her his office phone number.

When she hung up, she thought about his request. Hadn't Matt also mentioned something about documents belonging to his father? Should she call Lance back and tell him about that? No. She doubted Matt Sinclair would want Lance to know, given his negative feelings about Joanna. Still, both requests made her uncomfortable, though she couldn't explain why. The sense of being in the middle, between two men connected to Joanna.

There was little she could do about that, at least until she'd made a decision about selling or keeping Limberlost. No doubt that choice would become very clear once she visited the place. And although she'd dismissed any possibility of keeping it to Matt, she knew deep in her heart that if Joanna had wanted her to have it, she owed it to her to explore every option before discounting the idea of maintaining the camp.

She checked the time and, seeing she had a few minutes to spare, decided to make a telephone call. The information operator gave her the number for the Westchester County Police Department, and after several transfers and voice messages, she finally was connected to a real person in the right section.

"Tom Andrews? Hold on a sec, though the name doesn't ring any bells."

The officer returned a moment later. "Sorry, ma'am, there's no one by that name in this department."

"Maybe he's recently left to go to another police department."

"Well, I've been working here for twenty years, and I assure you the name doesn't register at all. Maybe you got the wrong police department."

Kate pursed her lips. She'd have sworn she got the right name. "Is there a central directory somewhere for police officers in the state?"

A low chuckle rolled down the line. "Wish there were, ma'am. It'd make my job a bit easier. The only thing I suggest is that you contact the New York City police. Maybe that's where the guy works. Anything else I can help you with?"

"No, no thanks. And thanks for your time."

After Kate hung up, she considered calling the NYPD, but suspected that would take more time than she now had. The mystery of Tom Andrews would have to wait for her return to the city.

"THIS IS SO COOL, KATE!"

Kate turned to smile at Carla, buckled into the passenger seat of the Acura. They'd just struggled through Brooklyn, where Carla lived, and had finally left city streets behind for the highway. That part of the trip had taken half an hour longer than Kate had anticipated. Not just because of the traffic, but because Carla had kept running in and out of her house to search for items that were too important to be left behind. Rita and Kate had exchanged amused smiles. It was nice to see the girl enthusiastic about something other than a music video.

"Have you figured out all the buttons on the dashboard now?"

"Yep. And more important, I know how to select certain songs from each side of the tape. That way, we won't have to listen to cuts we don't like so much."

"That's good," Kate agreed, hoping there'd be one she did like.

"It's okay that you couldn't get a car with a CD player, Kate. Besides, I haven't heard some of these tapes in ages."

"Play away, then."

It was a bright, sunny day, not a cloud in sight. She hoped the weather up north was as promising, if only to make Carla's first trip out of the city extra special. The cassette player occupied Carla's attention for most of the drive out of the suburban areas. When they changed highways, encountering increasingly larger sections of forested land, Carla's interest in the music waned. After a late lunch stop at a roadside diner packed with truckers and, according to Carla, featuring the best fries she'd ever eaten, the tape machine didn't get turned on at all.

Craning her neck this way and that, Carla finally sank into her seat and announced, "The world is a big place, isn't it, Kate."

Kate smiled. "It sure is, and I personally have seen very little of it."

"Really?"

"Yeah. I'm a city gal, like you."

Carla thought for a moment. "When you were a kid and going to all those foster homes, did you ever want to just be in another city? To just walk away from everything and see the world outside?"

"Sure. But you know, there's a whole world just in Manhattan. Growing up in New York isn't the same as in a small town somewhere. Besides, I had a goal."

Carla turned her face to Kate, her brown eyes shining with curiosity. "What was your goal?"

Kate hesitated. She'd never really talked about her childhood with Carla, only to share some stories about foster homes. The bad stuff she'd kept to herself, and besides, Carla had her own memories to deal with. But she wanted to tell the girl about Joanna, knew that was inevitable, given their visit to Limberlost.

"When I was eleven I was gearing up for adolescence in a big way. Caused all kinds of grief for my caseworker and my foster parents."

Carla's eyes widened. "Seriously? I can't picture you being, like, a big problem. Not doing stuff like I've been doing."

Kate reached out a hand to pat the girl's knee. "Kiddo, I made you look like an angel."

"Yeah, right."

"Really. And my foster folks were okay—not as nice as Rita, 'cause they had more financial problems and more kids of their own—but they weren't unfair or mean. They just expected me to do my share of the work, and I wasn't into that at all."

Carla laughed. "I know what you mean." Her voice sobered. "D'ya ever feel like that's all you were wanted for? To help out?"

Don't skirt that one, Kate. She'll catch you out in a second. Kate glanced across the seat, meeting Carla's frowning face. "Sure. All the time. At least, since I was ten or so. But I didn't always have it right."

"What do you mean?"

"When I got into my mid-teens, I began to see how things worked. That everyone had a job and a responsibility. Not just me, but my foster mom and dad and even their own kids."

The girl nodded. After a moment, she asked, "What was your goal then? To just get away?"

"Not quite, 'cause I knew that was going to happen eventually, anyway. When I was sent to Camp Limberlost, I didn't want to go at all. But my caseworker told me if I didn't, I'd probably have to go into a group home, because my foster parents couldn't cope with me over the summer."

Carla's gasp said it all, Kate thought. The girl could relate to that threat. Though she had to admit, a group home wasn't such a bad thing. Just that there was no fooling yourself that you were part of a family.

"So I went and I hated it. The girls in my cabin were

all from the same part of the Bronx, and there was no way they were going to let me into their little clique. I guess I was lucky they didn't do more than simply ignore me.''

''Yeah,'' Carla agreed solemnly.

Kate glanced at the girl's profile, her small pretty face fixed on the windshield as if she were watching a movie. And in a way she probably was, thought Kate. Harking back to her own recent experience with cliques. Knowing already at the age of thirteen things about bullying and anger and hate that most adults in the larger world would never know.

''Anyway, the first week was so bad I decided to run away. Then I met Joanna Barnes and everything changed.''

''Who's she?''

''I was swimming out to a raft to get away from some kids one day and she was there sunbathing. She was the daughter of the owners of the camp.''

''A kid?''

''No. She was turning thirty.''

''Oh.''

Kate smiled at the letdown in Carla's voice. The girl was already dismissing Joanna as an adult. ''But she was a very cool thirty-year-old, trust me.'' She and Carla smiled at each other.

''You keep saying 'was','' Carla pointed out.

''Yes.'' Kate sighed. ''Joanna is the person who left me the lodge.'' When the girl's face remained blank, she added, ''She died about ten days ago.''

Carla frowned. ''Oh, I'm sorry, Kate.''

''I know, sweetie. Anyway, after that first day we always seemed to meet at the raft. I knew when she'd be there and I'd swim out to visit her. It's hard to explain how a thirty-year-old woman and a girl of eleven could hit it off, but we did. I think, looking back, that we were both outcasts in a way.''

"What d'ya mean?"

"Just didn't have a group to hang with, you know? Kind of drifting on our own."

Carla nodded. "I feel like that sometimes."

"Yes, I know." Kate paused. "We would talk about all kinds of things. Not just how my life was going—we laughed a lot, too. That was the best part. I have to say, she was the first adult I'd ever met who treated me like an equal. After she left, the rest of my stay wasn't quite so bad because I swam out to the raft every day and pretended she was still there. And I'd have these conversations with her." Kate laughed. "I'm sure if anyone saw me from the shore, they'd have thought I'd lost my mind."

"Did you ever see her again?"

Kate had to wait to answer. Finally she shook her head and said, "No. We made this promise that we'd meet this summer on July 14. It would be a kind of reunion to compare how our lives turned out. But she died."

A great stillness settled over the car.

"Anyway," Kate continued, "Joanna kind of changed my life. When we'd talk, I'd start to think that I could do anything I wanted. That I had something to look forward to as I got older. She sent me these cards once a year from all over the world. There was never a big message in them, just a reminder that she was thinking of me and that she would be seeing me again. They kept me going through a lot of down times.

"Joanna likely didn't even realize it herself, but simply the thought of those cards made me feel special and valued. It made all the difference in how I began to view my foster home and my life there. For the first time, I could see that, even if they didn't love me as real parents, my foster mom and dad were really trying to help me. So I determined that I would succeed. That I would have a career and that I would become a decent person. Not someone who distrusted everyone.''

Carla reached out her hand to Kate. For a long moment they sat holding hands in silence, gazing out as the countryside began to roll toward the Adirondack foothills.

CHAPTER SIX

"I THINK I'M GOING to throw up," Carla moaned.

Kate wordlessly seconded the feeling. They'd been driving up and down hills and snaking around mountains for the past hour. "We're almost there," she said, trying to encourage the girl, who was curled up against the door, her head lolling in the crook between the back of her seat and the opened window.

"You said that an hour ago!"

The accusation might not be an exaggeration, Kate realized. She'd either taken a wrong turn or had miscalculated travel time on mountain roads. It was almost three o'clock and they ought to have arrived in Bondi at least half an hour ago. But just when she was certain she'd have to pull over and stick her own head out the window, she rounded yet another curve and saw a small white-painted sign perched at an angle on a wooden post: Welcome to Bondi Village.

"We're here!" she announced triumphantly, and had to look across to the now-silent Carla to see if she was still conscious.

Kate slowed as they approached a cluster of gray-and-white frame houses around a crossroads. If she'd gone too fast, she thought, she could have driven right through it without noticing. The village was obviously too small for street signs—were there even any streets?—and none of the houses sported numbers or even signs proclaiming the names of their owners. Though why bother when you know everyone and where they live?

Greg Collier had instructed her to ask for directions to Bill and Verna Tippett's at the Twin Birch Convenience and Gas store, the only such store in the village. And sure enough, there it was, just where the two-lane paved road forked about a hundred feet ahead of her. Kate took her foot off the accelerator and coasted into the graveled lot.

Carla rolled out of the car as soon as Kate turned off the ignition. "Is there a washroom here?" she croaked.

Kate took her by the hand and led her into the store. The man behind the counter gave them a friendly smile and, before Kate could say a word, pointed to the back. Kate led Carla to the door, closing it behind the girl.

"First time in the Adirondacks?" the man quipped.

Kate's smile might have been warmer if she herself was a hundred percent, but she made an effort. "I'm looking for Bill Tippett's place."

He pursed his lips thoughtfully, giving her a once-over with more care this time. "You the new owner of Limberlost?"

"Um..."

He grinned, holding up a palm in self-defense. "It's okay, ma'am. Up here in the north country we all know the doin's of everyone else. Outsiders seem to get riled by it, but that's the way it goes. Otherwise—" his grin became a hearty chuckle "—we'd all be gettin' cabin fever, if you know what I mean."

Kate stuck out her right hand. "I'm Kate Reilly, and I guess you could call me the new owner. For now, anyway."

He nodded, planting his own browned and wrinkled hand in hers. "George Miller," he said.

Kate guessed he was in his sixties and wondered if he'd known Joanna. Later, she told herself. All in due time.

"You'll find Bill down that other road, the one that forks away from the village. Go about four miles and make a sharp right onto the gravel road at a stand of tall cedars. There's a dirt lane that goes up to his house about another hundred yards farther. Stay in the car when you pull up, 'case his dogs are loose."

Great, thought Kate. *I've come to the wilds of the Adirondacks from Manhattan and the first animals I meet are man-eating canines.*

Carla emerged from the washroom, pale-faced but perkier, and after purchasing supplies, the two reluctantly got back into the car. "I really don't think we're going to have to make too many more winding turns now," Kate assured her.

The girl merely gave a wan smile and peered out the passenger window. "It's pretty here, anyway," she eventually said.

An understatement, Kate thought. Words like *rugged, magnificent* and *awesome* came to mind more readily. She suddenly recalled her first impressions of the area, seen from the window of the chartered bus she'd taken along with thirty-five other campers. Growing up in the city had exposed her to a sense of bigness, but she'd never seen such vast tracts of forested land. The sight had frightened her, made her feel small and even more vulnerable. Where were the stores? The streets and expressways? Were there even *people* up here?

She'd taken a reading from the odometer as soon as they drove away from the store, waving goodbye to George, who was leaning against the door frame. When the number four appeared, she slowed the car to a crawl, scanning the right side of the road. If only she'd asked George what a stand of cedars looked like.

"What are you looking for?" Carla asked.

"A bunch of cedar trees."

"Aren't they evergreens?" Carla's face was scrunched up. "I remember that from school."

"Oh, yeah," murmured Kate, thinking all the greenery outside the car looked the same to her.

"And you're the teacher!" scoffed Carla.

Kate grinned at her. "Yeah, but I didn't teach science. Just math, literature and history."

"Still," the girl teased, "you're supposed to know everything."

"If only...ah! What about those trees there? And there's a dirt path going into the bushes. That must be the turn."

"Doesn't seem like a road to me."

"It isn't, but then, I guess up here a road is anything that leads to somewhere."

Carla laughed. "Too right. And some of those roads I don't wanna see again." She thought for a moment before adding, "Too bad we have to go back. Isn't there a different way?"

"Doubt it," Kate said. "But maybe we'll be acclimatized or whatever you call it. Okay, hold on. I think this is going to be bumpy."

The Acura chugged and struggled the next hundred yards until it struck a clearing, in the center of which stood a ranch-style house with two sheds behind it. The lane wound around a small garden that had been planted several feet in front of the house and stopped abruptly at a side door.

Before Kate could turn off the engine, three dark shapes barking ferociously darted out from one of the sheds. She instantly rolled up the windows. "Stay in the car," Kate warned Carla.

"Jeez," muttered Carla. "What are they? Guard dogs?"

"Who knows? But they don't look friendly." By now, the dogs were leaping at the sides of the car.

As quickly as they'd appeared, the dogs bounded away. Kate craned her neck to see past Carla's head. A lanky man in jeans and T-shirt was walking their way from a clump of trees beyond one of the sheds. The dogs trotted obediently toward him and he led them into a kennel, which Kate noticed for the first time at the rear of the house.

"Thank goodness," grumbled Carla. "It's getting hot in here." She yanked open the door and stepped out. Kate followed, walking around the hood of the car just as the man returned from locking up the dogs.

"Kate Reilly?"

"Yes, and this is Carla."

He nodded toward Carla, hovering at Kate's side. "Howdy."

He looked to be in his mid-fifties and had probably been a bit of a rake in his youth, Kate bet, his weatherbeaten face reminiscent of magazine ads featuring cowhands and cigarettes.

"Sorry about the dogs," he said. "Believe me when I say their bark is worse than their bite."

"I believe you, but I'd just as soon not put it to the test."

He laughed, then said, "My wife, Verna, is away visiting her ma in Plattsburg right now. Otherwise I'd invite you in for a cold drink, but the place is a bit of a mess. My grandson, Kyle, and I haven't exactly mastered the art of housekeeping."

"Your *grandson?*"

"I'll take that as a compliment. We start breeding early up in the north country." He grinned at Kate. "Just kidding. But Vern an' me, we've been together thirty odd years. Grew up right here in Bondi." He paused a beat. "So...you related to the Barnes family?"

"No. I did know Joanna, though."

"Aah! Well, we *all* knew Joanna, that's for sure...."

The sentence drifted off, as if he couldn't find the words to say what he wanted. He crinkled his eyes against the sun, then looked back at Kate and Carla. "That lawyer fella

from New York said you'd be here a coupla days, so I got
the generator going for you, give you some power. But I'd
better show you how it works and the pump, too, in case
anything stops. It's been a while since the place has been
stoked up, so to speak. I'll go get the keys.''

As he walked away, Carla turned to Kate with big eyes.
''What's a generator? And why's there a pump? What kind
of place *is* this?''

Here it comes, Kate sighed. *Reality.* ''Honey, it's not a
posh resort. But don't worry, we're only here for a couple
of nights. If it's horrible, we'll leave. Deal?'' She wrapped
an arm around the girl and squeezed gently.

''Deal,'' Carla echoed, though her tone was doubtful.
But when she noticed Bill returning from inside the house
followed by a tall, skinny youth, she straightened up, moving slightly away from Kate.

''This here's Kyle,'' Bill said as soon as the two reached
earshot of Kate and Carla. ''Kyle, meet Miss Kate Reilly
and Miss Carla…''

''Lopez,'' said Carla.

''Make that Kate and Carla,'' added Kate, smiling at the
teenager.

'''Lo,'' he mumbled, obviously not happy about being
dragged out of the house. He hoisted up baggy khakis that
were losing a struggle with gravity.

''Kyle and I'll head out in the pickup so's you can tag
along. Just wait'll I back outta the shed.'' Bill started walking toward the largest of the outbuildings, then stopped to
turn around. '''Fore I forget, you bring any bedding or
anything?''

''Sleeping bags.''

Relief washed over his face. ''Great. There're some blan-
kets and sheets stuffed into a cedar box in the main lodge,
but God only knows what shape they're in. The place has

been closed up almost ten years now." He went on to the shed and Kate headed for her side of the car.

"Carla?"

The girl's attention was still focused on Kyle. Then she clambered into the passenger side as a rusting green truck shot out of the shed, spun gravel and came to a halt in front of Kyle. The boy climbed in and the truck tackled the dirt trail as if it were doing a lap at the Indy.

"Forget about tagging along," muttered Kate as she gunned the Acura.

Once on the paved road again, the two vehicles headed north. About five miles along, the truck's left signal flashed. Kate slowed down, grateful that this road was at least gravel and wider than the lane at the Tippetts'. The sun, golden now, slashed through the canopy of the forest. Ten minutes later, a sharp curve in the road ended in a huge clearing. Whitefish Lake.

Kate and Carla simultaneously cried out "Oh!" at the dazzling show of reflected sunlight from the lake. Like a thousand jewels, Kate thought.

As soon as the car lurched to a stop, she jumped out. The air was crisp and redolent of Christmas trees. Pine trees, Kate reminded herself. God, she was such a city girl. She and Carla crunched across the dried pinecones and needles to the largest of the log buildings with a big, old-fashioned wraparound veranda. Bill trotted up the three steps to the massive wooden door, fronted by a screen door.

"This is the main lodge," he said, "and the only building I readied for your visit. Figured it would be the most comfortable. Anyway, some of the cabins don't have any kitchen facilities, so this seemed the best choice."

Kate waited behind, scanning the cluster of cabins and sheds dotting the lawn all the way to the water's edge. "It looks smaller than I remember," she murmured.

The door creaked open and Bill turned around. "You've been here before?"

She nodded. "When I was about twelve. For two weeks."

"Come with your folks?"

"Nope. With a busload of thirty other kids from New York."

"Aah!" He studied her for a second longer, then said, "The Barneses were good about bringing city kids up here. Did it every summer for a month. Till the place had to close up, of course." He lowered his head as if in mourning. Then raising it, gestured outward with his right hand. "There are about sixty-five acres here, though most of it's bush. They always kept the lawn mowed, but I only cut a few trails between the cabins and down to the water. Hope you don't mind. Didn't see the point of gettin' it all ship-shape. Especially since that lawyer said you'd probably be sellin' it." He narrowed his eyes at her.

Waiting for her to deny it? Kate wondered. Instead, she moved past him to go inside. There was no foyer, just a large room with wooden floors that gleamed in the sun spilling through the windows. Shrouded mounds of furniture were grouped in bunches around the room. A massive fieldstone fireplace was the focal point in the far exterior wall.

Bill walked around, flipping off the sheets while Kate just stood there, transfixed by the sudden rush into the past. She was half-aware of Carla and Kyle coming in behind her, but said nothing.

Part of the room, especially the wide pine staircase, was so familiar she felt a physical pain at the memory flash. But at the same time, she had to admit most of it was new to her. The city kids hadn't been allowed in the main lodge and the only time she herself had stepped foot inside had been when she'd come looking for Joanna one afternoon to return her beach towel, left behind on the raft.

Then all she'd noted was how dark and cool the lounge had been. Wicker furniture with overstuffed cushions, gleaming tabletops and, most of all, the buck's head mounted on the wall opposite the fireplace. Instinctively she looked to that wall now, but it was empty.

"Lotta stuff here," Bill Tippett said as he joined Kate in the center of the room. "Yup. Guess you'll have your work cut out for you."

She turned to him, wondering what he meant.

"Now that it's yours, you'll have to decide whether to sell with contents or clear it all out. If you ask me, I'd get the whole thing off your hands with the first buyer that comes along. For the right price, of course," he added, giving her a shrewd wink.

She was startled by her quick rise of annoyance, but bit back a retort, sensing he'd only been teasing. It seemed that everyone who knew about her inheritance assumed she'd immediately sell the property.

"Perhaps," she murmured. "Where will Carla and I be sleeping?"

"Upstairs. I don't know if you know the layout of this place...."

"I don't. Want to give us a tour?"

"Sure."

He crossed the lounge to a shadowy hall at the north end. Kate started to follow, then looked back for Carla, still standing inside the door. "Coming?" The girl nodded. "Leave your things there with mine. We'll collect them once we know where we're going."

Carla caught up, but Bill's grandson stayed behind, sprawling on one of the sofas. Tippett led them along the hallway, pointing out that it would brighten once the outside window shutters were removed. "I took the shutters off the lounge windows and the ones in the kitchen so you don't have to turn lights on all the time.''

"Is the power on?" Kate asked.

"Not to worry," he said, picking up the anxiety in her question. "I've got the place running on what we call a demand generator. Everytime you switch on something electrical, the generator comes on. But I've left flashlights, a kerosene light and matches, so at night after you've gone to bed, you can use those to find your way to the washroom without having to turn on the generator. The thing is kinda old and unpredictable, but I rigged up the system for you, rather than get the whole place reconnected by Con Ed. Frankly I didn't see the point in going to all that trouble if you were just about to—''

"Sell the place," she filled in for him.

He stopped in his tracks and said, "You got it."

"What about the stove and fridge?"

"They're on propane and I filled up the tank for you. Both working fine. If Vern had been here, she likely woulda cleaned the stove, but I—''

Kate waved a dismissive hand. "That's okay. We'll only be here two days at the most."

"Is there a TV?" Carla asked.

"Nope. Sorry."

"Good thing I brought my Walkman," the girl grumbled.

Bill cast another wink at Kate. "Kids. All the same. Got to be entertained. In my day, we made up our own."

Recalling his remark about starting to breed early, Kate grinned and said, "I bet you did."

He flushed, cleared his throat twice and jerked his head to the left. "Kitchen's in here."

The room was at least a third the size of the lounge area, with windows along the exterior wall. Sun trickled through the trees behind the kitchen until the forest beyond became too dense for light to penetrate.

Kate wondered for one anxious moment if there were bears lurking in the dark woods. But Bill was saying something about the appliances, and she forced her mind away from its morbid imagining.

A large two-door refrigerator and the biggest stove Kate had ever seen formed an alcove in one end of the room, with a massive wooden island opposite. A porcelain sink with taps was set in the island and, along the same side of wall as the stove, a pair of huge stainless steel sinks flanked by tiled counters. Built-in shelves lined the perimeter. A round wooden table with chairs made a cozy eating nook adjacent to another doorway opposite the one they'd entered.

"That's where the staff ate, and the Barneses, on occasion. The dining room's through here." He started forward, asking on his way, "Didn't you city kids eat in the summer mess hall?"

"Is that in another building?" Kate asked, her memory working on a clearer picture of the resort.

"Yup. Down by those cabins on the east side of the property."

"I seem to recall being separated from the other guests here."

"The paying customers. Guess the Barneses had to make a living just like the rest of us."

"Oh, I didn't mean that in a negative way. When I think of all those kids—and I remember Joanna telling me her parents had been hosting city kids since she was a teenager—it's only now that I realize how much the venture cost them."

"The Barneses never thought of the money side of it. They liked kids and they knew how important it was to expose them to the north country."

Carla gave an impatient sigh, reminding them that the tour had slowed down. Bill pointed through the doorway beside the eating nook into a dark room stretching off the kitchen. "Main dining room with screened-in porch. I left it all shuttered up, figured you two'd eat in here."

"Or maybe outside," Kate said. "We can have a picnic, Carla."

The girl mumbled a reply. Kate glanced at her sharply, realizing she was probably tired and hungry.

"Can you show us the upstairs and then Carla can freshen up for dinner?"

"Yup. There's a staff staircase off the kitchen pantry here. Chambermaids used it." He led the way to a small door that Kate had missed entirely, next to one of the shelving units. Inside was a room the size of her apartment kitchen lined with more shelves, pots and pans, and a collection of dusty glass jars. A washing machine and dryer were tucked into a corner next to a narrow staircase.

"Is that where they did the laundry?"

"Just small stuff. Towels and the like. The rest they sent out to the laundry in Bondi."

"You know a lot about the running of this place, don't you?" Kate asked.

"I worked here as a teenager and so did Verna. In fact, Vern's folks owned the Laundromat. Not there anymore, though." Bill squeezed past Kate and headed up the stairs.

"Should we get our things? We left them in the lounge."

"Kyle can help you take them up the main staircase. We'll go down that way."

The upstairs was so dark Bill had to grope for a light switch. As soon as he flicked it, there was a low rattling hum from somewhere beneath them. "Hear that? The generator just came on. It's a bit noisy but you get used to it."

"Where is it?"

"There's a partial basement. The Barneses had the generator for emergency use only. And it came in handy, I can tell you.''

''The power used to go off?''

''Once in a while a big storm would knock a tree down, take out the hydro lines.'' He led the way along the dimly lit hall to the first doorway on their right.

''Thought one of you could take this room. The other's connected through that door there,'' he said, pointing into the shadowy interior. He ran his hand along the wall next to the door frame and flicked on a light switch.

An old-fashioned four-poster covered by a white sheet dominated the room. It was accompanied by a three-drawer wooden bureau and another smaller vanity on which sat a ceramic pitcher and basin. An alcove opposite the bed and next to the connecting door served as a closet, judging by the coat hangers perched over a wooden rod. Kate raised her eyebrows. Could this be the luxurious interior she'd fantasized about while sleeping in a bunk bed in a cabin down by the lake?

''I know it looks drab,'' Bill said, ''but all the little knickknacks and such that used to decorate the rooms were packed away. And when the shutters are off, you get a magnificent view of the lake from here. Did you want me to take those shutters off? 'Cause I can do it first thing in the morning, but I'll have to root around for the ladder first.''

Kate sighed. As dreary as the room was, she'd only have to sleep in it two nights. ''No, don't worry about it, Bill. Can you show us the other room? And Carla—'' she turned to the girl, who was sagging against the door frame ''—you can have first choice of the rooms.''

''Great'' was the unenthusiastic response.

The second room wasn't much better, featuring twin beds, instead of a double. But there was a skylight and a wedge of golden sun dappled by overhanging tree branches brightened it.

"I'll take this one," Carla quickly said.

Kate and Bill exchanged amused glances over the girl's head. "That's it for now, then," Bill announced. "Unless you want to see the rest of the rooms."

Kate shook her head. "We can explore later. We'll get our stuff up here and then I want you to show me how to light the gas stove."

"Okey-doke. There's not much to it, really. It's pretty modern. The Barneses updated all their appliances about—" he screwed up his face "—twenty years ago?"

Kate was still smiling as she and Carla descended the large central staircase leading from the second floor to the lounge. Kyle raised his head, an expression of "about time" stamped on his face. He and Carla carried the backpacks and sleeping bags upstairs while Bill demonstrated the features of the stove and fridge back in the kitchen.

Kate tried to pay attention as closely as she could, but was beginning to find his drawl hard to follow. She was relieved to know, however, that she and Carla wouldn't really be "roughing it" for their two-day stint; they wouldn't have to rely on a camp stove or worse, an open fire.

After the Tippetts left, she and Carla unpacked the food in the kitchen. Kate had chosen easy menus for their two dinners. Steak and salad one night; burgers the next. Carla opted for burgers first because they'd be quicker.

"I'm starving," she said.

Twenty minutes later, they carried their burgers, tortilla chips and salsa out to the picnic tables scattered under the trees at the front of the lodge. For a long time there was little noise but satisfied chomping.

"Mmm!" Carla moaned, sinking her teeth into her second burger.

Kate, also working on her second, could only nod. She couldn't remember feeling so famished. Nor so contented. She set the last third of her burger down and propped her head onto her elbows, taking in the view of lake, forest and foothills rolling into the horizon. It was only about seven, she guessed, and the sun would be strong till at least eight before changing to the reddish-gold hue of sunset.

"Want to go for a walk around when you've finished?" she asked Carla.

Carla nodded vigorously. Kate smiled to herself, thinking how a full stomach could mean all the difference in mood change for a teenager. *And you, too, Reilly. Aren't you feeling a heck of a lot more content than you did two hours ago?*

When Carla finished her burger and wiped her mouth on her sweatshirt sleeve, they set out, automatically heading for the water. As they approached the sandy beach that stretched along the main part of the shore, Kate said, "There used to be all kinds of lounge chairs on the grass here. Adirondacks, too."

"What do you mean, Adirondacks?"

"They're a style of chair, made of wood. I guess they originated right here, in the Adirondack Mountains. Anyway, they're very comfortable and also still very trendy. You can even buy them in Manhattan, if you want to pay a fortune."

"Huh. Here they're probably cheap."

"Certainly less expensive. The canoes were stacked on the lawn over there," Kate said, pointing in the direction of a wood-frame building on stilts perched over the water's edge. "Come on, let's check out the boathouse."

"Is that what that place is? A house made just for boats?"

Kate smiled at Carla's incredulous expression. She'd felt much the same when she'd first arrived here years ago. At the time the boathouse had likely been sturdier than the dwelling places of some of the kids at the camp.

Before leaving, Bill had mentioned that he'd left the boathouse unlocked. "There's an old cedar-strip canoe in there, great condition. Also some life jackets hanging inside. Didn't think you'd want to take the motor launch out. Besides, the engine'll need an overhaul."

"Motor launch?"

"One of those big old mahogany boats you never see on the lake anymore. Everything's fiberglass nowadays. There's also an aluminum fourteen-footer."

When she pushed open the door, Kate walked right into a spiderweb. She backed out, sputtering and brushing the sticky film from her face and hair.

"What is it?" Carla asked in alarm.

"Yuck. Just a spiderweb."

The girl jumped. "A spider? Where?"

Kate laughed. "Relax. I've a feeling the whole place is full of them. Don't worry, just be on the alert and brush the webs away if you see one. Come on, it's safe." She stepped into the boathouse, searching its gloomy interior from the wooden dock that rimmed the water inside. The water was dark and flecked with dead leaves and other bits of flotsam that Kate had no wish to investigate.

As Bill had said, the two larger boats had been pulled out of the water and propped on wooden stands. Three canoes were mounted on the opposite wall of the house, and oars, paddles, life jackets and other boat paraphernalia dangled from hooks along the end wall, near the door they'd entered.

"Wow!" Carla breathed. "I've never even seen boats like those in real life, let alone inside an actual boathouse."

Kate hugged the girl. "We're just two city slickers, I'm afraid. But maybe tomorrow if the water's calm, we can take down one of the canoes and go for a paddle. Like that?''

''Sure. But—'' she turned hesitatingly to Kate ''—do you know how to paddle?''

Kate shrugged. ''It shouldn't be too hard,'' she said.

SLEEP HAD BEEN a deep void. Like losing consciousness, Kate speculated, and regaining it in what seemed the blink of an eye. She felt like dozing some more, but something tugged her from sleep. She fumbled for her watch on the night table and, squinting in the dim light to see, realized it was almost ten. She shot upright, wondering where she was. But then she remembered. Camp Limberlost. The place where her life had been turned around. The place she now owned, however temporarily. She tiptoed to the opened connecting door and peeked in. Carla was a buried mound. Kate smiled. The girl must be tired, for she'd crept into Kate's room a couple of times not long after the lights were turned out to complain of rustling and other, more ominous sounds.

Kate could sympathize entirely, recalling her first sleepless night in the bunkhouse nineteen years ago. Of course, most of those sounds had been hushed giggles and crackling of candy bar wrappers.

Day was still a tantalizing streak, the sun not quite high enough to pour through the skylight. But the stuffiness of the room suggested it was going to be a hot one. Kate returned to her room to get her shower toiletries. There were only four rooms in the lodge with adjoining baths, Bill had explained yesterday. The guests in the rooms Kate and Carla were using shared a bathroom.

But what a bathroom it was. A great claw-footed tub with curtained shower ring, a large porcelain sink, a vanity counter with tiny chair and, beneath the wide gable, a window seat. Kate wished Bill had removed the shutter from the gable because she knew the white-and-blue tiled floor and walls would fill with light. For a crazy second, she thought she'd like to have a bath in that tub, windows wide open. *Get over it, Reilly. You're not likely to keep the place.*

Last evening's tour of some of the property before she and Carla had wearily collapsed on the chairs in the lounge had reinforced for Kate the extent of her inheritance—and the extent of the responsibility as well. Besides the main lodge with its six bedrooms, there were six guest cabins plus the four cabins used by the city kids who came every summer.

She sighed, slipped out of her nightie T-shirt and climbed into the tub. The water, when it came, chugged out rusty and dank, but by the time she'd fiddled with the shower attachment, the stream was brisk and hot. She washed quickly, drying herself and changing into shorts and tank top by the time Carla stirred from the other room.

"The shower's great," Kate called out. "I'm going down to warm up our waffles. You want blueberry or plain?"

"Blueberry." Then, after a pause, "Is there hot water?"

"Of course. I know this isn't the Ritz, but it's more than a shack in the woods." Kate chuckled. "Get up, sleepyhead. We've got waffles, real syrup, orange juice, coffee—God, I hope there's a pot somewhere—and some canoeing ahead of us."

And in spite of the late start they managed to finish breakfast and get the canoe off the boathouse wall and into the water well before noon. Kate had already opened the wide doors to the lake.

"I hope this is worth it," Carla muttered.

Kate grinned. "Cheer up. It'll be fun. You'll see."

"Yeah, right."

"Okay, we're at the water's edge. The rest is easy, but don't put your end down until I get it farther in." Kate sloshed through the mucky shallows, glad she'd had the foresight to wear her Tevas. "All right, steady…let it down gently. Okay. Good!"

Carla's face was bright red, but smiling.

Kate grabbed two life jackets and two paddles from a rack on the wall, then after they'd both put on the jackets, hunkered down beside the canoe. "Okay, Carla, I'll hold the canoe while you climb in."

Throwing Kate a "why me?" glance, Carla sat on the dock and began to shift her weight into the craft. "It's tippy."

"The trick is, you've got to step into the center and try to keep your weight centered," Kate said, recalling her own limited canoeing experience all those years ago. "Then you kneel on the bottom."

The plan worked and soon both were in the canoe, Kate in the stern, Carla in front. Using her paddle, Kate pushed the canoe out of the boathouse. In seconds they glided out into deeper water. Paddling was easy, too, she thought. "Just dip, pull toward you and lift. Do it over and over."

"How far are we going?" Carla asked.

Kate caught the anxiety in her voice. "Not far. We'll just go round that bend ahead and back." The canoe slid easily through the water, which sparkled in the bright sun. They might as well be the only people on earth, Kate thought, it was so peaceful. Just the gentle splash of paddles, the squawking of seagulls and other birds calling from the woods.

"Sure is quiet here." Carla turned her head to look back to Kate.

"Nice, isn't it?"

"Yeah," the girl replied, her voice doubtful. "But there's something about the noises in the city. I don't know."

"They're comforting because you know what they all mean. Here it's harder to identify sounds."

"Maybe." Carla paused, lifting her paddle out of the water. "Like, isn't that a car engine? Hear that?"

Kate stopped paddling, too. "I don't hear anything."

"Well, I do. A car."

"Maybe it's Bill coming over. I think he said he might."

"Oh." Carla resumed paddling as the canoe rounded a narrow peninsula, giving them a different view of the lake. "Wow!" she exclaimed. "It's beautiful."

Kate was breathless herself. The lake seemed to double in size, with islands dotting its shimmering surface. Fingers of land covered with trees poked out here and there, creating little coves and inlets. Kate realized for the first time that Limberlost itself was at the end of a large bay in the lake. The foothills and mountains behind seemed unreal, a painted backdrop to the immediate foreground of blinding light and cool shade along the shoreline.

"Uh-oh," said Carla, lurching off her knees and into the seat. "Kate...oh, my God—there's a humongous spider and it's crawling right toward me."

"Relax, Carla. Don't move around so much. This is a canoe, remember? Just flick it away if it comes too close."

"But, Kate, this is a serious spider. Like, there's hair on it. And spots. It's coming closer." She shrieked, dropped the paddle into the water and stood up.

"Don't!" Kate screamed as the canoe tipped over and they hit the water.

CHAPTER SEVEN

KATE HAD A SPLIT SECOND to gulp a mouthful of air before submerging. But not for long. The buoyancy of her life jacket brought her to the surface almost immediately. She gasped, water-blinded, head swiveling for Carla. The canoe was floating upside down a few feet away.

"Carla!" she shouted.

She didn't know how well the girl swam, only that she'd taken lessons at school. But she'd been wearing a life jacket and should be okay. Kate swam toward the canoe, to see if Carla was on the other side. She wasn't.

"Carla!"

Nothing. Then a muted sound of distress. Trapped under the canoe? Kate swam over to it. She put her face into the water and opened her eyes. Peering through the greenish water, she saw...yes! Carla's legs waving under the canoe. She ducked under the gunwhale and lifted her head out of the water. There was about a foot of air between the canoe and the surface of the water. First she saw Carla's hands clutching the upside down seat, then her face, white with fear.

Teeth chattering, Carla cried, "Kate! My life jacket... came off. Didn't do it up right."

"It's okay sweetie." She took another gasp of air. "You can wear mine." But the space under the canoe was too small to maneuver and she only succeeded in shifting the canoe and Carla. And the air space was growing smaller.

"Kate," the girl wailed, "I'm afraid. I'm not a good swimmer."

"All right. Then this is what we do. Hold on to the belt of my jacket. When I say go, take a deep breath and go under. Just hold on to me and trust me. It'll only take two seconds to get out from under here, okay?"

Carla nodded, her eyes huge in her pinched, narrow face.

"All right. One, two, three and *go!*" Kate saw Carla open her mouth and clamp it shut just as she ducked beneath the surface and, pulling Carla along with her, emerged on the other side of the gunwhale. Carla thrashed wildly, but Kate managed to grab one wrist and place her hand firmly on the side of the canoe. Immediately, the girl stopped thrashing and opened her eyes.

Kate smiled. "We did it. Now, just relax. As long as you're holding on to the canoe, you'll be fine."

Carla nodded, tendrils of hair drooping over her face like strands of seaweed. "But...it's...a...a long way to...to..."

"A few feet."

Carla's tight mouth cracked in a half smile. "Like a...a hundred...math teacher!" She gasped out the two words.

Kate smiled back, but she was worried. The girl wasn't very strong and the cold, mountain-fed lake was already taking its toll on her. She unclasped her life jacket and helped Carla get it on. It was too big for the girl and she cinched the belt as tight as she could.

"Can you do the breaststroke?" she asked.

"K-kinda," Carla said through chattering teeth.

"Just go slowly, honey, okay? Don't take your eyes off me, and if you get tired, just turn onto your back and kick. The jacket will keep your head out of the water. We're going to feel our way around to the other side of the canoe, 'cause that's where the shore is closest. Ready?"

The girl nodded and they began to slowly edge their way to the end of the canoe. As Kate came around, she saw the life jacket Carla had been wearing drifting toward shore. She gave Carla a thumbs-up and, lifting her hand off the canoe, began to swim. Carla hadn't been far wrong about the distance, she figured. She just prayed the girl could make it. Every few feet, she glanced back to make sure Carla was still following. About halfway to shore, she realized the distance between them was widening. She tread water, uncertain whether to go back and help Carla or wait.

The sun beat down, limning the water and blinding Kate as she watched Carla's head bob toward her. She closed her eyes against the glare. Nausea rolled up from her stomach. Her eyes blinked open. Everything was black and silver with huge red spots pulsing here and there. The light was playing tricks on her, she knew. She could swear there were two heads in the water. No. One. Wait. There *was* another. They bumped against each other, separated and came together again.

More nausea. Kate wanted to throw up. She was exhausted. Occasional laps in the school pool didn't cut it for lake swimming. She did what she'd told Carla to do, turning onto her back and staring up at the brilliant sky. Ouch. Mistake. Closed her eyes to see even more red spots. Moved her arms backward, clumsily pawing at the water. Too slow and uneven to keep afloat, she began to sag midbody. No good. Keep breaststroking.

But when she rolled over, her legs seemed to have turned into cement, dragging her lower body too far below the surface to get momentum. Treading water more frantically now, she pivoted around to look for Carla, straight into the sun. It was like staring at a camera flash. Closed her eyes. Opened them.

"Carla!" she called. Was that her voice? So high-pitched and reedy? Her chin dipped, filling her mouth with water. The shock jolted her. She shot up, choking. How far did she have to go? And was Carla still coming? Turned her head. Strange black shapes danced above the shimmer of water. Was one of them Carla?

"Carla!" she called. The name echoed in her ringing ears. Then something tugged at her bathing suit straps. She whirled around, beating the water with her hands. "Carla!" And the something raised her shoulders out of the water, pushing and pulling at her arms. A man's voice, soothing and calm, just there at the back of her head.

"Easy. Let's get you into this." A strong arm came up across the front of her suit, pressing against her breasts as first one of her arms and then the other was shoved roughly into the life jacket. Then Kate felt herself pulled from behind.

"Kick, if you can. It'll help."

And she did, letting her body relax, closing her eyes against the sun and skimming ever so slowly over the surface of the lake. She almost drifted off—would have, were it not for the labored breathing of her rescuer and the realization she ought to keep kicking even though she was so tired. Soon warmer water lapped beneath her, her backside scraped against sand and she was dragged up onto the shore, where she let her head drop, eyes still closed? But she was alive.

When she could open her mouth for more than just air, she licked her dry lips and murmured, "Bill?"

"Who's Bill?"

Kate rolled onto her side, squinting, and came face-to-wet-face with Matt Sinclair.

THEY MADE A PATHETIC sight, Kate thought, she and Carla. Soaked hair dangling, eyes ringed with fatigue. She was wearing a large cotton sweatshirt, and Carla, a fleecy jacket, pulled from the trunk of Matt's car.

She'd wanted to walk back to the lodge, but the look Matt gave her suggested "over his dead body." So they'd spread towels over the seats in his car and he flicked on the heater for a few seconds, though the sun streaming through the windows was soon enough to ease the bone-chilling shivers that had possessed both of them once out of the water. It wasn't until they were back at the lodge and in dry, warm clothing that he would answer any of their questions.

In fact, the only one of Kate's he'd responded to at the time was her gasped, "Where's Carly?"

And he'd pointed to the beach a few yards away where Carla lolled in the hot sand, seemingly none the worse for her swim to shore. Only then had Kate sunk back, squeezing her eyes shut to give a silent thank-you.

While she and Carla were dressing upstairs, he'd changed in the lounge. Matt had taken a small gym bag from the trunk of his car when they'd gone up to the lodge.

"In case I decided to stay overnight somewhere," he'd explained.

Somewhere? Was there another resort close by that she'd missed?

Afterward, he'd found the kitchen and boiled water for hot chocolate, a treat Kate had planned for an evening bonfire. Then he'd carried it out with a plate of cookies to the trio of Adirondack chairs he'd arranged on the lawn's only sunny spot.

As they watched him stroll from the lodge as if he'd worked there all his life, Carla hissed at Kate, "Who is he?"

"A friend of mine, it seems."

Carla frowned at the cryptic answer, then said, "Well, he sure looked hot in his boxer shorts."

And Kate's sputtering giggle rolled into belly laughter that both refused to explain to Matt when he reached them. They blew on the hot drinks, carefully sipping them, while Matt leaned back in his chair and watched.

Kate set her mug down on the wide arm of the chair and said, "Carla Lopez, meet Matt Sinclair."

Matt winked at the girl and said, "I believe we've met."

Carla giggled behind her mug of chocolate.

The he turned to Kate and asked, "Is it question time?"

She could only nod. His presence there was just beginning to register. Back on the shore, he could have been an alien and she'd have gladly accepted his arrival so relieved was she at being pulled from the water. But now a hundred questions buzzed her weary mind. Most of them starting with *how* and *why*.

He waited for her to speak, smiled knowingly and said, "Okay, then. I can see you're still recovering from your swim."

Kate heard Carla giggle again beside her and shot her a frown.

He went on. "When I woke up this morning it was such a beautiful summer day, I had an impulse to go out into the country. Then I remembered your trip to Limberlost and thought, why not take a drive up there?"

Kate turned her frown on Matt this time. *An impulse to go out into the country?*

"I had just turned off the main road and had stopped the car to take in the view at that point where you dumped. First thing I saw was the overturned canoe. Then I heard shouting and saw heads bobbing in the water. I drove as closely as I could get to the water and dove in. Carla...'course, I didn't know it was her at the time—" he threw a dazzling smile Carla's way and Kate ground her teeth at the girl's coy smile "—had almost made it to shore but was upset about you, Kate. When I got to her, she said you were swimming away from the point. You must've gotten disoriented from the sun."

Kate realized how it had happened. The sun and glare from the water had blinded her. No wonder the land had never seemed to get any closer. She hated to think Matt Sinclair might have saved her life. Not because of the man himself, though he still grated, but because she'd needed saving at all. It was humiliating. She also felt responsible for Carla's nearly drowning. She should've made certain the girl's life jacket was fastened properly.

"But what Kate isn't telling you," Carla put in suddenly, "is that I was trapped underneath and freaking out because I'd lost my life jacket and thought for sure I was going to drown. Kate came under, got me out and gave me her jacket."

"Really?" Matt stared thoughtfully at Kate. "Not bad for a city girl," he finally said.

"Two city girls," Carla said.

Matt caught Kate's eye over the top of Carla's head and smiled. It was almost a complicit smile, a sharing of common knowledge whose message Kate picked up right away. For the first time since she'd met him, she felt as though they were on the same wavelength.

After a long pause, Matt said matter-of-factly, "We still have to go back for the canoe."

Carla's eyes almost popped out of her head. "I'm never gonna set foot in another canoe in my life."

Matt laughed. "Now is exactly the time to do it. Kate can drop us off at the point and you and I will paddle it back." He waited, then added, "I'll show you how to do draw-and-sweep strokes. How many kids at your school know how to do them?"

"In Brooklyn? Like, prob'ly no one."

"Except for you," he said.

Carla sighed and stood up. "Okay, let's get it over with."

Kate followed them to the gravel driveway where the cars were parked, marveling at the way he'd finessed Carla into giving canoeing another try.

"Cool car," Carla pronounced as they passed Matt's. "I was gonna mention it before when you drove us back up here, but my teeth were chattering too much."

Matt grinned. "Right. Well, I got this little number about a year ago. Courtesy of my Christmas bonus at work."

"No kidding? Jeez, what's your work, anyway?"

"I'm a lawyer."

Kate rolled her eyes as she let herself into her own car. Although Matt had offered his, she'd taken one look at the gearshift and said no thanks. Carla had been mildly disappointed, she thought, judging by the furrowed brow. Still, Matt had definitely scored with the girl. Kate herself didn't buy his reason for following her to Limberlost. Though she didn't want to consider how the canoe outing might have turned out had Matt not happened by.

The trip to the point took less than three minutes by road. Kate watched as Matt swam to the nearby overturned canoe and pushed it to the shallows, where he managed to flip it over and empty it of water. As he patiently outlined the basics of getting in and out of a canoe, Kate had to admit that, as Carla had pointed out, he had looked "hot" in his boxer shorts. Matt glanced up then, catching her gawking at him, and she feigned sudden interest in removing a pebble from one of her sandals.

"Are you waiting to see us off?" he asked, cocking his head to one side and grinning.

"Of course."

"I think we'll be okay, Kate," Carla said. "Why don't you go back and get some lunch ready for us?"

Matt's grin transformed into an enthusiastic smile. "Great idea!"

And Kate, chewing on her lower lip, headed for the car.

THE FIRST THING she saw as she walked through the screen door into the lounge was Matt's gym bag lying open on

one of the wicker chairs. A tumble of clothing had spilled
out of it onto the arm of the chair, probably when he'd
rummaged for his dry shorts. She didn't want to poke into
his things, so she gently lifted up a polo shirt that was
heading for the floor. A small black leather address book
fell onto the floor when she moved the shirt. Kate bent
down to retrieve it and was about to place it in the gym
bag when a wicked impulse struck her.

She flipped through the book, finding her name under the
*R*s. There was an asterisk beside her name. Meaning what?
she wondered. On impulse, she looked in the *A* section but
found no reference for Tom Andrews. *Stop it, Reilly. What
you're doing is reprehensible, not to mention downright
sleazy.* But she couldn't stop. Flipped through the *B*s to
find Joanna's name and at least three telephone numbers
for her, all but one crossed out. Under *M*s, there were two
listings for Lance Marchant—business and home.

*Why would Matt have the phone numbers of people he
wanted nothing to do with? People he obviously hated?*

She turned the pages over quickly, noting an abundance of
female first names throughout, and almost closed the back
cover when she spotted, penned in red, the initial *T* with a
number beside it. *T for Tom?* Or maybe *T* for Theresa or
Trish. Kate shook her head, disgusted at her actions. She
placed the book inside the bag right next to a cell phone.

He'd come prepared, all right, she was thinking. All the
basic accoutrements of an affluent urban dweller. *Don't be
so smug, Reilly, especially after snooping through his personal things. And what did you get out of it, anyway? Other
than a creepy feeling about yourself and a couple more
questions?* She made for the kitchen to set out lunch,
though her appetite had waned considerably.

THEY ARRIVED just after she'd set the picnic table on the
front lawn. Paddling onto the sandy beach, Carla let out an

exuberant whoop. Kate sauntered down to the water as they hauled up the canoe and flipped it onto the grass. The expressions on their faces made Kate think of early explorers, discovering some new territory. She'd never seen Carla looking so pleased.

They washed up at the kitchen sink, Matt informing Carla with mock solemnity that he'd never do such a thing at home, only if he were camping or roughing it.

"This is roughing it for me," she'd complained, at which he'd sprayed her with a handful of water and told her she didn't know what roughing it *meant*.

Kate watched the whole thing with a mixture of curiosity, awe and, she reluctantly admitted, petty jealousy. She wished she could have the same carefree manner with Carla, but her own childhood kept getting in the way.

After a lunch of sandwiches, fruit and cookies, Matt suggested a walk around the resort property.

"Have you never been here before?" Kate asked as they set out on a path leading to the cabins at the farthest side of the resort.

"Nope. Heard about it from my father but never made it here."

"Where did you learn all about canoeing and rescuing people from drowning?" Carla asked.

"Camp," Matt explained. "I went every summer from the time I was eight."

Carla's lip curled in horror. "That's awful. Did you like it? Why did your parents send you?"

He held up a hand, laughing. "Whoa! I didn't like it the first year and apparently wrote begging to go home. But my folks didn't get my letters until the end of the summer after they'd returned from Europe."

"They went to Europe while you were at *camp*?"

Kate had to laugh at the shock in her voice, though she,

too, was appalled at the idea of sending such a young child away and then going abroad. Maybe that was what rich people did, she thought.

Matt shrugged. "After that first summer, I got used to it. In fact, learned to love it. Because I went to the same camp every year, I got to see friends I'd made, and some of them are still my best buddies today."

They stopped in front of two cabins. Matt wandered around the side of one while Carla and Kate gazed up at the wooden banner hanging lopsided now from above one door. It read Spruce.

"This is where I bunked with five other girls when I stayed here."

"Six of you in there!" Carla exclaimed.

"There were three sets of bunk beds. It was crowded, but we didn't spend a lot of time inside, anyway."

"What about washrooms?"

"See that building over there?" Kate pointed to a con-crete-block structure hidden in a clump of trees beyond the two cabins. "It's got toilets, sinks and showers inside. One side was for the girls and the other for the boys." She smiled, suddenly remembering something. "We hated go-ing out there in our pajamas or bathrobes 'cause the boys would always make jokes about us. So we'd throw our rain ponchos over us whenever we went to shower."

"Did you like it here?"

"Not at the time," Kate said. "But looking back, I'm sure it wasn't as bad as I made it out to be. The thing was, I really wanted to hang out with my friends in the city."

"I know the feeling."

Kate glanced down at Carla. "But you're glad you came here, aren't you?"

"Oh, yeah. I really am. Even the getting-dumped part."

Matt rejoined them to hear the last part of her reply. "Look at it as a great story to tell the kids when you go back to school,'' he told Carla. Then to Kate, ''You know, this is a terrific piece of property. I wouldn't rush to sell it if I were you. If you like, I'd be happy to go over financing details or refer you to an investment adviser.''

Kate's estimation of him rose a notch. He was the first person to actually encourage her to keep Limberlost. Though heaven knew how she possibly could.

''Kate?''

She turned her head toward Carla, whose mouth was gaping in a yawn.

''I'm real tired. Think I'll go back and have a nap. Okay?''

''Sure, sweetie.''

Carla began walking toward the lodge when she turned around to call, ''If Matt wants to stay the night, he could have your room and you can bunk with me. It'd be fun.'' Then she went on her way.

Kate knew from the heat in her face that she was blushing.

''Actually,'' Matt said, ''I thought I should be leaving soon. It's a bit of a drive back to the city.''

''You're welcome to spend the night,'' Kate said, feeling embarrassed and ticked off at being put on the spot. Hadn't he come prepared to stay, anyway?

''I did, it's true,'' he said.

''What?''

''Didn't you just say I'd come prepared to stay anyway?''

Oh, God, she thought. *I'm going to get in big trouble if I start verbalizing all my thoughts.*

''Well, I know Carla would be disappointed if you left now. And the steaks I bought are big enough to share.'' She stopped talking, aware of his intense study of her.

''But do *you* want me to stay?''

He never took his eyes off her, compelling her to meet his gaze and say, "Yes, I'd like it, too."

At his satisfied smile, Kate felt a rush of giddiness. "Shall we have a look at the rest of it?" she suggested, and he nodded, flashing a million-dollar smile this time. As they walked toward the cluster of cabins reserved for paying guests, Kate wondered if she'd really had any say in anything that had occurred since Matt Sinclair turned up at Limberlost.

CARLA PLUNKED HER FORK onto her empty plate. "That was for sure the best steak I've ever eaten in my entire life. Thanks for cleaning up that old stone barbecue, Matt. They are *so* much better cooked that way." She got up awkwardly from the picnic table and started to clear the plates. "I'll do the dishes tonight, Kate. You just relax."

Kate gaped at the teenager. She watched her carry the tray full of plates and cutlery toward the lodge before turning to Matt, sitting opposite her at the table.

"That incredible?" Matt asked.

Kate shook her head. "Absolutely. If you only knew."

"I guess this trip has done something for her, then."

"I think so. You're very good with her, by the way. That's a gift, you know. To be a natural with kids and yet have them respect you at the same time."

He tipped his head. "Thanks. But I don't know that I can take credit for anything special here. I learned how to get along with all sorts of people from boarding schools and holiday camps."

Kate ran an index finger along the rim of her glass. "It's funny, almost."

"What?"

"Well, you grew up in a bunch of different boarding schools away from your parents, while I went from foster home to foster home—and obviously, without real parents.''

''So?''

His expression made her uncomfortable. As if she'd said something indiscreet. She shrugged. ''I'm not sure what point I'm making here,'' she said, giving a nervous laugh.

''Maybe that we're not so far apart, after all? In some ways, we were both neglected as children?''

''Yes, I think that's what I mean.''

He reached across the table to refill her glass. ''Shall we take our wine down to the shore to watch the sunset?''

''I'd like that.''

She and Carla had put on long pants and sweatshirts, not only for the cooler night air, but the mosquitoes that were just beginning to make an appearance. He'd changed for the evening, too, into jeans and a long-sleeved cotton shirt that he left untucked, its tails flapping around him as he walked. Following him down to the water's edge and the grouping of Adirondack chairs they'd set up earlier that afternoon, she decided that he did indeed cut a fine figure in any kind of clothing. And she'd seen him in almost all kinds in the past twenty-four hours. She giggled at her trend of thought. Too much wine, she told herself, without really believing that was the source of the frisson of excitement she felt at being alone with him.

The sunset was stunning, illuminating the horizon in a blend of pink, scarlet and indigo blue. They sat down in silent awe, just taking in the whole breathtaking panorama.

''That blue would be great on you,'' Matt murmured.

Kate laughed, embarrassed at the unexpected intimacy in his voice. ''Maybe,'' she said. ''But better on a blonde, I think.''

He studied her face, then pursed his lips. ''Nope. You've got the perfect skin tone for that color. Kind of milky white with a hint of pink. And your hair with those streaks of chestnut. An Irish heritage, I guess, especially with a name like Reilly.''

She shrugged. ''I don't really know for sure. Maybe.''

He frowned, realizing his error. ''Oh, sorry. Do you know anything about your background?''

''When I was eighteen I requested my file from Children's Aid. There wasn't a lot in it. Apparently my mother was unmarried or had been left alone and she couldn't keep me. I was left with Children's Aid. Kate Reilly was the name on the birth registration. So presumably I could be Irish.''

''Ever think of searching for her?''

''Nah. Too much time and money. Besides, once I'd met Joanna I never really burned to find out.'' Kate paused, then said, ''For a time, I used to fantasize that Joanna would adopt me.''

''Joanna? Hah! Not bloody likely.''

The expletive stung. ''I realize how childish that fantasy was, but still—''

''Kate,'' he interrupted, ''it has nothing to do with your dreams, which are very understandable, believe me. It's just that you didn't know the real Joanna Barnes. She was a vain and self-centered woman who demanded a lot of care and attention for herself. There's no way she'd even have considered having a child usurp that limelight.''

''You remember one side of her, but I knew another. She really listened to me. She didn't judge me or give me gratuitous advice the way adults do with kids and their problems. And mine were not ordinary problems.'' Kate paused, unable to continue. Finally she said, ''She never once forgot to send me a card, in spite of the busyness of her life, because she knew how important a message from her was to me.''

Beside her, Matt heaved a loud sigh. He finished off the dregs of wine in his glass and set it on the armrest of his chair. "We each have our version of her, and most likely, it'll never change. There's no point in spoiling such a beautiful sunset. How about we agree to disagree, as the expression goes, and forget all about Joanna Barnes, at least for this evening." He stood up and extended a hand to her. "I don't know about you, but the mosquitoes are finding my flesh very tender tonight."

Kate had to laugh, in spite of her mixed emotions. She took his hand and got up, swiping away a squadron of bugs with her free hand. "I'm with you on that, at least."

Matt brushed at something on her forehead. "You're a good sport, Kate Reilly, I grant you that." Then he drew a line across her forehead with his finger, down the bridge of her nose to the tip, and making the short but breathtaking leap to her lips.

She flinched.

"Chilly?" he murmured, moving closer as if to warm her with his body.

"No," she whispered, "just…"

"Just what?" His breath fanned gently onto her face as he lowered his mouth to hers.

When his lips touched hers, she knew she ought to pull away. Knew that after his kiss, everything between them would change. Become complicated in ways she couldn't possibly foresee now. Experience warned her off. Still, his lips were full, urgent and oh so sweet. She opened her mouth and took him in, savoring the warm rush and the mind-spinning whirl of sensations.

At last, he lifted his mouth from hers and tucked her head into the space between his neck and chest. She felt the pounding of his heart matching her own and held on, as if he were saving her all over again.

"That's the real reason I followed you here," he murmured. "Unfinished business."

"I don't understand."

"Last night. When you were sitting beside me in the car in front of your place, all I wanted to do was kiss you. Not kissing you tormented me all night long. So this morning, I knew I couldn't go another day without making it happen."

Something in his tone gave her goose bumps. Kate couldn't decide if she was excited by his passion or spooked by his associating the kiss with business. *Then what am I?* she asked herself.

But the heady scent of warm skin beneath his opened shirt and his hands stroking her neck and lower back had her mind shifting into third gear, leaving all doubts in the dust behind. She raised her face to his, leaned back and said, "Well, if that kiss was for last night, what about tonight's?"

And his illuminating smile was the last thing she saw before his mouth found hers again.

CHAPTER EIGHT

HER EYES FLICKED OPEN. Kate smiled. She'd had a deep sleep induced, she was positive, by the narcotic effects of Matt's kisses. Only two, but as he escorted her back into the lodge, there'd been a tacit agreement of more to come. He'd insisted on bunking down on a couch in the lounge and she'd found a pillow and slightly musty quilt in a blanket box in her bedroom.

He'd seemed reluctant to let her go, holding on to her hand and gazing into her eyes.

"I'll make breakfast," he promised.

"There's only pancake mix and frozen waffles. But I brought real syrup."

His smile at this announcement was tender. He looked as though he wanted to say something then, but Kate let slip a wide yawn.

"Better go up now," he said. "You've had a big day."

She blushed at the double meaning and made a quick exit up the main staircase. When she was tiptoeing into her room, she noticed a dim light in Carla's room. The girl was reading in bed by a flashlight.

"It's late, Carly," Kate said.

"I was just waiting for you to come up. Where's Matt?"

"He's going to sleep downstairs on a couch, so I'll stick to my own room, after all. Okay?"

"Sure. As long as he's staying over." Her eyes swept Kate's face in a knowing appraisal. "You're glad, too, aren't you?"

"Of course," she said, keeping her voice even. "Sleep in in the morning if you like."

The flashlight went off and Carla snuggled into her sleeping bag. "He's nice, Kate. Don't you think so?"

"Yes, yes. Good night." She closed the door behind her, feeling a sudden need for privacy. And Matt's face—the charcoal-gray eyes that seemed to have a hundred different expressions—was the last thing in her mind as she fell asleep.

So when Kate awoke to the muted sound of cupboard doors and the clinking of pots and pans, her thoughts turned at once to breakfast. And perhaps—dare she hope?—another kiss. After all, it was another day. She threw on shorts and tank top and skipped down the pantry stairs to the kitchen. No sign of Matt. In fact, no sign of breakfast, either.

More mystified—she'd have sworn she'd heard dishes clinking—than disappointed, Kate wandered into the lounge. It, too, was empty, though the quilt lay in a hump on the couch and Matt's gym bag was still sitting on the chair. *Well, at least he hasn't left.* As she turned around, deciding where to look next, she spotted a half-open door at the opposite end of the lounge to the kitchen. It was an area that Bill hadn't included in his brief tour, and certain that she hadn't noticed the door ajar before, Kate headed for it.

She stood on the threshold, eyes straining to adjust to the dimness inside. The shutters had been left on the windows, but after a few seconds, Kate could see that the room was an office. A large desk sat against one wall, bookcases and two filing cabinets against another. A couple of wicker chairs and a small table stood in front of the window side. And in the corner between desk and filing cabinet, was another door, also ajar. Kate took a step toward it and hesitated.

There were rustling noises coming from the other room. Could a bear have gotten into the lodge? No. Not unless it was a bear with a light. A faint glow bobbed through the opening of the door. She moved closer to look inside the tiny room—a kind of ante-office, she guessed. There was a smaller version of the desk in the office behind her, and on the other side of it—on all fours and bent over something on the floor—was Matt. As Kate moved softly into the room, she saw that he was riffling through papers in a file.

It still hadn't occurred to her that anything was amiss, but when she asked, in a perfectly calm and normal voice, "Are you looking for something in particular?" the expression in his face erased any benefit of doubt she was ready to give. Shock, embarrassment and, worst of all, guilt. About what, Kate had no inkling.

He clambered awkwardly to his feet, kicking over the flashlight in the process. "Kate!" he exclaimed. "You're up!"

She hoped his observations as a corporate lawyer were a little more insightful. "Yes. I thought I heard the sounds of breakfast cooking, but…"

He raked a hand through his hair, which promptly reared up from his head in untidy clumps. "Ah, yes. I was just getting to that."

"In here?"

He didn't answer, but stooped to retrieve the flashlight. He clicked it off, throwing the tiny room into darkness.

Suddenly Kate felt uncomfortable. *I may have lost my head and allowed this man to kiss me—twice—but do I even know him?* Nervously she piped up, "What about the papers?"

"What papers?"

"The ones you've left on the floor."

The light came on again. Matt walked stiffly behind the desk and bent to pick up the file folder.

"What are they?" she asked, striving for a balance of interest and indifference in her voice.

"Nothing much. Here, have a look."

She ignored the folder in his extended hand, keeping her eyes fixed on his face. He dropped the folder onto the desktop and started to leave. Rather than be left in the dark—literally and otherwise—she followed along. Her bewilderment was quickly changing to anger.

He was partway through the outer office when she called after him, "Wait a sec."

She caught up to him in the doorway, where he waited patiently. The look in his face had also changed. Now he seemed completely oblivious to the situation. As if she'd merely interrupted him performing some puzzling but harmless task.

"What were you searching for in there? And is this what you've been doing all morning? Rummaging through cupboards and closets?"

"I...it's not what you think, Kate. Trust me."

"I don't know what to think, to be honest. Yesterday you said...you said you came here because you wanted an outing in the country. Then there was that other explanation—the one you gave me last night." Her voice fell. The memory of their parting made his sneaking around even worse.

He held up both hands, almost in supplication. "Please, don't get the wrong idea. Remember when we had coffee a few days ago? The day you met with Joanna's lawyer, Collier? I told you then that I'd been to see Marchant because Joanna had some papers of my father's. Remember? I suggested they might be here at Limberlost."

Of course. He *did* say that, she remembered. *God, did everyone have papers hidden away up here?*

"Then what was all this stuff about wanting to come up north? Why didn't you just tell me you came to look for the papers? Why all the secrecy, Matt?"

He averted his face for a moment. To compose himself, she wondered, or to avoid her while he concocted some other wild tale?

When he finally turned back, he said, "As improbable as it sounds, my number-one reason for coming *was* to see you again. Last night was no pantomime, believe me. The other—looking for Dad's things—was a secondary issue. I didn't even think of it till first thing this morning."

"And you just happened to have some fancy flashlight with you," she scoffed.

"I knew there might not be any electricity up here."

"How did you know that if you've never been here?"

He scowled. "I don't know. A guess. It's been closed up for years. What's with the interrogation? What are *you* worried I might find?"

"Me? How did I get into this?"

"You seem very paranoid about this place."

"Because I happen to be the *owner!*"

He rolled the flashlight in his hands. After a few seconds he said, "Maybe I should see to breakfast. Carla will be getting up soon."

Carla. The last thing Kate wanted was to have the girl encounter them arguing. She'd already witnessed enough domestic fights in her short life.

"Forget breakfast. I've lost my appetite. If Carla wants pancakes, I'll make them."

His eyes flicked away from hers, but not before she noticed the bleakness in them. He was feeling miserable, she realized. *But so am I.*

"Then I guess I'll...I should just..."

"Go?"

"Right." He shrugged and walked into the lounge.

As Kate made her way up the front staircase to see if Carla was awake, she noticed him tossing things into his gym bag. He was wearing the same shirt and jeans from yesterday, and while she watched, he unzipped the jeans to tuck in his shirt. He glanced up, catching her staring, but seemed too preoccupied to be embarrassed. She turned away and continued on up the stairs. When she reached the second-floor landing, she heard the hard thwack of the screen door as it closed behind him.

WHEN KATE HEARD the sound of an engine as she and Carla were washing the breakfast dishes, she almost dropped a glass.

"Maybe it's Matt coming back," Carla said. "Maybe he remembered he didn't have a business meeting, after all."

Kate flushed. The girl had immediately seen through the weak explanation Kate had made for Matt's absence.

"He doesn't seem like the kind of person who'd forget a meeting one day and remember it the next," she'd said, skepticism edging her voice. "Are you sure you two didn't have a fight?"

"A fight? I hardly know the man."

Carla had just snorted.

So Kate took her time finishing the dishes while Carla went out to greet their visitor. When she returned seconds later followed by Bill Tippett and his grandson, Kate was both relieved and disappointed.

"G'day," Bill said. He hovered in the doorway with Kyle and Carla behind.

"Hi, Bill. Like some coffee? There's some left."

"Don't mind if I do." He pulled out a chair and sat down.

"Carla? Do you and Kyle want anything? Juice? Pop?"

They shook their heads and then Carla unexpectedly turned to Kyle and asked, "Wanna go canoeing?"

The boy shrugged indifferently, but said, "Sure."

Kate managed to keep the surprise out of her face. Evidently Carla had regained her lost confidence from yesterday's mishap. She supposed she had Matt to thank for that, but the mere thought of the man made her feel queasy.

"The life jackets are back in the boathouse," she reminded Carla as the teenagers headed out of the kitchen.

"Nice to see that a city kid knows something about canoeing," Bill remarked.

"Well, she just picked up a few pointers yesterday, actually. I hope she'll be okay. I don't want to discourage her."

He pursed his lips and nodded. "Yep. Good for them to get some independence. Though some might be wantin' too much too soon."

This last statement was bitter. Kate waited for him to explain.

"Kyle's been with us since May and he's not very happy about it. His mom and dad—my boy, Richie—got divorced this year and they've had some problems with Kyle. Figured he'd be better off with us in the country 'stead of takin' that roller-coaster ride his folks've been on lately in Plattsburg, where they live. But to tell you the truth, none of us is enjoyin' it much."

"Divorce can be tough on kids. I guess he doesn't have many friends here in Bondi."

Bill snorted. "Hah! You've seen the village. Ain't what it used to be, when Limberlost was up and running. Made a difference, you know. Kids hung around to get summer jobs here, 'stead of hoofin' it to Plattsburg or Lake Placid or wherever." He eyed Kate over the rim of his coffee mug. "Be nice if the place were to open up again, y'know. Think you might be interested in doin' that, 'stead a sellin' it?"

Put on the spot, Kate stammered, "I...I don't know. I'm still getting used to being the owner. It hasn't even been a week since I found out and not even two since…since Joanna died.''

He gave this thoughtful silence, then said, ''Well, I know for sure the Barneses woulda hated to see the lodge torn down by developers and them pricey condos or chalets put up in its place.''

''Is that what you think will happen if I sell?''

''Prob'ly. I know Joanna was offered big bucks for the place a few years ago, right after her papa died. But she said no way.''

Mention of Joanna brought a rush of sadness. Kate felt a sting of tears and looked away. She wondered if Joanna had already decided at that point to leave Limberlost to her. Maybe she'd been saving it for her. She sighed. *What was the point of all this speculation? She'd never know for sure.*

After a moment Kate asked, ''Did you know Joanna well?''

''She was a coupla years younger. Guess she'd a been turning fifty this year.''

''Yes.'' The kitchen filled with silence and thoughts of Joanna.

''She wasn't very happy here in Bondi the last few years of high school. The kids were bused to the next town to school, and she hated taking that bus. Dunno why, though I guess some of the kids were kinda mean to her.''

''Mean?''

He shrugged, searching for words. ''She was always so different. Never wore the same fashions as other girls her age. Had real black hair and eyes like Elizabeth Taylor. A real beauty she was, but most of the guys were afraid of her.''

''Why?''

''Had a wicked tongue, she did. Hated any kinda nonsense or horsin' around. And believe me, teenagers in Bondi weren't all that sophisticated.'' He chuckled. ''She made it pretty clear to everyone that she was headed for bigger and better things. And she was!'' He fell into thought, then looked across the table at Kate. ''But you know, I always had the feeling she was never very happy. There were times, before her folks passed away, that she'd come here to hang out kinda. Just get away from it all.'' He shook his head. ''Nope, even though she was dead set against livin' here—even told me once she hated the place—she always turned up whenever things in her own life weren't goin' too well.''

Just like when I met her.

''Shame she died so young. Guess she couldn't take it no more—whatever was makin' her unhappy, I mean.''

''I can't believe she'd kill herself,'' Kate said. ''She loved life too much, even if it did make her unhappy at times.''

He pursed his lips again. ''Yep. She was always up for anything, was Joanna. One of her favorite sayin's was 'You only live once,' and I betcha she never turned down any chance at havin' fun.''

Bill set the coffee mug down on the table, slapped his palms against his thighs and said, ''Well, suppose I best be goin'. Reason I dropped by was to see if you had any instructions for the place after you leave.''

''Instructions?''

''Joanna asked me to make regular rounds, put off any vandals.''

''I haven't thought about any of this. Gosh…'' She let the sentence drift, unsure of what she ought to do.

''I can turn off the generator and propane. Make sure the fridge door is left open once you clean out all your leftovers. I'll put the shutters back on and that's about it.'' He paused. ''Till you let me know about the long-term.''

''The long-term? Oh, you mean what I intend to do. Oh, of course. Do you have any deadline for that? I mean, is looking after this place going to interfere with your own business?"

"Heck no! I work outta my home, doin' mechanical repairs and such. Driving around Limberlost once every two weeks is a pleasure, not a job."

"Still, Joanna must have been paying you." The responsibilities of ownership were just starting to sink in. The single thought going through Kate's mind was, did she have enough in her savings account to get her through the summer? Taking on an employee was way beyond her budget.

Bill said, "Joanna paid me a stipend—so much a year. To set your mind at rest, she's paid me right through till September. By then you might have a better idea what you want to do with the place."

"I appreciate that, Bill. Thank you so much. I'll let you know as soon as I decide."

His eyes fixed on her face, as if assessing her. "Appreciate that, mostly because there'll be a lot to do to get it in order for sellin', if that's the way you're gonna go. After Mr. Barnes died, Joanna came to pack up everythin'. There're boxes o' stuff stored all over this place—in the cabins and up in the loft here. Heck, I even got boxes of hers in my shed. So you'll want to go through things, keep what you want or toss out the worthless stuff."

Kate nodded, too overwhelmed by having to make a decision before the end of the summer even to consider the extent of the tasks involved. She followed Bill to the front door of the lodge. Down by the lake, she could see Carla and Kyle dragging the canoe up onto the sandy beach.

"The kids are back," she said.

"Yep. Looks like they enjoyed themselves." Bill crinkled his eyes against the glare of the midday sun. "Kinda nice to see Kyle talking to another human being. All Vern and I get are mumbled grunts."

Kate laughed. "Maybe I'll get a chance to bring Carla

back up here before…before I decide what I'm going to do. I guess I'll have to do that by September. After that, I'll be busy at work."

"What is your work?"

"I'm an elementary-school teacher in Manhattan."

Bill whistled through the gap in his front teeth. "I would say a spell in the north country is exactly what you could use. But come for longer next time—it takes at least a couple of weeks to get to know the place. I doubt you remember too much from when you were a kid up here."

"You're right. My memory of it is very sketchy."

He stepped off the porch and walked toward his pickup. As he opened his door, he said to Kate, "That friend o' yours show up? Fella from the city?"

"Oh, oh yes, thanks."

"He stopped in at George Miller's place to ask for directions—that's how I knew you had a visitor. Don't want you to think us nosey parkers up here are spyin' on you." His face broke into a big grin. "Anyhow, George wasn't sure if he ought to be givin' out that kinda information, but the fella insisted you were expectin' him. Plus," he added, a twinkle in his eyes, "the guy was drivin' one o' them pricey foreign cars and George has always been impressed by any show of wealth. Coulda been a bank robber, for all George knew, but the car was the ticket for him."

Kate smiled, but inside her blood pressure was rising. Obviously Matt Sinclair had a knack for coming up with the right lines in any situation. She stood by the truck while Carla and Kyle, deep in conversation, strolled up from the beach. Still seething over Matt, she almost missed seeing Carla reach out to furtively touch Kyle's hand. The movement was quick, just as Kyle was climbing up into the truck and waving goodbye. The truck roared into reverse and tore down the road.

"Have a good time?" Kate asked casually.

"Yeah" was all Carla said, turning away from Kate. "Is it lunchtime yet? I'm starving."

I'll bet, Kate was thinking, after charging up all those adolescent hormones. *Speaking of hormones.* She recalled with some chagrin how she'd looked forward that morning to the possibility of another kiss from Matt Sinclair. *No chance of that now, Reilly. Prob'ly, as Carla would say, not ever again.*

CARLA WAS LOST IN THOUGHT for most of the return trip, which was just as well, Kate figured. Take her mind off the winding roads. Not to mention the questions about Matt that had come at sporadic intervals throughout lunch. Deflecting neatly any mention about her canoe ride with Kyle.

They'd left after lunch, but not before Kate took a flashlight and returned to the small office where she'd found Matt earlier. She picked up the file folder on the desk, her face warming as she did. Why did she care, anyway? But her curiosity was aroused. As Matt had said, there was nothing much in the folder. A collection of receipts going back several years. Kate pulled open the desk drawers. There were a few other files, all about the same. Old papers, bills and receipts. Nothing that would interest anyone any longer.

Kate wondered why he'd thought his father's papers would be in a file folder in what was obviously the resort's office. *Because the office is simply the first place he looked, that's why.* She closed the door behind her and went to see how Carla was doing with her packing.

There was a brief run of conversation after a stop at a service center. Carla asked Kate why Joanna had never operated Limberlost after her parents died.

"I don't know, Carly. Maybe she figured it would be like taking a giant step backward. She wanted to leave so bad when she was young. Besides, she was a big fashion writer and then editor of some very well-known fashion magazines. It would be impossible to have a career like that and run Limberlost.''

"Why couldn't she pay other people to run it for her?''

"I don't know. I guess she could have, but even that would have required management and so on.''

"Why do you think she left it to you?''

"I don't really know, Carla.''

"I guess she was thinking of you a lot even if she only sent you one card a year.''

Kate felt a lump in her throat. *Out of the mouths of babes.* "I guess she was, Carly. I guess she was.'' And there was nothing else to say, just recalling the memory of all nineteen years of waiting for Joanna's note to arrive and the thrill of even such minimal contact. *The sad thing is,* Kate realized, *I never asked for or expected more. As if I always knew I'd only fit into a very small part of Joanna's life.* Still, it was enough.

By the time they pulled up to Carla's triplex in Brooklyn, it was just after seven and they were both exhausted. Carla tumbled out of the car, oblivious to Rita's warm welcome. She barely took time to set her backpack down on the pavement, give Kate a quick hug and a thank-you for taking her before rushing up the steps inside.

Rita watched her disappear. "I was just going to ask her if she had a good time. Does that mean she did? Or not?''

Kate laughed wearily. "I think so, it's just that we're…''

"Tired.''

"Right. But it went very well and I imagine she'll be more talkative after a good night's sleep.'' She said goodbye to Rita, got back into the car and drove to the rental agency. When she finally arrived home, splurging on a taxi because she couldn't face the subway, it was almost eight o'clock.

There was a message on her telephone from Lance Marchant, inviting her to dinner the next night if she was available. The mood she was in, she didn't feel like dealing with anyone connected to Joanna. She stood, zombielike, under a cool shower, ate a container of yogurt and went to bed.

IT WAS LATE MORNING by the time Kate got back to Lance Marchant about dinner. She was in a better frame of mind, in spite of a sleep broken by recurring images of Matt in all the various scenes of the past two days.

Soaking wet beside her on the shore, behind the wheel of his flashy car and wearing nothing but boxer shorts, or scrubbing the stone barbecue prior to cooking their steaks. But the image that appeared most often was Matt's face when she'd turned from the staircase to look back at him. The silent rebuke in his eyes blended with a challenge. *I'm here, waiting. Come back.*

Kate inhaled deeply, dispelling the vision. An overactive imagination, she reminded herself, had always been her downfall.

Apart from a telephoned thank-you from Carla, the day dragged. Heat emanated from every surface. The air-conditioning unit was operating at maximum capacity, yet Kate could only feel its effect when she was in the kitchen itself. When she finally got through to Lance, his cheerful breeziness was refreshing. He sounded delighted at her acceptance and said he wanted to hear all about her trip. They spoke briefly, as he was on his way to a press conference where he'd officially announce his decision to run for Congress.

When Kate hung up, her unexpected pleasure at being asked to dinner by someone like Lance almost completely overshadowed her qualms about going out with him. So she decided to wear the same dress she'd worn at her dinner with Matt. *No reason to keep it special, was there?*

Lance's approval was gratifying, too, when he picked her

up the following evening. "I brought the Chrysler tonight, instead of the convertible," he said as Kate locked the apartment door behind them, "for the air-conditioning. And now I'm delighted I did. It would be a shame to ruffle one bit of such perfection. You look stunning."

Kate blushed. For an instant, she questioned her decision to date Joanna's husband. Then reminded herself the evening was about companionship, not romance. Matt Sinclair's face resurfaced in her mind. *Forget about romance.*

On the way to the restaurant, Lance asked her several questions about her teaching job and her background in an interested, rather than intrusive, way. Once they arrived, the attentiveness of the staff and good wishes bestowed by several of the patrons added to the aura surrounding him. Kate could see his gift for politics as he handled both compliments and questions with warmth and ease.

But once they were sitting down and had ordered, his attention was devoted to her again. Kate found she enjoyed the spotlight, even the furtive glances from some of the people who'd come up to wish Lance well in his campaign. Her earlier doubts vanished and she relaxed, sipping first champagne and then wine with dinner.

"How did you find the lodge? Was it in good shape?" he asked, after listening to some of her teaching anecdotes.

"Not bad, though I didn't exactly make an inspection. I had a friend with me."

"Oh?"

"Well, she's only thirteen. She's a foster child and I'm her big sister, as in the organization." He nodded. "I thought it would be a chance for her to get out of the city, if only for a couple of days."

He nodded. "And what about this Tippett character?"

"Bill? He was great! He'd opened up some of the rooms for us and turned on the power and so on."

"Power? Oh, I suppose everything's been closed off for years."

"There's a generator and propane for the fridge and stove. It was a bit like camping, though not as rough. Not that I would know," she said, laughing, "having never really camped in my life."

Lance raised his wineglass to her. "Precisely my sentiments. My idea of roughing it is staying in a three-star hotel, instead of a five."

"Exactly." Kate returned his smile with an unexpected rush of pleasure.

"Did seeing the lodge restore any memories of your visit there?" he asked.

Kate thought for a moment. "I had these memory flashes, you know what I mean? When I went inside the main lodge and saw the staircase, I remembered my first time in it. We city kids were more or less limited to our sleeping cabins and our own dining hall. That way, I guess the paying customers didn't have to be exposed to some of the antics of the kids. That's my impression now, though as a kid I figured we were less than worthy. Charity cases." She smiled at the recollection. "I was pretty uptight in those days about everything."

"You managed to shirk off those traits very effectively," Lance murmured, tipping his wineglass to her. After a pause, he asked, "What do you recall of Joanna?"

"She was fabulous. Beautiful, as you know, but also flamboyant. Ambitious, the way she talked about her plans for making it big when she came to Manhattan. Also very down-to-earth. I didn't get the sense that she was a snob, certainly not by the way she used to mimic some of the wealthier people who stayed at Limberlost."

"Yes, she was definitely down-to-earth, as you say." Deep in thought, he ran a finger along the rim of his glass.

Then he raised his eyes to Kate. "I miss her very much," he said, his voice husky all of a sudden.

Kate didn't know what to say, so she reached out and patted his hand.

The waiter arrived to take Lance's credit card, breaking the mood. After he left, Lance said, "So I suppose you didn't have an opportunity to see if any of Joanna's personal items were lying around?"

"Oh, no I didn't. As a matter of fact, I didn't think of looking around for stuff like that. I...there was so little time." She stopped, hesitating to mention that Matt Sinclair had turned up. Somehow she didn't think Lance would like that. "But Bill told me there are all kinds of boxes packed away in the cabins and even in his shed. He and Joanna cleaned up a lot of things after they closed the lodge when her father died."

"Oh? Maybe I can arrange to look at things later. Did your visit help you to make a decision about the place?"

"Not really. I wish it had, actually. But I did promise Bill I'd let him know before September."

"Why then?"

"Joanna had paid him to look after the place till then. And I'll be starting work again, so if I have to look after selling it, I'll have more free time to do everything this summer."

"Sounds like you're leaning that way," he said.

"I suppose so. Although..."

"What? Doubts?"

"Kind of. I can't help but think that Joanna obviously wanted me to have Limberlost. Wouldn't she have wanted me to keep it?"

He shrugged. "Since I knew nothing of Joanna's bequest, I can't say. Perhaps she simply wanted you to have it as some kind of insurance for yourself. An investment can be realized many ways. Either operating the resort for a profit, if that's even possible now, or selling it and investing the money. Joanna was a great one for recognizing and appreciating the value of a dollar, believe me.'' He said this dryly, with some humor.

Kate smiled. "I hadn't thought of that possibility, though of course it makes sense. Well, I guess having a deadline for a decision is good. Otherwise, I'd put it off forever.''

The waiter brought Lance's receipt. "Shall we go?'' Lance asked.

"Yes. I still haven't recovered from the road trip.''

"Maybe another reason to sell,'' he said. "It's certainly not exactly commuting distance if you chose to live up there.''

"No,'' Kate said, dismissing the idea at once. "I'm too much of a city girl to settle in Bondi village.''

On the way to her apartment, Kate thanked Lance for the evening.

"Maybe we can do it again some time,'' he said, "though my life is going to become a lot more frenetic in the next few weeks.''

He walked her to the bottom of the steps of her row house. On the way home, Kate had been debating whether or not to ask him up. She'd enjoyed the evening and found herself liking Lance. Even his remark about being busy had mildly disappointed her. But she felt enough discomfort about being close to Joanna's husband that it was a relief to have the decision taken from her.

"It's been a wonderful evening,'' he said, "but I've a lot to do tomorrow. Perhaps I can call in a few days?''

When he leaned over to kiss her gently on the cheek, she patted his arm. "Thanks again, Lance. The evening was lovely.''

He smiled, gave a jaunty wave and got back into his car.

She stood and watched him drive off, then turned to go up the stairs.

"Kate?"

She wheeled around, recognizing the voice instantly.

CHAPTER NINE

MATT STEPPED OUT from the shadows at the corner of the row house. She knew from his face that he'd seen Lance kiss her.

"Kate," he said again, walking toward her. He was wearing rumpled tan slacks and a pale blue short-sleeved shirt opened at the neck. He looked as though he'd just awakened from a long sleep—slightly disheveled, baggy-eyed, hair going in all directions.

When he was standing in front of her, he forked his fingers across his head, as if only just now aware of his appearance. He kept staring at her, his eyes bloodshot. Tossing and turning last night? she asked herself.

"I have to talk to you," he said.

"Now? I'm really tired, Matt."

Annoyance and something darker—anger?—flickered in his eyes.

"Not too tired, it seems."

"Say again?"

"Never mind." He placed a hand on her forearm. "Please, Kate. It's important to both of us."

And against her better judgment, she agreed. "All right. We'll go upstairs. I'm too beat to sit in some coffee shop."

Her apartment was sweltering because she'd turned off the air-conditioning when she'd left. Throwing down her handbag, she headed for the kitchen to flip the switch. "Would you like a cold drink?" she called out to Matt, still in the living room.

When he didn't answer, she walked back into the other room and found him standing in front of the window, staring bleakly out. At least, she thought that look in his eyes could be called bleak. Or miserable.

He turned around. "Did you say something?"

"Cold drink?"

"No, thanks. You've got a nice place here, Kate. It suits you."

"Thank you, but I'm sure you weren't lurking around my building at eleven o'clock to find out about my decor."

That raised a ghost of a smile. "I think the more appropriate word would be *waiting*."

"Whatever." She sat down in her favorite chair.

"You're wearing that dress," he said, running his eyes across her as if she were some kind of lab specimen.

"Yes," she replied, gritting her teeth but determined to wait him out.

He began to pace. "I don't know where to start. The thing is, I don't much care for Lance Marchant. You may have gathered that already."

"Or Joanna," she said.

"Or Joanna, though I admit my feelings for her are biased. Founded on the sensitivity of an adolescent boy who'd recently lost his mother and then saw his father marry a gold digger."

"A *what?*"

"Okay, it's an old expression. You get my drift."

"I didn't see Joanna that way."

"How could you?" He wheeled around to her, scowling in anger. "You were a kid. Not competition. Not someone she could use to get what she wanted."

"If you're going to raise your voice, you can leave, because frankly, to use another old expression, 'I don't give a damn.'"

He smiled at that. "You're right. May I sit down?"

"If you can make it short. I'm really tired."

"From Lance? Or present company?"

She ignored him and he sat down, anyway.

"Okay, sorry. I'll get to the point." He paused, then said, "I've told you I was only about seventeen when my Dad and Joanna got married. Lance Marchant had introduced them just a few months after my mother's death. So yes, I was negative about Joanna from the start. Fortunately I was in boarding school in Switzerland at the time and had little to do with either of them. But being away also cut me out of the loop as far as what happened later. I've had to piece it together over the years, and there are a few gaps."

"Piece what together?" Kate toyed idly with her dress strap, wishing she'd changed into something more comfortable. She also wished she'd asked him to come back another time.

"The whole story. The land swindle that eventually destroyed my father."

"Matt," she said, leaning forward in her chair. "I'm really exhausted and hot. I understand better your feelings about Joanna, but all of this happened years ago. What relevance does it have now? Shouldn't you just put it behind you?"

His face clouded. "Of course, and I had. Very effectively, I thought. Until I had a phone call from Joanna."

That got Kate's attention.

"About two weeks before her suicide," he continued. "She was almost hysterical on the phone. Kept talking about some news article she'd just seen. The body of a man had been found upstate. Joanna said the discovery had to do with my father and the land-fraud case." He leapt to his feet to pace again.

Kate watched, mesmerized. He was charged by some unseen force. Revved up. There was no stopping him now.

"I didn't want to hear about it. As you said, I'd put it

behind me. But then she said she had something that would
clear my father's name. And that got my interest. I agreed
to meet her the next day at some café downtown. Near her
office.''

''And?''

''I was late getting there—got tied up in traffic. No more
than twenty minutes late, but she wasn't there—perhaps
had never shown up. Who knows? Two weeks later, I read
her obituary in the paper.''

Kate leaned forward. ''When did she call?''

''Uh, around the end of June.''

''Did you call her back to find out why she didn't meet
you?''

A red stain moved up into his face. ''No. And I regret
that. To me, it was all typical Joanna. Even though I hadn't
had any contact with her for years, it was exactly like something she'd have done. Promise to be somewhere and just
not show up. So I wrote it off.''

''Wrote it off,'' Kate repeated with disbelief. ''And she
died on the fifteenth, wasn't it?''

''Well, that's when Marchant came home and found her
in the garage.''

''In the *garage?*''

''In her car. Carbon monoxide poisoning.''

A harsh sound erupted from Kate's mouth. A sense of
loss overwhelmed her. What if Matt had met with Joanna?
Would that have made any difference?

''Are you okay?'' he asked, peering at her. ''Can I get
you a drink?''

''I was supposed to meet her on the fourteenth,'' she
whispered. Then, hearing him for the first time, glanced up
and said, ''Please. There's ice water in the fridge. Glasses
in the cupboard beside the stove.''

He was gone and back in an instant, handing her a frosty
glass and standing in front of her while she sipped. When

she set the glass down, she looked up at him and asked,
"How?"

"She closed the garage doors and left the car running."

Kate turned her head away from him, toward the window. An image of Joanna's lovely face, her violet eyes rimmed in pain, swam before her. *She loved life too much. She must have been desperate.* "Did you go to the police?" she murmured. "About Joanna's phone call?"

He stepped back so abruptly he almost stumbled. "The police? Why?"

She looked at him again, puzzled by the incredulity in the question. "You've just told me she had some evidence in that case involving your father. She was hysterical. She didn't turn up at your meeting. Then she's dead. Supposedly a suicide. Why *wouldn't* you have called the police?"

He sat down opposite her. Finally he said, his voice low and troubled, "As I also said, I dismissed the whole thing. I didn't put it all together."

"But not after? Not at the funeral or even later?" She frowned. She couldn't believe he'd be so uncaring. "There was that police officer at the funeral. Remember I asked about him? You were standing right beside him when I left." She wanted to shake him, jolt loose his memory.

He got up again and walked over to the window. His back to her, he said, "I might have met him. Anyway, the police did make a formal investigation. I recall reading that in some news report shortly after."

"But wouldn't your information have made them check more carefully or something? I mean, it might have made a difference to their investigation. You're a *lawyer.* Didn't you think of that?"

He spun around. She saw the indignation in his eyes.

"Of course I thought of it. But I also knew Joanna. Or thought I did. Anyway, I decided to find out on my own. That's why I went to see Marchant that day. And why I asked about my father's papers at the coffee shop. See, that's what Joanna had said. That there was something in my father's papers, which she had, that might clear his name.''

"Clear his name of what? You've been hinting at horrible deeds committed by Joanna, but haven't told me what she was supposed to have done."

"True. I don't know if we've got all night, though." His voice was bitter.

"Just the basic details."

He sat down across from her. "A few months before my mother died, Dad bumped into Lance Marchant in Princeton. That's where my folks lived at the time. Marchant was with friends who belonged to the same club as my dad. Lance and Dad had met at university as students and they had mutual friends but were never close friends themselves." He paused. "Most of this I've inferred from letters from my parents. My mother had just been diagnosed with cancer, so the next half year my father devoted to her. He took a lot of time off work, although he'd just been made head of the bank." Matt rubbed at his face.

"I should make this short, but there are so many things I realize now, looking back. There was just that one accidental, or *coincidental* meeting, however you want to look at it. Then nothing more until after my mother died. Lance sent a card and they had lunch. Soon there were invitations to play squash or golf or what have you. Dinner invitations. It was like he was courting my dad—ingratiating himself with him."

"Or maybe just being nice to someone who was grieving," Kate said.

He ignored the suggestion. "Marchant introduced Dad to Joanna scarcely four months after Mom died, as I've said. I think my dad fell head over heels right away."

Kate nodded. She doubted any man could have resisted

Joanna. "How long ago was this?" she asked, wanting to put the date in context with her own first meeting with Joanna.

"Nineteen years ago when they first met. They got married a few months after that." He fell silent, his face settling into the memory. Finally he said, "I was resentful of her and I behaved badly. Typical insecure jealous teenager, I suppose."

He smiled, but she didn't respond. She was thinking that Joanna and Matt's father might have first met that same summer. She could still hear Joanna tell her that she was "between marriages." Had she already cast her eye on Matt's father?

"I seldom saw either of them the year after they married," Matt continued. "When I finished prep school, I took a year off and traveled around Europe working here and there. I was on some Greek island when my mail caught up to me. By then, the whole land-fraud scandal was in full play in the papers, but of course it never made the international ones."

"How was your dad involved?"

"I still don't have all the details. As I told you, there are a few gaps. Basically, Lance and some other guy persuaded a New Jersey city councillor to okay the sale of some land. It was supposed to be developed into low-rental housing and so went cheap. Lance got my dad to organize the details, the financing and so on. I think my dad took it at surface value, believing everything his friends told him." He paused, adding, "Certain banking regulations were overlooked in the transaction. But then Marchant persuaded my dad to sell the land for a small profit to a numbered company which turned out to be owned by his partner. There were official papers with company letterhead, the whole works. The councillor who'd authorized the actual land transfer disappeared and the land was almost immediately flipped for a sum more than ten times what the city had sold it for. Suddenly the police were investigating because the company that bought the land cheap and flipped it was alleged to be run by a mobster—Marchant's unknown partner. The whole deal had been set up just to launder money.''

"I can't see that Lance Marchant would have been mixed up in something like that. I mean, he's running for Congress!''

"Yeah, precisely,'' Matt drawled sarcastically. "The thing is, after the smoke cleared the only people whose names were on any of the documents were my dad's and that city clerk's. And he'd disappeared. My dad's whole career in the bank took a dive. It was as if he'd never been a respectable businessman with integrity and honor. All the values Jim Sinclair stood for, all his accomplishments were simply erased.''

"But couldn't he prove his innocence?''

"Eventually he would have, but eight months into the investigation and less than two years after his marriage to Joanna, he had a fatal heart attack. I'd just turned nineteen and didn't have a chance to see Dad before he died.'' Matt stopped then and struggled to his feet.

She watched him walk around the living room. His shoulders slouched, his profile etched in misery. After a moment, she dared to ask, "How was Joanna involved?''

"I think the whole thing was a setup from the start. Lance purposely introduced Dad to her—Marchant and Joanna had been friends, maybe off-and-on lovers—for years. When he came to Dad with this scheme, I know for a fact Joanna pushed Dad to be part of it. He mentioned that in one of his letters. Something about Joanna being accustomed to an affluent lifestyle and this would be a chance to ensure a rich retirement for them. Obviously he, too, had been taken in by the deal.'' He returned to the chair, slumping into it with a loud sigh.

"But she couldn't have known about everything—if any of this is even true—because you said she called you to say she had something that might clear your father's name. If she'd been a real participant in the fraud, as you want to believe, she'd have done nothing.''

"That's the part I can't figure out, of course. She had to have known. She and Marchant were so close they could've been joined at the hip. Whatever she had, she must have just found it. Or realized she had it.'' He shrugged. "I don't know. So much of this is…''

"Conjecture.''

He shot her an exasperated look. As if she still wasn't getting it. "Maybe that's why she committed suicide,'' he said. "Guilt over her part in the whole thing.''

"Then she would've done it years ago, right after your father died,'' she snapped. She was getting tired, the whole story was too complicated to digest at that time of night.

"There is something, I know it,'' he repeated, more to himself than to her.

"That's what you were searching for? At the lodge?''

"I *told* you that. At the lodge.''

She winced at the rebuke. "But you never found anything.''

"No.''

"Bill Tippett said he and Joanna packed up all kinds of stuff. Your father's things could be up there.''

He shrugged. "Maybe. I'm not so sure now that she had anything.'' He stared at her for a long moment. "I've kept you up longer than I intended. I should go.''

"Do you want to go back to Limberlost to look? Is that what you want?''

"To be honest, I don't know. When I was there, it seemed like a good idea. Until you walked in on me.''

His smile was unexpectedly sheepish. Kate felt herself pulled in by it. "I can let Bill know, if you want to go," she said, her voice softening.

"I'll think about it. Thanks." He stood up and stretched. "I've a big day tomorrow so I'd better leave." Still, he seemed to be waiting.

Kate got to her feet, stiffly because she'd been sitting so long. "Think about calling the police, too. To tell them about Joanna's phone call. It can't hurt."

He moved toward the door, pausing with his hand on the knob. "I will."

She could tell he wanted to say something more.

He removed his right hand from the door and brought it up to touch her lightly on the forehead. His index finger ran along her brow and down along the side of her cheek, where it paused.

"He kissed you," Matt murmured.

A blast of heat shot through her. "Only on the cheek. He was being kind to me."

"He's a womanizer. Always has been. And he's sixty years old."

"He's very good-looking. And charming," she whispered, refusing to step back from him. His face was so close, she could feel his breath fanning against her skin.

"He's a slick manipulator with his own agenda." Matt inched forward.

"He's a politician," she countered. If she tilted her head, her brow would meet his lips. She kept very still.

"He kissed you," he repeated.

"A peck on the cheek," she repeated, her voice edgy now.

Matt shifted his body, brushing up against hers. "I can do better." His hand cupped her chin, raising her mouth to his.

Kate wanted to resist. *Keep the game going,* she told

herself. But her body betrayed her, molding itself into his as his tongue parted her lips. She lifted her arms, bringing his head and neck down. His mouth now moving to the hollow of her neck and shoulder. She felt her body shudder, a throbbing deep inside urging her to press closer.

He lingered there in that warm, shivery place for what seemed ages. Then withdrew his head, stepped back, his face pale. "I'd better go," he whispered, and reaching for the knob, pushed open the door.

"I'll call you," he promised in a voice so throaty she scarcely heard him. Then he was gone.

She leaned against the door for several long moments. But when she convinced herself he wasn't coming back, Kate moved into her bedroom, tugging at the dress as she went. The blinds were still open, so she left the light off. Pulled the dress over her head and went to close the blinds. Bending over, peering through the slats, she saw a figure standing on the pavement below. Strained her eyes, touching the glass with the tip of her nose to get a clearer look.

It was Matt. Talking on his cell phone again. Kate frowned. Who could he be calling at this time of night? And why hadn't he simply used her phone?

Unless he didn't want her to hear the conversation.

HE PUNCHED IN the number blindly, his anger at himself, at her, at Marchant escalating to the point of carelessness. While he waited, he glanced back at her windows. Her bedroom, at least he assumed it was her bedroom because he hadn't seen a fire escape from either living room or kitchen, was in darkness. She couldn't be in bed already, he thought. Then told himself not to think about that even for a second. As it was, the first thing he wanted when he got home was a cold shower to sober up from the intoxication of her kiss.

He'd waited in the hall outside her door a full two

minutes after he'd left, hoping she might fling it open. But she hadn't. Of course, he could have knocked. But he'd known where that would lead. As it was, he was already in way deeper than he ought to be. Or ever planned to be.

He could still taste her lips, their sweet fullness. He groaned. And her body crushed into him. Who'd have thought anyone so slender could have such softness? Be so full in all the places any man dared dream about?

The other end picked up, saving him from running immediately back upstairs. "It's me," he said, facing the street now, away from her flat so those dark windows could no longer reproach him for his cowardice. *His betrayal.* He moistened his lips, dry now.

"Like I said, I don't think she knows anything," Matt insisted. "I know, I know. It *is* suspicious, her turning up with him like that. Yes. Again tonight. No, he didn't go upstairs with her." He paused then, considering the possibility. Not liking it.

He listened to the spiel on the other end. He'd heard it all before, anyway. Finally he said unhappily, "Yeah, I told her. Of course not everything. What we agreed on. Her reaction? She seemed confused. As if she wasn't really taking it all in."

Matt waited again, daring one last glance behind him and up. Darkness still. "Okay, I *know* it could all have been an act. But it wasn't. Believe me. Because I've got a gut feeling. Ha, ha," he countered. "No, I haven't! Everything is…is aboveboard, as you say. So now what?"

He listened, not liking what he was hearing. "I think it's better if we just level with her. Why not right now? Dammit all, she's an innocent pawn in this whole thing." Matt frowned. "Go ahead, then, do your check. You won't find anything. Yeah, yeah. Okay. I'm leaving. Going home. No, not tomorrow. It'll have to be the day after. Think about what I said, though. Please." Matt turned off his phone,

took one last look up at Kate's flat—all in darkness now—
and headed for his car parked down the street.

If only he'd met Kate Reilly someplace else. Anyplace
but at Joanna Barnes's funeral.

KATE MULLED OVER what he'd said all night long. At least,
what she could remember. She was beginning to think he
might be one of those conspiracy theorists who saw plots
behind every event or chance encounter. *Next thing you
know, he'll be implying Joanna befriended me for some
ulterior motive.* The idea was laughable.

By morning she had to concede that Matt's father likely
lost his money in the land deal because of a lack of judgment. Perhaps it had been like a pyramid scheme, where
those who started it up got out early with their investment
not only intact, but increased. Whereas others...

And she had to admit, as little as she'd known Joanna,
she bet that her lifestyle demanded fresh supplies of money.
But Matt's suggestion that it was all a setup from the beginning, when Lance had introduced his father to Joanna,
was absurd. Plus, he hadn't offered any evidence other than
his own suspicion.

No, Kate decided over her second cup of coffee. Lance
Marchant had too much to lose by involving himself in
shady deals, even if they'd happened almost twenty years
before. And while Joanna might have been ambitious, she'd
also been a hard-working career woman who'd been highly
successful. She hadn't needed to swindle people to get to
the top.

The phone rang while she was in the shower. By the
time she rushed to it, dripping water all along the hardwood
floor, the caller had hung up. Annoyed, Kate slammed the
receiver down. Whoever it was, probably some telemar-
keter, hadn't bothered leaving a message on her voice mail.

She dressed in shorts and T-shirt, cleaned up her break-

fast dishes and considered the long day ahead. After last
night's meeting with Matt, it promised to be long and full
of self-analysis. The kind of activity that both compelled
and revolted Kate at the same time. She'd always had a
tendency to anguish over her actions. If only she'd put in
as much thought *before* charging headlong into a situation.

What she ought to do, she reasoned, was prove Matt
wrong about Lance Marchant. Kate paced between the
kitchen and living room. She was restless and full of energy, in spite of the heat. She hadn't told Matt about Andrews following someone. Matt's suspicion about Lance,
based on a dislike stemming from his adolescence, might
not be so convenient if he was forced to consider another
possibility. Such as the partner he'd referred to.

And did Tom Andrews have anything to do with all of
this? He certainly was no police officer in Westchester
County, as he'd claimed. Kate's head was spinning with
ideas so she latched onto the nearest one. She'd try to find
the same bar in Little Italy where she'd seen Lance Marchant, Tom Andrews and the man in the black limo. She
congratulated herself on the brilliance of it.

She had a vague notion where the bar had been and was
able to pinpoint the subway stop by backtracking her route
home that day. Pausing only long enough to get her baseball cap and a bottle of water, she locked up and headed
for the subway station. It felt good to play an active part,
rather than rely on others to feed you the information you
sought. Besides, how could she trust any of the data that
was coming in, it was all so conflicting. And had a few
gaps, as Matt had said.

Matt. If she let her defenses down, she could still feel
the tingle when his fingers had touched her skin, the hard
insistence of his lips on her mouth, at the base of her neck.
She had to stop to take a swallow of water. She must keep
in mind that what had happened between them stemmed

from pure physical desire. Lust, as her least-favorite sister at St. Patrick's School would have said, wrinkling her nose in distaste.

Call it what you like, it was pretty compelling. *Magical. Exhilarating.* She didn't want to think about what might have occurred had he come back. Especially since her resolve never to let him exert such physical control over her body again. No, sir. If he even kissed her once more, it would happen only if she wanted it to. Definitely. She took another swig of water and dug into her fanny pack for her subway pass.

Twenty minutes later she was above ground again on a sidewalk crowded with people. The bar had been a couple of blocks away from the outfitter store where she'd bought her sleeping bag, between the store and subway station. Fortunately she'd kept the receipt and to be on the safe side, she exited the subway one stop beyond the store's address. Then she walked back toward the store and, standing outside, began to trace her steps. She didn't recall crossing the street and it seemed she'd only jogged a block or so when she collided with the baby stroller.

The problem was, Little Italy was full of sports bars and they all looked the same. She could see the next subway stop one block away and decided to check in at every place she came upon.

But she was intimidated by the first place, aware as soon as she crossed the threshold that, except for the ninety-year-old woman knitting at the very rear, she was the only female on the premises. At least thirty pairs of dark eyes frowned at her until she babbled some excuse and backed out the door.

So the next place she found, she resolved not only to walk right in but to ask if anyone there knew Lance Marchant or someone called Tom Andrews. As she walked along, she saw ahead a fruit and vegetable market on a

corner. *That must be where I ran into the stroller.* Just two
stores beyond was a rather dingy-looking shop. The windows were clouded with grime and an open sign swayed
back and forth on the inside of the door's window. She
took a deep breath, walked up to the door and pushed it
open. A bell clanged.

There must have been ten or fifteen men inside. Most
were playing some kind of board game, with glasses at their
elbows. A couple were reading newspapers and a handful
more were in deep conversation at the rear of the shop. It
was from this group that a heavyset man got up from his
chair and sauntered over to Kate, waiting by the service
bar.

"Help ya?" he asked.

"Yes, I'm…uh…I'm looking for a couple of…of friends
of mine. They sometimes come here."

"Oh, yeah?" His expression said he doubted it.

"Uh-huh. Uh…Tom Andrews is one and the other is
Lance Marchant."

The first name drew a blank, but she saw a flicker in his
eyes at the second. Still, he kept her waiting a full ten
seconds before answering. "Nope, never heard of neither
of them."

The teacher part of her wanted to point out the double
negative. *You mean you* have *heard of one of them?*

"Oh? I could swear this is the place where I bumped
into them a few days ago," she said, instead, trying for a
cheery note.

He didn't budge, resting one hand on an ample hip while
the other drummed impatiently on the bar.

"Okay, then, no point in hanging around," she said, her
attempt at a laugh echoing like a belch at a dinner party.
"Thank you, anyway," she said, then turned and, going
out the door, stumbled over a chair leg in an exit only a
clown could have bettered.

Out on the sidewalk, Kate walked a few feet from the entrance before halting to catch her breath and gather some semblance of dignity. She took another mouthful of water, tempted to dump the bottle over her head, she was perspiring so badly, when she noticed in her peripheral vision something white pull up to the curb beside her. A door slid open just as she realized it was a white van.

"Well, well, we meet again, Miss Reilly."

Tom Andrews. Not in a rumpled suit this time, but in navy blue work pants, a lighter blue shirt and a baseball cap perched rakishly on his balding head. His stomach bulged out of his shirt, and Kate noticed, on its breast pocket, an oval-shaped crest with an unrecognizable logo on it.

"I was hoping to find you," she said, taking the offensive quickly.

"Were you now? And why is that? Lost your car again?" He laughed delightedly at his joke.

"And where's your police uniform?" she countered.

"Haven't worn one for years. Now it's my turn. This is a little out of your area, isn't it?"

"How do you know where I live?"

"Remember signing the guest book at Joanna Barnes's funeral?"

That silenced her reply.

"They don't call me a detective for nothing, Miss Reilly," he continued. "Seriously, why are you here? More important, how come you've decided to invade all the men's clubs along this strip? Part of a feminist agenda or something?"

Kate's face burned. "I went in to ask if anyone there knew you." She waited, letting that sink in. When she got no response, she added, "Or Lance Marchant. Furthermore," she continued, deciding to keep the upper hand as long as she could, "I know for a fact that you are *not* a police officer in Westchester County, as you told me."

"Yeah?" He looked mildly interested. "And how do you know that?"

"Because I called them and they've never heard of you."

"Aah." He nodded, then smiled. "Maybe you should be a detective, too."

It was the last straw for Kate. "Mr. Andrews—that's probably not even your real name—I don't know who you really are and I've no idea what you are, but I do know that somehow you're connected with Lance Marchant and...well, maybe some other people."

"I guess I should fill you in, then." He leaned forward, his voice taking on a conspiratorial tone. "I *am* a cop and I'm working undercover. As you can see by my clothes. Unless you really do think I work for Standard Electrical Appliances."

Kate pulled her head back, but not before catching a whiff of sour breath mixed with tobacco. "And your connection with Lance Marchant?"

He frowned. "Lance Marchant?"

"Lance Marchant! He's running for Congress!"

"No kidding? Good for him."

She sighed, frustrated at the persistent game-playing he obviously liked. "He was Joanna Barnes's husband."

The grin disappeared. "Oh, yeah. Thought the name was familiar. Well, I was at the funeral for two reasons, Miss Reilly. One, to check out unknown visitors like yourself and, two, to keep an eye on someone there we are currently investigating. And no, sorry, I can't reveal the name of that gentleman because that would seriously hamper our undercover work. So, was there anything else I can do for you?"

She made a wild stab. "Do you know Matt Sinclair?"

His face was blank. "Doesn't ring a bell. Fill me in."

"His father was once married to Joanna."

"Aah. Is that it, then?"

She couldn't think of anything else to ask, knowing she'd already made a complete fool of herself and gained absolutely nothing by it. Kate nodded, wishing she could simply slink away.

"Yes, thank you. If I think of anything, how can I get in touch with you?"

He pursed his lips. "At the Westchester County Police Department. You've got the number."

Kate blew out a mouthful of air. "Fine," she muttered, and turned to walk away.

"Oh, Miss Reilly, just curious, did anyone in that bar know me? Or Lance Marchant?"

"No," she said.

That brought a wider grin. "Okay. Well, maybe we'll bump into each other again sometime. Oh, and another thing, I wouldn't cast my vote for Lance Marchant, I was you."

"Oh? And why is that, Mr. Andrews?"

"The guy's a real scumbag, that's why. In fact, I wouldn't even go for lunch with a guy like that, I was a nice young girl like you."

"I'm not a girl, Mr. Andrews, though I assume that inappropriate remark was meant as a compliment. As for the advice, you'd never have an iota of worry in a million years of being nice, young or female, and last of all, I can't imagine anyone *wanting* to take you out for lunch."

He tipped his hat, the grin still firmly in place, though it had left his small pale eyes.

"Well put. You gotta be an English teacher. Just take my advice, *Ms.* Reilly."

As she walked away, Kate heard the van door slam shut, then the van squeal away from the curb. Or so she thought. Her teeth were chattering so loudly she couldn't be sure.

CHAPTER TEN

"URGENT CALL FOR YOU, Mr. Sinclair, on line three. He refuses to be put off."

Matt scowled. He had fifteen minutes to scan the documents one last time for the largest merger he'd thus far negotiated in his career. He'd already used up five precious minutes first thing that morning anguishing over telephoning Kate and then had chickened out when the brisk hello of her voice mail answered. Put the receiver down in a cold sweat. Just like a teenager.

Still, his secretary was excellent at fielding calls, so he knew he'd have to take this one. He checked the time again. The team should be finishing their prelunch snacks in the boardroom. He forced himself to relax. The whole Marchant-Barnes business couldn't have come at a worse time. Not to mention the added complication of one Kate Reilly.

He sighed. Maybe the million-plus commission he'd snare from the merger would give him an advantage there. Sighed again. Doubted it. Not with someone who appeared as genuine as Kate Reilly. Which was precisely what attracted him to her. Along with a few obvious other traits, of course...

"Mr. Sinclair?" his secretary prompted.

"Yeah, yeah. I'll take it. And, Paula, I've approved the press release. I'll have it delivered to you as soon as the papers have been signed. Thanks, I appreciate it. We *all* worked hard. Oh, and can you confirm those luncheon reservations for us? Two o'clock at the Ritz. I think about ten of us. Not counting you. Of course I want you there. Okay, thanks, Paula.''

He pressed the phone button and, clutching the receiver to his ear, resumed skimming the merger documents. ''Sinclair here. What can I do for you? *What?*''

He tossed his pen onto the desk. ''Are you sure? You *talked* to her? Damn.'' His stomach roiled. ''She actually asked outright? God, what was she thinking? *What's that?* I don't believe it. Say what you want. She's not the type. I told you—'' He stopped, his mind racing.

He couldn't think clearly at all, the figures from the documents and Kate marching into the bar swirling together in a nauseating concoction. He took a calming breath, then said, ''So now what? Uh-huh. I don't know…it's your call. Your show. Yeah, yeah. Call me tomorrow.'' Matt set the receiver down and lowered his face into his hands. Great timing.

He was torn between throttling Kate and begging her to take a nice long holiday somewhere—anywhere—away from Manhattan. And now there was this other, unpredictable side of Kate. One he didn't dare contemplate. Not now.

The intercom buzzed again. ''Mr. Sinclair? They're ready for you.''

Matt groaned. ''Okay. Be right there.'' He inhaled deeply, forced Kate Reilly out of his mind, shuffled the papers in order and headed for the door. Hoping he wasn't about to blow a million bucks.

THE FIRST THING Kate did when she got back to her flat was check her voice mail. For some reason she'd hoped there'd be a message from Matt. But nothing. She felt like flinging the phone across the room. She was still shaking from her encounter with Andrews. What an odious man! And she hated to admit he'd managed to pull every one of her strings.

She flicked on the air-conditioning and poured herself a cold drink. It was almost noon and she'd accomplished nothing so far. Certainly had been a bust as an amateur detective. She blushed just thinking about the way she'd strode into that bar and then practically fallen out of it seconds later. And she hadn't handled Tom Andrews or whatever his name was any better, either.

Impulsively she headed back to the living room and the phone. Found the number for the Westchester County police where she'd scribbled it on the inside cover of her address book and tapped in the numbers. This time when she asked for Andrews, she was put on hold. After what seemed ages, a man's voice said, "Sorry, ma'am, he's out at the moment. Can I take a message?"

She said no and quickly hung up. So now there *was* a Tom Andrews in the department. Very puzzling indeed. Or clever, she thought. Rather than clarify anything, she only felt more confused than ever.

After a lackluster lunch, her appetite defeated by the heat and the morning's activity, she sprawled on the sofa opposite the kitchen door, enjoying the spillover of the air conditioner. Maybe she ought to purchase another one for the living room. No, not yet. It would only block the one window with the best view. Maybe, she thought, she should just head out of the city altogether. Didn't she own a mountain resort?

Kate thought suddenly of Carla, realizing she'd hardly talked to her since their return from Limberlost. She wondered if she had returned to the old gang. She forced herself off the sofa and over to the phone, getting Rita on the second ring.

"She's been quiet. Kinda moping around," Rita replied after Kate inquired about Carla.

"Really? Any sign of Toni and friends yet?"

"Someone from that gang called once, but I heard Carla

say she was grounded.'' Rita laughed. ''I don't mind taking the blame for something I haven't done if it means she stays away from them.''

''It was probably a safe way for her to turn them down, without forcing a confrontation. Well, good for Carla. She's figuring it out.''

''Maybe.'' Rita sounded doubtful. ''But she doesn't seem very lively these days.''

''Maybe she's bored.''

''She is that, for sure, but she won't take me up on any of my suggestions. I even offered to take her into the city one day, and that barely even drew a response.''

''Hmm.'' Kate frowned. She ought to do something. But what? Take Carla back to Limberlost?

When she mentioned the idea, Rita said, ''That might be what she'd like. I know she's been raving about the place—even the spiders and canoe tipping have become favorite stories. Talks about it nonstop. To that boy, too.''

Kate's ears pricked up. ''What boy?''

''The one from up there. Kyle, I think his name is.''

''Carla's been talking on the phone to *Kyle?*''

''At least a couple times a day. I put my foot down when I found out it was long distance, so now he phones her.''

''But we just got home from there the day before yesterday.''

Rita sighed. ''I know. I've been wondering if she's got a crush on him.''

''Is she there now? Can I talk to her?''

''Sure, hang on.''

When Carla got to the phone, her voice sounded wary. ''Is something wrong?''

''Heavens, no. Just wondered how you're doing. What's up?''

''Not much.''

''Want to do something tomorrow?''

"Like what?"

Kate gritted her teeth. *Try to sound a little more enthusiastic, Carla.* "I could meet you somewhere and we could see a movie, go shopping or whatever. And if Rita doesn't mind, you could sleep over."

"Well...maybe. Can I call you back later today and let you know?"

Kate sighed. "Sure, Carla. By the way, Rita says you've been talking to Kyle Tippett."

There was a brief pause before Carla muttered an expletive.

"Pardon? I didn't get that."

"I *said* there's no such thing as privacy here. Anyway, have to go now. I'll call you later, Kate."

Kate replaced the phone, smiling at the last part of the conversation. Yes, she thought, that girl has a crush, all right. Then she remembered last night's parting kiss with Matt. *You and me both, Carla.*

THE PHONE WAS RINGING. Kate struggled awake. Where was she? On the sofa. She'd fallen asleep reading next year's history curriculum. A bad sign, she thought, rolling onto her feet and reaching for the phone. When Lance Marchant's pleasant voice boomed across the line, her first sense was disappointment.

"I've just been talking to Greg Collier—we had a squash game this morning and the subject of Limberlost came up."

"Oh, yes," Kate replied.

"He was wondering how your visit there went and so on. I didn't realize you hadn't got back to him about it."

"Uh, no. I didn't realize I was supposed to." Was he laying some kind of bizarre guilt trip on her?

"Oh, well," he blustered, "I suppose as a courtesy... At any rate, I told him you thought you'd like to wait until the end of the summer. Isn't that what you said last night?"

"Yes. If you're talking to him again, could you pass that on?" She suspected the request was unnecessary. What was it with those two?

"Certainly. I simply wanted to get your permission. Now that I'm running for Congress, I have to be extra careful about these things. Conflict of interest issues and so on."

"Of course. By the way, thank you again for dinner. It was lovely."

"I enjoyed myself, too. I'm…I'm hoping we can do it again. Unfortunately things are already starting to get very hectic around here. The people working for me have set up a campaign office—not too far from you, actually, near the border of SoHo and Little Italy."

"Oh?" She had a sudden thought. "Actually I was in Little Italy a couple of days ago. I'm positive I saw you there."

"Good God! Where was this?"

"I don't know the name of the cross street, but I think you were coming out of a bar."

He laughed heartily. "I don't think so." There was a long pause. "Although…well, it would have been an incredible coincidence, but I was in that general area checking out sites for the headquarters. Real estate is so much more economical there."

"I was positive you came out of a bar."

"Perhaps from a place quite close. There are a lot of vacant stores in the area. I must have seen more than a dozen when I was there."

"I suppose that was it, then," she said. Another dead end. Impulsively she asked, "Do you know a police officer by the name of Tom Andrews?"

"No, should I?"

"I met him at Joanna's funeral. He said he was with the Westchester County police."

"Ah, well. A number of police were there at my request. Helping with the parking and so on. I was expecting a great number of people."

"He wasn't in uniform. He said he was a detective. And when I left, he was standing in the parking lot with Matt Sinclair."

"Matt Sinclair?"

"Yes." She had a sensation of falling into the deep end of a pool. Thinking fast to distract him, she blurted, "Actually Matt doesn't know him, either. But the strange thing is, I've seen this detective twice in the last few days, and both times he was near that bar. The one where I thought I saw you." She waited. "Lance? Are you still there?"

Finally he came back on the line. "Sorry, but there was an incoming call and I'm still figuring out this new machine of mine. As I've said, I don't know any Tom Andrews. No doubt his presence was just coincidence."

Come on! Kate wanted to exclaim. But she was still treading water after her faux pas about Matt. Lance wasn't letting that pass, apparently.

"I didn't realize you knew Matt Sinclair."

"Um, I met him at the funeral. And we bumped into each other the day I went to Greg Collier's office about the will."

"Oh, that's it. For a moment I had the horrible thought that you were dating him."

She uttered a nervous laugh. "Hardly" was all she said. But she wondered why he cared. And if so, why was the idea "horrible?" Maybe he really was the womanizer Matt insisted he was. He was certainly charming enough to attract any number of women.

"I ought to go now—important meeting coming up—but I'd love to see you again. How about drinks tomorrow?" he asked.

"Uh, I'm not sure about my plans tomorrow," she said, remembering Carla. "Can I get back to you?"

"Of course."

He gave her his campaign office number "—I'm here all the time and might have to move a cot in—" and extracted a promise from her to call the next day. When she hung up, Kate had a strong sense of déjà vu, thinking back to her earlier conversation with Carla. She also knew that she'd committed a major blunder mentioning Matt's name to Lance. Or was it her reference to Andrews? Whatever, he'd sounded a lot tenser at the end of the conversation than he had at the beginning.

IT HAD BEEN A LONG LUNCH, but a festive one. Matt was the first to return to the office, encouraging the others to stay behind and celebrate at the law firm's expense. The deal had gone through. His first million. At least, the first million he'd actually earned in a lump sum on his own merit. His mother had left a sizable estate in trust for him. It was a move that had guaranteed his father hadn't lost that income, as well. Sometimes Matt wondered if his mother had suspected his father would remarry. She'd had a favorite saying that too often came true: *Women mourn and men replace.*

At any rate, the whole merger deal, along with his trust fund, made him a wealthy man. He could retire right now, he thought, and still live comfortably for the rest of his life. But he loved work—the challenges of highs and lows all exhilarated him. It wasn't about the money, though that was a definite perk, but about the challenge. That and the power that went with winning.

That was what he admired about Kate. At Limberlost when she'd allowed him glimpses of her past, he realized that she had never been a quitter, either. In spite of her belief that Joanna had been instrumental in turning her around, Matt guessed Kate would have succeeded, anyway. She had the same burning desire in her to fulfill herself as he'd had. And although they were miles apart in terms of family background and experience, he knew at heart they were—or could be—soul mates. He hated to use such a trendy expression, but it fit.

So when he got back to work and saw the message that Tom Andrews had called—very urgent—he decided not to spoil his mood by talking to the man again. The whole business was wearing him down. He wanted out of it. If it wasn't too late. Most of all, at that very moment, he wanted to be with Kate.

He finished off some work, scribbled a note to Paula telling her he might be late the next morning and left. Stopped on the way for flowers, champagne and gourmet delicacies from the local Dean & DeLuca and drove toward SoHo as fast as the law allowed.

KATE STARED AT the kitchen clock. Six. Too hot to cook, although the kitchen itself was pleasantly cool now. Pizza or Thai? she asked herself. Neither appealed. What was happening with her life, anyway? Usually the summer holidays were filled with friends, social events and summer school. This year everything had been turned upside down.

Granted, there were friends she could call. Even men friends. But she didn't have the energy, much less the inclination. *Snap out of it,* she told herself.

She marched to the phone and ordered Thai before she changed her mind again. Then she dashed into the shower. If she was still feeling restless after dinner, she'd go out. Maybe try that new wine bar down the street. Resolved, she took her time in the shower and so was unprepared for the downstairs door buzzer. She towel dried haphazardly, throwing on her cotton robe and ran to the intercom.

She pressed the button and called out ''Come up!'' and

had time only to tighten the robe sash before knocking signaled the arrival of her dinner. Wallet in hand, she opened the door to Matt Sinclair, his arms full of bags and flowers.

"I hope you were expecting me," he quipped, "and not someone else."

Kate shaped an answer around her gaping mouth. "Only the Thai-food guy."

"Did you order enough for two? No matter," he said, holding aloft two shopping bags, "I can supplement it."

"Then I guess you'd better come in," she said, standing aside to let him pass. She watched him head straight for the kitchen. "I'll just go dress," she murmured.

"Not on my account," he said, sticking his head out the kitchen door.

She blushed, glad he couldn't see her face. The problem was, once she'd closed her bedroom door, she couldn't decide what to put on. Finally she settled for a flowing batik skirt and an Indian-cotton top.

When she returned to the living room, Matt was paying the deliveryman for the takeout. She noticed he'd found a vase for the flowers and had a bottle of champagne with wineglasses all set up on the coffee table. Had she taken that long, or was he really a dream come true?

The door closed behind the deliveryman, and when Matt turned, bags in hand, he froze on the spot. "Now I know what the word *ravishing* means," he murmured.

She blushed again. "Thank you for the flowers," she said, shifting her eyes from the expression on his face. "And champagne! What's the occasion?"

"Does there have to be one?" He carried the Thai food into the kitchen and she followed, watching helplessly while he opened cupboards and drawers for plates and cutlery.

"No, I guess not. Just that, in my experience, limited as

it is, mind you—'' she laughed giddily ''—there usually has been. An occasion, I mean. For champagne.'' She closed her mouth then, hating the sound of babbling.

He passed her the dishes and cutlery, grasping her hands as he did. He gazed deep into her eyes and said, ''Then I shall have to broaden your experience.''

She sensed he was talking about more than just champagne and felt a shiver of both apprehension and pleasure.

''Where do you want to eat?'' he asked, still clutching her hands and the plates.

The question roused her from the stunned state she'd been in since his arrival. She *was* hungry, she thought.

She pulled her hands and the plates from his and motioned toward the kitchen table. ''It's cooler in here.''

He nodded. ''Cool is good—for now. How about champagne and appetizers in the living room?''

''You have *appetizers?*''

He laughed, shaking his head at her surprise. ''Always, with champagne. Come.''

Kate set the plates down onto the table and followed him once more.

''Take a seat while I get them organized in the kitchen,'' he said.

''I feel silly having you wait on me like this,'' she protested. And finding her normal voice again, added, ''You still haven't told me what you're celebrating.''

''I negotiated a big merger that was signed today. It'll be in the papers tomorrow.''

''Congratulations,'' she said, smiling at the pleasure in his face. She knew that heady sense of accomplishment. ''What does this mean for you and your career?''

''Another step up, of course. More responsibilities and challenges. More money,'' he added.

''It's a good feeling, isn't it?'' she said.

''The best.'' He stood watching her for a long moment,

then, "I'll get those appetizers. Do you have a sound system? Shall we have music?"

"I'll get it going," she said, glad for an excuse to do something—anything—rather than sit and be treated like some rare hothouse flower. She thumbed through her CD collection, selecting a couple she thought he might like, and from the smile on his face when he returned, knew she'd chosen well.

He'd removed his tan linen suit jacket as soon as he'd entered her flat, and at some point, in the kitchen, had rid himself of the tie. His sage-green shirt was now unbuttoned partway down his chest and he'd lifted the ends out of his trousers. "Excuse the casual look," he said, setting a tray onto the coffee table. "But suits weren't meant for hot spells."

"Have you come here right from work?" she asked.

"Yeah. We signed the papers shortly after noon and then went for a long lunch. I probably should've stayed on at the office longer, but everyone was still out celebrating and I…I don't know. I just wanted to share what I was feeling with someone, and I thought of you."

A thrill shot through her, though she wondered why his first choice had been someone he'd only recently met. Was that a compliment to her or a sign that he didn't have any close friends? She remembered his address book and guilt about what she'd done brought a rush of blood into her face. She looked away from him.

"Those look wonderful," she exclaimed, scanning the appetizer plates.

"Dig in," he said. He uncorked the champagne and poured it. Handing a glass to Kate, he raised his to hers. "A toast is in order."

"To you and continued success, of course," she said.

"And to this night," he murmured.

He wasn't very subtle, Kate was thinking, realizing at

the same time that she didn't care. She tipped her glass toward his and then sipped slowly, forcing herself to keep her gaze fixed on his.

They ate hungrily and silently. Kate began to relax, sinking into her swaybacked canvas chair and indulging all her senses at once. The sweet-and-savory assortment of gourmet delicacies, the soft rhythm of music, the heady scent of summer flowers and the mellow pulsing deep inside her. And of course, there was the compelling image of Matt himself, perched on the edge of the sofa. Every time he leaned forward to take something from a plate, his shirt gaped.

As she watched, Kate wondered about stroking that smooth, taut chest and the strong arms that had not only dragged her out of a lake, but hoisted a canoe out of the water. Arms that had wrapped around her mere days ago.

He glanced up, catching her staring, and grinned. "Had enough?" he asked.

"Uh…yes," she stammered, not sure if he meant the appetizers or her looking at him. Had the champagne gone to her head already, or was it simply his presence that left her befuddled and confused?

"Dinner, then?"

And she trailed behind him into the kitchen, standing like a guest in her own apartment while he put away the rest of the appetizers and began setting the hot food onto the table. When he finished, he came back for her, leading her to the table as if she were a child. She giggled.

"What?" he asked, a smile lighting his face.

"This is so strange. I'm supposed to be waiting on you."

"Oh? Why is that?"

He moved closer, the smile tinged with something else now.

Kate shrugged. "You're the one celebrating, that's why.

And…and this is my place. So I should be, you know, cleaning up and…and stuff.''

He was inches away from her now and still smiling. "Let's focus on the 'stuff,'" he murmured.

A faint hint of garlic mixed with chili filled the tiny space between her face and his. He placed a finger on her lips, tracing their outline and then parting them. Kate caught the tip gently between her teeth. She thought his smile seemed nervous now. But when she curled her tongue around the finger, he brought his arm up to the small of her back and pressed her against him.

She released his finger as his mouth came down on hers. He backed her away from the table and up against the kitchen counter, his right hand—now free—sweeping up and under her top. She wasn't wearing a bra and Kate gasped at the touch of his skin against hers. She heard him moan from some distant place—or had it been her?—when his hand found a breast. He kneaded it gently, rolling his thumb across her nipple as he pressed his hips into hers.

Kate held him to her, her hands up inside the back of his shirt. When he pushed a knee between her legs, she straddled it, holding him tight against her. His mouth had moved on, down her neck and along the curve of her collarbone. She tilted her head back, letting him have as much of her as he wanted. With his other hand, he pulled up the bottom of her top and pulled it up over her head.

Her breasts spilled out, ready for his lips. "Oh, God!" he groaned, and buried his face between them. Then he settled on one and sucked slowly, drawing her nipple out until she thought she'd faint with pleasure.

She slipped her hands around to his chest and down to the waist of his pants. Felt the hard swell and fumbled blindly at his belt buckle. Suddenly he pulled back, his eyes glittering with desire. Tendrils of hair were matted along the border of his forehead.

"Your bedroom," he said, his voice husky and uneven.
She brought her arms up around his neck. "Dinner?"
"Got a microwave?"
When she nodded, he swept her up into his arms and
carried her out of the kitchen.

MUCH LATER, when the sun had long slid beneath the horizon, Matt slipped out of bed and made for the kitchen.
His whole body was still tingling, but the unbearable throbbing from earlier was now a warm glow all over. He padded around, placing containers of Thai food in the microwave and setting up a tray to take back into the bedroom
where Kate was still asleep. In dreamland, he hoped.

He thought about what she'd said, about him waiting on
her. She just didn't see it, he realized. How he wanted to
do everything for her. Now more than ever. He'd been surprised at her passion, her rapid abandonment of the usual
inhibitions he'd encountered in other women he'd gone to
bed with. She was either loving his every touch, he thought,
or hadn't been made love to for a long time. He hoped
both.

When he returned to the bedroom Kate was stirring under
the sheet. Her eyes flicked open and she smiled. His pulse
quickened. God, she was beautiful.

"Is this breakfast…or what?" she asked.

"Dinner—if you're still hungry."

"I am. For food and…other things." She made a teasing
purring sound at the back of her throat.

He carefully placed the tray on top of a small vanity
table. Then he faced the bed and said, "I'm ready, too…"

"I see that," she murmured, and extended her arms to
him.

He lowered himself onto the bed, resting as lightly as he
could on top of her, the sheet between them. "A second
helping?" he asked, grinning.

"Please," she whispered, and helped him get beneath the sheet until the whole length of his body covered hers.

Matt buried his face in the crook of her neck, inhaling deeply all the combined scents of skin, sheets, soap and her. He rocked slowly back and forth, savoring the gentle beat of their two bodies moving together, the sensory overload kicking in, urging a faster rhythm. And faster. *Easy now,* he warned himself. *Not yet, not yet, but soon,* and then he pushed between her legs and found her open, warm and moist. He gave in to it then, the flow, and felt himself swept along deeper and deeper until the almost painful shudder of release. From somewhere a long way off he heard a cry, but wasn't certain if it had been her or him or both of them together.

After a shower, they sat up in bed, containers of food littering the spaces between them.

"The nice thing about Thai food," Kate announced around a mouthful, "is that it's just as good hot or at room temperature."

"Mmm," Matt agreed, forking another shrimp into his mouth. "And so are you."

She smiled and ran her tongue provocatively around her lips. "Are you ready for dessert?"

There was that tingle again, right up his spine. But he knew there was no way. Ten years ago, maybe. Ah. If only he'd found her ten years ago.

"I'll have to take a rain check," he admitted.

"A rain check? A strong, virile man like you?" she teased.

"That's the operative word, Kate. *Man.* Not *boy.* Not any longer."

She gave him another achingly sweet smile and then said softly, "What kind of boy were you, Matt?"

And because no one had ever asked before, he loved her at that very moment. He tossed aside the containers between them and moved over next to her. Placed a bare arm around her shoulders resting against the headboard of her bed and said, "I'll tell you." And he did. It was a poignant summary of a privileged, but often lonely childhood spent in various boarding schools. Sports became an outlet for both his competitive drive and his need for companionship.

When he was finished, she simply got up from the bed and walked over to a closet. Opened it and reached up to bring down a scrapbook. He watched her every movement, reminded again of the spontaneous intimacy that had sprung up between them. As if they'd been together for years. As if he'd seen her nakedness many times before. That was when Matt knew he wanted to see her again and again. Wake up with her. Read the morning papers in bed. Sip coffee together. Make love. Over and over.

"This is sort of my childhood," she said.

Almost shyly, he thought, waiting patiently as she began to turn the pages.

"But the beginning is really nineteen years ago, in July. Here, on this page, is a pressed wildflower that had fallen from Joanna's hair. She and I collected armfuls one day and made crowns. I wish I had a picture—we looked so funny. And this is my bus ticket stub—to the camp," she explained when he asked.

As she flipped through pages of little mementos, Matt felt a lump rising in his throat. He looked across the room to her vanity and three framed photographs of Joanna, Carla and Kate's favorite caseworker, an older woman who'd died three years before. Matt realized that the small grouping represented the only family Kate Reilly had. No pictures of parents or grandparents, siblings or uncles. The sum total of her "family" were those three people. Suddenly he understood how important Joanna's memory was to her. He only hoped that he wasn't going to be the one to tarnish it in the days ahead.

He leaned over her shoulder as she turned another page.

"This is the very first card I got from Joanna, on my twelfth birthday, just a few weeks after she left Limberlost."

Matt read the card and the inscription a young Kate had scrawled beneath. He was touched by it and wanted to say something about how he could see what Joanna had meant to her. But then his eyes wandered farther down the page to a bottom corner where a small faded photo—it looked like a Polaroid—had been glued.

"This one," he said, placing the tip of his finger at its border. "Where was this taken?"

Kate brought the scrapbook closer. "Joanna and me at Limberlost." Her brow wrinkled. "You know, I think this picture was taken the day she left. I remember she'd told me to meet her in the parking area behind the main lodge to say goodbye. I sneaked away from some basket-weaving class or something—" she laughed up at him, then looked down at the photo "—and when I got there, those men were there, too. I remember being disappointed and almost embarrassed, because I'd wanted to say a private goodbye to Joanna, but I never got the chance." She raised the scrapbook right to the end of her nose. "You know," she said, "one of those men looks very familiar."

Then realization dawned, as it had for Matt seconds earlier. Kate lowered the book, stared openmouthed at him and asked, "Isn't that Lance Marchant leaning against the limo and talking to that other guy?"

CHAPTER ELEVEN

"IT IS," MATT SAID. His voice sounded peculiar and Kate glanced at his face. The cocky grin from seconds ago was gone. Even the tender smile he'd given her when she'd opened the scrapbook. There was no smile now. Just a cold, hard look.

"You know, I'd forgotten about this picture. I guess because it's so small and I always read the cards. Anyway, I haven't looked at this book since the night of Joanna's funeral."

"Oh?" He shifted his gaze from the photo to her.

"I guess I was feeling nostalgic, certainly sad. Reading the cards was a way of getting in touch with her again."

He nodded, but didn't seem to be really listening. "Tell me again about that picture," he said.

"Sure. Joanna had said to meet her at ten, but she hadn't told me she was driving to New York with those men. I foolishly thought she was taking the bus!" She laughed at her naïveté. "I might have known that wouldn't be Joanna's style."

"No, not her style," he repeated, his voice hollow. "Go on."

"So when I got there, these men were hanging around. There was a big black limo—that's the rear end of it in the picture—and I remember being totally impressed when I realized Joanna was going to the city in a limo. I really wanted to have a closer look at it, but the men put me off."

"How so?"

"I don't know. They were so serious and just the way they stuck by it. The driver and another man never even got out of the car—only Lance and the guy he seems to be talking to. 'Course at the time I didn't know his name or who any of them were."

"Do you now?"

She turned to look at him, surprised by the question. "Of course not."

"You're sure?" he persisted.

Something in his voice triggered a warning bell. "Only Lance. I *told* you," she said slowly, to clarify any confusion he might have.

He nodded, but still didn't smile. "Who took the picture?"

She thought for a moment. "Another man. There were four...no, wait...five of them. There was a chauffeur. He sat up front and never moved the whole time they were there." She paused, trying to re-create that scene from so long ago, but all she remembered were snippets.

"The one who took this picture came in another car. That's right." She was recalling more now. "And there was a disagreement just before they all left because he wanted Joanna to go with him, but the others wanted her in their car. I thought it must be nice to be so popular." She smiled up at Matt, but he was engrossed in the photo. Almost transfixed by it, she thought.

"Do you remember who she went with?"

"Yes, because I was so disappointed. I'd have chosen the limo."

"So she went with the other man. The one taking the picture."

Kate nodded.

"Is there anything else?"

She shook her head. "Matt, this happened nineteen years ago. I didn't—and still don't—know any of these people, except for Joanna and Lance. And you've told me they were friends for ages, so it can't be much of a surprise that he's there except that—''

"What?"

He shifted so quickly she almost fell off the bed. His manner was beginning to irritate her, mainly because she was bewildered by it. But she wasn't about to dampen the aftermath of their lovemaking.

She answered, striving to keep her voice calm. "I'm positive Lance told me the day we had lunch together that he'd never been to Limberlost." She mulled over that for a second, then added, "I guess he'd forgotten."

"He doesn't deserve that benefit of doubt," Matt said bitterly. He pushed aside the sheet and swung his legs off the bed, then turned to look almost wistfully at Kate. "I should go," he murmured unexpectedly. "It's getting late."

She was astounded by his abrupt change in mood. "Is there something wrong, Matt? What's bothering you about that picture?"

"Nothing, why?"

It came out a snarl. She felt herself shrinking against the headboard. Automatically she raised the sheet, covering her bare breasts. "Because you're so upset. Tell me why."

"I'm not upset." He forked his fingers through his hair, trying to push it into place. Then he peered down at the floor, reaching to retrieve his undershorts and trousers. He pulled them on without a second glance at Kate. When he stood to zip the fly, he turned to look at her.

"I'm sorry I have to go, but it's late. I do have work in the morning," he said, his voice softer now.

Coaxing her to understand? But she didn't. "I...I thought you'd stay over," she whispered.

He grabbed his shirt from the back of her vanity chair and shoved his arms into it, his eyes fixed on her face the whole time. "Stay all night?" After a nod from her, he asked, "Do *all* your men friends stay over?"

He might as well have doused her with cold water. Something frightening began to grow inside her. Some fear that the magic of the past few hours was rapidly souring and she didn't know how to stop it.

"No," she said, her voice so low he leaned forward to hear.

"Not Lance?"

Her eyes shot up to his. "Even if I understood the question, I wouldn't answer it."

"Why not?"

"Because it's insulting."

"But you've been seeing him. You're always defending him."

She raised her arms in a helpless gesture. "I don't know what you mean by any of this. I can't believe it's all coming from some attack of...of..."

"Of what?"

"Jealousy."

He snorted. "Hardly. But you've got to admit, the guy is always hanging around."

"And so are you!" she blurted.

He buckled up his trousers, gave her a quick, cool look and said, "Not anymore." Then he walked toward the door, turning once to say, "I'll call."

"Don't bother!" she cried after him.

MATT SPENT THE ENTIRE drive home replaying the last hour at Kate's, analyzing where he'd gone wrong. He hated himself for the way he'd treated her. There was no way to rationalize, much less excuse, his behavior.

It all began to fall apart when he'd seen the Polaroid photo. What had really troubled him was the man, barely visible, sitting by an open window in the back seat. In fact,

Matt didn't really want to contemplate what it would mean to Kate if he *was* right and the man was indeed Joe Levin, the city councillor whose body had recently been found upstate.

The first thing he did on his arrival, after pouring himself a Scotch, was to phone Andrews.

"It's me," he said when the other end was eventually picked up.

"Jeez, it must be about four in the morning," complained Andrews.

"A quarter to, actually. You called me yesterday, but I wasn't able to get back to you," Matt said, closing his eyes briefly as if to shut out what he'd been doing last night.

"Yeah, well, that woman is causing us all kinds of grief. She's really done it now. Thrown the whole operation in jeopardy. If I didn't know any better, I'd swear she's working for Gallini himself."

Matt's stomach sank. "What now?"

"She's gone and told Marchant about meeting me at the funeral and then again outside the sports bar. Basically she's blown the surveillance, if you want the bad news all at once."

Matt swore.

"Yeah, you can say that again."

"You blew your own cover, Andrews, when you confronted her at the bar."

"I'd no choice. I had to find out what the heck she was doin' in there. Anyway, me and the guys are trying to come up with a fall-back plan. Any ideas? And by the way, why are you calling me at this godforsaken hour?"

"I…uh, I just got home."

A loud sigh. "Catting around, eh? You lawyers. Bet when you get behind the wheel of that Lamborghini or whatever you drive, all the babes come out of the woodwork."

"Yeah, well, not quite. And it's only a Jaguar. Tell me exactly what Kate said to Marchant."

"Come on over this morning and I'll play you the tapes. Maybe by then we'll have some strategy, see if we can save this operation. Okay? See ya about ten." And he hung up.

Matt replaced his receiver and rubbed his forehead. It was ironic that when he'd finally convinced himself Kate was an innocent bystander, she'd managed all on her own to get right into the very thick of it. And the only way he could get her out of the mess she was now in would be to admit to her that much of what he'd been telling her had been a lie.

KATE COULDN'T GO back to sleep. There was a stunned silence after Matt left. Then anger took over. His arrogance and indifference had stung her, but even more, she knew there'd been something in that photograph that had triggered his reaction. The fact that he couldn't—or worse, wouldn't—talk about it didn't bode well for their relationship.

Relationship? Ha! What relationship?

By ten, after a long hot bath and a breakfast of toast and peanut butter that she forced herself to eat, Kate had begun to view the whole incident as a lesson well learned. She dressed and decided to call Carla early, so that they could plan something for the rest of the day. Perhaps the diversion of a teenager, even one as moody as Carla could be, would help her get through the day.

Rita picked up the phone after the first ring. "Oh, Kate, I was about to call you." She sounded frantic.

"What is it? Has something happened?"

"Carla's taken off."

Kate closed her eyes and swore under her breath. *How*

could you do this to us, Carla? And now? "Has she gone to see Toni and the gang?"

"Worse. I think she's gone to see that boy, Kyle."

"What?" Kate sat down. "Tell me."

"He called a few times yesterday. Then I noticed when she went to bed that she seemed jittery, almost as if she wanted to talk to me about something but couldn't do it. You know Carla. She seldom shows her feelings. But last night was different somehow. I can't explain it."

"So then what?" Kate tried to stay calm for Rita, who tended to panic, but her pulse was pounding in her ears.

"I went to wake her this morning because she'd promised to go shopping for me and she hadn't come down to breakfast. This was just half an hour ago! She wasn't there and so I assumed she was in the shower. But when I checked there a few minutes later, the bathroom was empty. I still didn't think anything of it until I looked in her room again and noticed that her backpack was gone. Clothes and toiletries from her dresser are also missing."

"But how do you know she went to see Kyle?"

Rita gave a deep, resigned sigh. "Because when I went to call a couple of the friends she's been hanging out with, I found a note from her tucked underneath the telephone."

"Can you read it to me?"

"Sure, I've got it in my pocket. Here it goes.

'Dear Rita, I hate to do this to you and I know I'm going to get into deep trouble, but Kyle really needs me right now and I want to be a good friend so I'm going to see him for a couple of days. I'll be okay so don't worry and please please don't call the police, though I probably deserve it. I'll call you when I get there. And can you call Kate to let her know and tell her not to worry? Also that none of this is her fault because I'm old enough to know what I'm doing, even

if it is a dumb thing in your eyes. Please don't tell
Kim but I'll understand if you have to.'

　　　　　　　　　　　　　　'Love Carly.'''

Rita sniffled. ''She said 'love Carly,' Kate. She's never
said 'love' to me before. What should I do?''

Kate felt sick at heart. This was the most serious act
Carla had pulled and it could mean a group home for sure,
but her motives for taking off stemmed from loyalty to a
new friend—maybe a first-time crush—rather than an out-
burst of anger at some rule. She deserved a chance to re-
deem herself, especially now, when she'd been doing so
well staying away from Toni and the gang.

''Rita, I know we shouldn't be doing this, but to give
Carla the benefit of having good but misguided intentions,
can you postpone calling Kim long enough for me to try
to track her down?''

There was a long pause before Rita said, ''I want to give
her a chance here, too, Kate, because she's shown so much
improvement the last couple days. Okay, I can do that, but
promise to keep me informed.''

Kate made arrangements with Rita, and the first thing
she did after hanging up was to call Bill Tippett. There was
no answer. And no answering machine, either. But then,
Bondi was a small village whose residents could walk their
messages to one another as easily as telephone.

Her only option, she knew, was to drive up to Bondi
herself. The thought of another marathon session into the
Adirondacks set her teeth on edge, not to mention her stomach. But she had no choice, unless she wanted to alert au-
thorities to help her. And she'd never do that to Carla. She
quickly phoned the car-rental place, then threw some
clothes into a bag. The scrapbook she and Matt had been
looking at mere hours ago was lying on the vanity, and on
impulse, she tossed the scrapbook into her bag, as well.

Bill Tippett, who could have been working around the lodge that summer, might recognize the other two men in the photo. It was a long shot, but she was determined to find out what had produced such a mood change in Matt. He had information about the case and the people involved that he wasn't revealing to her. Obviously he didn't trust her. His remark about Lance certainly supported that.

For that matter, why should I trust him? She locked up her apartment and hailed a taxi to take her to the rental place. By late afternoon, she was driving through Bondi, which was dead quiet. She didn't need to stop in at the convenience store, but thought she saw the owner—George?—stick his neck out the door as she passed. Bondi grapevine at work.

Kate expected to see Bill's dogs come charging out of the bushes as she drove up his lane, but they were nowhere in sight. When she pulled up beside the shed and stepped cautiously out of the car, she heard the dogs baying from their kennel behind the house. That was one problem out of the way. No sign of a pickup so she walked up to the front door and knocked.

When she called Bill's name, she only succeeded in making the dogs howl louder than ever. She dashed off a note for him to stop in at the lodge as soon as possible, adding that she'd come for Carla. Assuming he knew Carla had come up north. Frustrated by the inability to do anything further, Kate headed back to her car and drove to Bondi again. She'd have to buy some provisions and might as well get them now. Also, George might know where Bill had gone.

"Sure do," he said when she asked him. "Went to Plattsburg. That grandson of his took off early this morning, hitching to the city, his note said."

"Do you know if a girl was with him? Remember the young girl with me earlier in the week?"

He shook his head. "Bill didn't say anything about a girl. But he did say anyone asking about him should leave a note for him."

"I left one at his house, so I guess he'll get it. But just to be sure, if he stops by here first, will you tell him I'm at Limberlost?"

"Will do, Miss Reilly. You gonna be stayin' a coupla days?"

"I don't know." She paid for her purchases and returned to the car. Inside, she blew out a mouthful of sour air. She had a bad feeling about the whole thing.

"TURN IT OFF," Matt muttered. He'd heard enough. At least the tape had confirmed that Kate was no more than an innocent bystander who'd blundered into the investigation. Problem was, she was now mired in it. Especially since she had the one piece of evidence linking Marchant with Joe Levin.

The other thing that had stuck in his craw had been her reply to Marchant's stupid question about her dating Matt. "Hardly" wasn't the response he wanted to hear. Though reason reminded him that the telephone conversation had occurred before they'd made love.

Don't go there, fella. He wanted to put last night out of his mind—at least until this whole mess was cleaned up. Maybe then he could explain to Kate how it all happened. If it wasn't too late.

He rubbed his face. He was exhausted and still had to go back to the office. "So now what?" he asked the man sitting in the swivel chair opposite.

"Like I said, we're into damage control right now. The one thing on our side is that Marchant and Gallini don't have a clue what I look like."

"But they know they're being watched and, presumably, taped. So—"

"Yeah," Andrews put in, "so there won't be any more tapes, that's for sure. We've changed our surveillance vehicle just in case, though she didn't mention anything about Standard Electrical." Andrews laughed. "I gotta hand it to the babe, she can be tough when she wants to be. She may a schoolteacher, but she don't take no guff, if you know what I mean."

Matt forced a smile. "No, she doesn't."

"So what's this about boxes that Joanna Barnes has stored up there?"

The question jolted Matt back to the present. "Boxes?"

"Yeah. We picked up a reference to boxes on one of the tapes between Marchant and his lawyer, Collier. He was asking if they legally belong to him or to Reilly. You know anything about these boxes?"

Matt shrugged, evading Andrews's eyes. "Sort of. I told you I had a look around when I was up there and didn't find anything."

"If I was Joanna Barnes and I wanted to hide something important, I wouldn't leave it at the lodge where anyone could rummage around for it." Andrews drifted off into thoughtful silence. "That guy looking after the joint. What's his name?"

"Bill Tippett."

"Yeah. If Joanna trusted him, maybe she'd leave her important stuff with him."

"Maybe." Matt wasn't sure where Andrews was going with this.

"Tell me again what Barnes said to you when she called."

Matt sighed. "Do we have to go over it again? God!"

"Hey, you came to us, remember?"

"Okay, okay. She said she'd found something linking Gallini with Levin. Putting him at the scene roughly at the same time Levin disappeared and that she could swear to this meeting herself.''

''But she didn't say exactly what she had? A credit-card receipt? A picture? A letter?''

Matt turned his head, sensing that the white lie he was about to tell would be instantly picked up by Andrews's mental radar. ''No, she didn't.'' *And she hadn't.* Though he knew now what it was, because he'd seen it in Kate's scrapbook.

Kate had told him that the unknown photographer—his father?—had taken two Polaroid snaps that day. One for her and one for Joanna. But he wasn't about to tell Andrews. Not yet. Not until he could figure out how to get Kate out of the situation safely.

Andrews frowned, his eyes fixed on Matt. Finally he said, ''How about you go up there again and check out this Tippett? See if you can get Miss Reilly to let you have a look at those boxes.''

Yeah, right, Matt thought. *Miss Reilly would be happy to have me turn up again primarily to inquire about the boxes.* ''I doubt whatever Joanna had is up there. It'd be a waste of time.''

''What's the big deal? You and the lady have a lovers' quarrel?''

A surge of heat flooded into Matt's face. ''I don't know what you're talking about.''

''Are you telling me you didn't leave her place in the wee hours today?''

Matt had to restrain himself from hitting the guy. Especially with that know-it-all leer in his fat little face. He bit down on his lower lip, refusing to let the man draw him into revealing something. The guy was good at getting information. He'd seen enough of him in action in the past month to know.

"Didn't you guess we'd have someone on her place?" Andrews continued.

"Thanks for the vote of confidence," Matt muttered. He hated the cocky tone in Andrews's voice and was tempted to tell him about the photo just to rub in that Matt himself had found what the agent had been seeking.

"Hey, don't be so touchy. It's not about you. It's about her. We had to check her out, remember? That's why we had you cozy up to her. It's not my fault if you took things a step further." At that, Andrews chuckled.

Matt jumped to his feet, ready to punch the man or leave. He settled on the latter and was partway to the door when Andrews stopped laughing long enough to say, "Check out those boxes. You've got the perfect excuse. And she's going up there today."

That froze Matt in his tracks. "What do you mean?"

"The guy who's tailing her followed her to a car rental. She took off just before noon for the Adirondacks. That's what she told the clerk at the rental place. Said she might not be back for a couple days."

Matt took a calming breath and continued on his way to the door.

"Here's your chance, Sinclair. Finish the job for us and have something for yourself on the side."

Matt slammed the door against Andrews's hearty cackling. By the time he got back to his office, most of his anger had changed into a determined resolve to fix things however he could. He refused to let Andrews goad him into doing his dirty work. The last thing he wanted to do was go back to Limberlost to rummage through Kate's things again. Besides, he wanted to confirm something he couldn't ask Andrews about. The identity of the third man in the Polaroid photo. The one beside Lance Marchant.

SOMEHOW DRIVING ALONG the dirt road leading to Limberlost wasn't as magical this time. Both Carla and Matt had competed with each other for space in her mind the whole trip. And they both got equal time, Kate figured.

The place was closed up, but Bill had given her a spare key before she'd left the other day. He'd also replaced the shutters so it would be dark inside. As she let herself into the front door of the lodge, Kate wondered if the generator had been shut down. When she reached for the switch inside the door and no light came on, her heart sank.

The opened door let in enough sunlight for her to grope her way into the kitchen, where she'd left the flashlights and lanterns from the last visit. By the time she returned to the car for her backpack and sleeping bag, the sun was losing most of its brilliance to early evening. She figured she'd have another three hours before dark. Plenty of time, considering all she had to do was wait.

Before the sun had set completely, she got up her nerve to check the generator in the basement. Bill had shown it to her and had even demonstrated how to start it. She wished now she'd paid more attention. There was a kind of pull cord, but when she tugged at it, nothing happened. She gave up, resigned to using the lantern. Dinner proved just as futile. The propane had also been turned off and she had to eat her frozen pasta entrée at room temperature once it thawed.

By the time she'd set up her sleeping bag on a sofa in the lounge, deciding against stumbling around upstairs with a kerosene lantern, Kate had come to the realization that camping and roughing it were not for her. She could completely relate to Lance Marchant and his preference for five-star hotels.

The thought of Lance took her in a rapid circuit to Matt and the early hours of that morning. Strange that he could be jealous of a man like Lance, the type of man Kate could never be seriously attracted to. Although considering the story he'd told about his father and Joanna, any reference to Lance Marchant was bound to raise hackles. She doubted he could be objective about the man if he tried. Not that she wasn't sympathetic. It was easy to see how a teenager would have viewed the woman who'd taken his mother's place so quickly. And as much as she'd adored Joanna, she herself had known that the woman wasn't the maternal type.

But so far everything he'd told her about the land swindle had come from his own perception of the story. What he read and concluded from letters and from news clippings. Only Joanna's recent phone call to Matt indicated that there might be some substance to his beliefs. And even then, would she have implicated Lance, her own husband?

Kate sighed. She was exhausted, and examining all the possible explanations to Matt's story had only drained what little energy she had left. Bill still hadn't arrived and she could only assume he hadn't returned from Plattsburg. Not for the first time that day, she wished she owned a cell phone. She hated the feeling of helplessness and not knowing what others were doing.

Where was Carla right now? Was she safe? Afraid? Kate refused to let her mind wander down that path. Carla was a city kid who could handle a lot of tough situations for a thirteen-year-old. She had to have faith that the girl would use her common sense and get help if she needed it.

And what about Rita? Was she lying awake, too, regretting her promise not to call the caseworker? Kate had said she'd call as soon as she knew anything, but had also warned that the call might not come until the next day. There'd be a phone at George's store, or she could use Bill's, whenever he arrived home.

Last, there was Matt. Was he alone and wishing last night had ended differently? Not likely, she figured. Probably out celebrating his big merger again. With someone else? *Well, if so, then you're lucky to be out of his life, Reilly. And if not, then...*

She crawled into her sleeping bag. The sunset she'd hoped to see had been a nonevent, as dark clouds gradually covered the evening sky. There was a cold front moving in and a likelihood of rain. But all the shutters were up and the door closed. She hadn't locked it, hoping Bill might still turn up. The wind picked up outside, but Kate was warm and snug curled up on the sofa. The very one, she recalled as she dozed off, that Matt had slept on less than a week ago.

THUNDER CRASHED right above her. Kate bolted upright, heart racing, forgetting for one terrifying moment where she was. Rain poured down, drumming against the lodge, and brilliant white strobes of lightning pulsed through the chinks and gaps between windows and shutters.

Storms had always troubled Kate, made her feel anxious and restless. She burrowed deeper into her sleeping bag, covering her head. After a while, the center of the storm moved on and the rumble of thunder grew distant, less threatening. Kate threw back the top part of the sleeping bag and stretched out. Definitely not a camper, she thought, knowing that indoors was where she wanted to be in any stormy weather.

She closed her eyes, hoping to hitch back into the nice dream she'd been having before the storm hit. A kind of replay of Matt holding her in his arms, but without the cold-shower ending. Drifting into it, allowing herself to remember the taste of his lips, the strength of his arms, she almost missed the creak of floorboards on the veranda. But the distinctive sound happened again, between muted rolls of thunder.

Kate sat up, ears straining in the dark. Some animal had wandered up to the lodge and was prowling around, except the heaviness of the noise discounted any small mammals. A bear? she wondered, her throat catching on that thought, which rapidly led to another—could bears open doors? Then, had she locked the door or not? Her mind raced, reenacting the moment of arrival and her mental debate about whether Bill might turn up that night.

Maybe he has! She welcomed the idea, immersing herself in it as if in a warm bath on a winter night until the shuffling sounds reached the main door of the lodge and halted. Kate slid out of the sleeping bag, grabbed the flashlight on the table beside her and tiptoed into the center of the room. She was afraid to use the flashlight, afraid of what she might see.

Move forward, her mind urged. One step, two—keep going. Wait! The screen door, its hinges protesting loudly, swung open. She waited for a knock, but none came. Her breath echoed in the big room, her lungs begging for more oxygen to feed her heart, furiously pumping adrenaline to every nook and cranny of her body. Every cell screamed for some kind of evasive action. *Run, Reilly,* her brain coached from the sidelines, but her legs, stubbornly acting on their own, carried her like a dead weight closer to the door.

Her eyes flicked back and forth as she sought some defense, then settled on an umbrella stand tucked into the corner just to the left of the door. The door whose outside latch clinked up. The inside knob was now turning slowly. Kate raised the umbrella stand and waited. The knob reached a full revolution and stopped. The heavy wooden door groaned as it was pushed forward, scraping the floor in a damp, widening arc.

Kate screamed and threw the umbrella stand at the same time.

CHAPTER TWELVE

THE UMBRELLA STAND caught the intruder in his midsection. The dark figure crumpled to the floor with a whoosh. Kate waited for a sign of movement and when none came, she fearfully moved closer, still clutching the flashlight. Her hands were shaking so badly it took two attempts at the button to get light. The beacon swept up and across the room before she managed to hold it steadily on the person on the floor. The man began to rouse himself, lifting his head.

"Lance," she cried, and bent over him, relief that she hadn't maimed Bill Tippett flooding through her, "are you all right? What are you doing here?"

He moaned, rolled onto one side and struggled to a cross-legged position. After a few moments, he gasped, "What did you hit me with?"

"An umbrella stand."

"Oh, God! I feel like I've been run over by a tank."

Kate had to smile. Her throwing arm wasn't that good. But she was happy to see him alive and breathing, even if shocked at his presence. *The man was breaking into my lodge.* She decided not to feel too sorry for him.

He reached out for a handhold and she grasped his forearm, helping him to his feet. Using the flashlight, she guided him to the chair next to where she'd been sleeping and sat him down. Then she found the kerosene lantern and lit it. The pale yellow light flickered in the room, making everything seem bigger and scarier. Even Lance Marchant.

His face, though pale, was lined with anger. The snowy white hair swooped up in peaks and, in the lantern's light, made him look like a deranged wizard. Or madman, Kate thought, her anxiety stirring again.

"Did you have to throw *anything?*" he asked, patting at his hair with both hands.

"Well, you didn't exactly knock."

"I didn't know anyone was here."

"You didn't notice my car?"

"No. Too dark and raining out."

Kate sat on top of her sleeping bag, tucking her feet up beneath her. "Why are you prowling around at this time of night? In fact, why are you here at all?"

His breathing was still ragged. He held up a hand, motioning for her to wait. Finally he sagged back into the chair. "It's a long story, Kate, and first, I apologize for my actions tonight. I called your place, but obviously you weren't there. The other day when I was talking to Greg, he told me that anything of Joanna's of a personal nature belonged to me. Anything that came from the lodge and had been used here belonged to you. And I got to thinking…"

"Yes?" she prompted.

"See, there was this time about a year ago when Joanna and I were having some problems. Marital problems." He sighed heavily. "The truth is, I had an affair and Joanna found out. The other woman, whom I'd broken up with, had written a malicious letter to her. When Joanna showed it to me, I broke down and confessed. We went to a counselor—the whole ball of wax—and things between us improved. But I never saw that letter again and never knew what Joanna had done with it." He paused. "Mind if I take off my jacket? It's a lot warmer inside than out."

"Why not? Now that you're here," she said sarcastically.

He fumbled with the zipper and awkwardly pulled off the nylon sport jacket, flinging it to the floor. Underneath he wore a jersey turtleneck and he tugged at the neck, as if it was too tight. "That's better," he finally said. "Where was I?"

"The letter."

"Right. After Joanna's death I remembered it. I'd just announced my candidacy, and I realized that if anyone got their hands on the letter, well, it could make me look bad."

I'll say, Kate thought.

"I looked everywhere at home for it, even in Joanna's safe-deposit box."

"How do you know she just didn't throw it away?"

A bitter half smile crossed his face. In the strange light, it made him look like a satyr. "Joanna wouldn't have. Believe me."

Strangely enough, Kate did. The more she learned about Joanna Barnes, the more she realized how complex the glamorous fashion editor had been. "So you thought it might be here at Limberlost? But why here?"

"Because she came here sometime in the year after she got the letter. I can't recall why. She and Bill had packed up everything long before. But she just said she wanted to visit the place and was vague about the reason. When you mentioned that there were boxes of stuff stored here, I thought she might have hidden the letter during that visit."

"But according to Bill, there are boxes everywhere. In most of the cabins. You could spend a week looking for it."

"I know, but you also said he had some in his garage. I got to thinking that maybe that's what she did when she was here. Took it to a place that might not be as accessible or obvious as Limberlost."

"That's ridiculous, Lance! Why would she go to all that trouble? It doesn't make sense."

"It does if she knew I wanted it back," he murmured.

"What do you mean?"

"She was in a strange frame of mind this past year. Pre-menopausal, I think. Paranoid. Accusing me of lying to her about several things. All of them petty. I'd been talking about running for Congress, and at first, she didn't seem to care. Only to say that her job was too busy for her to help with my campaign, but I knew that, anyway. Then she said not to expect her to be one of those smiling politician's wives who have nothing to say." He stopped a second, shaking his head sadly at the memory. "When I asked her what she meant, she said if a reporter ever asked her about any affair I might have had, she'd make it perfectly clear that…well, certain events had happened."

Events. The man can't even refer to the act for what it is. Infidelity. Suddenly she remembered Matt's whispered comment the night of the kiss. *The man's a womanizer.* Who could blame Joanna?

"I asked if she'd disposed of the letter. She refused to say, and I knew she hadn't. That she'd use it against me whenever she wanted to."

"I don't believe that," Kate said. "Joanna must have loved you. She'd known you for years, you said. She wouldn't be so callous."

"No? Unfortunately your own recollection of her is that of a child's."

She wasn't about to be sidetracked by a discussion about Joanna. "Let's get back to why you were compelled to come in the dead of night looking for something that probably isn't here at all. And chose not to wait to get my permission to be on my property."

"I was at a local candidate's campaign start-up today—a place outside Plattsburg—and since I was in the area, thought I'd drive by to see if you were here. I had called your apartment from my cell phone, got no answer and made my decision very impulsively. I'm sorry about that.''

He managed to add a whole new dimension to the notion of dropping in, she thought. In the Adirondacks? What did he take her for? But the part of his explanation that lingered was the cell phone. ''Do you have it with you or is it in the car?''

''What?''

''Your phone.''

''Uh, it's in the car. Why?''

''Can I use it? I need to call someone.''

His brow furrowed. ''Who?''

''Carla's foster mother,'' she said. ''Another long story we don't have time for. Can you go get it?''

''In a minute. Now that I'm here, I'd like to have a look for that letter, if you don't mind.''

Kate made a sweeping gesture with her hand. ''Be my guest. Where will you start?''

''I thought at the caretaker's place.''

Her jaw dropped. ''Are you kidding?''

He made a strange laughing sound. ''Why would I be? I didn't drive through the mountains in a rainstorm and risk my political career by breaking into someone's place on some whim.'' He practically barked the last word.

Kate shivered. The edge in his voice reminded her that she knew him even less well than Joanna. ''Bill isn't there. He's gone to Plattsburg and I doubt he came back tonight.''

''All the better. That means we won't have to wake him up. Besides, we're not breaking into his house. You said they might be in a shed.''

Oh, yeah. That's okay, then. ''We should wait until the morning. What's the big rush?''

''Because I've a very important meeting in the city and I don't know when I'll get a chance to drive back up here.

Come on, Kate. Be realistic. We're only going to pick up what legally belongs to me, anyway.''

"Call him on your phone first in case he's back now."

"All right. Let's go out to the car."

"Why both of us?"

He sighed. "Because," he said, as if speaking to a child, "if he's not there, I'd want you to come along to witness my taking the box. Just in case."

She could only shake her head at his blithe disregard for private property. "I'm sorry," she said, "I can't be part of this. Even if the boxes are yours, it's not right."

"Fine." He shrugged. "I'll go on my own."

"Do you know where he lives?"

He shook his head. "But I can call someone—that fellow who runs the convenience store. Miller. Greg gave me his number just in case."

There was no stopping him, she could see that. She hated the thought of poor old George Miller being awakened in the dead of night. Lance was determined to go regardless. Besides, she wanted to let Rita know what was happening. The poor woman was probably still awake, waiting for any word about Carla. "Okay," she said, sighing loudly as she got to her feet.

IT DIDN'T TAKE HIM LONG to find what he was looking for. He had a name, just needed a face to match the one in Kate's photo. Matt thanked Paula for her help in obtaining disks of several back copies of newspapers.

Andrews hadn't told him a whole lot about the operation he and his team had been mounting. They'd been trying for years to pin something on Vincent Gallini, a reputed New Jersey racketeer. When Matt had contacted the police right after Joanna's death, Andrews had been eager to hear his story.

He spent most of the afternoon scrolling through the disk

until he finally came across a picture of Gallini. It was the
same man in Kate's Polaroid, with about thirty extra
pounds on him. Matt's dilemma now was what to do with
this information. He knew he ought to take it to Andrews
immediately, but then Kate would learn right away about
his involvement. And he really wanted to prepare her for
that. To have a chance to explain how it had all come about.

Except she wasn't home, gone foolishly to Limberlost,
miles away. So he filed the printout of Gallini's photo in
his office desk and called for Paula.

ONE OTHER THING she didn't like about country life, Kate
was thinking as Lance's car bumped along the dirt lane to
Bill's place, was that without streetlights the roads were as
dark as the inside of a coffin. Not that she knew or ever
wanted to know what that could be like. But she could
certainly imagine it. It didn't help that there were no stars
or moon or any other celestial lights. At least the phone
call to Rita had removed some of her anxiety.

"Kate," Rita had shouted gleefully into the phone, "I
was hoping you'd call. Carla telephoned. She's all right. In
Plattsburg with Kyle and his grandfather, that man who
looks after your place. He made Carla telephone me. They
tried to call you, too. Anyway, I told them you were at the
lodge. They're driving from Plattsburg to Bondi tomorrow."

The car headlights swept across the property as it pulled
up to the house. When they struck the shed, Lance braked.
"That it?"

"Well, the one he keeps his truck in. But I remember
another building behind the house."

"We'll start with this one, since I can keep the beams
on it." He opened his door. "Coming?" he asked.

Reluctantly she dragged herself out of the car.

Lance raised the shed door and at once the silent night

filled with the uproar of barking. Kate couldn't resist a smile as he ran back to where she was standing.

"What the hell is that? Are there guard dogs here?"

"Sort of. But it's okay," she said quickly, worrying from his red face he might have a heart attack. "They're locked up in a kennel."

He bent at the waist, hands on his knees as he caught his breath.

"Are you okay, Lance? Want to forget about this?" She was beginning to feel real concern for him.

He raised himself and met her gaze. His face was white now and lined with worry. And something else she couldn't define. "Too late for that, Kate. I wish it could wait. I wish a lot of things. But…as I said…too late. Stay there." He hobbled back to the shed like a man twenty-five years older.

Kate wrapped her arms around her, shivering. She knew it wasn't the cool night air that was bothering her. What would Matt think if he knew what she was doing? Would he have accepted Lance's story about the letter or put some twist on it? Make it look like another piece of the larger plot? It was perfectly credible to her that Lance would want to dispose of evidence linking him to adultery, especially since he was running for Congress. What wasn't so believable was Lance's urgency, his need to find it in the middle of the night.

She saw the flashlight beam bob around the shed as he searched for the boxes. Suddenly he gave a shout from inside, rousing the dogs even further. Kate could scarcely hear him over their howling.

"I've found the boxes. There are only three. It won't take me long."

But now she had another idea. One she wished she'd thought of earlier. She walked to the door of the shed. Lance was bent over a box that he'd lifted onto a worktable.

"Why don't you just take the boxes with you?" she

asked. "They're yours, anyway. When Bill comes tomorrow, I'll tell him you came for them. I'll…I'll try to make it sound legitimate," she said, hating herself for even a minor deception to Bill. But all she wanted was to go back to the lodge and get some sleep. And be rid of Lance Marchant at the same time.

"Why didn't I think of that myself?"

Kate snorted. Did he think all the smart ideas came from him?

She helped him lug the boxes into the trunk of the sedan he was driving. "I don't take the Porsche to candidates' meetings," he'd confided when they'd left Limberlost. "It doesn't look good."

And immediately she'd thought, neither does break and entry, but kept the remark to herself. As they bumped back along the lane, Kate could hear the dogs still baying.

"I'll drop you off and then head back to the city," Lance said. "It's almost two. I can make my eight o'clock meeting with time to spare for a shower."

"You should take care, Lance. You don't look very healthy."

He turned his face toward her. A smile lit his eyes. "Why, Kate Reilly, I didn't know you cared."

"I don't, trust me. But seriously, why don't you find a motel and go back early in the morning? Your meeting can't be that important."

He laughed. "I take it you're not inviting me to stay the night at Limberlost. Should I be flattered that you don't trust yourself around me or—"

"Definitely the 'or,'" she interrupted.

He laughed harder. "I didn't realize humor was another of your many talents." He paused, then, lowering his voice, said, "I've probably messed up my chances of taking our acquaintanceship into another stage."

"If you're trying to say you've no chance whatsoever of knowing me in any real way, Lance, then you're dead on."

The car pulled up in front of the lodge. He shifted into Neutral and said, as she opened her door, "I'm very sorry to hear that. And, Kate, steer clear of Matt Sinclair. You won't want to be around him the next few days or so. Some unpleasant things are going to be happening."

She froze. "What do you mean?"

"Just that he's been getting involved with some pretty questionable characters. People linked with the mob. Maybe it has something to do with his business, I don't know. All I can say is, he's made some enemies, and those around him are going to be affected. Take my advice and keep away from him."

"And of course you're an authority on exemplary behavior yourself," she retorted. "Give me a break." She climbed out of the car.

"I'm telling you the truth, Kate. And remember, those boxes belonged to me, anyway. Ask Greg Collier."

"Give me my flashlight," she snapped. When he handed it over, she slammed the door behind her.

"Remember what I said," he called after her. "Matt Sinclair is going to bring you nothing but trouble."

HE ALREADY HAS was the answer rolling around in her head all night long. In spite of her fatigue, the night's adventures had left her physically spent but mentally on the alert. She went over every word Lance had uttered, searching for ambiguities, exaggerations and half truths. But he was a politician and had "the gift of the gab," as Kate's former caseworker had once remarked of Kate herself. She sighed.

Maybe it took one to know one. But whereas she'd outgrown her defensive storytelling as an adolescent, she suspected Lance Marchant had developed a whole credo around his.

She was trying to light a fire in the fireplace to boil water for instant coffee the next morning when a horn tooted from the drive. She ran outside to see Bill's pickup lurch to a halt at the edge of the lawn.

The passenger door was flung open and Carla leapt down. Kate kept running, grabbing Carla in a bear hug and swinging around with her.

"Hey, little sister!" she cried. "Good to see you!" Then she paused, standing still to look down at the young girl. "Really good to see you," she said softly.

Carla squeezed harder, looking up at Kate with tears in her eyes. "I'm so sorry, Kate."

Kate wrapped an arm around her and pulled her close. They stood there, unmoving, while Bill and Kyle climbed out of the truck.

"Miss Reilly," said Bill, his face drawn and serious, "Kyle here has somethin' to tell you." He gave Kyle a nudge.

The boy stepped forward, head down and shoulders slumped. Kate might have felt sorry for him if he hadn't caused so much worry for everyone. But she was willing to listen.

When he was standing right in front of Kate and Carla, he looked up and mumbled, "I'm sorry I got Carla into some trouble. I didn't mean to. I only wanted her to help me try to persuade my mom not to get divorced from my dad." He ducked his head again. "It didn't work, anyway," he added.

Kate reached over to pat him on the shoulder. "Thanks for the apology, Kyle. And thanks for watching out for Carla in Plattsburg, because I'm sure you must have."

He raised his head, and his face flushed at her comment. He managed a faint smile and stood off to one side as his grandfather approached. "Seems like Kyle called Carla and convinced her to take a bus to Plattsburg. They met there early yesterday morning but didn't turn up at his mama's place until after lunch. She called me right away and I tried to phone you from home, but you musta already left for here.'' He shrugged. ''Anyhow, that's what happened. When I got there, we tried calling you again and then I had Carla phone her foster mother. We learned you were here. Sorry to put you to all this trouble, Miss Reilly.''

''Please, Bill, it's Kate. And thanks for acting on this right away. It helped that you were in Plattsburg to get the kids back home.''

He nodded. ''Well, then, guess Kyle and I should get goin'. He's got some chores to do for me, help get the place ready for Verna. She's coming home tomorrow and likes a clean house. Anything I can do for you before I go?''

She almost said no, but remembered her efforts to light a fire for coffee. ''The generator?''

''Heck, why didn't you say somethin'? Come on, I'll get it started and show you again what to do.''

Kate followed him to the basement and paid strict attention this time.

''If you keep the place, you'll want to get reconnected to the hydro. Make your life a lot easier,'' he said, wiping his hands on his jeans. ''That it?''

''Well, there is one more thing,'' she began, faltering under the man's steady gaze.

''Yes?''

''Last night I had a visit from Lance Marchant. Did you know him? He was—''

''Married to Joanna. Yep. Met him once, years ago. Didn't much care for him. Why?''

She flinched at his sudden curtness. Did he think Lance had come to see me for personal reasons? She set the record straight. ''Lance had been asking me about some things that belonged to Joanna. I'd mentioned to him that you had some of her stuff in your shed—'' she saw Bill's eyebrows shoot up ''—and he asked his lawyer if it was legally his or mine.'' She stopped to take a breath.

Bill nodded thoughtfully. ''Take your time.''

''Well, he turned up in the middle of the night demanding these boxes and refused to leave without them, so I had no choice but to—''

''Get them for him,'' he filled in.

She nodded, feeling as chastened as a schoolgirl caught in a prank.

''I see,'' he said, ruminating over the situation. ''You really had to give them to him or he'd still be here, right?'

Another nod.

''Then thank you for doing that. I got rid of the boxes and I didn't have to see Lance Marchant myself to do it.''

Kate was grateful for the kind response. She followed him outside to the truck.

''Will you be staying on a few days?'' Bill asked.

''I wish we could, but I think Rita would like to have Carla safe at home. Right, Carla?''

The girl nodded.

''But I'll let you know soon about the property,'' Kate said. ''Definitely before September.''

''Okay'' was all he said as he and Kyle climbed back into the truck. The engine turned over and they waved goodbye as it took off down the gravel road.

''Want a swim before we head back?''

''How about going out in the canoe?'' Carla asked, and Kate knew everything was going to be just fine.

Later, when they were on the road, Kate remembered that she'd forgotten to have Bill take a look at her scrapbook. She murmured a faint expletive that brought a questioning look from Carla.

''Can I see it?'' the girl asked after Kate's partial explanation. And while Kate drove, her mind drifting back to the recent past, Carla delved further back, to nineteen years ago.

KATE SPLURGED ON A TAXI from the car rental. She'd ended up staying for dinner at Carla's, a pleasant but tumultuous experience, with Rita's toddler and baby wanting their equal share of Carla's attention. She enjoyed watching Carla with the younger children. The girl was a natural caregiver, Kate thought, though she'd have turned up her adolescent nose at such an observation. In spite of the rocky beginning the summer had had for Carla, Kate could see now that she was awakening to her good fortune in having Rita and family. *If only my own summer was shaping up to be as positive.*

She lingered on that dismal thought all the way home, swaying back and forth in a cab whose driver had a penchant for zigzagging through traffic. She scarcely had both feet on the curb when the taxi was off again, leaving her stumbling over her backpack. She dragged herself upstairs, stopped momentarily by Ginny, whose unexpected question, ''Have you been away?'' puzzled Kate—until she reached her door and stared.

It was ajar. She lowered her pack and sleeping bag to the floor and gently pushed the door, which swung open. Her clammy hands tingled as adrenaline surged through her, and she could almost feel her blood pressure soar. She took a deep breath, reached a hand around the doorjamb and flicked on the light.

The living room was a mess. Drawers opened, cushions tossed onto the floor and a lamp toppled. She didn't want to go inside, but closed the door and ran downstairs.

Ginny insisted that Kate telephone the police from her apartment. Then she guided her into the kitchen and put the kettle on. Kate was taking her first sip of hot herbal tea when there was a hard knock at the door. She jumped, sloshing the hot liquid onto her knee.

"I'll get it. It's likely the police," Ginny said.

There was the muted sound of voices. Kate carefully set the mug on the kitchen table. She was feeling better now, the shock of discovering a break-in subsiding. In fact, the irony of the situation hadn't escaped her. She'd been helping Lance Marchant in a quasi break-in mere hours ago, perhaps while her own place was being ransacked. *Is this my punishment?* Kate asked herself.

A familiar voice left that question hanging. Kate rose from her chair and headed for the living room. There was no NYPD officer standing in the doorway. Only Tom Andrews.

CHAPTER THIRTEEN

FLASHING A LEATHER billfold at Ginny, he approached Kate and asked solicitously, "Shall we go upstairs to your place, Miss Reilly? Or would you prefer to stay here?"

"Where are the *real* police officers?" she asked, catching Ginny's startled glance at the same time.

Andrews smiled broadly. "They're on their way, Miss Reilly. Let's go have a look at the damage." Then he grasped her by the elbow and steered her out the door.

Kate jerked her arm from his the second they were on the landing. He went ahead, waiting for her in the open doorway of her apartment.

"Certainly looks a mess," he said. "We'll go in, but I'll have to ask you not to touch anything. Though fingerprints seldom help with break-and-entry perps. If they're pros, they wear gloves." He stepped inside. "Coming?"

She lingered in the hall, reluctant to be alone with him. "Why are *you* here?"

"You called in an alarm. I picked it up on my scanner and since I was in the area, thought I'd drop by."

Shades of Lance Marchant, she was thinking. "Where are the police?"

He smiled again. "Miss Reilly, I *am* the police. The uniforms are coming." He beckoned. "You can trust me."

Kate retrieved her pack and sleeping bag and stepped gingerly into the living room.

"Why don't we walk through the rooms and see how the guy got in. There a fire escape?"

"My bedroom," she said. She rushed ahead of him, horrified at the thought that her bedroom—her refuge from the stresses of work and city—might have been violated.

Even more disorder here. Every drawer in her bureau had been removed and upended, their contents scattered all over the floor. The closet door gaped to reveal clothing heaped onto the floor. The boxes on the shelves inside had been emptied onto the same heap. The entire room looked as though it had been hit by a tornado.

Kate sat on the edge of her bed. She fought back the tears, refusing to cry in front of Andrews. But the knot in her stomach was working its way up into her throat. She could hardly breathe and forced herself to take long slow inhalations of air. As the fear abated, anger set in. *Why me? Why did this have to happen now, when so many weird things were going on? Is this some kind of test?*

"He didn't use the fire escape to get in," Andrews said as he ran his fingers along the window sash. "Everything's secure here." He turned toward her. "You okay? You look a bit pale. Put your head down between your knees."

And because she knew he was right, she did.

"That's it. Just keep it there a couple minutes." He wandered about the room, eyeing the damage without putting a finger on any of it.

When Kate raised her head, she felt better, though still wobbly. From beyond the room, she heard the thud of ascending footsteps.

"Uniforms are here." Andrews noted. He walked over to Kate and squatted on his haunches in front of her. "Miss Reilly? After they've finished with their questions, they'll want you to have a look, find out what's been taken. Then they'll call back tomorrow to finish their report and so on. You may wanna call your insurance company meanwhile. I gotta go now." He held on to the bed to pull himself up.

Then added, "One more thing. Maybe it'd be a good idea to visit a friend for a couple days."

She turned her face from the window to him.

"People find they feel uncomfortable stayin' in their places after a robbery." He poked around in his suit jacket pocket and withdrew a pack of cigarettes. "Know what I mean? You may be feelin' threatened." He tapped the pack against his other hand and grabbed a cigarette as it dropped out. "Other thing is, and I don't wanna frighten you, but whoever did this may come back." He held her gaze, tucking the cigarette behind his ear. Then he gave a quick nod and left the room.

Whoever did this may come back. The thought of herself lying here in the dark when that happened clutched at her throat and choked her. She lowered her head between her knees again and breathed deeply. The footsteps grew louder, accompanied by voices now. Andrews talking to the others. Then they came her way, halting just at the bedroom door.

"Miss Reilly?"

A uniformed female NYPD officer stood patiently in the doorway. "Are you all right? Can I get you something before I start my report?"

Kate was grateful for her thoughtfulness. "No, no, I'm okay. Can we go into the living room, though? I...I have to get out of here."

The officer nodded and backed out the door to let Kate by. There were three men in the living room. One was walking carefully around the litter and jotting notes, while the other two opened cases and began pulling out strange-looking tools and objects.

"The technicians are going to try to lift some fingerprints," the officer said. "Why don't we go in the kitchen while I ask you a few questions? I wouldn't mind a cup of tea, myself."

Kate followed her, childlike, into the kitchen and sat silently while the officer efficiently found kettle, tea and mugs. She couldn't help thinking of the night Matt had been here, setting out dinner for her. Except that night anticipation had been coursing through her veins, rather than this overwhelming flood of helplessness.

"Okay?" the officer asked, placing two mugs of hot tea onto the table. "I'm Officer Brady, by the way. You're feeling vulnerable and helpless right now, but that will pass. We can take our time with this and when we've finished, we'll see if someone can come and stay the night with you. Or maybe you can go to a friend's."

Kate nodded, picked up the mug and blew on the hot tea. The other woman's manner was already having an effect on her. Her heart rate was slowing and the awful nausea had gone. She sipped carefully and let the soothing liquid flow into her, easing her tension as if she'd stepped into a hot bath.

"All set?" Brady asked.

"Yes," Kate said, and straightened in her chair, ready to answer the officer's questions.

It only took twenty minutes to go through them, there was so little information Kate could provide. She had definitely locked up and, no, she didn't have any known enemies. That particular question reminded her of Lance's parting shot at Limberlost. But his warning had been focused on her involvement with Matt. And Kate had now resigned herself to the fact that *involvement* was hardly a word that applied to her and Matt Sinclair.

She drank the last of her tea while Officer Brady wrote her report. Wandering over to the kitchen window, Kate stared out at the remnants of a brilliant sunset, thinking how much more stunning it would be at Limberlost. Her eyes swept across rooftops to the street below. A man was standing on the pavement, smoking a cigarette. Tom Andrews.

Hadn't he said that he had to go, implying some other business? Kate pursed her lips. *Guess that business was a cigarette.* She glanced back at Officer Brady, who was now shuffling her report form and snapping it into her clipboard folder. Then she turned once more to the window and saw another man, his back to her, approaching Andrews. Kate leaned closer to the window. She must be mistaken, she thought.

But when the man nodded and swung around, her suspicion was confirmed. *Matt.*

HE TOOK THE STAIRS two at a time, his fury mounting at the same pace. He'd been working late when he got Andrews's call and had left the office immediately. But in spite of his plea to see Kate first, the man had barged on ahead. God only knew what he'd told Kate. How had he been so naive to think he'd been working with Andrews when it was so obvious he'd been used by him all along?

Two technicians in white coveralls brushed past him on the landing. Matt hesitated in the doorway, taking in the scene. His stomach hit the floor. What if Kate had been here at the time? Two uniformed police were talking in the middle of the room and looked up quickly at his arrival.

"Help you?" the male officer asked.

"I'm here to see Kate," Matt said, stepping inside.

"Watch where you go," the officer cautioned.

"Are you a friend of hers?" the female officer asked.

"Yes."

She jerked her head toward the kitchen. "She's in there. Pretty upset. See if you can find somewhere for her to spend the night."

Unnecessary advice. She's coming home with me.

He paused on the threshold, taking in the slump of her spine and the dejected droop of her head. This wasn't like

Kate, he thought. And felt a surge of anger again at who-ever had done this to her.

He walked slowly across the tiles and pulled out a chair. She raised her head and stared at him with eyes that were tired and sad and something else. Disappointed?

"How did you know?" she asked. "And please don't say you were passing by."

Blood rushed into his head. "I...uh...I..."

"He called you, didn't he? Tom Andrews."

The roaring in his ears muffled his own reply. "Yes."

She started to get up, but he reached out a hand to her arm. "Please, Kate. I think I deserve a chance to explain."

"What makes you think I want to hear it?" Her face was tight with anger.

"Please."

She sat down, brushing his hand off her arm.

He closed his eyes, knowing he couldn't evade or be ambiguous any longer. This might be his only shot at con-vincing her. "Everything I've told you about how and when Joanna Barnes married my father, the land fraud, all that was true."

Her eyes flashed, but she remained silent.

"I was working at my merger deal at the time. When she failed to call to apologize for skipping the meeting she'd begged for, I—"

"Wrote it off."

"Sorry?"

"Wrote it off. Isn't that what you said before?"

He ran his fingers through his hair, a nervous habit he'd picked up as a kid. He hoped that slight smirk on her face didn't mean she thought all this was a joke. *No. Get seri-ous, Sinclair. The woman's on the brink and it's up to you to bring her back.*

"Yes." No point equivocating. "I was busy. I hadn't heard from her in years. I didn't really believe her." After a moment he said, "I was wrong. And I was stunned when I read her obituary, because like you, I doubted Joanna would ever kill herself. Though I think my reasons were less generous than yours." He tried for a small smile, but she wasn't interested.

"A while ago I told you I didn't go to the police with that story, but I did." He waited for a reaction, but she'd already figured that out. "A few days after I called NYPD, I got this phone call. From Tom Andrews. He said he'd received my message and wanted to talk to me about it. Asked me to meet him downtown in some office building. It wasn't even a police station." He stopped, his mouth dry. Whether from the blank expression on her face or the labor of telling the truth.

"Mind if I get a drink?" he asked, and when she mumbled some response he couldn't quite catch, he opened her refrigerator door. There was one beer and a can of Coke. He reached for the soda, flipping the tab as he pulled out his chair and sat down again.

"Did you want something?"

She shook her head. "No. Just go on."

He gave a brief account of how Andrews persuaded him to attend Joanna's funeral and pass on any information he might have about any of the guests.

"But why was Andrews interested in all of this, anyway?" Kate asked.

"Oh, right. I missed that bit." Matt set the can of pop onto the table, running a finger along the rim. "Andrews— by the way, he's FBI—had been working with Internal Revenue and a bunch of other federal agencies accumulating evidence against this guy, Vincent Gallini, who's been involved in all kinds of criminal activities for years. But they've always missed getting enough to indict him and have never been able to link him directly with anything serious. The most the guy has done is a year inside for failing to report all of his income.'' Matt took another drink.

''Remember I told you that Joanna had read about a body being found upstate?''

Kate nodded.

''The body was eventually identified as Joe Levin—the city councillor I told you about who'd been part of the land swindle. Once he was officially identified and it was determined that he'd been shot—execution-style—the feds decided to reopen the case in hope of connecting Gallini to the murder. When I phoned to say I had information about Joanna Barnes, my inquiry triggered some kind of computer warning system, I guess.''

''What's Joanna got to do with this murder?''

Matt hesitated. This was where the story got tricky. He'd resolved not to lie. But he also knew there was no way he'd tell her about the Polaroid right now. She was already traumatized by the break-in. The photo thing could wait until he had a chance to talk to Andrews about security for Kate. So far, he was the only one besides her who knew about it. And she wasn't aware of its significance.

''No one knows for sure. She might have known all about it from the start—'' he paused, noting the disbelief in her face ''—or maybe she found out later and wanted to fix things. Looking back on her phone call, that might be the case.''

Her eyes stayed on his. He could almost see the domino action of her mind putting it all together. She moved her lips, murmuring something he couldn't hear.

''What's that?'' he asked.

She ducked her head. ''Nothing important. It's just, well, hard to believe.''

''So now you know why you saw Marchant in Little Italy at that bar. It's where he meets Gallini.''

"How do you know about that?" she asked, her eyes now like saucers.

Matt had to perform a mental two-step. Was this part of what he safely could reveal? Yes, he decided. "Andrews told me. He and his team picked it up on tape when you were talking on the phone to Marchant."

"They've tapped my phone?" Incredulity raised the pitch of her voice.

Matt let slip a smile. "No, Kate. They've been tapping Marchant's phone."

"Oh." She waited a moment and then, her voice low and troubled, said, "This has all been very...overwhelming. I don't know what to make of any of it. Your story—and now this." She motioned toward the living room. "It's not that crime is something new to me. I mean, I grew up in Queens and saw a lot there. And I've lived in Manhattan all my adult life. I've even had my purse snatched! But today when I came home—" she swiped at the corner of her eye with the back of her hand "—I felt so...so exposed. This is my home!" she cried. "The only real one I've ever had."

Matt couldn't sit still a second longer. He jumped up, his chair clattering onto the floor, and went to her, pulling her up out of her chair and hugging her. Which is what he'd wanted to do since he'd first walked into the kitchen. She collapsed against him, starting to weep. It was a soft, muted sobbing, but it sent slivers of pain through him.

Matt sat down again with her still in his arms. He stroked her head, which she'd buried in his chest. When her body ceased trembling and her sobs quieted, he tipped up her chin to look into eyes that were red-rimmed and swollen.

"You're coming home with me tonight," he said firmly, and planted a kiss on the end of her damp nose.

KATE STOOD in the center of the marble-floored foyer of Matt's condo. She hoped she wasn't gawking. The foyer fanned out into a huge living room, an entire side of which was window. The condo was on the thirtieth floor and afforded an amazing view.

"Is that the Hudson?" she asked, pointing to the ribbon of river beyond the skyline.

"Yes, it is," Matt said as he carried her backpack through the room and disappeared into a hallway. When he returned seconds later, she was still perched on the edge of the foyer.

"Are you coming in?" he asked, folding his arms and smiling.

"I was just trying to take all this in. It sure is different from my brownstone. Right down to the guy in the lobby with all the TV monitors."

"There's a good security system here. But at least *you* don't have to come up thirty floors in an elevator with a load of groceries."

She thought that over for a second. "Yeah," she agreed, "you've got a point. I guess I'd rather live in my three-story row house."

He let out a small chuckle as if he wasn't sure if she was kidding or not. "Come on," he said, "I'll show you around."

The rest of the two-bedroom condo was as magnificent. For the first time, Kate realized that Matt Sinclair was seriously wealthy. Of course, the car had been a clue, along with his designer clothes and references to boarding schools. But she remembered he'd said his father had been financially ruined in the land deal.

When they returned to the living room, Kate sank into one of the many overstuffed white sofas and chairs grouped around the windows and a built-in gas fireplace at one end of the room.

"I'm pouring myself a Scotch," Matt said, standing in

front of a polished wood cabinet, which he'd opened to reveal a collection of bottles. "What will you have?"

"I don't know. Do you have any beer?"

"I do," he said, "but not cold. Besides, I think you need something more soothing. Try a Scotch. If you don't like it, I'll pour it out."

He walked over to where she was sitting and handed her a crystal tumbler with amber liquid sloshing over an ice cube. "Sip it," he warned, as she coughed and grimaced.

Then he sat down on the love seat beside her, placing an arm along the back of the sofa. "Like it?" he asked.

She'd stopped coughing enough to try a second sip. "It's strange. Like smoke."

"Good taste buds. It is. A single malt from the Isle of Islay off the coast of Scotland."

Kate grinned. "You sound like an advertisement."

"That's what I like about you," he said, toying with a lock of her hair, "you bring me down to earth. And you're not impressed by...stuff like this." He gestured with the hand holding the glass into the room.

"Oh, I'm impressed," Kate said.

Matt laughed. "Seriously. I assure you that as much as I enjoy the perks of wealth, money itself isn't what drives me. And making it isn't what gets me up in the morning. I really like what I do."

"You don't have to justify yourself to me, Matt." She kept her eyes on his, wanting him to believe the sincerity of her comment. "But I am curious. You said before that your father was financially ruined in that land deal. Did you acquire all this on your own?"

"A lot of it, but I wouldn't have a condo in this building if it hadn't been for a trust left to me by my mother. Her family were old wealthy Easterners, the kind who owned property in the Hamptons before it was trendy. She left her money to me, rather than Dad. I suspect she feared he might run afoul of some 'gold digger'—'' he smiled ''—and he did.''

Kate looked away. She wondered if their differing views of Joanna would always come between them. He'd turned to face her and kept staring at her as if she were some delectable item on a dessert cart. The Scotch infused her with warmth, or was it his nearness, his presence...?

He brought his fingers to her cheek, ostensibly to brush a strand of hair away, but Kate knew from the way they lingered that he simply wanted to touch her. And she wanted him to.

When he leaned over, she was ready. But instead of kissing her, he said, ''How about if I run a hot bath for you and show you your room?''

She stared at him. No one had run a bath for her since she was a toddler. But she nodded meekly and followed him down a hallway, the hardwood floor of which gleamed in the soft lighting from wall sconces.

''This is the guest room,'' he said, opening a door and flicking the light switch. ''I apologize for the decor. It's not my style, but I was too busy when I bought the place to do things myself. Had an interior decorator come in, as well as the wife of a close friend of mine, but the place needs the touch of a woman who's...well, connected to me.'' He looked down at Kate and lowered his voice. ''If you know what I mean.''

Her shrug was noncommittal. ''It looks okay to me.'' She scanned the room, its double four-poster bed and dresser set complemented by early-American accessories. ''That's a beautiful quilt. Handmade?''

''Yes, apparently. And antique,'' he added dismissively. ''There's an en suite bath through that door. You unpack your bag while I get it going for you.''

''Matt! Really, I can run my own bath.''

''You don't understand, Kate,'' he murmured. ''I want

to do it for you.'' Then he disappeared through the door and soon she heard water gushing from a tap. She wandered around the room, feeling slightly uncomfortable. Her style was more thrift shop with the rare splurge at a high-end chain store.

''Are you unpacked?'' he asked, returning.

She laughed, gesturing to her backpack still on the floor. ''I don't think that'll take long.''

''Then I'll leave you to it,'' he said. ''Are you sure you're okay? I know it'll take a while to get over the intrusion of that break-in, but do you feel better now?''

She bit down on her lower lip to stop its trembling. His caring was exactly what she'd needed, and that he'd provided it so spontaneously was even more moving. Especially in light of their parting two days ago. Turning away to pick up her backpack, she managed to say, ''Yes, thank you, Matt. You've been wonderful and I...I don't even know how I can ever thank you enough.''

He took the pack from her and dropped it onto the bed. Then he placed his forefinger on the end of her chin and turned her face toward him. ''I don't want you to thank me,'' he whispered. ''I want you to be safe and to feel safe—with me.'' He kissed her brow and said, ''It's not very late, but I think you need a good rest tonight. My room is right next door if you want anything. I have to fly to Toronto in the morning for an early meeting, but you sleep in. There's coffee, juice and breakfast-type food in the kitchen. I'll have the doorman get a cab for you—my treat,'' he added, smiling.

''I'll be fine and don't worry about the cab. I did bring my wallet,'' she joked. But the sense of vulnerability was beginning to surface again. ''I guess I'll be spending the day cleaning up. Officer Brady said she'd call in the afternoon to find out what's missing.'' She frowned suddenly, thinking of something.

"What is it?"

"The thing is, Matt, I've nothing worth stealing outside of my CD sound system and that was still there. Aren't burglars supposed to steal those things? And my TV-VCR was there, too. It doesn't make any sense."

"No, it doesn't," he agreed.

She watched his eyes crinkle in thought. He glanced at her quickly as if about to say something else, but then changed his mind. "Good night Kate" was all he said, and left the room.

After a long bath—to which some kind of herbal oil had been added—Kate dried herself with a thick, fluffy bath towel and crawled between crisp sheets. The type she'd seen in specialty magazines and only imagined sleeping in. She extinguished the bedside lamp and stretched out, thinking that in spite of her protestations otherwise, she could learn to feel comfortable around such luxury without a lot of effort.

The last thought she had before succumbing to sleep was that she hadn't told Matt she'd been to Limberlost. Nor had she mentioned Lance's midnight visit. A twinge of guilt nudged her, but she was too drowsy to listen.

FOOTSTEPS. THUDDING, shuffling, ominous ones closing in. At her bedside now. A presence. Someone hovering in the dark. Then a hand reaching down.

Kate shot up, choking, her gasps cutting the silence. Gradually the pounding in her head eased to a mere pulse, and her heaving chest slowed down. She turned on the light and looked at her watch. Only two o'clock. She'd been out for less than two hours, but the depth of the sleep had been almost as terrifying as the nightmare itself.

When she was a child, she'd gone through a phase of bedtime phobia. It had occurred after an abrupt move from the foster home she'd been placed in the longest period of time. She hadn't been afraid of dreams, but of dying in her sleep. Years later, she found out that the grandmother in that home had passed away in her sleep while Kate was still living there. The family had subsequently decided to move, and Kate had been sent to another foster home.

Tonight she felt as if she was eight years old again—the same heaviness in her limbs, the pulsing beat in her ears, the cold sweat trickling down her back. After half an hour, eyes sifting the black room for familiar reference points that weren't there, she threw back the sheet and padded across the floor to the door. Opened it to a ribbon of ghostly light cast by the moon through the panorama of windows in Matt's condo. There were no city noises up here in the clouds, she thought, missing them acutely. As ever-present and annoying as they could be, they were always a sign of life even in the dead of night. She hesitated in the doorway, peering at Matt's closed door a few feet away. Then she walked toward it.

MATT HANDED his boarding pass to the hostess and strode along the narrow walkway to the small Dash-7 that was taking him to Toronto. His mind wasn't linked to his body, which was still feverishly entwined with Kate's back in his bed.

When he buckled into his seat and gratefully accepted his first cup of coffee, he sank back, watching the last bits of sunrise fade into early-morning light as the plane soared toward the border. And his mind soared back to predawn. He closed his eyes and smiled, reliving the night visit.

What had awakened him was the rustling of sheets as she slid into bed beside him. He'd almost jumped out the other side until his brain kicked in, reminding him Kate was on the premises.

''I had a bad dream,'' she'd whispered, and he'd pulled her to him.

They'd lain still, hearts beating against each other, for several minutes until she'd raised her head and said, "You told me to let you know if I wanted anything."

"Yes?" he'd asked, sleep still clogging his synapses. Not getting her drift.

"I want to be with you. Here."

And still not tuning in he'd murmured dozily, "Sure," and nestled his face into the crown of her hair beside his on the pillow.

It was only when he felt the feathery sweep of her fingertips along his side, up across his bare chest to the hollow of his neck that he guessed what she'd come for.

"You sleep naked," she'd whispered, her tongue flicking at his ear.

Goose bumps rode up and down his spine. "Aah!" he'd groaned. Synapses now making a hit.

"Makes it easier," she'd continued, shifting beside him. There'd been a brief flurry of movement in the darkness and she was back, stretching alongside of him. Naked now herself.

Matt moaned.

"Sir?"

His eyes flew open. The hostess was standing next to his seat. "More coffee?" she asked with a perky smile.

How about a cold shower? he wanted to say, but settled on a quick no to get rid of her. He had to focus on the business meeting ahead of him, rather than the pleasures of the night. That Kate was an ardent and uninhibited lover was a special bonus. He knew he'd never find another woman like her. Not with her emotional balance, her unpretentious intelligence, her feistiness blended with a vulnerability that made him ache. All that with a body, skin and face Hollywood starlets spent a fortune to achieve. And breathtaking in bed.

He sighed. Could his life get any better? he wondered

until the first cloud appeared in his dreamy horizon. *Tom Andrews.*

The passenger warning prior to landing came on. No cell phone use now. He had to remember to call the FBI agent as soon as he was on the ground to make sure the surveillance was still on Kate. After the break-in, she needed it more than ever. And he wasn't going to try to conceal his relationship with her any longer. If Andrews didn't like it, too bad. The sooner he was free of the man, the better.

CHAPTER FOURTEEN

KATE UNLOCKED her apartment door, pushed it open and let her backpack drop. She felt the well of tears again, but knew there was no way she'd get the mess cleaned up if she sat around weeping all day. Thank goodness she'd had a solid jolt of coffee at Matt's.

When she'd finally rolled out of bed there it was almost nine. She hadn't even heard him leave. It was strange waking up alone in another person's home, but this morning she hadn't felt like an intruder. More like a regular guest. She'd giggled at the idea, liking it.

He'd thoughtfully left a note on the kitchen counter, informing her where things were located. And ending with what he'd loved best about their lovemaking, as well as what he'd like to do next time. She'd quickly folded up the note, as if someone might read it over her shoulder, and tucked it into her jeans pocket.

As usual, he'd thought of everything. He'd said to let the doorman know when she was coming down in the elevator and, like magic, a yellow cab had appeared. She'd been ushered into it as if she were a celebrity. Had the doorman winked? she asked herself as the cab pulled away. Maybe this was simply all part of Matt's regular routine.

She decided to hide that ugly thought away. For today she planned to cling to her dreamworld as long as possible. Although she saw some of it fading darn fast when she opened her apartment door.

By ten-thirty, she'd only finished her bedroom. She

stopped to take a break and have a cold drink. The day was going to be another scorcher and the air conditioner was already at max. The cool, clean altitude of Limberlost was beginning to look pretty good. Too bad she had to sell it, she thought. Then realized at once that somehow, without any analysis of the situation, she'd come to that inevitable decision.

There was a sudden loud knocking. Kate froze, hand still clutching her cranberry juice. *Get a grip, Reilly. Burglars don't knock.* She set the glass down and went to the door, opening it to a forty-something, plumpish and dark-haired woman who smiled broadly at Kate as if she were some long-lost relative.

"Hi!" Her rich voice boomed in the hallway. "Are you Kate Reilly?"

Kate nodded.

"I'm Maria da Costa," she said, extending a chubby hand. "Mr. Sinclair sent me."

"Sent you?"

"To help you with the cleaning. I'm his cleaning lady on Mondays and Fridays. He left a message on my machine this morning to ask if I could come here and give you a hand." She stepped into the room. "And you certainly can use it. What happened?"

"A break-in," Kate answered. Then stupidly added, "Today is Thursday."

The woman laughed. "Yes, it is. This is a special job, just for Mr. Sinclair." She winked at Kate. "Because he's so cute. Right?"

Kate knew her own smile was a bit stiff. She was beginning to feel as if she'd been swept up in a flash flood right into Matt's world. Still, the woman was here and looked able. Kate worked at the smile and said, "Come on in," although Maria had already deposited her satchel and was removing from it a large floral apron.

IT WAS LATE AFTERNOON by the time Matt had a chance to call Kate on his cellular. He'd been unable to raise Andrews on arriving at Pearson International in Toronto, but had left a message telling the agent to be sure to keep watching Kate's place.

Then he'd gone to his meeting, which had been successful, leaving him high and ready to fly out by lunchtime. Except that he'd been booked on a five o'clock flight and, due to lack of cancellations, had to kick his heels in downtown Toronto for several hours. The opportunity took him to a trendy shopping area where he impulsively bought a pale yellow satin negligee for Kate. Then, worried that she might consider the gift too seriously intimate, purchased a fluffy stuffed animal, as well.

When the saleslady had cheerfully asked, "Presents for the family?" he'd realized she was referring to the gifts separately, and the image that formed instantly in his mind gave him a warm glow inside. "Yes," he'd replied without hesitation. As he wandered around the shopping area, that vision of what could be overwhelmed him. That was the moment he knew he loved Kate Reilly enough to want to spend the rest of his life with her. It was a realization that both excited and frightened him.

He waited to call Kate until after an early check-in at Pearson because he'd wanted some privacy. She answered after the third ring, and his heart raced at the sound of her voice.

"It's me," he said, turning into a corner, away from the terminal's noise.

Her return hello was breathless and he clenched the phone. God, he could hardly wait to hold her in his arms, to tell her what he'd discovered.

"Where are you?" she asked.

"I'm still in Toronto, calling from the airport."

"Oh," she said, sounding disappointed.

"Listen, my plane leaves at five so I should get into JFK about six-thirty or so. I'll give you a call from there. Maybe we could have dinner…or something."

"Okay." Her voice picked up. "Matt, thank you so much for sending Maria over. She was fabulous. We got the place all fixed up." A quiet giggle. "It looks even better than it did before."

"That's great. Was there anything missing?"

A pause, then, "Nothing I can find. Strange, isn't it?"

"Yeah." A thought occurred to him that he didn't like. Maybe the burglar had been looking for something in particular to steal. "Have you talked to that police officer yet?"

"Uh-huh. She said it was peculiar, but that sometimes people don't notice things missing for several days—especially jewelry and other small things." She paused again. "But you know, I only own a few pieces of costume jewelry, and they all seem to be there."

Matt made a mental note to himself to get on to Andrews about it. But then he'd have to tell him about the Polaroid. Damn. His life was getting too complicated.

"She may have a point, though, Kate." In a lower voice, he asked, "Did you get my note this morning?"

"Yes." That breathlessness again. If only he were closer.

"You're amazing," he murmured. "And you know what I'm talking about." Just then a loudspeaker announced his boarding. "Listen, I've got to go. It won't be long. Till dinner?"

"For sure," she said.

"And Kate, I just want to say that I…I can hardly wait to see you again."

A brief silence and then, "Me, too."

He rang off and headed over to the boarding gate. He felt like he was walking on air.

KATE REPLACED the receiver. She sensed he'd been about to say something else. Something more meaningful than he could hardly wait to see her, but then she had to ask herself if she was ready for that. They were from such different worlds and their opinions of Joanna alone could be cause for argument. *Don't get all serious and analytical now, Reilly. Just get ready.*

Five o'clock. Time for a long bath and some pampering. The place did look great, she thought, going from room to room. Maria's help had made all the difference. At first, Kate had worried that she'd have to constantly tell the woman where to put things, but years of experience must have provided Maria with a good mix of logic and intuition.

The woman had told Kate she'd been working for Mr. Sinclair for three years. He was a wonderful, generous employer. That was it. Kate had almost been tempted to ask her questions, but recognizing the loyalty shown by Maria, had refrained. Still, she thought she'd detected a few sly glances every now and then, as if Maria were sizing her up. She hoped she passed inspection.

Just before Kate ran her bath, Carla called, all excited about qualifying for a basketball team at a local community recreation center. Kate congratulated her and arranged to meet her the day after next for a shopping expedition. When she hung up, she reflected how much the girl had changed over the past couple of weeks. A month ago she wouldn't have been caught dead near a community center—they're for geeks, she used to say—and now she was even talking up the possibility of summer camp next year.

That took Kate's thoughts around to Limberlost. It was already August, and September—and a decision—loomed. Her hand hovered above the telephone after she finished talking to Carla. Maybe she ought to phone Greg Collier right now and get it over with. Still, another visit there would be nice. The place was growing on her, despite her aversion to roughing it. Instead, she called Bill Tippett.

"No, everything's all right here and with Carla," she said at his first concerned question. "How're you guys doing? Oh, your wife's back. Kyle's moving back to Plattsburg to stay with his dad? Is he happy about that? Good. Sure, I'll ask Carla if he can write to her." She nodded, listening to him fill her in on local news as if she were now a local herself. It was a pleasant sensation.

"Bill—" her voice changed tone, as she decided to ask something that had been on her mind "—do you recall Joanna going up to Limberlost sometime in the year before she died? Maybe six months or so before?"

"Can't say about six months before—that woulda been round January, and I doubt she'd have driven up at that time of year. But she was here just about two months before. Guess about first of May or so," he said. "Why?"

"When Lance came to get her things, he said she'd been there. When she was there in May, did she go to your place to put anything in her boxes?" she asked, thinking of the letter Lance had been raving about.

"Nope." A slight pause. "But she went into the shed and took somethin' out of one of the boxes."

"*Out?* You're sure?"

"Sure as I have a mortgage payment tomorrow. Saw her myself, though she did it real quick like, as if she didn't want me to notice. Don't know why she'd care 'cause they were her boxes, anyhow, but Joanna always loved a little drama in her life."

Kate smiled. "Yes, I've a feeling she did. And, Bill, I may want to come back up there for a few days—before September. Can I just give you twenty-four hours' notice or something so you can get the generator and propane going for me? Ah, you're sweet. Okay, talk to you when I've picked a date."

And she already had one in mind, she thought as she hung up. But not a calendar date. She headed for the bathroom and the tub, anticipation about seeing Matt again increasing with each minute and completely overshadowing the information about Joanna and the letter.

MATT PRACTICALLY LEAPT over the railing after clearing Customs. He'd purchased a bottle of expensive champagne at the duty free, and the officer on duty, who must have had a boring day, insisted on performing a baggage inspection for no apparent reason. But experience with various Customs people in various countries had taught Matt argument and anger would only lengthen the process. So he gritted his teeth, dashing out into the main terminal as soon as he could to hail a cab.

En route into the city, he suddenly decided to call Paula. If he had a light day tomorrow, maybe he could take it off. Last time he'd done that—he didn't count Joanna's funeral as a day off since he'd been working for Andrews—had been the day he'd driven to Limberlost. He hated to call Paula at home—it was almost seven—but had to know now so he could plan for the evening. Then he'd call the Ritz, see if he could get reservations.

He took his cell phone out of his briefcase and tapped in his secretary's number.

"Hi, Paula, it's Matt. No, everything's fine. Yup. Great meeting. Went smoothly and successfully, I might add." He laughed. "Yeah, another good Christmas bonus shaping up. Can you do me a favor? Can you remember if I had anything important tomorrow? No? Hey, great. I was thinking of taking a day off. No, I'm not sick. Just that something's come up." Matt's eyes flicked to the rearview mirror where the cabbie was looking and grinning.

"Nope, something good. Okay, thanks. What's that? A security check? No, I don't know anything about it. Not me. Maybe one of the associates ordered it. Why don't you look into it tomorrow? Okay then, bye.''

As he replaced the phone in his case, he remembered that he still had to call Andrews. But that would have to wait. They were already in SoHo.

SHE'D JUST STEPPED OUT of the tub when her door buzzer rang. Shades of the last time he was here, she thought. The man always seems to be early, and why hadn't he called as he'd said he would? Drying herself on the way to the intercom, she simply pressed the buzzer to let him in. Then she dashed back to the bathroom to get her robe, tying it up as he knocked.

Unlatching the chain, she had a horrible thought that she ought to have checked to see who was at the door, rather than assume it was Matt. As the chain dropped and the dead bolt unsnapped, the door was pushed open from the other side.

Kate fell back, her hand reaching out to slam the door. But Lance Marchant was standing in the way.

''Lance! What are you doing here?''

''At least I didn't break in this time.''

''That isn't funny,'' she said, drawing her robe sash tighter.

''I've got to talk to you, Kate.'' He charged into the center of the room without another word.

She closed the door reluctantly. Hard to act tough in a bathrobe. ''I'm just going to change, okay?''

''No, don't bother. I won't be long,'' he said as he began to weave frenetically back and forth around the furniture.

It was then that Kate noticed how awful he looked. His hair was disheveled and his eyes ringed with dark pouches. She was certain his clothes were the same ones he'd worn the night he came to Limberlost, and his face sported a two-day beard. It was the face that troubled her. Chalky, lined with fatigue.

"I've gone through those boxes," he said, riffling his hair as he paced, "and found nothing. I'm at the end of my rope, Kate, in more ways than one."

"You haven't found the letter," she said flatly.

He gave her a blank look as if he didn't have a clue what she was talking about. Then his expression shifted. "Right," he mumbled. "No letter." A sudden harsh laugh. "No letter." He plunked down onto the sofa and lowered his face into his cupped palms.

Kate stared, wide-eyed. "Lance," she finally said, trying to sound calm and rational, "what's the big deal? The letter's been hidden somewhere for ages. It's not going to surface now. What does it matter?"

When he raised his face, his eyes were haunted. "It does matter. In fact it *is* a matter of life and death." His laugh ended in a half sob. "I'm here to beg you. Do you have anything at all of Joanna's I could look through? Anything she might have sent you or told you about?"

"Lance, you're not making any sense. Why would I have that letter?"

"Forget the letter!" he shouted. "I don't care about the goddamn letter. There *is* no letter."

Kate froze, barely registering what he'd shouted. Matt would be arriving any moment. How could she get rid of Lance in the state he was in? She decided on the straight approach.

"Look, I've been getting ready to go out. You've got to explain yourself or leave."

That sobered him. "Someone has been blackmailing me. About a fraud case I was involved in years ago. It's been going on awhile now and I have to get out of it. Especially with my election race coming up."

Kate sat down on the edge of a chair. "Did this case involve Matt Sinclair's father?"

He looked sharply at her, his eyes narrowing unpleasantly. "You know about that?"

Disconcerted, she turned her face away. "A bit," she said, downplaying it now, unsure what his reaction would be. "Only that his father and you and some other men were under investigation."

"What else did he tell you?"

She shrugged. "Not much. He thought his father had been set up by you and the others. He suspected Joanna was in it, too."

He snorted. "Joanna wouldn't have stooped so low. She had class, in spite of what some people might say about her. She had class," he repeated. His voice drifted off as if he'd gone into some reverie.

About Joanna, Kate guessed. She checked the time. Almost seven. She had to get him out of her place. "Lance, how about if you call me tomorrow? Let me know exactly what you're looking for and...and I can help."

"How can you help? No one can help. And I don't really know what I'm looking for, anyway." He paused on his way to the door. "That's the irony. All I know is, Joanna had found something connected to the land deal. Just before she died." He slouched toward the door, stopping again as he opened it. "That's all I know." And then he left.

His last words ricocheted in her head, their similarity to Matt's flashing like neon warning signs.

Without thinking, she ran after him down the stairs. She caught up to him, breathlessly, as he was about to get into his car parked in front of her house.

"Wait! There may be something."

Lance turned around, his grim face brightening. "What? You've remembered something?"

And then some instinct warned her off. His response was

too eager, too hungry. Had his eruption upstairs been a performance? Kate sensed it was neither wise nor safe to let him know that Joanna had contacted Matt before she died. Clutching at a reply, she said the first thing that popped into her head.

"I…I was talking to Bill Tippett today and he said Joanna went to Limberlost in May. I…I asked him—you know—if she'd put something into the boxes in his shed, but he said no, he thought she'd taken something out. Don't you see? Whatever it was, it could have been what you're looking for."

His body seemed to sag, though she couldn't say if it was relief. "I haven't found it," he protested.

"But it's got to be somewhere. Look again."

He moved toward her and she stepped back, remembering his instability moments ago. "You're right," he said, his face unexpectedly breaking into one of his politician smiles. "I should look again. And I will. I guess I just haven't been looking in the right places."

He stood in front of her, so close she could smell the stale odor of alcohol. She would have pulled back, but he grasped her hands and held them. Then he reached up a palm to her cheek, brushed it lightly.

"I wish things had turned out differently, Kate. I truly do. Don't forget that." He walked toward his car, opened the door and climbed in.

She stayed on the sidewalk until the sedan disappeared, fearful he might come back. Then shivering, she ran back into the house.

WHEN THE TAXI PULLED OVER to the curb partway down the street from Kate's, Matt reached inside his suit jacket pocket for his billfold. He was thumbing through it when the cabbie murmured, "Will ya lookit that."

"Hmm?" Matt peered up at the rearview mirror, but the

driver was facing ahead. Matt looked in the same direction
and saw Lance Marchant stumbling down the front stairs
of Kate's row house. He squinted against the sun, low in
the sky.

"Is that guy drunk or what?" the cabbie muttered.

Matt leaned forward, staring over the man's shoulder.
Then his heart skipped a beat. Kate, wearing nothing but
the skimpy robe she'd been in the other night, was running
after Lance, trying to stop him.

"Uh-oh," said the cabbie. "A domestic scene. This may
get interestin'."

Matt opened his mouth to say something but instantly
thought better of it. Besides, he couldn't move, every cell
in his body frozen in disbelief.

Kate seemed to be trying to convince Marchant of something. But what?

"Now look—" the driver was still into his running com-
mentary "—she's begging him not to leave, but he's not
havin' it. Oh, see." He pointed through the windshield.
"Now she's sayin' somethin' he likes 'cause he's suddenly
all smiles. Hey—" he craned his neck to grin at Matt
"—there's gonna be a happy endin', after all. See? He's
holding her hands and brushing her tears away. He's drivin'
off now, but you can tell she's not unhappy anymore."

And Matt, his stomach churning, watched Kate skip back
into her house.

The cabbie shook his head. "Thank goodness. For a minute, I was afraid there was gonna be a tragedy or somethin'.
Know what I mean?"

Not getting a response, he craned his neck around again,
his eyes sharpening. "You gettin' out here or what?"

Matt swallowed a mouthful of bile. He shook his head,
waited, then said, "No, I've changed my mind." And he
gave the driver his office address, knowing he couldn't yet
face walking back into his condo. Not until his head had

cleared and he'd managed to figure out what he'd just witnessed.

AN HOUR AFTER MATT was supposed to arrive, Kate decided he wasn't going to. She got ready for bed, thinking even if he was simply late, she wasn't up for going out on the town. Especially after the scene with Lance. By the time it got dark, Kate knew she'd been stood up. A sense of helplessness added to her mental inertia. She realized she didn't even have Matt's phone number and therefore couldn't ease her fears that something might have happened to him. Except that he could have called her, couldn't he?

When she finally gave up all hope of seeing him, Kate had a bowl of cereal as a makeshift supper and went to bed at midnight, her mind swarming with Lance's rave about the letter—no, not a letter—and her unsatisfied stomach rumbling. As for the dull ache centered in her very being, only sleep could ease that pain.

MATT SAT AT HIS DESK, head propped up on his elbows as he stared at the telephone. Several times he'd lifted the receiver to call Kate, and each time, he'd plunked it down. No matter how he tried to work the little drama he—and the cabbie—had seen, he couldn't come up with a logical explanation for why Marchant and Kate would be out on the street with Kate in her night wear, for God's sake, acting out some quarrel. The aura of intimacy was what had stunned him.

Or had he been too influenced by the cabbie's take on the scene? Now he wasn't so sure. It was already nine o'clock and she must have assumed he wasn't coming. He hated himself for his cowardice, but so many doubts had been scattered into the air between him and Kate he was at a loss as to his next step. When the phone rang, he jumped at it.

Tom Andrews. Matt's stomach sank. "Yeah," he muttered.

"Sittin' on the phone, were ya?" Andrews gave a little chuckle. "Been tryin' to get hold of you, Sinclair. You got your cell turned off? Finally thought I'd better try your office."

Matt sat back in his chair. "Yeah, I…uh, have a bit of work to do."

"Got your message about Kate Reilly's surveillance. Good thing we kept it on 'cause my man saw an interesting number between her and Marchant tonight. Right out on the street. He said it was like watchin' TV."

Matt chomped down on his lower lip. He knew what was coming and hated having to sit and be quiet about it. Andrews was goading him. He held his tongue, refusing to be drawn into the agent's weird notion of fun.

"Somethin' between those two, I bet. Gotta be. Tonight's episode confirms it for me. Especially after Marchant's detour to that lodge of hers."

"What? What are you talking about?"

"The night before she came home to find her place had been burgled. She'd been up at that resort she inherited from Barnes. Marchant was there, too."

Matt went for the bait. "How do you know that?"

"We had a guy on Marchant at this candidates' meeting in some joint outside Plattsburg. The tail lost him afterward, but it didn't matter 'cause we put a tracer on Marchant's car. Just had to sit back and watch a computer screen. He went to the lodge, stayed a couple hours, then made a detour to a place outside Bondi where he stopped briefly. After that, he drove back here for an early-morning meeting with Gallini."

"At the bar?"

"Nah, they got a new place, but it don't matter because we can follow Marchant wherever he goes." Andrews paused. "So far, we haven't been able to bug their new meeting place 'cause it's some deserted cargo shed on Roosevelt Island. Owned by a numbered company that will most likely be traced back to Gallini."

Matt was hooked now. "Do you have any idea why Marchant was at Kate's?"

"Not really. Few hunches. We know from old tapes that Gallini and Marchant have been looking for whatever Barnes had on them." He paused. "Y'know, I can't figure how Reilly's connected. I mean, she's gotta be. Why else would Marchant be hanging around? And before he and Gallini had clued in on our taping, they talked about her a couple times. Almost as if they were worried about her. She's gotta know somethin'."

Matt bit down on his tongue. Now was the moment to reveal the information about the Polaroid photo. But he hated turning Kate's fate over to a guy like Andrews when he knew he could look after her so much better. *Yeah, like you're doing now. Leaving her all alone. Suspecting the worst without giving her a chance to explain. Isn't that what she's done to you? Now you're going to pay her back in kind?* A wave of self-loathing engulfed him.

"You still there?" Andrews was asking.

"Uh, yeah. So, anything else?"

"Not yet. Let's play this one by ear, see what turns up next. I know Marchant left there empty-handed. Seems Reilly doesn't have whatever he's looking for."

Matt tightened his grip on the receiver. "How do you know that?"

"Oops." Andrews laughed. "I'm givin' away the trade secrets here. Reilly's place was clean, that's how."

Realization was sinking in. Matt's stomach churned again. "You were responsible for that break-in!"

"Well, not me personally. A couple of our guys who were too impatient to get a warrant."

Matt squeezed the receiver, picturing Andrews short, thick neck in its place. After a long, painful moment he managed to ask, "Why did you have to do that? *Why?*"

Andrews heaved a loud sigh, as if annoyed at such a naive question. "Just exploring all the angles, Sinclair. Too many people interested in that gal. Including you," he stressed. "My advice to you is, stay clear for a few days. If Gallini and Marchant are going to make a move—with or without Reilly—I don't want them seein' you and gettin' spooked off. Got it?" The line went dead.

Matt slammed the receiver down. His association with Andrews was already jeopardizing any chance at making peace with Kate. If she found out the truth of the break-in and thought he'd known all along, she'd never forgive him. And he could hardly blame her. *Thank God I didn't tell Andrews about the photo. The man would do anything to anyone to get what he wanted and damn the consequences. No way am I going to entrust Kate's safety to that creep.*

He checked the time. After midnight. She'd be asleep. Tomorrow, he thought. I'll explain everything, including the photo. His only hope was that she'd be willing to listen.

CHAPTER FIFTEEN

KATE SURRENDERED to insomnia by daybreak, crawling out of bed to watch the sunrise. The sleeplessness had given her plenty of time to think. Not that she wanted to think about why Matt hadn't come or even called.

Later, she'd gone over and over Lance's visits, both last night and at the lodge. He'd been searching for something to do with the land swindle. To stop a blackmailer, he'd said, which fit with Matt's assertion that Lance had been a participant in the fraud. Both Lance and Matt had claimed that Joanna had found something regarding the case. Matt believed that whatever that something had been, it would have cleared his father's name. Lance's panic obviously stemmed from fear that whatever Joanna had discovered would implicate him and cost him votes in the coming election.

Kate ran the tip of her forefinger along her upper lip, lost in thought. What was it Joanna had found? More important, and the idea was taking alarming shape in her mind, did it have anything to do with her death?

She sighed, lowering her forehead onto her hands. Lack of sleep had brought on a headache. She thought of Lance again, wondering what had become of him after he'd roared away last night. Her mind touched down briefly on Matt. There was no way she was going to sit around and mope. It was only eight-thirty. A good time for a brisk walk in the city, before the heat of the day kicked in. Fresh air and exercise would not only help her headache, but halt any further self-torture about Matt Sinclair.

Kate bustled around, preparing for a long walk. Her destination was yet unknown. Someplace away from her apartment was the only requirement. About to leave, she made an impulsive decision and called information to get Lance Marchant's campaign office phone number.

The woman who answered was vague about his whereabouts. He hadn't been in and she didn't know when he would be. She refused to give out his home phone number and suggested Kate try his office. When Kate hung up, she knew where her morning walk was going to take her.

She grabbed a water bottle and strapped a fanny pack around her waist. Carefully locking up, she left the building, stopping outside to consider her options. Lance's office, according to Matt, was in the same high-rise as Greg Collier's—in Midtown near the New York Public Library, just off Avenue of the Americas. She'd take the subway partway and exit a few blocks short of Forty-second Street.

About a hundred feet from her front door, she noticed a small buff-colored car parked at the curb. There was a man sitting behind the wheel reading a newspaper. Kate stopped beside the car and pulled up her sock. Was it her imagination or had that same car been outside her place, parked in different spots, for the past few days? As she stood up, she quickly glanced inside, noticing a lot of debris littering the seats. The man lowered his newspaper suddenly, staring directly at her with a curious expression that reminded her she was being nosy. She waved a few fingers and continued on to the subway.

"DON'T TELL ME you've been here all night!"

Matt opened his eyes and sat up. He groaned. The sofa in his office looked great, but was no substitute for a bed.

Paula was standing in the doorway connecting her office to his, her arms akimbo and a frown on her face.

"I thought you were taking the day off. Are you okay? Is everything all right?"

Matt perched on the edge of the sofa, rubbing his face. "I'm fine, Paula, thanks. I may stick around here for part of the day, but consider me absent for any real work. I've got too many other more pressing demands." He stood up, stretching and yawning. Noticing the alarm in her face, he quickly reassured her. "It's okay, really. Personal issues, not business ones."

She smiled and said she'd be back with coffee. Matt headed for his private bathroom to wash his face and brush his teeth. He'd shower at his condo before seeing Kate. When Paula returned, he was already behind his desk, the telephone receiver in his hand.

"Thanks, Paula, I appreciate it. Say," he said, "let me know if you find out anything about that security check and why it was ordered."

Paula nodded and left, closing the door behind her. Matt punched in Kate's phone number and waited, sipping the hot brew. When the answering service came on, he hung up, deciding a message wasn't be appropriate under the circumstances. Checking his watch, he saw that it was just after nine. She must be in the shower, he thought. He'd try again later.

He decided to finish his summary of yesterday's meeting for Paula before leaving and was working at it when Paula opened his door.

"I know you don't want to be bugged, but a man called Tom Andrews said he'd come down here personally to talk to you if you didn't take his call."

Matt sighed. He dropped his pen onto the desk. "Okay, Paula."

"He's on line one. By the way, I talked to security, and

as far as they know, the alarm system is fine. No one seems to know who ordered the inspection.''

"Right, thanks, Paula." Matt picked up the receiver.

"How about turning your cell phone on, buddy," Andrews complained. "I've been trying to get hold of you."

"What is it, Andrews?" He was still ticked off at the man after his admission to Kate's break-in.

"No need to get testy. Just thought you might be interested to know that Miss Reilly has spotted our tail."

"What do you mean?"

"She walked right up to the car and waved at the guy. Cheeky."

Matt muttered an expletive under his breath. "So now what?"

"Just checkin' to see if you were the one told her she was under surveillance."

"I didn't tell her, though frankly, I wish I had."

Andrews chuckled. "My, my. Developing a conscience, are we? The thing is, there's no point in keeping the guy parked outside her place if she knows he's there."

"Don't pull him off," Matt said. "Be reasonable. She's still at risk."

"I'm beginning to think she's more at risk from you than Marchant and Gallini."

Matt swore aloud this time, telling Andrews what would happen to him personally if any harm came to Kate. "Why don't you change cars, for God's sake?" he added, making a last pitch.

"Not worth the expense, Sinclair. We've got men on Gallini's warehouse on Roosevelt Island and other places I can't tell you about. Except for some interesting scenarios with Marchant, the watch on Reilly turned up very little. As I said yesterday, the guys who tossed her place found zip.''

"Maybe they just didn't know what they were looking for," Matt mumbled.

"What's that supposed to mean?"

But Matt hung up, too upset to spend another word on the man. When the telephone button started flashing, he pressed the intercom to Paula.

"If that guy Andrews calls back, tell him I've left. And I really will be leaving, Paula, as soon as I make one more call."

When he got Kate's answering service again, Matt knew he had to leave some kind of message. Especially since her place was no longer being watched.

"Kate," he said, his voice precise but urgent, "this is very important. The Polaroid photo that we were looking at in your scrapbook is what I think Joanna was referring to. The man talking to Marchant in the picture is Vincent Gallini, and he's under investigation right now." He hesitated, then said, "I'm sorry I didn't tell you about it sooner, but I thought you'd be safer not knowing how important it is. I'm at work now and leaving for my condo any second. Call me there as soon as you get this message." He rattled off his number and hung up, grabbing his suit jacket on his way out the door.

LANCE MARCHANT'S secretary looked almost as harassed as her boss had been when Kate had last seen him. She politely but firmly told Kate that Mr. Marchant was unavailable and refused to say whether he was on the premises or not. Kate wouldn't leave a message.

Did she want Lance turning up at her place again? No. What she wanted was to talk to him in person in some neutral place and find out exactly what he knew about Joanna, the land swindle and Matt's father. She was tired of having only bits and pieces of the story.

Waiting for the elevator, Kate saw Greg Collier with a

group of men heading her way, but he abruptly turned around and headed in the other direction. Her elevator came and she stepped on, wondering if the lawyer had purposely avoided her. She couldn't imagine why and decided she was being as paranoid as Lance Marchant had been lately.

Out on the pavement, Kate realized that, even if her visit had proved fruitless, she'd had a chance to get some exercise and most of all, to get out of her apartment. She wandered toward the subway, prolonging the return home and the inevitable waiting by the telephone she knew she would do. If Matt had been upset about something last night, surely he'd have phoned first thing in the morning to clear the air.

Window shopping, browsing through a couple of bookstores and a lunch at an outdoor café filled hours that Kate knew would otherwise have been spent tormenting herself about why Matt wasn't calling. It was after two by the time she got back. When she walked toward the entrance to her row house, she scanned the parked cars on both sides of the street, but the buff-colored car was gone. *See? Another example of your growing paranoia.*

She purposely didn't check her messages until she'd showered and changed. There were two hang-ups and then Matt's baritone voice filled the room. Kate tightened her grip on the receiver and listened, with mounting anxiety, to Matt's message. When it finished, she replayed it, making sure she'd heard every word. Then she played it a third time, ensuring she understood what he was saying.

She pressed Save and hung up. Her hands were trembling. She wasn't certain what his information meant to her personally, but the urgency in his voice was both scary and annoying. If this photograph was so important, why hadn't he said so days ago when he'd first seen it? Why hadn't he been waiting here for her to tell her in person?

Kate called the number he'd left at once, but after the

third ring hung up, deciding to try to reach him in person. Then she headed to the bedroom to get her scrapbook. It wasn't in her closet. Thinking it had been stolen during the break-in, she was about to call the police when she remembered.

She'd taken it with her to Limberlost. Carla had been looking at it in the car on the way home. Kate searched her memory, but couldn't recall seeing the scrapbook since. Carla must have taken it home with her.

Fumbling at the telephone buttons, she finally got through to Rita. Carla was at the rec center and wasn't expected home until dinner. Was it an emergency? Kate hastily said no. Could Rita ask Carla if she had Kate's scrapbook and call her back when she got home?

Kate tried Matt's number again without success. She paced the living room, her frustration increasing with each footstep. The impact of Matt's message was starting to hit her. Especially knowing that Joanna had had the same picture. Kate plunked down into the canvas-back chair, drumming her fingertips on its wooden arm-rest. She had to resurrect as much of that last day as she could. She closed her eyes, trying to relax and let memory take charge....

"I'm leaving tomorrow," Joanna unexpectedly said as Kate was about to dive off the raft and swim to shore. And she must have seen the shock and letdown in Kate's eyes because she quickly added, *"I have to go, love, because I've a chance at a job in Manhattan. It just came up, through a friend of mine. He's driving up here tomorrow."*

She reached a long, tanned arm to Kate. "Come on, no pouting. Remember our promise? I'll send you the first card on your birthday. August 15, right?"

Kate nodded, fighting the tears.

"Why don't you come say goodbye? Meet me in the parking lot behind the main lodge about ten." She laughed.

"An ungodly hour, but there you are. I can't afford to turn down the job."

Kate felt the sting of tears. She remembered swimming blindly back to shore and racing to her cabin, throwing herself on her bunk-bed and weeping. The rest of that day was still a blur, but she could see herself approaching the parking lot the next morning. The heat and reflected glare from the row of cars had her squinting, shielding her eyes with her cupped hand.

"Kate," Joanna called. "We're over here."

She was leaning against a dark-colored car, parked at an angle away from the others, just inside the wooden gates that opened to the gravel road leading to the lodge. A man in a short-sleeved shirt and long pants was standing very close to her, holding something up to her face. When Kate got closer, she saw that he was lighting a cigarette for her.

Joanna straightened and waved to Kate. "Come and meet my friend," she said as she tucked her free arm through the man's.

"Kate, this is Jim. And this," she said with a grand sweep of her other arm, cigarette still in hand, "is the very special Kate Reilly all the way from New York City."

He was handsome, Kate thought, but old. He couldn't be Joanna's boyfriend. But his handshake was friendly and his smile welcoming.

"Darling," Joanna said to him, "I've got to say goodbye to someone in the kitchen," and she'd swayed toward the back door of the lodge.

Kate and the man watched her until she disappeared through the screen door. Then he went to the rear of the car and raised the trunk. Kate peered around, noticing luggage that must belong to Joanna. Just then someone called out and Kate realized, for the first time, that another car was parked near the gate.

She couldn't understand how she could have missed it

because it was a long, shiny limousine. Two men got out of it, one blond, the other dark and kind of chubby. The blond man called again, asking where Joanna had gone. Jim sauntered toward them and stood chatting.

Curious to see a limousine up close, Kate meandered over. It was a beautiful car. She approached from the front and saw a man sitting behind the steering wheel. A real live chauffeur in a hat and uniform. She moved to the driver's side to get a better look, bending her head to the open window. The chauffeur turned to her and said, "Get lost."

Before she straightened, Kate noticed a man crouched in a corner of the back seat. He had a black mustache and messy gray hair. He was wearing a suit and she thought he must have been hot. He looked sick, too, pale and sweaty. His small eyes darted at her with an expression in them that troubled her.

The chauffeur rolled up the window, shooing her away with his hand. When Kate stepped back, she thought she saw one of the two men talking to Jim at the rear of the car move toward her. But just then Joanna came out the lodge door and everyone looked at her.

She was beautiful with her raven hair and deep blue eyes, Kate thought.

"All set?" Joanna asked Jim when she reached the limo.

"Aren't you driving with us?" the blond man asked.

"No, I told you I was going with Jim. I didn't even know you guys were coming."

"Treat yourself to an air-conditioned ride. You can sit up front with Tony," said the chubby man.

"No way. I'm going with my new guy." And she took hold of Jim's hand and gave him a dazzling smile. Suddenly looking at Kate, she said, "There you are. Come, Jim's going to take our picture, aren't you, darling? One for Kate and one for me."

Kate followed them back to the other car, waiting as Jim retrieved a Polaroid camera from the back seat.

"Where shall we take it, Kate?" Joanna asked. "Near the limo, so you'll be able to see it in the background?"

And Kate, disappointed that Joanna had chosen not to ride in the limo when she had a chance, nodded eagerly. Joanna grabbed her hand and they walked a few feet from where Jim was standing, swinging their arms together as they moved. Just like real girlfriends, Kate thought.

They stood close together for the two pictures, Joanna's arm draped across Kate's shoulders. She couldn't remember the last time she'd felt so happy. Then Joanna leaned down. "I won't forget. Nineteen years from now." And kissed Kate on the cheek.

Joanna waved to the two men who were getting into the limo and climbed into Jim's car, which rolled toward the gate. She turned around once inside the car and was still waving at Kate when it drove onto the gravel road, followed by the limousine.

It was the last time she'd seen Joanna Barnes in person. And the man she'd driven off with, Kate realized now, had been Matt Sinclair's father.

WHEN MATT FAILED to reach Kate a second time from his condo, he showered and, passing his king-size bed, mused wistfully that the last time he'd been in it, Kate had been with him. The bed was still unmade, because Maria had left a message on his voice mail to say she wouldn't be in, her son was sick. Matt sprawled on it, breathing in the lingering delicate scent of Kate, reminiscent of tropical flowers.

His eyelids closed. A short catnap, he thought, will get me revved for the rest of the day. And just before dozing off, he reached over to yank the phone cord from its jack, not wanting Tom Andrews to intrude on his much-needed sleep. When he awoke, it was noon. He plugged the phone in, brewed a cup of coffee and tried Kate again, hanging up before her voice mail picked up.

Matt hated not having something to do. He wasn't the type to relax with a good book unless it was on the sundeck of a yacht and someone like Kate was lying beside him. Not someone *like* Kate, he amended his fantasy. But *Kate*. After the other night, he couldn't imagine being with another woman.

He was restless, consumed by his need to be with her, to explain what had driven him away last night. The scene with Marchant had played in his head for hours. There must be dozens of explanations for what he'd seen, he concluded, but the one he'd been influenced by had been the cabbie's. Surely the woman he loved deserved better than that.

KATE KNEW SHE WAS BEING foolhardy, but she also knew that only Lance Marchant would be able to answer her questions. If he wasn't at his office or campaign headquarters, she figured he might be at the bar. He might have gone there to meet with Gallini. She decided she would simply leave a message for Lance to contact her. *How risky could that be?*

This time, the stares of the bar's all-male patrons didn't deter her from inquiring about Lance. The man behind the bar was the same one who'd said he didn't know Lance when she was last there. But Kate now knew all of that was a lie.

She walked straight up to the bar, placed an order for iced coffee and asked to leave a message for Lance Marchant.

The man raised an eyebrow but only said, "Latte or espresso?"

"Latte," Kate said. "I also said I'd like to leave a message for Lance Marchant. I know he may come by here today."

"Like I said the other day, miss, I don't know any Lance Marchant. Now, do you want that coffee or not?"

What she wanted was to grab him by the collar of his flashy Hawaiian shirt. "If you want to continue this charade, that's fine with me. Yes, I do still want the iced latte, and please tell Lance to call Kate Reilly as soon as possible. It's urgent."

He shrugged and went about making the drink. After he handed it to her and took the money, he disappeared into the kitchen area behind the bar. Kate took the iced coffee to a vacant table and, ignoring the smirks of some of the customers who'd been listening in, sipped slowly.

She wanted to find Lance to talk to him about Joanna. How could she have gone on, even years later, to marry someone who'd been implicated or, worse, might have been a key player in the swindle? Someone who had led to her husband's downfall. Not possible, Kate decided. Joanna couldn't have been so cold-blooded or hungry for money or power.

It only made sense if Lance was more of an unwilling partner. She recalled the bizarre things he'd said and his behavior. The midnight trip to Bill Tippett's shed to get those boxes. His frantic and erratic manner at her place the other day. *No one can help. I wish things had turned out differently.* These were not the threats of an evil person. Not even the mutterings of a madman. More like the despair of a man who'd given up.

Kate finished her drink. She'd exhausted all of her ideas and now had nothing to do but go home and wait. Wait for people to call or come around. On her way out the door, she turned around once to see if the bar man had returned from the kitchen, but he hadn't. Hopefully he'd get the message to Lance.

She stepped out into the glare and heat of late afternoon. Almost four and the sun had no intention of giving the citizens of New York a reprieve. Kate walked toward the subway, but had to stop for a light at the first intersection beyond the bar. The very same corner, she realized, where she'd tripped over the baby stroller and seen Lance Marchant. The place where Tom Andrews had stopped in his white van. She scanned the parked cars. No white van today.

The light changed and she stepped off the curb. A car shot out of nowhere, squealing to a stop inches from her. A black limo. The rear door swung open and Lance Marchant staggered out. He clutched onto the door handle and said, "We have to talk, Kate."

CHAPTER SIXTEEN

LANCE DIDN'T LOOK WELL, Kate thought. His gray face was waxen, and his eyes were bloodshot and furtive.

"Please, Kate. Get in."

She glanced down at the limo's tinted windows but all she saw was a shadowy reflection of herself. "All right, Lance. Maybe you could give me a ride home."

He cracked a weak smile and opened the door wider.

Kate stooped down to get in and was pushed from behind by Lance onto the single seat facing the rear of the car. She realized too late that there was another passenger sitting directly opposite.

He filled up all of the corner and a good part of the middle seat. Although his hair was gray, his large florid face was relatively unlined. He was a big man, and his white-shirted belly swelled over his waist onto his lap. Unaffected by the heat wave because the air-conditioning was going full blast, he wore a two-piece navy-blue pin-striped suit. His thick black eyebrows were drawn together and he didn't look friendly.

Lance climbed into the other corner seat and slammed the door behind him. The limo pulled into the traffic.

"Lance? What's going on?" Kate asked, her eyes flicking from the big man to Lance.

The stranger waved a hand at Lance, shutting him up. "This is what's going on, Miss Reilly. We're going to your place to pick up your scrapbook."

"Who are you?"

The man smiled. It was a reptilian smile, Kate thought, if there could be such a thing. Slow-moving and predatory.

"Vincent Gallini," he said. "And now the formalities are done with, I will tell you what I expect. When we arrive at your apartment, we will go quietly inside without attracting any kind of attention. You will give us the scrapbook and we will leave—quietly. It will be simple and quick. It all depends on you."

The smile vanished and he narrowed his eyes at her, daring her to protest. She didn't. But she turned to Lance and said, "I've been trying to find you all day. Why are you here with him?"

"*Him?*" Gallini drawled, his voice breaking into a hoarse chuckle. "You talkin' about *me?* That's rich."

"I was speaking to Lance."

"And *I* speak for Mr. Marchant here," Gallini snapped. "I tell him when to talk and what to say."

Color climbed into Lance's face. "Kate," he said, "it's best to simply do what Vincent says. That way, no one will be hurt."

The possibility of being hurt, rather than merely inconvenienced, registered in a sobering instant. Kate risked a glance at Gallini, who gave a tight smile.

"Exactly what I was going to tell you to say, Lance." He cocked his head at Kate. "I hope you got it all?"

Her throat and chest were constricted. She nodded and stared down at her hands, folded together on her lap. She wondered what they would do when they found out she didn't have the scrapbook.

MATT WAS ON HIS WAY OUT the door to go to Kate's place when the phone rang. After he listened to Paula's message, he wished he'd kept on walking out the door.

No one at the office had ordered the security check, she'd said. And the firm's own security people had subsequently checked the premises, discovering a "bug" on Matt's office telephone. When Matt learned that his was the only telephone bugged, he also knew he had to call Andrews.

"Figures," Andrews said when Matt finally tracked him down. "I'm sitting out here on Roosevelt Island and nothin'—absolutely nothin'—is happening. So what this means is that Gallini is on to you. And how'd he find that out? From your very own Miss Reilly."

Matt had already figured that out. What got his blood pressure soaring was that now Gallini knew about the Polaroid. *And where the hell was Kate?*

"You still there, Sinclair?"

"Yeah. What about putting a tail on Kate now?"

A pause. "What's the point? Is she more at risk now than half an hour ago?"

Matt licked his dry lips and massaged his temple with his free hand. The headache that had begun when he'd learned about the security check had increased tenfold. "She might be."

"Oh? Why's that?"

Andrew's voice was still calm, but Matt heard the added edge. "Uh, because she has something I think Gallini's been looking for. A Polaroid photo taken nineteen years ago—the summer Joe Levin disappeared—with Marchant, Gallini and a third man who appears to be Levin altogether."

There was a sharp intake of breath from Andrews. "All of them in the same photo? Can you prove when it was taken?"

Matt's stomach heaved. "I can't, but another person in the picture can."

"Quit the game playin', Sinclair. Who is it?"

"Kate's in the picture with Joanna Barnes." He held the receiver away from his ear, at Andrews's shouted expletive.

"Oh, wonderful. Just wonderful. This is what happens

when amateurs get involved. All right. Listen up. I'm sending a car to Reilly's right now. Don't you call her or do anything stupid like going over there. When my men arrive, they'll call you. Okay?''

"She's not there, Andrews. I've been trying to get hold of her all day.''

A loud sigh. "Maybe they've already got her, then.''

Matt broke out into a cold sweat. He hung up and ran for the door.

THE LIMO WAS TWO BLOCKS away from Kate's place when she realized she'd have to speak up now or cause a greater commotion when they got to her place. She couldn't think properly. Her mind was fragmented with frightening possibilities of all that could happen. What she wanted more than anything was to get out of the car. She'd feel safer and more confident in her own place. What could they do, anyway, once they found out? Wouldn't they just leave?

Maybe not. Gooseflesh rose on her bare arms. The limo reached Kate's block and double-parked in front.

"I'll go up,'' Kate offered.

Gallini's smile was indulgent. "We will *all* go up, except for Mario here who's waiting in the car. Remember what I said about makin' it nice and easy?''

Kate nodded. She had to think of a plan but her mind refused to cooperate, choosing instead to focus on minor and irrelevant details, like the black mole sprouting a single hair in the corner of Gallini's mouth or the tufts of bristly hair on his chunky knuckles.

Lance opened the door and got out. Stiffly, Kate noticed. Gallini gestured at Kate to follow and she did. Then Mario got out from the driver's seat, walked around to the rear and opened the door for Gallini.

"Sure you don't want me to go with them, boss, and you wait in the car?''

"Nah. I need to be with Mr. Marchant," he said, wheezing out a laugh at the same time. The chauffeur shrugged and returned to his place. Kate headed for the stairs and opened the front door. She watched the portly Gallini struggle up the three cement steps and wondered how he was going to tackle the flight of stairs inside. But it was Lance who was panting and gasping when they reached her floor.

As soon as she stepped inside, Kate headed for the kitchen.

"Where you going?" Gallini demanded from the doorway.

"To get Lance a drink of cold water. And I need one, too."

"He don't need a drink," Gallini said.

Kate ignored him. When she returned and handed Lance a glass, Gallini glared at her. She looked away, taking a long, slow drink herself and trying to come up with a plan. Like what? Overthrow a man who must weigh three hundred pounds?

Reading her mind, Gallini said, "Get the scrapbook, Miss Reilly, and don't be thinkin' of doing somethin' foolish."

She set the glass down on the table. "I don't have it," she said, enjoying for a tiny second the sight of Gallini's jaw dropping.

He quickly recovered, reached into his suit jacket pocket and withdrew a gun. "This ain't no social visit, Miss Reilly, so I'd appreciate no more niceties or jokin' around. Get the book."

"Kate—" Lance warned.

The telephone shrilled. Kate flinched, staring at the phone. Why now?

"Get it," Gallini ordered Lance.

Lance picked it up. "Yes?" He listened for a second,

then cupping a hand over the receiver, said to Gallini, "It's a kid."

Carla. Calling about the scrapbook. Blood rushed into Kate's head. She couldn't think straight.

"Take it and get off the line quick," Gallini said.

Kate took the receiver with a hand that felt weighted. Her mouth was dry and her tongue seemed to have doubled in size. The one objective her spinning mind could center on was keeping Carla safe.

"Hi, Carla?"

"Hi, Kate. Who was that guy?"

"Oh, uh, a friend of mine."

"Yeah? He sounded real weird. Is everything okay there?"

She had to dispel the suspicion she heard in Carla's voice. And get off the phone quickly, as Gallini's eyes were reminding her. "Oh, just fine. What can I do for you?"

"Well, Rita said you called me. About the scrapbook. I'm so sorry. I don't even remember putting it in my backpack. I think it was when we stopped for a cold drink, you know, and I kinda tucked it inside and then I forgot about it. So, like, I didn't even remember still having it until Rita reminded me. I'm real sorry. D'ya want me to bring it over? Rita said I could if you do."

"No!" Kate said sharply. "Don't worry about it. In fact, just keep it. You can have it, okay? It's all yours. Anyway, got to go now. See you soon." And she hung up.

The two men were staring at her. "So?" asked Gallini.

"My little sister. She just wanted to return a sweatshirt I'd lent her." Kate picked up her glass of water and swallowed a big mouthful.

"What was the 'no' all about?" Gallini asked.

"She wanted to bring over the sweatshirt right now."

He nodded, keeping his small eyes fixed on hers. "Okay, so get the scrapbook."

"I told you, I don't have it."

"Kate, this is serious," Lance said. "The picture is what I've been looking for. I just didn't realize what it was until this morning."

"This morning?"

"When Matt called and left a message for you. Gallini's men tapped Matt's office phone."

Kate sank into a chair. She thought of Matt's call from Toronto airport and wondered if they'd overheard that conversation, too.

"Fer cryin' out loud, we don't got all day here, Marchant. Get me the damn scrapbook and let's go," Gallini grumbled.

"Kate?" Lance was perched on the edge of his chair. His pallor was worse than ever. "Seriously, where is it?"

"You don't have to do this, Lance," she said, searching his face for some sign of agreement. "You can just refuse to help and—"

"He'll go away?" he asked, his voice flat. "You're very naive for a former street kid, Kate. I wasn't exaggerating when I told you it was a matter of life and death. Two people have already died over this. So get the picture." His voice rose, clipping off each of the last four words with deadly meaning.

She knew they'd never leave, not without tearing her place apart—again?—or figuring that if she didn't have it, one of her friends might. Such as Matt. Or Ginny. *Or Carla.* No, she wouldn't risk that. Suddenly she had an idea.

"I left it up north. At the lodge."

Lance went crazy. "But I was there. You never said a word."

"You said you were looking for a letter!"

"Jeez," Gallini muttered. "No wonder you couldn't find nothin'. A letter! What kinda cockamamie story is that?"

Lance opened his mouth.

"Don't bother," Gallini snarled. "C'mon, let's go."

"Where?" Lance asked, struggling to his feet.

"To the lodge, where do you think?" Gallini was half-way to the door. He jerked his head at Kate. "Bring her, too."

Lance looked from Kate to Gallini. He shook his head and mumbled, "I tried to warn you, Kate. I really did." And grasping her elbow in his hand, led her out of the apartment. As they were going down the stairs, Kate's telephone rang.

"Nobody's home," Gallini said in a loud theatrical whisper, breaking off to laugh.

"ARE YOU LOOKING for Kate?"

Matt turned to the young woman on the landing below. She looked familiar. The downstairs tenant, he decided. He'd seen her the day of the break-in.

"Yes, I've been trying to get hold of her all day. She's not answering her door." He ran fingers through his hair. "I'm a bit worried."

"She was here just about an hour ago."

"She was? Did you talk to her?"

"No, I'd just taken my cat in and saw her open the front door as I was closing mine." She thought a moment. "I think there were two men with her."

Matt reached out a hand to the doorjamb to steady himself. "What did they look like?"

The woman frowned, pursing her lips. "One had silvery hair and the other I didn't get a good look at. But he was a big man. Is something wrong?"

Everything's wrong, he thought. Wrong and incredibly screwed up. "Look, do you have a key to her place? Just in case she left something behind that…that might give me an idea of where she's gone?"

Her frown deepened. "I do, but I don't think Kate would be wanting me to give it out. Especially after the break-in."

"But you've met me. I was here the day of the break-in. Don't you remember me?"

She pulled her head back, giving him a long look. "There were so many police around..."

"I'm her fiancé!" he cried, desperate now.

One corner of her mouth rose. "Kate would've told me if she was engaged. Not that we're best friends, but we do talk regularly. She'd have told me."

Now she was casting suspicious glances at him and Matt figured she'd soon be calling the police. "Forget it, then," he said. "Do me a favor. If Kate comes back, tell her Matt was here. And let her stay the night with you. Something's come up. Her life may be in danger."

He was back on the sidewalk when the patrol car Andrews sent showed up. Matt walked over to greet the officers. "She's not home. Her neighbor said she arrived with two men, both matching descriptions of the men Andrews is looking for."

"Who's Andrews?" one officer asked.

"Sergeant Tom Andrews. The undercover cop who sent you here."

The officer raised an eyebrow at the other, then said to Matt, "Our precinct got a call to check a possible B and E. That's why we're here."

Matt silently cursed Andrews for continuing to play his cloak-and-dagger games while Kate was in real jeopardy. "Mind if I come up with you to look around?"

"Sure as heck do, mister. In fact, you can disappear altogether." The officers walked up the steps and rang the first-floor buzzer. The tenant let them in, glancing quickly at Matt before closing it behind the police.

Matt sank down onto one of the front steps. He didn't

know what to do, short of searching for Andrews and throttling him. It was close to six o'clock. He refused to believe
Kate had willingly brought Marchant and Gallini to her
place, much less willingly left with them. Would they have
taken her to Roosevelt Island? He wondered if Andrews
and his men were still watching the warehouse there.

Andrews. The bastard. He hadn't called a car at all. He'd
only said that to put Matt off. But why? To get him out of
the way for some reason. But what? What was the creep
up to? He stood up, so rattled now he wasn't thinking
straight. He felt like a mad dog, consumed with an urge to
run in circles and howl. A voice hailed him as he started
walking to his car.

"Matt! Mr. Sinclair!"

Turning around, he saw Carla running toward him, followed by a woman. When they got closer, he said, "Carla,
what are you doing here? Are you looking for Kate?"

Breathless, Carla nodded. Then she said, "Matt, this is
my foster mom, Rita, and this is Kate's boyfriend."

Matt shook hands with the woman, not bothering to clarify his status. Not wanting to.

"Is Kate home?"

"No. But the police are up there because they got a
break-and-entry call."

"That was us!" Carla beamed. "It was Rita's idea."

Matt frowned. "What's going on?"

Carla explained about Kate's strange response on the
phone. "I mean, she would never give her scrapbook away,
would she?"

Matt agreed. "So *you've* got the scrapbook?"

"Right. Anyway, the man who answered sounded kinda
scary, so when I hung up, I told Rita. We sat around worrying about it for a while, then we called back. But this
time there was no answer, only Kate's machine, so we

thought maybe the burglar had come back. That's why we called the police.''

His mind ran through various strategies and options, discounting most immediately. No way was he telling Andrews about Carla's having the scrapbook. Nor did he even feel like telling him about Kate leaving with Marchant and Gallini. The guy should've kept the tail on her.

"How did you end up with the scrapbook?" he asked.

When Carla explained, a glimmer of understanding flickered in Matt's mind. He knew that Kate would want to draw the men away from Manhattan and possible hiding places for the scrapbook. Away from Carla, especially. And what better, more logical place to keep something safe than Limberlost?

He had to admire her guts, though was now so fearful of her safety he scarcely thanked Carla. But he did warn her and her foster mother to say nothing to anyone about the scrapbook, promising to call them the instant Kate was found. As they headed to the subway, he sprinted to his car.

IT WAS ALMOST MIDNIGHT when they drove through Bondi. Kate peered through the limo window, hoping to see any sign of life. Lance directed the driver down the gravel road leading to Limberlost. When they pulled up in front of the lodge, trapped in a ghostly halo from the full moon, Kate's heart sank. Now what?

The men got out and stretched. There'd been only one stop for refreshments, with Kate chaperoned to the washroom by Mario, the chauffeur. He was almost as frightening as Gallini. The way he looked at her, especially when he'd hovered outside the door. She'd hoped for some opportunity to get a message to someone there, but the service center was almost empty at that time of night.

Now they were finally here and she still had no idea what

she was going to do. Pretending she'd misplaced the scrapbook might give her an extra fifteen minutes. No, she thought, remembering Gallini's shrewd, beady eyes, make that five minutes. The men followed her up onto the veranda to the front door. Kate fumbled the key, dropping it onto the porch. She heard someone swear softly behind her as she crouched to feel for it.

"Fer cryin' out loud," Gallini muttered. "Mario, get down there with her and find the damn key."

But Kate's fingers located the key and she stood up to try again. This time Mario snatched the key from her hand and deftly inserted it into the lock. He pushed the door open.

"Lights?" Gallini snapped.

"There aren't any," Kate said.

"Whaddaya mean?" he shouted.

"The place is run by generator and—" she hesitated "—the generator's broken."

"What kinda place is this, no lights?"

Lance stepped in. "She's right, Vincent. The night I came, there were no lights. But she's got lanterns and flashlights inside."

"So get in there and get them goin'. I wanna be outta here in twenty minutes, max."

Lance proceeded through the door. Gallini gave Kate a hard nudge in the middle of her back. "Go on," he muttered.

There was enough moonlight spilling through the open doorway for Lance to grope his way to the center of the lounge. Unfortunately, Kate noted, he remembered exactly where the lantern and flashlight had been sitting and in seconds was strobing the room with the flashlight, looking for matches.

Mario handed him a pack, and after a false start, Lance managed to light the kerosene lantern. When its pale yellow glow highlighted his face, he looked like a character from a horror movie, Kate thought. Like one of the walking dead.

Gallini nodded toward a love seat and ordered Mario to uncover it. Then he slowly settled into it, grunting softly as he sank into the cushions. He waved a hand at her. "Get the scrapbook. Mario, take a flashlight and go with her."

Kate's heart rate accelerated. She didn't want to go into any dark rooms with Mario. "It's just upstairs in my bedroom," she said. "I can grab it and be right back." Her voice sounded like a stranger's. High-pitched and cracking.

Gallini snorted. "Yeah, right. Mario, go."

Mario picked up one of the flashlights from the table and motioned to Kate with it. The grin on his face in the arc of light was grotesque—lips drawn back over small crooked teeth, his black eyes like tiny lumps of coal in a snowman. Kate shivered. Might as well get it over with now than have him groping her in some dark hallway.

She threw off the hand that Mario had placed on her forearm, stepping away from him. "I don't have the scrapbook," she said. "It's not here. I was lying."

"Kate, don't do this!" Lance cried. "Just give it to them and we can all go home."

"I'm serious, Lance. I was lying all the time. It was never here."

Silence shrouded the room. Silence except for Gallini's wheezy breathing. After a long, suffocating moment, Gallini said, "Sit down, Mario. You, too, Kate."

She took the nearest seat, noting his change from "Miss Reilly" to her first name. Did that mean he was relenting? Softening toward her?

"Okay, let's get all this straight. Maybe we shoulda done this before leaving Manhattan, eh? 'Stead of rushing up here. Now. We know that you've got a scrapbook with a picture in it of me, Lance here and Joe Levin. We got that on tape and I'm asking you—dead serious—am I correct?"

"Yes," she said, then cleared her throat and added, "and Joanna Barnes and me."

"Yeah? You and Joanna, too? And this photo was taken when and where?"

"Right out back. In the parking lot the day Joanna left here."

"Right. She came up here with that loser Jim Sinclair."

Kate winced. "I doubt he was a loser," she objected, "since he married Joanna."

Gallini laughed uproariously. "So Joanna Barnes would never team up with a loser, that what you're sayin'? What about old Lance here? Didn't she marry *him?*"

"Matt's father wasn't a loser."

"Nice sentiments, but I gotta say you have a bit of a bias here. Eh, Marchant?"

Lance sat up in his chair. He seemed groggy, and when he finally answered, spoke slurringly. "Yeah, that's right, Vincent. Whatever you say."

Gallini laughed again. "Poor Lance, he's at the end of his rope. 'Course, he's got no one to blame but himself. If he hadn't've come runnin' to us when Joanna found out about that sucker Joe Levin, she might still be alive. Ain't that right, Marchant?"

Lance's yes was barely a whisper.

"He could've just kept his mouth shut, like we was all doin', and the feds would never have found anything. But oh no, he had to confess to the little woman how I had to get rid of Levin 'cause he was going to tell all. She told Lance here he'd better come clean with the feds or she'd tell them what happened to Levin. Said she could prove he'd been up north with me, too."

An icy dread filled Kate. "You killed Joanna, didn't you?"

Both Mario and Gallini snorted. "Hey, the schoolteacher's finally figured something out," Gallini said.

Kate's throat swelled. She turned to Lance. "How could you let them? How could you cooperate with these men? They killed your wife!" she cried.

"I didn't know," he said, his voice dull and flat. "I didn't find out until the next day."

"But you knew…at the funeral, when you were giving your big, loving eulogy."

"She was already dead. It didn't mean I'd stopped loving her. I wanted to honor her."

"You're disgusting, Lance. You didn't deserve Joanna." Her voice fell off. Tears stung her eyes.

"Well, I gotta say, I've had enough of this soap opera. How about you, Mario?"

"Me, too," agreed the chauffeur.

Gallini struggled out of his chair. "Frankly, I don't care about the picture. So long as it can't be backed up by a date, who can say when it was taken? Joanna and Sinclair no longer can. Marchant for sure won't be sayin' a word. Levin's long gone. That only leaves you, Miss Reilly."

"Me?" She hadn't picked up the thread of his rave yet.

"Aren't you one of the people in the picture who's still alive?"

"Uh, yes…with you and Lance."

Gallini smiled. "And I been through all that. Do you remember when that picture was taken?"

"July, nineteen years ago."

"Kate, be quiet," Lance moaned. "Don't say another word."

"Hey, haven't we all figured that one out already?" Gallini asked. "So you see what I'm gettin' at, don't you? The picture don't really matter so long as you're not around to put a date on it. That's the way I make it. Right, Mario?"

"That's right, boss." He moved toward Kate.

She jumped out of her seat, backing into the shadows.

"No, don't hurt her. She's done nothing to you. Please,

Vince!'' Lance rushed at the big man, who placed one large palm on his chest and pushed back. Lance hit the floor, crying out in pain. His body went into uncontrollable spasms.

CHAPTER SEVENTEEN

"HELP HIM!" Kate cried. "He's having a heart attack!"

She ran to Lance's side. He was foaming at the mouth, his face contorted with pain. His lips moved, shaping words that Kate couldn't hear. She bent her head down to his, planning to start the CPR she'd been trained for but never used.

"No....just go...run if you can...go..."

She pivoted around to Mario and Gallini, standing a few feet away. "Get your cell phone! Call 911 or whatever it is up here."

Gallini snorted. "Hey, this is all gonna work out for the best. Lance don't have to stand trial or worry about his election campaign. 'Cause there ain't gonna be one now." His laugh ended in a choking fit that reddened his face. His hands rummaged through his suit pockets pulling things out onto the table. He gasped, "Mario! My puffer! In the car." And Mario dashed out the front door.

Kate lowered her mouth to Lance's, but he shook his head. "Go now...go..."

She took a quick look at Gallini, still trying to catch his breath. An asthma attack, she guessed. And realizing that very second might be her only chance, she grabbed the flashlight from the table and sprinted toward the kitchen and the back door. When she reached it, her stomach hit the ground.

Bill Tippett had shuttered it up. Desperate, she tore through the screened-in dining area. She could hear the slam of the front screen door. Mario. Coming back or going out after her, hoping to head her off? She forced herself to keep calm. Think. Escaping is about using the brain, too. Except that she'd never had to run for her life before.

No exit through the dining room except into another lounge area. Her only option was to backtrack, try to sneak past Gallini and out the front door. Yeah, right. He can't run, but he does have a gun. Or go upstairs. No. Bad idea. No escape there, except out a window and they're all shuttered. *A window.* The skylight in Carla's room.

She tiptoed back into the kitchen and dashed up the pantry stairs to the second floor. Below, she heard Mario prowling around the kitchen, moving slowly, expecting her to be hiding somewhere. Taking one stealthy step at a time, she worked her way down the hall to Carla's room. Peering up at the skylight, she felt nauseous thinking about what she was planning. She'd no idea if the thing would even open, but she was running out of options. She carried a chair underneath the skylight and stepped onto it.

Aiming the light at the frame of the skylight, Kate saw a simple sliding-bolt mechanism. She tucked the flashlight between her knees, hoping their trembling wouldn't release it to crash to the floor, warning Mario below. And just then, he called her name. She froze, fingers at the sliding lock. Afraid to move. Afraid to breathe.

He called again, imploring her to come out so they could all talk. *Yeah, right. Does he think I've never seen any of those movies?* His voice drifted off as he headed through the screened-in dining area. Any moment he'd realize it was a dead end. Go back to the kitchen. See the pantry. Find the stairs.

She pushed at the bolt, but it wouldn't budge. *Damn.* She twisted the end of the bolt back and forth between her index finger and thumb. Then pushed it as hard as she could. It scraped forward. Tried again. With one last shove and ignoring the excruciating pinch of her fingertips, she unbolted the window.

No time for celebrating. The other bolt. This one was easier, now that she'd figured out the little trick of turning and pushing together. Wait. Noises downstairs. Mario? Someone calling. Gallini, maybe. Giving instructions. Then she heard the metallic click of a door opening. The pantry. *He's found the pantry stairs.*

She reached up to the glass and thrust upward. Heavy. But it was moving. Up, up and stop. On its hinges now. An opening of at least a foot. Fingers clutching the window frame, she pulled herself up. Every nerve in her body screamed *stop* as her skin scraped against the rough shingling around the skylight's frame. Then she was out, creeping along the edge of the roof. Heading for the rear of the lodge where the roof sloped. Not too much of a jump. At this point, who cared about a broken ankle?

You can't run with one, the little voice in her head warned. Kate forced her mind off the future ten minutes, focusing on the next five seconds. Thank God for the full moon. Easy to see where she was going to land. *But easy for Mario to see her, too. Don't slow down. Keep going.* Crouching crablike, she scuttled across the sloping roof until she came to the end of it. Right above the kitchen back door. From there, the roof soared to a peak.

She thought she heard swearing behind her. Mario trying to crawl through the skylight? Maybe it was too narrow. If he used his brain, he'd go back down and outside, catch her coming off the kitchen roof. *Please, Mario. Don't use your brain right now.* Kate lay down on the roof, peering over the edge for a way down other than simply jumping.

The drainpipe from the eaves curved down from the roof alongside the door frame. At some point in time, someone had screwed in a hook near the top of the door frame for a hanging plant. Kate swung a leg over and stretched to place one foot on top of the hook, tested it, then swung her other over and, holding on to the drainpipe, slid down firepole-fashion.

When the ground was within leaping distance, she pushed herself off from the pipe, banging her shin and landing on her bottom on the gravel parking lot. Then she heard yelling from inside and the thump of heavy footsteps charging in her direction. *Mario had used his brain.*

No time for an injury check. As long as all of her limbs moved, she was okay. Kate jogged across the lot away from the lodge and into the woods. She didn't stop to catch her breath until she reached the treeline. There, she discovered the flashlight had fallen out of her pocket. The moon at least could guide her several feet into the trees. After that, she was on her own.

SOME INSTINCT WARNED Matt away from the lodge veranda. Not that he'd ever had any kind of military training, but common sense told him if you're planning on sneaking up on bad guys, you don't use the front door.

He vaguely remembered an entry at the back. Off the kitchen? But was it shuttered up, too, like the windows? Probably. He suspected Tippett was a thorough man. He decided to circle the lodge to check out the situation before going over his options. If he had any at all. Coming round to the kitchen area, he heard someone crunching across the gravel. He crouched against the cement foundation of the lodge, waiting.

Then a man appeared, backlit by the moon. Matt figured the guy was a good five inches shorter than he was, but the outline suggested a powerful body. The man turned to scan the parking lot, and when he did, Matt jumped.

He knocked him to the ground and rolled with him, trying to get an offensive position on top. But the guy scrambled to his feet and came at Matt. He raised his fists in front of his face and when the guy was mere inches away, feinted, landing a vicious blow right in his solar plexus. The man doubled over, punctuating the still night with an explosive *whoosh*, crashing against the shuttered door and slumping to the ground.

Matt bent over the prone figure to feel for a pulse and, finding a faint but steady one, left him to search for Kate.

KATE SHIVERED. The air was denser in the shadows and colder, too, already heavy with dew. The night was eerily quiet. From where she was standing, she could see the section of the parking lot where it merged with the main drive and the gravel road. If she could make it to the road, she'd stand a better chance of reaching Bondi by road than through the forest. She pictured herself wandering through the labyrinth of trees for days, maybe weeks.

Kate scanned the parking lot. Where was Mario? The idea of him creeping around in the dark terrified her. But standing there, waiting for him to find her in some deadly game of hide-and-seek was even more unthinkable. She had to get moving. She half ran, half walked at a crouch along the edge of the parking lot and came to a sudden full stop when she saw the limo. Had Mario left the keys in the car? Could she be that lucky?

She paused, eyes sweeping across the expanse of lawn. Then, ducking low, she ran across the bare stretch of land to the limo's driver side and wrenched the door open.

"Get in, Miss Reilly," Gallini said.

He was in the front passenger seat, aiming his gun directly at Kate. She did as she was told, closing the door behind her.

"There's gotta be some philosophical expression for this, don'tcha think? Like, if you wait long enough for somethin' it'll drop into your lap."

His laugh was loud, though less hearty than before. Kate noticed a puffer lying on the dashboard.

"Where's Mario?" she asked, curious and weighing her odds at the same time.

He shrugged. "Mario shmario. Who cares? Maybe he fell into a hole out there."

She was afraid to ask, but had to. "And Lance?"

"Gone from this life, hopefully to a better one."

The brief stab of regret this news brought had more to do with sorrow that someone Lance had obviously known for more than twenty years was so unmoved by his death. As calculating and conniving as he'd been, Lance deserved better. Kate sighed. Her odds were looking bleaker than ever.

"Now what?" she asked wearily.

"Now we do what we shoulda done all along. We go back to Manhattan to my place. We pick up a few of my guys and we go to your place and tear it apart. Then we visit all your friends' places and do the same thing. It's not very subtle and Marchant wouldn't have picked it, but it works, Miss Reilly. So let's go, you're the driver."

Her hand moved over the steering wheel column. "No keys. Mario must have them."

"You think the chauffeur's the only one with a set of keys?" he scoffed, digging his free hand into his suit coat pocket. Then he grimaced and swore. "Musta left them on the table inside when I emptied my pockets looking for my puffer. Let's go." He opened his door to get out.

"I'll wait here," Kate offered.

Gallini smirked. "Yeah, sure. We'll see if you're still makin' the wisecracks when we're back in the city."

She'd have said she wasn't being flippant, she just couldn't bare to see Lance Marchant lying dead on the floor. But Kate already knew Gallini had no concept of the word *sensitive*.

She got out and walked ahead of Gallini to the veranda. Once there, she hesitated. *Hoping for a knight to come to your rescue?* her mind sneered. *Like your white knight, Reilly? Where is he when you need him most?*

Gallini waved the gun at her. "Go on."

She pushed at the screen door and saw Lance right where she'd left him. Kate averted her face and skirted round him to the sitting area of the lounge. She sank into one of the sofas, exhausted and nauseous.

"What're ya doin'?" Gallini asked, making for the table where the lantern still flickered.

"I don't feel well," Kate whispered. "I think I'm going to be sick."

"What a useless buncha amateurs I've been dealin' with," Gallini grumbled. He pocketed the items from the tabletop and, cupping a hand to his mouth, hollered, "Mario! Where the hell are ya? Mario! Get in here!"

Kate groaned. Her stomach heaved.

Gallini took one look at her and said, "Get outta here. Don't do it in here, fer cryin' out loud."

And she ran for the veranda, slamming through the screen door. Rushed to the nearest piece of railing and, leaning over, threw up. Once was enough, but she waited for her stomach heaves to lessen. Then she wiped her mouth with the bottom of her T-shirt and counted to ten. Gallini must be waiting for her inside. Funny, she thought, that a man who could kill as easily as he, would also recoil from someone vomiting.

She thought of running again, but her legs wobbled like jelly. The limo was no good to her—Mario and Gallini had the keys. There was nothing to do except hope that Gallini would keep her alive long enough to get back to Manhattan. Then she recalled the scene when Lance had his attack. Gallini didn't need the picture if she and Matt were dead. She thought of the drive back to New York along dark and isolated mountain roads. A hundred places for her to disappear. Just like Joe Levin.

They must have brought him along that summer purposely to get rid of him way up here, where his body might never have been found. Even then it took nineteen years. Maybe Joe Levin didn't have an inkling that day about what was going to happen to him. But she flashed onto her peeking inside the limo, catching a quick glance at the man in the rear corner. His face. His eyes. A shiver traveled up and down Kate's spine. She took a deep breath, steadying herself to go back inside.

And then a man's hand sealed her mouth, cutting off her exhalation as he dragged her away from the railing.

CHAPTER EIGHTEEN

KATE THOUGHT she was going to suffocate. The hand clamped over her mouth was strong and unyielding. The arm that pulled her into the dark corner beyond the screen door bit into her waist. So when the hand came away, the first thing she did was take a deep breath. The second thing was whirl around.

Her face was inches from his, but she couldn't move. Her sharp, rapid breathing filled the night but the roaring in her ears was all she heard. Then she reached up a hand to his cheek and sighed.

"Matt," she whispered. "Where have you been?" She felt, rather than saw, his grin. Her fingertips explored his face as if to reassure herself this was no fantasy.

"Thank God," he breathed. "This moment has been driving me on for hours." And he grasped her to his chest.

"Reilly? Aren't you finished out there? Get in here!" Gallini called out.

Matt's fingers dug into Kate's shoulders. "Gallini?" he whispered.

"Yes. And he's got a gun."

"Okay, you go and stand by the railing right in front of the door. Then call him out, make like you're desperate. When he comes out, I'll take him from the side."

"There's another one. Mario. He's out there somewhere."

"We don't have to worry about him for a few more minutes, okay?"

She nodded, slipping out of his arms and over to the rail.

"Reilly? You hear me? Don't go gettin' me madder'n I already am."

Kate gave a loud groan. "Please help me. Something's wrong with me." She started keening, lowering her head over the railing.

"Oh, fer cryin'—" Gallini stepped through the doorway.

Matt flew at him, propelling the heavy man into the door frame, then spun him around before he could recover his balance, sending him reeling backward onto the veranda floor. The gun Gallini had been holding clattered across the porch in Kate's direction. She leapt for it, retrieving it just as Matt straightened up.

Gallin clambered onto all fours, his breathing harsh and laborious. "You're gonna regret this, the two of you. Big time."

Kate might have laughed at his bravado had she not been trembling so badly. Matt took the gun from her and pointed it at Gallini.

"Stay there and don't move." Then to Kate, "Is there any rope around we can use?"

"I think in the boathouse."

"Can you get it?"

Kate moistened her lips. It would mean running into the dark night again.

"Mario should still be out," he added.

She dashed into the lounge, pausing long enough to pick up the flashlight Gallini had been using. Then she tore out again, flying past Matt and Gallini, frozen like chess pieces in a stalemate. Heading for the boathouse down by the lake. Across the lawn, past the guest cabins. The moon was still hidden, but the flashlight was enough for her to see her way. Panting, she reached the closed door and prayed Bill hadn't locked it up.

The padlock was on, but hadn't been pushed all the way

through. Maybe Kyle had been helping his grandfather. Kate wanted to laugh. She flung open the door and swinging from a hook on its other side was the rope she'd spotted the day she and Carla had gone canoeing.

She ran back across the lawn toward the veranda, slowing down to ease the cramp in her stomach. When she reached the corner of the lodge, an arm shot out and yanked her into the shadows.

Mario.

His breath was hot and sour on her face. Kate felt the nausea roll up again. *So close. I was so close.*

"Give me the flashlight," Mario hissed. "And the rope."

Kate handed them over. She started to talk, but his hand covered her mouth.

"Where's Gallini?" he whispered.

She pointed at the veranda.

"Is he alone?"

Kate hesitated, then nodded.

"Okay, you'n me are gonna walk up the stairs together. When I take my hand away, you're not gonna scream or cry out or anythin' stupid. Got that?"

She nodded again.

He removed his hand and used it to pin Kate's right arm behind her. "Remember, just follow my lead." Then he began to guide her to the veranda steps.

"Kate?" Matt asked from the shadows above.

Mario's lips hissed in her ears. "You said Gallini was alone."

"Who's there?" Matt called out again.

Mario yanked her arm higher. "Tell him not to turn around, I gotta gun on you."

A gun. She hadn't noticed a gun, but maybe he'd had one tucked away somewhere.

"Matt? It's me and...and Mario's with me. He has a gun." She heard a muttered expletive.

Then Gallini broke in. "I knew this was my lucky day. Mario, get up here and take care of this guy for me, will ya? I'm dyin' sittin' on the floor this way."

Mario nudged Kate up the stairs. When she reached the top, she caught Matt's quick glance from Gallini to her. Frowning, she shook her head. "I'm okay, Matt. Really."

"Matt Sinclair?" Mario asked. He released Kate's arm. "You must be the guy who took me out back there."

Matt edged closer, keeping the gun fixed on Gallini, his eyes darting to the man behind Kate. "Who're you?"

"Mario, what is all this crap?" Gallini snarled. "Get my gun."

"Sorry Mr. Gallini, no can do."

Gallini roared a string of expletives, most aimed at Mario and his unfortunate family.

Mario laughed, his white teeth flashing. "There's another gun in the glove box of the limo," he told Matt. "I left it there purposely to stall for time if I needed to. As it turned out, everything went all haywire anyhow."

"Who are you?" Kate asked, moving close to Matt. His free arm came up and clutched her to him.

"He's Mario Pirelli, and get the damn gun or you're gonna be real sorry," Gallini warned.

Mario shrugged. "You still don't get it. But any time now, you will. As you like to say yourself, boss, 'big time.'"

"I don't get it, either," Kate said.

"Undercover?" Matt asked.

"Nope. I'm really Mario Pirelli and I've been working for Mr. Gallini here since I was a teenager, and my father before me."

"Your father was a loyal man," Gallini roared. "Good thing he can't see the treachery in his son."

"Yeah," Mario muttered, bitterness heavy in his voice. "But I'm hopin' he'll see his son get revenge for him. The way you shot him in cold blood after you killed that Levin guy. That's what this is about, *Mr.* Gallini."

"He became a liability to me. Nothing personal," Gallini mumbled.

"Matt," Kate murmured, "do you have your cell phone? Can we call the police now?"

"No need to, Miss Reilly," Mario said, pointing to the gravel road.

Car headlights zigzagged through the trees, bouncing up and down as they drew closer. In seconds a string of vehicles drove up onto the lawn, wakes of gravel spraying behind.

"You'll regret this, Pirelli. Just you wait. I can reach you even from a jail cell."

"I know, boss. That's why Mr. Andrews there—" he gestured to the man striding across the lawn to the veranda "—is taking me and my family into the protection program."

Andrews bounded up the steps with more agility than Kate would have considered possible. For the first time since meeting the man, she was actually glad to see him.

He viewed the little tableau and said, "Nice work, Sinclair, Pirelli." Then to her, "Miss Reilly, in spite of your determination to muck things up, we did it. So I'll congratulate you, too." He took the gun from Matt and handed it to the first officer who sprinted onto the veranda.

In deference to Kate, who didn't want to sit and talk in front of Lance's body, they retreated to the end of the long veranda. Mario was led to a squad car while two officers brought out chairs for them. Other police carried on with crime-scene protocol.

"An ambulance is on its way," Andrews told Kate, "but

it's not rushing. Sorry about Marchant. Wish he'd come to us himself.''

"Gallini killed Joanna!" Kate blurted. "He admitted it."

Andrews sighed, rubbing at his face. "Hopefully we can nail him on the murder charge, thanks to Mario's wiretap.''

"How long has Mario been involved?" Matt's voice was low and grim.

Andrews shot him an appraising look. "I know what you're thinkin' Sinclair. Why did we need you when we had Pirelli? But he only came to us after the Barnes funeral. Until then, Mario didn't know for sure Gallini had shot his father. Apparently Tony—that was the father—was the only actual witness to Levin's execution. When Mario overheard Gallini talking about it to Marchant, he came to us and offered to wear a wire, the whole thing. I knew you were pursuing other—" his eyes lit briefly on Kate's face, then flicked back to Matt "—avenues, so to speak. So yeah, I still needed you.''

Matt reached over to clasp Kate's hand in his. "How did you know we were here?" he asked.

"Well, it's a long story. When I got to Miss Reilly's place and I found out you'd been and left, I was pretty ticked off, I have to tell you."

"So was I. You didn't send a car."

"I did, but it got rear-ended two blocks from Kate's. I got over there as fast as I could and found two precinct guys checking out a false burglary report.''

Matt nodded. "I can explain that later."

"So the tenant downstairs—what's her name?"

"Ginny," Kate supplied.

"Right. She comes out and tells me about Kate showing up with two men who were definitely Marchant and Gallini. Then she tells me about Matt and I gotta say, Sinclair, she was highly suspicious of you. Said she'd never heard Kate was engaged.''

"Engaged?" Kate echoed, turning her head to look at Matt.

"I was trying to get into the apartment," Matt explained.

Andrews laughed. "Whatever you say, boyo. Well, it took us a few minutes to trace the burglary report, and that led to Miss Carla Lopez and her story of Kate's scrapbook. Once we got that nice tidbit, I figured out where everyone was heading."

"Is Carla okay? You didn't frighten her, did you?" Kate asked.

"That kid!" Andrews scoffed. "Not likely. However, we did take your scrapbook into police custody for evidence. I'll get you a receipt for it later."

"How'd you get here so fast?" Matt asked.

"Ordered up a helicopter and flew to Plattsburg, where we picked up these guys. Stopped in Bondi to get directions from a guy owns a store there. He'd already noticed a lot of traffic driving through the village and had called the sheriff in the next town, down the road. Don't recall the name. Anyway, probably in about ten minutes the whole damn village will be out here gawking, so if you don't mind, I'm gonna oversee Gallini's return to Manhattan."

He got up, nodded a curt goodbye and headed for a waiting squad car.

Matt bent over Kate and murmured, "I'm taking you home." He pulled her gently to her feet and wrapped his arms around her, holding her so close she could feel his heart racing against her cheek.

She sank her face into the thick cotton pile of his sweatshirt, breathing in his scent, letting it rejuvenate her, make her feel alive and safe. After a long moment Matt led her down the stairs. They walked slowly without talking. Headlights came at them and a truck screeched to a halt right next to Kate. The window rolled down and Bill Tippett stuck his head out.

"You folks okay?"

"Hi, Bill. Now we are." Kate's voice was stronger now.

"Drove over soon as I heard from George about the go-ings-on. Verna's at home, and we were wondering if you wanted to come back, spend the night with us."

Kate was touched by his thoughtfulness. "Bill, thank you. And your wife, too. But I...I just want to go home. Thanks, anyway."

"Sure enough. Want me to stay and lock up for you after the police are through?"

"Would you? That would be wonderful." She said an-other goodbye, promising to call him in a few days. As they passed Bill's truck, Kate said, "I told Bill I'd let him know by the end of the summer if I'm selling Limberlost or not. Might as well let him know sooner," she said to Matt.

"Don't make any rash decisions. Especially after a night like the one you've just had. Come on, the car's up the road a bit. Think you can make it?"

"If you're helping," she said, meeting his gaze.

"You know, Kate, from what I've gathered about the night's events, I don't think you need my help at all. Come on, I'll fill you in on everything on the way home."

"I might fall asleep."

"That's okay. As long your dreams include me."

Once settled in the cozy luxury of Matt's car, Kate was relaxed but mentally alert. She listened as he filled in the gaps for her, ending with why he hadn't explained the full significance of the photograph. "I wanted to make sure Andrews could come up with some protection for you, but as things moved along, I began to distrust him. Did you know that it was his own men who broke into your place? It was after I mentioned you might have something."

Kate was shocked but not surprised. "Somehow I don't

think Gallini and Andrews are very far apart, morally, I mean.''

''Yeah, you might have a point.''

She yawned, then thought of something. ''Why didn't you come to my place, Matt? After you called from the airport. Last night. God, was it only last night?''

''Technically no, since it's already three in the morning.'' He paused, lowering his voice. ''I did. In a taxi. We drove up just as Marchant was leaving your place. You were running after him in your robe. You looked…it looked like a domestic argument. Know what I mean?''

Kate stared at him in disbelief. ''You seriously thought that? After what we…after the night before, at your place?''

Matt turned from the windshield to her. ''I know. Foolish of me, wasn't it.''

''*Foolish* is an understatement,'' she sputtered. ''I can't believe you could…''

The car suddenly slowed, veering onto the shoulder. Matt shifted into Park and turned off the engine. ''Come here, Kate. I want to show you how sorry I really am. I'm willing to do whatever penance you can come up with as long as—''

''It involves just the two of us,'' she interjected. She unbuckled her seat belt and shifted as close as she could. ''That gearshift is in the way,'' she murmured as he bent his head to hers.

''Mmm,'' he murmured, ''but this is just what they call a pit stop. For light refreshment. I know a great little inn about a two-hour drive from here.'' His mouth closed over hers.

''Oh, yeah?'' she countered seconds later. ''What's it called?''

''Uh…the Plattsburg Best Western?''

''Mmm,'' she said, tasting his lips on hers. ''Sounds terrific. Drive on.''

CHAPTER NINETEEN

"WHY NOT THROW A DART at your two choices?" Carla suggested. "You can blow up two balloons, label one I Sell Limberlost and the other, I Don't Sell Limberlost."

Kate shook her head and sighed. This is what came of asking a thirteen-year-old a serious, life-altering question. Two weeks had passed since Gallini's arrest at Limberlost. September was looming and Kate knew her decision couldn't be put off any longer. She and Carla had been debating the issue over a pizza lunch, but in spite of the teenager's firm belief that Kate could do whatever she wanted with the property, Kate knew otherwise. There was no way she could afford to run it on a schoolteacher's salary.

Carla checked the time, swallowed the last of her soda and said, "I should be going—big game tomorrow. So, are we still going back to Limberlost before the end of the summer? Like, there's only two weeks left."

"For sure, Carly," Kate said, smiling. "And I'll be at your game tomorrow. Two o'clock?"

Carla nodded. "Bring 'you know who' if you want."

Kate laughed. "You know his name. What is all this, anyway?"

Another eyeball roll. "Okay, okay. *Matt.* Bring him with you, if he's not busy or anything."

Kate got up to see Carla to the door. "We'll see. And we'll talk to Rita tomorrow about a good date for Limberlost before school starts."

"School. Yuck. I don't even want to think about it." Carla gave Kate a quick hug, then sashayed out the door.

While she cleaned up their lunch dishes, Kate thought about how much Carla had changed and how much she herself had changed. Not in any obvious way, but inside she felt different. The days in the aftermath of that night at Limberlost had been hectic and emotional.

Tom Andrews, redeeming himself slightly in Kate's eyes, had popped around a few times to keep her informed. Vincent Gallini had been denied bail, in spite of his expensive lawyer's efforts. Mario Pirelli and his family were safely in a witness relocation program.

"What about Joanna? What exactly was her involvement in this whole thing?" Kate asked, needing to know.

"We've put together what happened from the phone taps and from what we got from Matt and Mario. Joanna had read about the discovery of a body in the Adirondacks, near Bondi. It caught her attention, as you can understand it might. When the body was finally identified as Joe Levin weeks later, Joanna confronted Marchant. Said she'd remembered meeting him at Limberlost. That much we got from conversations between Marchant and Gallini. When Joanna called Sinclair and said she had evidence to clear his father, she must have been referring to the same photograph you also had." Andrews pulled out his cigarettes from his jacket pocket, eyed Kate and tucked them away again.

He went on. "By the time she found her picture—the one that matches yours—she no longer trusted Marchant. We figure she threatened to go to the police with her evidence. Marchant in turn confided in Greg Collier—who by the way, works for Gallini, too—and he was the one who passed on the tidbit to Gallini. By then, it was all out of Marchant's hands. One of Gallini's men paid a visit on Joanna the day before her body was found—"

"The fourteenth," Kate whispered. "The day we were supposed to meet."

Andrews nodded. "This guy knocked Joanna out and rigged up her car."

"And the picture?"

"Our guys found it in the car under the floor mat on the driver's side. She musta hidden it there at some point."

Andrews's revelations had left Kate feeling hollow and sad. Not only for Joanna, but also for Lance, whose lack of judgment had led to his wife's death.

Kate sighed, still trying to piece together all the puzzling parts that had been Joanna Barnes long after Andrews's talk with her. Whoever Joanna had really been—gold digger, schemer or simply a woman with ambition—she'd cared enough for Kate to pass on Limberlost Lodge.

She checked the time. Almost three and her meeting with Matt was at four. She rushed to finish cleaning up, then changed into the peacock-blue silk sheath dress Matt had bought for her two days ago, adding the pearl dewdrop earrings he'd given her on their return to Manhattan, after the drive from Limberlost and the overnight detour in Plattsburg.

Kate had relived that night dozens of times in the past two weeks. They'd talked all night long before making love at daybreak. For the first time he'd told her he loved her, and she, him.

She left her apartment and hailed a taxi to his office. Matt was waiting for her when she stepped off the elevator. The smile in his face told her she looked great. He kissed her lightly on the lips and, holding one hand, led her around his floor and introduced her to so many people Kate's head was spinning. Then she was alone with him in his office, standing by the window and taking in the view that seemed to cover half the city.

"Come here, love," he said, grasping her hand and leading her to a sitting area. On the coffee table was a bucket with a bottle of champagne and two glasses. He poured them each one and handed her a manila folder.

"I want you to take your time reading this," he said. "And if you like the idea, then sign on the dotted line." He paused as if suddenly unsure of himself. "If you don't, well, we'll finish the champagne and go on to dinner."

Mystified, Kate set her glass down and opened the folder. As she read, she was certain her eyes were getting bigger and bigger. Finally she looked at Matt, sitting opposite her.

"I don't get all that lawyer mumbo jumbo, but tell me if I've got the gist of this." She set the folder down and leaned forward. Her excitement at what she'd read was escalating. She tried to think straight. "You want to set up a foundation that will operate Limberlost as a camp for inner-city kids every summer and you want me to run the foundation."

Matt nodded. "You've got the gist of it, all right."

"But...but the money..."

"It will come from the trust fund my mother left me. I can't think of anything she'd have wanted more," he said, his voice low.

Kate gazed at his face, flushed now with emotion. "It's very generous of you, Matt. Does...does this mean you want to buy the lodge?"

"No. The lodge is yours. Always will be. Just that the money to operate it will come from the nonprofit foundation."

"That you're setting up."

"Yes. What do you think?"

"I think you're incredibly generous. I...I just don't think I can accept this kind of generosity from...well, from a friend."

"A *friend?*" His smile was ironic. He got up from his chair and, reaching for her hand, pulled her to her feet. His hand tenderly stroked her cheek. "This is just part of the deal, Kate. The other part isn't written down anywhere."

She tilted her head questioningly.

He ran a fingertip along her jaw, up to her lips. "This is a contract for Limberlost—for its future. To benefit other kids, the way it did you and Carla. It's my gift to you. A wedding gift."

She had a foolish urge to quip, "Who's getting married?" but his eyes had already answered her question. She raised her face to his and let her kiss say all that needed to be said.

CREATURE COMFORT

A heartwarming new series by

Carolyn McSparren

**Creature Comfort, the largest veterinary
clinic in Tennessee, treats animals of all
sizes—horses and cattle as well as family
pets. Meet the patients—and their owners.
And share the laughter and the tears with
the men and women who love and care
for all creatures great and small.**

#996 THE MONEY MAN
(July 2001)

#1011 THE PAYBACK MAN
(September 2001)

*Look for these Harlequin Superromance titles
coming soon to your favorite retail outlet.*

HARLEQUIN®
Makes any time special ®

HSRCC

Harlequin truly does make any time special. . . . This year we are celebrating weddings in style!

A Walk Down the Aisle

WEDDING CELEBRATION

To help us celebrate, we want you to tell us how wearing the Harlequin wedding gown will make your wedding day special. As the grand prize, Harlequin will offer one lucky bride the chance to **"Walk Down the Aisle" in the Harlequin wedding gown!**

There's more...

For her honeymoon, she and her groom will spend five nights at the **Hyatt Regency Maui.** As part of this five-night honeymoon at the hotel renowned for its romantic attractions, the couple will enjoy a candlelit dinner for two in Swan Court, a sunset sail on the hotel's catamaran, and duet spa treatments.

Maui • Molokai • Lanai

To enter, please write, in, 250 words or less, how wearing the Harlequin wedding gown will make your wedding day special. The entry will be judged based on its emotionally compelling nature, its originality and creativity, and its sincerity. This contest is open to Canadian and U.S. residents only and to those who are 18 years of age and older. There is no purchase necessary to enter. Void where prohibited. See further contest rules attached. Please send your entry to:

Walk Down the Aisle Contest

In Canada	In U.S.A.
P.O. Box 637	P.O. Box 9076
Fort Erie, Ontario	3010 Walden Ave.
L2A 5X3	Buffalo, NY 14269-9076

You can also enter by visiting www.eHarlequin.com
Win the Harlequin wedding gown and the vacation of a lifetime!
The deadline for entries is October 1, 2001.

HARLEQUIN®
Makes any time special ®

PHWDACONT1

HARLEQUIN WALK DOWN THE AISLE TO MAUI CONTEST 1197
OFFICIAL RULES
NO PURCHASE NECESSARY TO ENTER

1. To enter, follow directions published in the offer to which you are responding. Contest begins April 2, 2001, and ends on October 1, 2001. Method of entry may vary. Mailed entries must be postmarked by October 1, 2001, and received by October 8, 2001.

2. Contest entry may be, at times, presented via the Internet, but will be restricted solely to residents of certain geographic areas that are disclosed on the Web site. To enter via the Internet, if permissible, access the Harlequin Web site (www.eHarlequin.com) and follow the directions displayed online. Online entries must be received by 11:59 p.m. E.S.T. on October 1, 2001.

    In lieu of submitting an entry online, enter by mail by hand-printing (or typing) on an 8½" x 11" plain piece of paper, your name, address (including zip code), Contest number/name and in 250 words or fewer, why winning a Harlequin wedding dress would make your wedding day special. Mail via first-class mail to: Harlequin Walk Down the Aisle Contest 1197, (in the U.S.) P.O. Box 9076, 3010 Walden Avenue, Buffalo, NY 14269-9076, (in Canada) P.O. Box 637, Fort Erie, Ontario L2A 5X3, Canada.

    Limit one entry per person, household address and e-mail address. Online and/or mailed entries received from persons residing in geographic areas in which Internet entry is not permissible will be disqualified.

3. Contests will be judged by a panel of members of the Harlequin editorial, marketing and public relations staff based on the following criteria:

    - Originality and Creativity—50%
    - Emotionally Compelling—25%
    - Sincerity—25%

    In the event of a tie, duplicate prizes will be awarded. Decisions of the judges are final.

4. All entries become the property of Torstar Corp. and will not be returned. No responsibility is assumed for lost, late, illegible, incomplete, inaccurate, nondelivered or misdirected mail or misdirected e-mail, for technical, hardware or software failures of any kind, lost or unavailable network connections, or failed, incomplete, garbled or delayed computer transmission or any human error which may occur in the receipt or processing of the entries in this Contest.

5. Contest open only to residents of the U.S. (except Puerto Rico) and Canada, who are 18 years of age or older, and is void wherever prohibited by law; all applicable laws and regulations apply. Any litigation within the Province of Quebec respecting the conduct or organization of a publicity contest may be submitted to the Régie des alcools, des courses et des jeux for a ruling. Any litigation respecting the awarding of a prize may be submitted to the Régie des alcools, des courses et des jeux only for the purpose of helping the parties reach a settlement. Employees and immediate family members of Torstar Corp. and D. L. Blair, Inc., their affiliates, subsidiaries and all other agencies, entities and persons connected with the use, marketing or conduct of this Contest are not eligible to enter. Taxes on prizes are the sole responsibility of winners. Acceptance of any prize offered constitutes permission to use winner's name, photograph or other likeness for the purposes of advertising, trade and promotion on behalf of Torstar Corp., its affiliates and subsidiaries without further compensation to the winner, unless prohibited by law.

6. Winners will be determined no later than November 15, 2001, and will be notified by mail. Winners will be required to sign and return an Affidavit of Eligibility form within 15 days after winner notification. Noncompliance within that time period may result in disqualification and an alternative winner may be selected. Winners of trip must execute a Release of Liability prior to ticketing and must possess required travel documents (e.g. passport, photo ID) where applicable. Trip must be completed by November 2002. No substitution of prize permitted by winner. Torstar Corp. and D. L. Blair, Inc., their parents, affiliates, and subsidiaries are not responsible for errors in printing or electronic presentation of Contest, entries and/or game pieces. In the event of printing or other errors which may result in unintended prize values or duplication of prizes, all affected game pieces or entries shall be null and void. If for any reason the Internet portion of the Contest is not capable of running as planned, including infection by computer virus, bugs, tampering, unauthorized intervention, fraud, technical failures, or any other causes beyond the control of Torstar Corp. which corrupt or affect the administration, secrecy, fairness, integrity or proper conduct of the Contest, Torstar Corp. reserves the right, at its sole discretion, to disqualify any individual who tampers with the entry process and to cancel, terminate, modify or suspend the Contest or the Internet portion thereof. In the event of a dispute regarding an online entry, the entry will be deemed submitted by the authorized holder of the e-mail account submitted at the time of entry. Authorized account holder is defined as the natural person who is assigned to an e-mail address by an Internet access provider, online service provider or other organization that is responsible for arranging e-mail address for the domain associated with the submitted e-mail address. **Purchase or acceptance of a product offer does not improve your chances of winning.**

7. Prizes: (1) Grand Prize—A Harlequin wedding dress (approximate retail value: $3,500) and a 5-night/6-day honeymoon trip to Maui, HI, including round-trip air transportation provided by Maui Visitors Bureau from Los Angeles International Airport (winner is responsible for transportation to and from Los Angeles International Airport) and a Harlequin Romance Package, including hotel accomodations (double occupancy) at the Hyatt Regency Maui Resort and Spa, dinner for (2) two at Swan Court, a sunset sail on Kiele V and a spa treatment for the winner (approximate retail value: $4,000); (5) Five runner-up prizes of a $1000 gift certificate to selected retail outlets to be determined by Sponsor (retail value $1000 ea.). Prizes consist of only those items listed as part of the prize. Limit one prize per person. All prizes are valued in U.S. currency.

8. For a list of winners (available after December 17, 2001) send a self-addressed, stamped envelope to: Harlequin Walk Down the Aisle Contest 1197 Winners, P.O. Box 4200 Blair, NE 68009-4200 or you may access the www.eHarlequin.com Web site through January 15, 2002.

Contest sponsored by Torstar Corp., P.O. Box 9042, Buffalo, NY 14269-9042, U.S.A.

PHWDACONT2